The Maple Bakery Murder

Also by R. L. Killmore

A Cinnamon Falls Mystery
Death at Daffodil Inn

The Maple Bakery Murder

R. L. KILLMORE

SIMON & SCHUSTER

London · New York · Amsterdam/Antwerp · Sydney/Melbourne · Toronto · New Delhi

First published in Great Britain by Simon & Schuster UK Ltd, 2026

1 3 5 7 9 10 8 6 4 2

Simon & Schuster UK Ltd, 7th Floor
199 Bishopsgate, London EC2M 3TY

Simon & Schuster Australia, Sydney

Simon & Schuster India, New Delhi

www.simonandschuster.co.uk
www.simonandschuster.com.au
www.simonandschuster.co.in

The authorised representative in the EEA is Simon & Schuster Netherlands BV, Herculesplein 96, 3584 AA Utrecht, Netherlands. info@simonandschuster.nl

A CIP catalogue record for this book is available from the British Library

Paperback ISBN: 978-1-39855-035-3
eBook ISBN: 978-1-39855-036-0
Audio ISBN: 978-1-39855-037-7

Typeset in the UK by Palimpsest Book Production Ltd, Falkirk, Stirlingshire
Printed and Bound in the UK using 100% Renewable Electricity at CPI Group (UK) Ltd

FSC www.fsc.org
MIX
Paper | Supporting responsible forestry
FSC® C013604

for me, here's proof you can do hard things

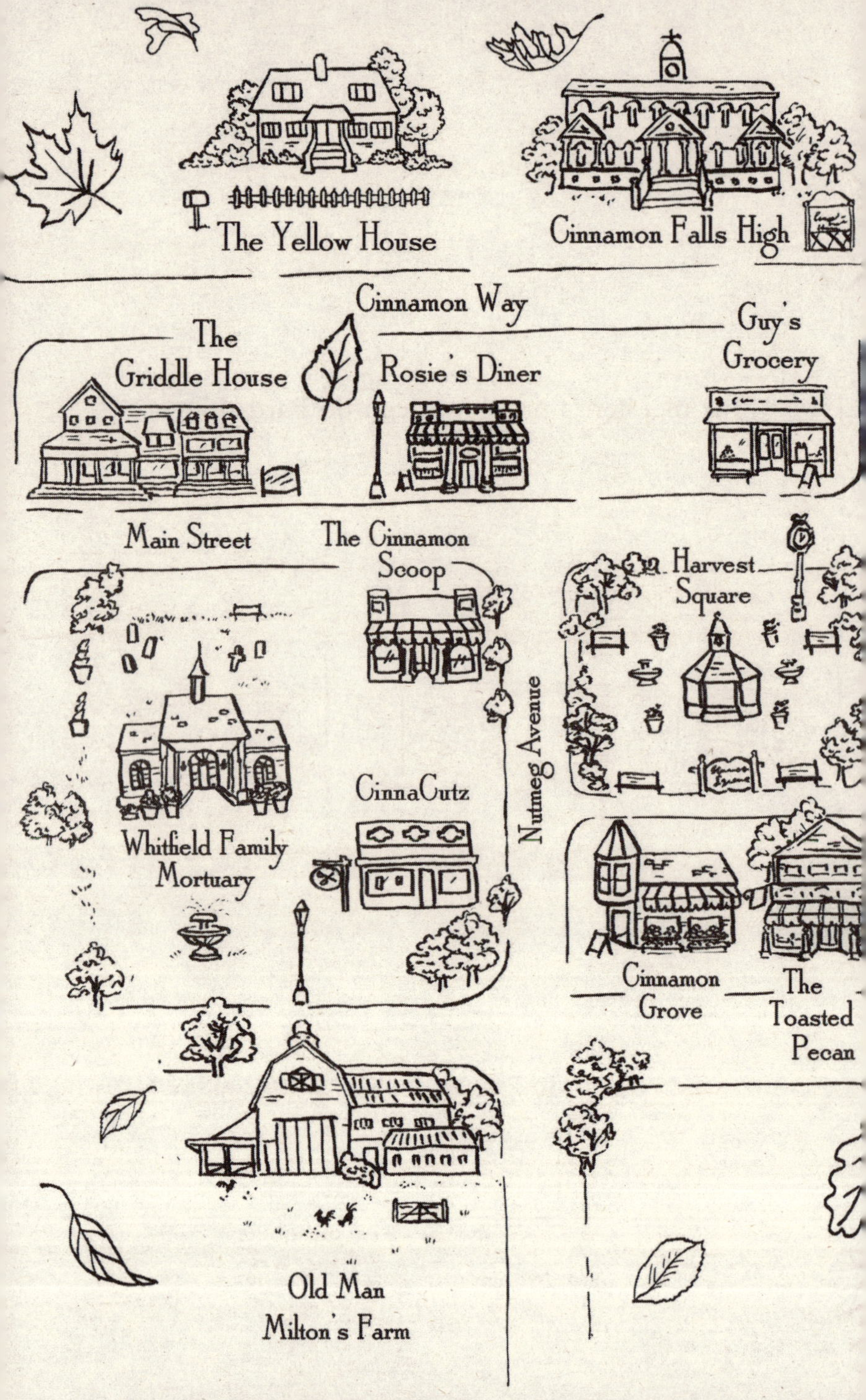
The Yellow House
Cinnamon Falls High
Cinnamon Way
The Griddle House
Rosie's Diner
Guy's Grocery
Main Street
The Cinnamon Scoop
Harvest Square
Nutmeg Avenue
CinnaCutz
Whitfield Family Mortuary
Cinnamon Grove
The Toasted Pecan
Old Man Milton's Farm

To Asheville
Bones' Barber Shop
Maple Bakery
General Store
Police Department
Town Hall
Cinnamon Falls
Paws & Whiskers
Vets

Chapter 1

Saturday

Ginger

Ginger Mills couldn't stand how right her cousin, Alexis, had been. Cinnamon Falls really *did* look like a fairy tale. A gentle wind pushed crimson and butterscotch leaves tumbling over the toes of Ginger's scuffed leather combat boots as she wandered up Main Street's busy sidewalk. She gripped her coffee cup tighter, her gloveless fingers knitting together around the paper sleeve. A hint of cinnamon drifted between the storefronts, and she tipped her face toward the warm morning sun, letting her eyes shutter closed. This place looked like what dreams were made of, but she'd never admit it. She couldn't give Alexis the satisfaction of saying, 'I told you so!'

If someone had asked Ginger six months ago what she'd be doing on the second Saturday in October, she would have rattled off her normal to-do list: tennis lessons in the morning with Jorge at the country club, then brunch with Camille who would have accidentally-on-purpose missed the early morning lesson. Afterward, the two of them would spend the afternoon shopping for new athleisure for said lessons, and then she'd round the day out with a new hairstyle, just in time for dinner reservations with Harrison at some swanky new restaurant he'd been invited to downtown.

None of the aforementioned included cinnamon or falling. A little country town like this had never been on her radar.

Back then, Ginger didn't care to pay attention to trivial matters like the sun-kissed treetops casting an ethereal glitter over the busy street, the sweet song from playful birds zipping overhead, or the chilly bite of air that swept around her exposed neck, prompting her to pull her leather jacket tighter around herself. But, suddenly, her life had changed.

Now she realized just how much she'd been missing back in Atlanta; before Harrison Caldwell became unrecognizable, and she'd turned her cushy life – that any other woman would have killed for – upside down.

Hindsight, as they say.

She didn't know who she hated more, Harrison, Camille, or herself.

Ginger shook the harrowing memories out of her head. Today was the grand opening of her bakery –

a new beginning – and nothing, not even thoughts of her controlling, manipulative ex, would taint that.

According to Alexis, the Fall Festival was the best time of the year here and Ginger could see why. Main Street stretched ahead, a vibrant, wide road boasting all The Falls' entrepreneurial ambitions. Brick-laid storefronts and hand-painted signs featuring smiling scarecrows and falling leaves, were haphazardly sandwiched together, one right after the other.

The street was a flurry of activity as Fall Festival vendors carefully unloaded goods from idling cars and worked diligently to assemble tables and display stands. The festival crew, in neon vests, controlled the never-ending stream of cars, shouting orders, while others balanced on high ladders, making sure every lamppost and archway had a string of mini paper pumpkins firmly secured. Ginger was sure her cousin was somewhere in that crowd. Alexis Chambers took her role as Head of Hospitality very seriously. By midday, the street would be closed off completely, the festival underway, and the usual hum of traffic replaced with wandering footsteps and raucous laughter. If there was a bullhorn within a five-mile radius, Alexis was likely holding it.

Ginger stepped carefully around a stack of hay bales being unloaded from a pick-up truck. She was a few blocks away from her bakery when the door to CinnaCutz Hair Studio burst open. A woman sporting a gray mohawk nearly collided with Ginger, catching herself just in time, her hands smoothing down the tapered sides.

'Sorry, honey, didn't see you there,' she said, turning back toward the open glass door. 'Ethel, I mean it, now. You know I'm going to miss you! Take it easy, you hear me?'

Inside, framed by the doorway, stood the woman named Ethel; petite and narrow-shouldered, swallowed by a black cardigan. Her silver hair had been set into soft curls. Her skin looked pale, fine like pressed paper, her thin mouth lifted in a pained smile. Ethel offered the woman a small wave with a veined hand.

'You drive safe, Delores,' she called back, her voice thick with rasp. Delores blew her a kiss and lowered herself into a midnight blue Cadillac and sped away.

Through a wide pane of glass, Ginger watched Ethel move slowly back inside. The hair studio was modest but tidy; two styling chairs, mirrors framed in gold-painted wood, a shelf lined with hairsprays and curl creams. The black and white tile floor gleamed. Ethel bent down to pick up a broom and paused halfway through, her shoulders dipping slightly, as though the effort was costly. She straightened, one hand bracing her back, and huffed out a labored breath. Then, she reached into her pocket and pulled out an inhaler, bringing it to her mouth and taking a puff, closing her eyes.

Ginger glanced at the paper sign in the window: Ethel Lawson – Styling Cinnamon Falls for 30 years. Delores said she'd miss Ethel. Was she closing her shop?

Ginger didn't know how long she would stay in Cinnamon Falls, but she hoped she would have the kind of success that would sustain itself for the next thirty years like Ethel's had.

As Ethel slumped in the nearest chair, her gaze drifted to the window, and her eyes met Ginger's through the glass. For a brief second, Ginger felt caught, like she'd intruded on a private moment. Ethel looked at her with a quiet, assessing calm, almost like she was expecting her to come inside, and smiled. Ginger returned the gesture with a small bend of her fingers.

A forklift beeped behind her, snapping Ginger back to the present.

'Move it, people!' someone shouted down the block.

Ginger tore her eyes away from Ethel, adjusted her bag, and continued up Main Street.

After traveling a few blocks, she reached The Maple Bakery. A woman in wide-legged, moon-print pants was covering a long folding table in a thick, velvet cloth. With practiced patience she placed what looked to be a silver bowl in the center, hollow in the middle and high on the sides. Ginger stepped closer, realizing it was a sculpture of two hands clasped together, palms open to receive. As she watched, the woman drew a gleaming sphere from a satchel, its surface swirling with an inky black fog inside. She gently lowered it into the bowl's hollow middle and affixed a banner across the front of her table that read: *Moonlight's Howl Apothecary* in curling script. Beneath it: *Herbs for the body, moonlight for the soul.*

A long, red scarf floated loosely around the woman's neck, its tassels fluttering in the wind like a ribbon of flame behind her. As Ginger approached, the woman looked up; her sharp nose held a pair of circle-framed glasses outlined in silver, making her soft brown eyes comically larger behind the lenses. Her lips parted slightly, and she batted a mess of unruly dark curls out of her face and revealed an easy smile.

'Care for a reading before the festivities?' she asked, gesturing to the ball. The inky mass inside swirled faster.

'Sorry, no time. I just took a quick coffee break.' Ginger turned back to her building and shoved the key into the bakery's seafoam green door beside her. It halted, catching in the lock. Ginger pushed and tugged, but the key didn't budge.

Of course, Ginger thought.

The woman stood, blinking, the expectant smile still on her face.

Ginger gestured to the stubborn door, silently threatening it to open as she rammed her shoulder against it. 'Just . . . going to get back to baking now.'

'So *you're* the new baker in town that I've been hearing about! I heard Marsha Pickens moved to Asheville and you renovated her space in a matter of months!' the whimsical woman announced loud enough for the entire block to hear. People slowed, pretending not to watch their interaction. Ginger wished she could disappear. Defeated by the door, she had no choice but to give in to the conversation.

'I'm Rowan Bell,' the woman boomed. 'I run the herbal apothecary over in Juniper Heights.' Rowan flourished her arms over her table that was now crowded with bottles with handwritten labels, several decks of cards of ranging sizes, jewelry with colorful stones, and that curious, swimming black ball. She stuck out her hand, fingers ringed in silver, while her bangles jingled melodically on her wrist.

Ginger hesitated, worried that once Rowan's palm collided with hers, she'd be able to see every lie and every painful memory that she was trying to bury. Even though she considered Alexis Chambers family, if more than one person in this little town knew her business, it'd be too many.

Ginger also knew how quickly word could travel. If she snubbed the weird tarot chick in front of everyone, she'd be *that bakery bitch* by morning. A bad reputation was not ideal for a new business. She had to make this work; and if that meant making small talk through gritted teeth with the locals, that was what she had to do. Besides, there was no turning back now. Atlanta was not home anymore. She had nowhere else to go.

Ginger swallowed down her apprehension and stuck her hand out, too.

'Ginger Mills,' she said proudly, as she pumped Rowan's hand twice, hoping to muster up some confidence.

'Gingerrrrr,' Rowan purred. 'You must dye your hair to match your name. You have the perfect skin tone for it.'

She hadn't considered it before, but it would be a nice change of pace from her normal wavy, natural black. She'd prayed for a new beginning, and what better way to celebrate than a new hairstyle?

'All the ladies around here get their hair done by Ethel Lawson over at CinnaCutz.' Ginger followed Rowan's finger as she pointed down Main Street, past Rosie's Diner, where she'd just gotten her coffee from. 'If you don't mind her chain smoking out the back door or reruns of *Paternity Court*, you should let her give you some face-framing layers, it'll give you a *whole* new look.' Rowan winked.

'Thanks, uh . . . I'll think about it,' Ginger responded before trying the key again.

This time, the front door unlocked with ease. She waved politely to Rowan, grateful for the reprieve. Stepping inside, the aroma greeted her like a warm embrace; vanilla, maple, brown sugar, and a whisper of cinnamon clung to the air from the morning's prep.

Ginger inhaled deeply, setting down her first vanilla latte of the day, and pushed up her sleeves. She stepped behind the service counter and ventured down the narrow hallway toward the kitchen where everything was just as she had left it earlier that morning.

The kitchen was Ginger's favorite part of the bakery, with bright polished countertops that gleamed beneath hanging copper pots and pans. The stand mixer waited for its orders beside bowls of rising dough and a half-empty bin of flour. She'd need more soon but was thankful that she had a delivery scheduled for the following morning.

She unclipped her apron from the hook on the wall and tied it around her waist, double knotting the strap, and then reviewed the to-do list she'd written on the dry erase board as she washed her hands. She'd pared her menu down to six signature items – more than enough baking for a staff of one; and all six had check marks beside them, noting that all the prep had been completed before she'd had her coffee break.

A small disbelieving smile tugged at her lips. She was finally here. Opening day. After months of dust and delays, she was finally here. She'd come straight from Atlanta in a tinkering hoopty with two suitcases, her mother's recipes, and a lease she'd signed on faith, pouring everything she had into this space. There were days that she thought the flooring would never get installed, nights she'd fallen asleep in Alexis' kitchen sketching layouts, and moments where she thought it'd never happen – but she pushed through it all until this point.

And now, the timing couldn't have been more perfect: the Fall Festival. The biggest day of the year for Cinnamon Falls. While the town descended onto Harvest Square and Main Street, she would be opening her doors for the very first time.

She felt a surge of pride that she was ahead of schedule. After months of worrying and wondering if she'd made a mistake leaving everything and everyone behind, fate was aligning exactly as it should. Baking was a marathon, not a sprint, and with just a few hours until the celebration officially started, perfection was her destination.

She started where she always did, with dough. The first batch of cinnamon pecan pull-apart bread had finished its rise, the scent of brown sugar and butter already perfuming the kitchen. She punched it down gently, the soft hiss of escaping air grounding her more than caffeine ever could. She flipped the dough out of the bowl and patted it into a rectangle, using her rolling pin to create perfect corners. She brushed on melted butter and sprinkled the cinnamon sugar and pecan mixture all the way to the edges. She cut the dough into squares and layered them into a greased pan for a second rise. She moved on to preheating the convection ovens, her movements practiced and precise.

Next were the donuts. Ginger had roasted her sweet potatoes yesterday and they were now the perfect texture: soft, pillowy and caramelized. She pulled the cooled candied bacon out of the chiller and shamelessly popped a piece into her mouth. The salty sweet flavor kicked her brain into high gear as she chopped the meat into fine pieces.

She spooned the donut batter into the mold with a quick flick of the wrist, just like her mother had taught her. Claudine used to say you could tell the mood of a baker by the texture of their dough; too dense meant too anxious, too soft meant distracted. Even though it was her debut, baking soothed her, and judging by her dough, today was shaping up to be perfect.

As her first batch of donuts cooled, she started on the maple glaze; bringing powdered sugar, butter, vanilla, a generous helping of authentic Canadian maple syrup and a pinch of salt together in a large bowl. She dipped each donut into the mixture and finished with an indulgent topping of the candied bacon.

In just an hour, the kitchen had transformed into a musical of whisks, clinks, and sighs. Maple oat muffins baked on the top rack while another batch of donuts rose on the bottom. Steam fogged the windows as the first timers buzzed.

While she worked, Ginger would occasionally glance through the window, catching the distant sounds of vendors still setting up their booths, the soft hum of laughter drifting up Main Street.

As opening time neared, she could feel the tension build in her chest, and she pushed air through her teeth, trying her hardest to tame the negative thoughts that bubbled up anyway: *What if they hate my desserts? What if I make no money?* Or worse, *what if Harrison shows up and drags me out of here?*

It'd been several long months since she'd left Atlanta to hide out in Alexis' guest room with no future plans. She was safe now. There was no more room for doubt, only execution.

She moved on to finishing the salted caramel apple cheesecake bars, her mother's favorite. If she was being honest, the recipe was her favorite too, which was why she prepped it first and saved the finishing touches for last. Yesterday, she'd layered ribbons of cheesecake filling over a graham cracker crust and let the cheesecake stiffen overnight. Now, she sprinkled the apple and oat crumble over the creamy filling and sliced it with a hot knife, before swirling the salted caramel mixture over the top.

She hoped the people of Cinnamon Falls would love them. She was giving them a piece of her heart in a baking dish.

'Make Mama proud,' she whispered as she set the bars aside.

When the timer chimed, she remembered her vanilla latte on the counter and took a long sip. Wiping her hands on her apron, she started her final challenge: the maple walnut cake with brown sugar frosting.

It was the bakery's showpiece, the recipe she'd spent weeks perfecting. Moist maple walnut cake layers rested on a cooling rack, rich and fragrant from this morning's prep. Ginger whipped brown sugar frosting until it turned fluffy, then spread a liberal amount between the layers. She decorated the border with walnut halves, and the result was her childhood in cake form. If he'd been alive, Uncle Maple would've been attempting to sneak a piece behind her back. She wondered if he was looking down on her with pride.

By nine-thirty a.m. she stood back, surveying her kingdom: trays of muffins lined in neat rows, donuts cooling by the window. The cinnamon pull-apart breads had just finished baking. Ginger poured the glaze, watching it dance between the layers like ribbons. The scent of roasted nuts, maple, and cinnamon engulfed her and she felt her chest loosen. Maybe, just maybe, this could work.

As the clock neared ten a.m., she pulled out the final batch of sweet potato donuts from the oven. Then she found her chalkboard sign and markers, and began to work on today's menu, detailing each dessert, its ingredients, and price.

As her final step, she flipped the sign over her front door to OPEN, and smiled for what felt like the first time in a while.

If Cinnamon Falls was the fairy tale her cousin claimed, that meant it held a happy ending for her. She squeezed her eyes shut and made a wish that today would be as magical as she dreamed.

When she opened them again, she realized the gods had sent her request to voicemail.

With hands cupped around his eyes, pressed against the front window like a kid at a candy store, was Austin Jacobs, her annoying contractor. His grin stretched wide, bound to fog the glass.

'Of course,' she muttered.

He didn't wait for an invitation. Before she could leap behind the counter and hide, he was through the door.

He was dressed the same as always; faded jeans that stretched over his athletic thighs, a branded fleece-lined jacket that hugged his corded arms, not that she'd been paying *that* much attention. His rosy lips were framed by a sharply maintained beard, housing an infuriatingly easy grin that sometimes briefly made her forget how annoying he was. Briefly.

His silky brown skin matched his eyes, a warm and intense hazelnut that lingered a bit too long when they landed on her. He filled the room effortlessly, his stature – broad shoulders and tree trunk legs – were too big for her quaint bakery; his personality, too bright for her quiet, busy morning. She didn't have time for the distraction he was sure to bring.

'Mornin', Sunshine,' he sang, his baritone striking the walls, reverberating in her skull.

She sighed, the corner of her mouth twitching despite her iron will.

'Perfect. My very first customer, and it's you.'

Chapter 2

Austin

Austin Jacobs used to think the Fall Festival was as close as you could get to magic: the soothing sound of soft, lo-fi music permeating Harvest Square, laughter gliding over the treetops and the comfort of warm cinnamon buns fresh from Rosie's Diner.

It was when Cinnamon Falls truly came alive; the crown jewel of the season, when Main Street was transformed into a harvest dream. Burlap banners fluttered from lampposts, pumpkins of all sizes lined the curb in neat, cheerful rows. Overhead, a string of lights had been weaved between the storefronts. Once the sun dipped lower in the sky, he knew his hometown would sparkle through the night.

Now, as an adult, the feeling still lingered, but different, tucked deeper in his chest. It made him think of Rosslyn Rose and Maggie Shilling. He would have seen Maggie by now, clipboard in hand, barking orders in a walkie-talkie. Although Alexis Chambers was doing a stellar job in Maggie's absence, this time of the year would never be the same. Cinnamon Falls without Maggie's organization and Rosie's cinnamon buns felt a little duller, like the place had half its heart. Still, life pressed on.

It was just past ten-thirty a.m., and Alexis had opened the Fall Festival floodgates. The crisp morning air swept through the town carrying the scent of brown sugar, roasted nuts, and the ever-present undercurrent of earthy spice from the forest of wild cinnamon trees miles away. Austin stepped through piles of scarlet and gold leaves, their papery crunch echoing underneath his boots. Half the town was already out, bundled in flannel, mugs of cider clutched to their chests, noses rosy from the chill.

Up further, Harvest Square sat at the heart of it all, where generations of families who owned Main Street businesses set up their booths beneath a canopy of trees showcasing everything from homemade jams, to natural body butter, carved woodwork, and baked goods. Vendors from neighboring towns lined the sidewalks, their tents spilling color onto the pavement; burnt orange, deep reds, golden yellows fluttering in the breeze. He stood, taking it all in. There was nothing quite like this: a perfect fall morning, his hometown alive with color, and the satisfying sight of his handiwork at the center of it all.

While the crowd stopped at the shops along Main Street, Austin made a beeline for The Maple Bakery, his latest baby in a long list of renovations. Just two years ago he'd worked tirelessly alongside his father while they restored The Cinnamon Scoop, and after Marsha Pickens decided to move CinnaSudz to Asheville, he'd been recommended to take on Ginger Mills' bakery.

From the street, the bakery looked exactly how he pictured the empty space mere months ago. The pink and white striped awning grabbed his attention first, making him want to stop and look in. It stood out proudly next to Sly James' brick-laid General Store. It took a while for Ginger to come around to the idea of it, but in the end, he'd gotten her to see it his way. The town needed new life after so much loss, and Ginger's bakery was bound to bring it more flavor.

He leaned closer, cupping his hands to the window, hoping to catch a glimpse of her working; expecting to see her in the kitchen he'd built, completing her finishing touches before the day's first rush. Instead, she was standing in the middle of the floor, her eyes narrowed in his direction.

Judging by the look on her face, Ginger was, once again, not very happy to see him. During renovations, Austin had grown used to her scowling and could tell her expressions apart by now. This one, with her hands crossed over her chest and her lips flattened in a disapproving line, let him know that he had about ten good minutes of her time before she reached her maximum annoyance level. That was plenty of time to tap dance on her nerves.

As always, she was all sour, no sweet. He wondered how a woman *that* fine could always look so mean, especially when her eyes landed on him.

Ginger Mills was hard to miss. She stood tall without trying to, long lines and quiet confidence giving her a statuesque presence. Her brown skin was deep and luminous like warmed honey under the peach-tinted pendant lights overhead. The glow caught the curve along her cheekbones and the bridge of her nose where a faint constellation of freckles gathered.

Her long, naturally wavy hair was pinned up in a loose bun at the crown of her head, though the style had begun surrendering to the day already. Soft coils escaped near her temples, a few stubborn tendrils curled at the nape of her neck, brushing along the collar of her sweater.

When she moved, there was something deliberate about her, like every gesture had been pre-planned. She wore all black; a fitted soft sweater hugged her narrow waist and skimmed her hips, sleeves pushed up just enough to reveal graceful wrists dusted with flour. Her dark jeans were sculpted to her long legs, tucked neatly into a pair of worn combat boots that gave her a rebellious edge. The monochrome look made her eyes impossible to ignore; sharp and suspicious, the kind that could see through people. There was something about her mouth, too. Full and expressive, but rarely careless. She might've looked like every man's dream, but she also looked like she'd bite if you got too close.

Austin cleared his throat and forced a grin, something that would surely piss her off.

'Mornin', Sunshine,' he sang, stepping inside, plastering on his widest smile.

'Perfect,' Ginger commented, rolling her almond-shaped eyes. 'My first customer, and it's you.'

Austin placed a hand over his heart in mock offense. 'It's been four weeks since I handed over the keys. You didn't miss me at all?'

Ginger shot him a look before slipping off her flour-stained apron and placing it on its hook on the wall. As she moved behind the counter, her hair caught the light like spun silk. She sighed and reached up to untie her bun, letting her hair tumble around her shoulders in soft waves.

Austin cleared his throat, his mouth suddenly dry. 'You know I had to see the place open,' he said, taking another long look around at the bakery, distracting himself with the pens on her counter that had maple leaves dancing along the barrel. 'Since you threatened to fire me at least twice during construction.'

'Three times,' she corrected. 'And if you hadn't installed the flooring I wanted, it would have been a fourth.'

He barked out a laugh and leaned backward, surveying the shelves, the soft pink walls, and the desserts in the display cases that made his stomach rumble. The bakery looked even better than he could have imagined. The pink checkerboard tile floor gleamed, every detail a reflection of her mind; from the vintage sign outside to the chalkboard menu where she'd written 'Life is what you bake it' in romantic, loopy calligraphy.

As uptight as Ginger was, Austin was impressed. He'd given the bakery its bones, but in just a few weeks she'd brought it to life. 'You did great, Ginger. It looks amazing, just like your sketches.'

She gave a small shrug, but he saw something flicker in her face; relief, or maybe pride, but it vanished fast, replaced by her cool composure. Did she *ever* smile?

'Thank you,' she said flatly, like the words had to be forced. After a beat she offered, 'You were right about the awning. It really does stand out.'

Austin bit back a grin, the memory of their first introduction, 183 days ago, swimming into his memory.

It had been a Sunday. He'd just finished lunch at Rosie's when Terrance and Alexis Chambers called and asked to meet him at CinnaSudz. Once there, he had been introduced to Alexis' cousin, Ginger, who had just moved to Cinnamon Falls from Atlanta and had bought Mrs. Pickens' old laundromat. She wanted to turn it into a bakery, fast – in time for her grand opening at the Fall Festival.

It was a huge ask; one that would push all his other projects to the back burner. Jacobs & Sons had been running a full-throttle, two-man operation up until his father's accident the year before. Now, all the big jobs fell to Austin. He had been laying flooring and running wires since he could walk, but he was skeptical about Ginger's turnaround time. He thought it'd take much longer than six months to complete the water line overhaul, structural modifications, and electric upgrades, not to mention the permitting and inspections, but Ginger refused to adjust her expectations, or her budget, and Austin loved a challenge.

Ginger had been all business for the next six months, describing her vision in great detail. She'd known exactly what she wanted: the shelving here, the counter there, a corner nook for cafe tables, two convection ovens, and a walk-in chiller. No hesitation, no fluff, all certainty. He didn't know much about her, or why she'd chosen Cinnamon Falls, only that she was determined to make Fall Festival her opening day. And the harder she pushed him, the more intrigued he became.

Along the way, he'd tried the small talk angle – weather, coffee, or local gossip – but she'd met every joke with a steely gaze that could freeze drywall into place. He quickly learned that Ginger Mills was a one-woman storm. She had vision, laser-sharp focus, and enough balls to go toe to toe with him about anything, from paint samples to flooring. He'd always been the man with the answers, and Ginger was refreshing in a maddening way.

Now, he rubbed the back of his neck, glancing toward

the counter where she was arranging a tray of donuts that were topped with bacon. He had to sample the goods.

'You planning to share any of those with your favorite contractor?'

'Depends,' she said, never looking up at him. 'Is your dad around?'

Austin guffawed, shaking his head. 'I'm more of a chocolate guy, anyway,' he quipped, shrugging his shoulders.

Ginger slid a donut onto a napkin and handed it over, but the look in her eyes made it clear that it was less an act of kindness and more of a nudge to get him to leave.

'This is Terrance's favorite, the "You Autumn Know". It's a sweet potato donut baked until golden brown, dipped in maple glaze and topped with candied maple bacon.'

Austin had a joke about police officers and donuts, but he kept it to himself. He took a slow bite. Pillowy dough melted in his mouth while the maple glaze had a sweetness that danced on his tongue. The salty sweet crunch of bacon was the perfect addition. He could've eaten the rest of the tray if he was in his bulking season.

'Damn, Ginger. This is . . . *you* made these?' he asked, before devouring the other half of the donut with a snap.

'What do you think, I'm AI or something? Of course

I made those.' She looked up at him, a storm in her eyes.

He swallowed, licking the glaze from his thumb, chuckling at how easy it was to get under her skin. She rolled her eyes, but he caught the ghost of a smile before she turned away.

Austin watched the festival crowd move past the window; kids chasing leaves, vendors calling out. His gaze shifted back toward her. She looked different now, softer, though the guard was still there. She worked quickly, filling the case with the last of her donuts.

'Bet this place'll keep you busy all day,' he commented.

'Oh, it will if people stop standing in the way of paying customers,' Ginger retorted.

Austin pointed to himself. 'That's my cue, huh?'

Just then, the bell jingled overhead. A couple stepped through the doors – the Bennetts' youngest son, Niles, and Ms. Pearline's great-niece, Shawna Daniels.

Austin had gone to high school with Niles' older sister, Nia. He didn't know Niles as well since he was younger, but they were friendly enough in passing, especially after Austin renovated The Cinnamon Scoop. As the first business in Cinnamon Falls, the Bennetts were practically royalty; everyone knew and respected them. Niles held out a fist to Austin, who gave it a friendly bump with his own.

'Mornin', Austin. How's everything?'

Shawna offered him a polite nod, leaves sweeping in behind them as the door closed softly. Shawna took a long sip of the coffee cup she held from Rosie's Diner, the signature red rose printed on the side.

'All good,' Austin replied. 'Enjoying the Fall Festival?'

'You know it. Wait, this is the old laundromat, right?' Niles mumbled, glancing around like he was attempting to conjure up the memories of CinnaSudz's heyday.

'Yeah, that's what my sister said. I told you, it's a bakery now.' Shawna bounced on her tiptoes, craning her neck to read the menu against the wall.

Ginger's face brightened, her eyes growing softer, her posture open and friendly.

'Welcome to The Maple Bakery! I'm Ginger, what can I get for you?'

So she *could* be nice. Austin had been convinced she was allergic all this time.

'Is this the "I Loaf You A Lot"?' Shawna asked, pointing toward a loaf of glazed layers of bread the size of Austin's palm.

'Yes, this is my take on a cinnamon bun—'

'No one's cinnamon buns are better than Rosie's,' Niles cut in, crossing his arms, skeptical. He took inventory of the space, analyzing every nook and cranny with a slow, concentrated gaze.

Austin watched as Ginger didn't falter under Niles' remarks. Alexis must have briefed her on Cinnamon Falls' fierce love for Rosslyn Rose, even in death.

'I don't doubt that. I've heard all about Ms. Rosie's cinnamon buns, trust me, I could never. This is a maple pecan pull-apart bread.'

Shawna *oohed*, stepping closer to the case. Ginger continued with her captivated audience. 'It's a buttery dough glazed with maple brown sugar and toasted pecans. It'll go perfect with your coffee.'

Niles looked between Shawna, Ginger, the pull-apart bread, and back, drumming his fingers along his biceps, considering. He leaned closer to the glass, pacing. He stepped back suddenly and said, 'Give me five slices, one "Crumble and Get It", and two "You Autumn Know's".'

Ginger clapped her hands in satisfaction and started on his order. She pulled a flat box down from the counter and folded it upright, swiftly loading his desserts inside while she and Shawna bantered back and forth about Niles' insatiable sweet tooth; to which he responded, 'My first word was vanilla. What do you expect?'

Austin backed toward the door and lifted his hand in Ginger's direction, letting her know that he was leaving. When they met eyes, he gave her a hopeful thumbs up. Ginger shooed him away in response.

He stepped out, stumbling onto the busy sidewalk. A group of teenagers brushed past him and spilled into the bakery, their laughter crowding the lobby. Austin paused outside the window, watching as Ginger charmed her new guests with an easy laugh that brightened her whole face and made her eyes sparkle; one she never used with him.

Something in his chest tugged – the dull ache he'd

grown familiar with whenever his thoughts trailed to Samantha. Her name wasn't a wound exactly, not anymore, more like a scar that ached when the weather turned. It'd been ages since he'd heard her laugh that could fill up the room. He once believed he'd remember that sound forever, but now he could barely summon the echo of it. Their memories had faded, only one stubborn one remained – the one he couldn't shake.

A child's scream sliced through the air, bringing him back to the present, as a group of little kids barreled past him, their sticky candied apples raised above their heads like trophies. A vendor steadied the items on her table as the children zoomed by. Austin recognized her immediately; the eccentric style – a strangely long scarf fluttering in the wind, loose fitting clothes with varying prints and colors, and wild glossy curls – could only belong to Rowan Bell, her vendor table stationed directly across from the bakery.

She arched one brow behind a pair of glasses that overtook her face and grinned like a fox who'd stumbled across an unfortunately lost chicken. He hadn't noticed her earlier, too single-minded, eager to get to Ginger. She'd seen him staring into the bakery, he was sure of it.

'Well, well, well,' she drawled, leaning forward, resting her elbows on her table, which looked like a miniature replica of her shop: dark, moody, and whimsical. 'You've been staring into that window like—'

'I wasn't staring,' Austin faltered, heat crawling up

the back of his neck. 'I was admiring my craftsmanship,' he countered, crossing his arms hoping to hide the way his face was flaming. 'I built the place, you know.'

'No surprise there,' she deadpanned, pointing to the logo on his chest: a hammer and wrench crossed with the letters J & S stitched underneath. 'Jacobs & Sons has practically built everything on Main Street.' She flicked her sugar-encrusted fingers toward Ginger's window while she picked through the bag of pecans. Just then, a young customer crept toward Rowan's table, curious and quiet, coming to Austin's rescue.

'Have fun at the Fall Festival, Mr. Countertops!' Rowan yelled after him, as he backed away to make room for the customer.

Austin picked up his pace and merged into the traffic of festival goers. He passed a couple leaning into each other, sharing a steaming cup of cider. Another pair of teens posed for a picture under the pumpkin archway as he strolled through Harvest Square, in the thick of it all. Just ahead, a little girl tugged on her father's coat sleeve, insistent, eager to show him the leaf she'd found.

And suddenly, Samantha was in his mind again, uninvited like a draft through a cracked window. He recalled the last time he'd seen her, so clearly in his mind, standing in the doorway of the quaint yellow house he'd built with his own two hands.

The house he thought would be theirs forever. The house she left him in.

He could still see the half-full boxes behind her,

twenty-seven of them to be exact; the look of genuine shock when he'd returned home early, the way she'd avoided eye contact when she told him she needed 'more than this'. More than him. How she'd slipped off the ring he'd saved for three years to buy and sat it gently on the kitchen table. Catapulting it at his head would have hurt less.

He blinked hard, focusing on the bright streamers ahead, the crunch of the leaves under his boots, the swell of Rodney McIntire and the Mac's jazz trombone, but none of it distracted him from Samantha's memory, except one thing.

He glanced backward at Ginger's bakery growing smaller in the distance, its pink awning jutting out against the brick background; something new for slow-moving, traditional Cinnamon Falls.

And maybe something new for him, too.

Chapter 3

Ginger

Ginger made a mental note to wear different shoes tomorrow. The combat boots she'd pulled on at three o'clock that morning had made sense to her still-sleeping brain at the time. But now, she realized it had been the wrong choice. Her feet throbbed; a dull, pulsing ache that radiated from her heels to her calves, but she didn't dare stop moving, not now; not when the bakery was still buzzing with the last wave of Fall Festival traffic.

Outside, the late afternoon sun spilled gold across Cinnamon Falls. Ginger finally had a break in customers, who'd visited steadily throughout the morning and afternoon, following the scent of brown sugar and maple past Rosie's Diner and straight to her door. She took the time to refill the display case, which was nearly empty now, save for a few lonely blondie bars that she was sure would sell soon. Her pull-apart bread and walnut cake were the most popular, flying off the shelves faster than she'd anticipated. She smiled, taking a moment to appreciate that she was living an answered prayer.

The bakery's bell chimed overhead and Ginger blinked, taking in the woman with honey-brown hair and the tiny white Pomeranian sticking out of her handbag, its tongue lolling out of its mouth. Its long white fur was styled into a ponytail on top of its head secured by a pink bow, and it sported a pink gingham printed bandana tied beneath its neck. The little dog let out a curious yip when Ginger introduced herself.

'Hi!' Ginger greeted both of them. 'I'm Ginger and this is my bakery. I've got a few of the Butter Me Up Bars left. It's a chewy brown butter blondie.' Ginger watched as the woman leaned closer to the display case and the Pomeranian did too, stretching its nose toward the counter, sniffing eagerly. It placed its paws on the edge of the bag and Ginger noticed its nails were painted hot pink.

'Apparently, someone is interested.'

The woman smiled, adjusting the bag on her shoulder as the dog wriggled inside. 'This is Princess Pawlina. She thinks everything is for her.'

'She has excellent taste,' Ginger replied.

'Well, don't just sniff around, say hello.' The woman stepped closer to the service counter, enough for Princess Pawlina to extend her paw toward Ginger, who shook it fervently.

'Very nice to meet you, Princess,' Ginger said. She gestured toward the display. 'You two are in luck. I just pulled a fresh dozen of the sweet potato donuts out of the oven. I call them "You Autumn Know". They're my last batch of the day if you're interested.'

The woman's eyes flicked between the pastries. She smiled good-naturedly and patted her very flat stomach through her sweater. 'I'm full of smoked turkey legs and I'm still digging the kettle corn out of my teeth. I couldn't eat another thing, but thank you.' She glanced over her shoulder but there was no one behind her. 'I was just checking to see if my son caught up to me.' She leaned closer, lowering her voice. 'I actually came to ask if you make birthday cakes?'

Ginger bounced on her toes excitedly because she hadn't expected her first custom order so soon.

'I'm Rachel Greene.' She pushed her hand over the counter for Ginger to shake. 'My husband came in this morning with our son, Dougie, and we had one of your *An Apple A Day* cheesecake bars; the one with the apple filling and salted caramel.' She paused, her eyes lighting up. 'We literally debated over who would get the last bite . . .' Princess Pawlina let out a small bark as if she was chiming in.

'I won,' Rachel finished proudly; her eyes flashed when she smiled. 'Dougie's birthday party is tomorrow, and we were just going to pick up a plain ol' vanilla sheet cake from Heather over at Cinnamon Grove tonight, but I would love to buy one of your cheesecakes right now, if I can. Dougie would be so surprised!'

Ginger hesitated. Heather Hughes had been nothing short of a godsend when Ginger had first bought the bakery. When she'd started testing recipes she'd found herself spending a small fortune on flour and sugar, until Heather generously shared her food supplier's details, Valley View Wholesale Foods. It cut Ginger's costs almost in half. Since then, they'd become good friends in the months leading up to the Fall Festival. Ginger never thought she'd be close with a woman twice her age, but she knew from experience that good friendships were hard to come by.

She didn't feel good about taking money from Heather's pockets, but a bland vanilla sheet cake was no match for her salted caramel masterpiece. She knew Heather would understand.

'I'm afraid I'm all sold out of *An Apple A Day* cheesecake bars right now . . .' Rachel's face fell, and Ginger panicked; she didn't want to lose the sale. It wouldn't take too much effort to add one more batch to her prep list tomorrow. A good reputation was worth the sacrifice. 'The quickest I could have one ready for you is tomorrow morning. Is that okay?'

Rachel's face lit up instantly. 'Perfect! Thank you! I'll come and pick it up around ten a.m.?'

'You'll be my first customer of the day,' Ginger responded happily.

She whipped out a notepad, writing down the details. Once the price was agreed on, Rachel clapped her hands excitedly. 'Dougie's going to be so happy!'

As Rachel and Pawlina skipped out of the door, Ginger allowed herself another small, quiet moment of pride. She didn't need the Caldwell name. She didn't need Atlanta. She had this now. A tiny town where no one knew her name or her background. She could be anyone she wanted to be. She decided she could spend the rest of her days here as Ginger Mills and bake to her heart's content.

The bell chimed over the door again. This time her cousin Alexis bounced inside, her husband, Terrance, at her side as always. They sported matching knit scarves and rose-printed mugs full of spiked cider, Ginger was sure.

'Look at this place!' Alexis exclaimed, arms wide, eyes glassy. Her gaze landed on the empty display case. 'Sold out on your first day? I'm telling everyone I know my little cousin is a baking legend! You know Daddy would be so proud.'

'He'd be telling anyone who would listen that he had a bakery named after him,' Ginger added with a nostalgic laugh. She raised her latte in the air and Alexis did the same with her mug.

'To Uncle Maple,' Ginger and Alexis said at the same time.

Uncle Maple, Alexis' father, was originally from Michigan. Every Christmas he would show up to

Ginger's mother's house with a case of authentic Canadian maple syrup. The sweet syrup meant the start of the holiday season for their family and always held good memories of her childhood. Maple meant safety and she needed that more than ever right now.

Ginger leaned over the counter, giving her cousin a deep hug.

Alexis pulled back, palming her cheek. 'I'm so proud of you, Ging. You left your toxic life behind and now look at you.'

'I couldn't have done it without you.'

'I told you, Cinnamon Falls is the perfect place for happily-ever-afters.'

Ginger knew her cousin was going to cash in on her 'I told you so' debt any day now.

Terrance let out a cough and zeroed in on the fresh batch of donuts. 'You got any leftovers for law enforcement?'

Alexis rolled her eyes. 'Here comes his cop-donut joke—'

Terrance raised a finger in protest. 'I'll have you know I won first place in the Dad Joke contest this morning with that very joke.'

Alexis twisted her lips. 'You're the only one who enters.'

He pulled her in close to his side, nuzzling his nose against her neck. 'And I'm not even a dad yet.'

Ginger waved them away. 'Take all that out of my bakery. This is a no-love zone, okay?'

The door swung open again, a burst of laughter spilling in. Two couples and a young girl filled the front lobby; Ginger recognized them from Alexis' pictures on social media, especially Terrance's partner at the police department, Jesse Shaw.

Jesse was clutching hands with a brown-skinned beauty that he couldn't tear his eyes away from. Her tailored brown trench coat was buttoned neatly around a cream cowl-neck sweater. Ginger felt her face lift into a smile that, for once, she didn't have to fake.

'You must be Ginger!' the woman said, grinning equally as hard. 'Alexis has told me all about you! We have been *dying* to try your pastries all day, but I've been held up at the shop.'

'Welcome to The Maple Bakery!' Ginger responded, her arms spread wide.

The little girl pressed her face to the display case and whispered, 'It smells like heaven in here.'

'I'm sorry it's just a few items,' Ginger said apologetically. 'But you're welcome to have what's left.'

The girl beckoned a man next to her down to her level and he bent over to meet her. They shared the same eyes. He had to have been her father.

She pounded a finger into her open palm, demanding, 'Next time, we stop here first.'

'Yes, ma'am,' he answered back. It was clear who ran the show. Ginger liked her already.

Alexis made the introductions. 'This is Nia Bennett,

her family owns The Cinnamon Scoop further down Main Street, just a couple of blocks from here.' Ginger recalled the ice-cream shop with the googly-eyed mascot on the far corner. Alexis had made sure to let her know all about the princess of Cinnamon Falls.

'My brother and his girlfriend raved about the pull-apart bread, said it was neck and neck with Rosie's cinnamon buns—'

'You're Niles' sister!' Ginger asked, finally connecting the dots between Nia and her first customer this morning. 'You two look so much alike.'

Nia groaned. 'He wishes he looked as good as me.'

'You know Jesse already,' Alexis continued, gesturing to the stocky gentleman whose hand stayed permanently glued to Nia's. Ginger tried not to gawk at the diamond on Nia's finger. It made her think of the emerald she'd given up so easily. Ginger's thumb grazed the empty spot on her ring finger as Alexis rattled off more introductions.

'This is Will Reed. He cuts hair just across the way at Bones' Barbershop.' The caramel-skinned man nodded his head, pushing the runaway locs out of his face.

'Nice to meet you,' he said with a friendly smile.

Alexis moved on, gesturing to the other woman. 'Morgan Taylor. Her family runs the Daffodil Inn up on the hill just before you reach Asheville.'

When Ginger rode into town she vaguely remembered a sign for a 'quaint bed and breakfast with relaxing riverfront views'.

'We want everything,' Morgan cut in, all smiles. She was dressed in monochrome purple, down to the shoes, no easy feat, but Ginger was impressed at her dedication.

'I'm the only person you need to know,' the little girl said with an air of importance, her eyes barely visible over the counter's edge. 'I'm Angel Reed.' On her tiptoes, she stuck her hand out with the confidence of a grown woman. 'Investigator extraordinaire.' She flipped a piece of torn notebook paper out of her jacket pocket and handed it to Ginger. 'If someone you love dies, call me.'

Will slapped his palm to his forehead as the room erupted in laughter. Ginger unfolded the crayon-riddled paper, realizing it was her version of a business card with only her name, Angel Reed, and nothing else.

'I'll remember that,' Ginger said, tucking the paper in her pocket and stifling a laugh, because it was clear the little girl was very serious about her business, and Ginger was a girl's girl.

Between her seven customers, 'whatever's left' in the display cases quickly turned into nothing. Jesse snatched the remaining donuts before Chambers could claim any, before generously deciding to split them, while Morgan and Will took the last two blondie bars.

'You coming to the parade?' Jesse looked at Ginger, while Nia swiped at a bit of maple glaze on his chin.

Ginger froze. 'Oh, I . . . well, I was going to finish cleaning up and—'

'Nope,' Morgan interrupted, beckoning for her. 'You must come to see the new Cinnamon King and Queen. It's basically Cinnamon Falls law.'

'We'll save a spot for you right up front,' Nia added brightly.

'Trust me, it's worth it. You into cars?' Will asked.

Ginger hesitated. She was into cars as much as she was into space; just enough to make small talk. 'I think so? It'll just take a second to close up.'

The group's cheers filled the bakery like applause, and Ginger couldn't help but smile. As they exited, Ginger stepped into the kitchen and stood alone in the quiet, warm space, staring at all the dishes piled in the sink. Not in a bad way, but from a place of gratitude. She'd made something that people wanted. Something that mattered.

She unhooked her apron, washed her hands, and pulled on her coat.

Outside, music drifted through the air, a steady thump of drums, while clusters of townspeople pressed in along the road, laughing, chatting, and waiting. Main Street was shoulder to shoulder now, festival energy swelling as the announcer tested the microphone near the stage at Harvest Square.

Ginger scanned the crowd, her eyes trained for familiar faces. She didn't see the man running toward her until he was almost on top of her.

'Whoa, Ginger!' Landon Lawson skidded to a stop in front of her. 'Standin' in the middle of Main Street like a tourist.' He laughed; that familiar and easy chuckle that she'd heard every Sunday morning when he delivered ingredients to her bakery. Landon was a driver for Valley View Wholesale Foods and was always punctual for his weekly delivery.

He was out of uniform today, dressed in light wash jeans and a red buttoned flannel shirt that exposed his forearms, which were pure veined muscle. His close-cropped haircut was hidden beneath a Cinnamon Falls branded baseball cap. Several inches taller, he glanced over Ginger's head, looking for someone out of her sight.

'In a rush?' Ginger asked, noticing the tension in his stance.

'Trying to be,' he admitted. 'My wife's waiting for me.' He pointed his chin in a general direction behind her. 'She's getting older . . . not feeling her best tonight.' His voice softened a touch. 'Trying to get her home before Main Street backs up when the parade starts. You know how it gets.'

'Older?' Ginger questioned. 'I bet the pair of you don't look a day over forty.'

Landon barked out a laugh. 'I'll be sure to tell her that. She'll get a kick out of it. Listen, I better go before I'm late for my shift tonight.'

She stepped out of his way, allowing him to walk around her. Before he got too far, he pointed at her. 'I'll see you first thing tomorrow morning. Got a fresh order comin' in for you.'

'Drive safe,' she called as he turned away. He gave her a quick salute and began weaving through bodies with ease, someone clapping him on the shoulder good-naturedly as he passed. Then, Landon disappeared into the crowd, swallowed by the celebration.

Ginger found the group waiting a few meters away. Nia looped her arm through Ginger's and tugged her toward the front of the crowd with the confidence of a born local.

'You can't watch your first parade from the back,' she insisted, clearing a space for her right at the lip of the sidewalk. The rest of the group fell in easily around her like they'd always been a unit. Ginger wasn't used to feeling folded into something warm; something communal that didn't expect anything in return.

When she'd first started dating Harrison, his mother had peppered her with questions about her background; her parents' lineage and her education, as if she couldn't believe her son could take interest in someone so . . . common. Here, Ginger didn't feel like such an outsider, even though it was clear she had a lot of catching up to do. Admittedly, she hadn't spent a lot of time socializing when she first moved to Cinnamon Falls. She was laser-focused on building a future she wouldn't have to run from, not making friends with the locals.

Nia and Jesse greeted everyone around them, shaking hands and making small talk. Ginger found it annoyingly impressive. Maybe Nia really was Cinnamon Falls royalty. Ginger glanced around the crowd, taking all the people in, until she ran across a familiar face; a goofy smile she'd memorized against her will. Austin Jacobs.

He stood directly across from her on the opposite side of where Main Street met Cinnamon Way, front and center, but hadn't looked in her direction. His phone was pointed down the street where a line of old-fashioned cars were idling.

He leaned too far out in the road and a woman clawed for his jacket, yanking him safely backward on the curb. She had the same smile as him, wide and joyful. His mother, Ginger guessed. Their resemblance was irrefutable. Next to him, his father maneuvered his wheelchair with ease, positioning himself for the best view. Pride practically radiated off him. Ginger had only met Mr. Jacobs once during the renovation; a kind man with stone eyes, a salt-and-pepper beard, and a calm spirit.

'Is Austin's little sister the Cinnamon Queen this year?' Nia asked, leaning back into Jesse's arms intimately. It pricked something tender inside of Ginger. She shifted her gaze to the pavement.

'Yeah,' Jesse answered, nodding his head toward Austin. 'Can't you tell?'

Ginger followed his line of sight just as the first

car in the line eased forward, turning onto Main Street, sunlight glinting off its polished hood. Sitting on the backseat next to a young man, waving shyly, was a girl who couldn't have been older than seventeen; crown slightly askew in her pile of curls, cheeks glowing pink.

Austin came alive. He whistled so loudly Ginger was sure Old Man Milton had been woken up out of his sleep. She watched as he clapped, shouting his sister's name, 'Lillian!' When the car rolled closer, Lillian straightened her back, her wave growing bolder, her smile stretched wider; powered by nothing more than the pure, explosive pride shining from her family on the curb.

Austin was yelling so hard he nearly tripped over a hay bale, catching himself with the kind of dorky enthusiasm that usually would have made Ginger roll her eyes. But, against her better judgment, she found herself waving with the rest of the crowd as Lillian cruised by, the moment effervescent, taking flight in her body. It swept her up, carried her, filled her as her cheers fused with the crowd's. The unbridled joy of a family celebration was something she hadn't experienced in far too long.

She glanced back across the street and noticed that Austin was looking right at her, not with his usual grin, but with something softer, something knowing. His smile eased down into a quiet, confident curve.

Heat climbed her throat. She swallowed hard and

unhooked her gaze from his, tucking her hands deep into her pockets, forcing her breath steady again. Then, without saying goodbye, she dipped backward out of the crowd and headed toward the bakery, back to safety.

When Ginger returned, she was sad to see that the dishes hadn't washed themselves while she'd been away. The sink was still piled high with mixing bowls, spatulas, measuring cups, and sticky pans that smelled of maple and sugar. Pushing up her sleeves, she turned on the warm water and let the familiar rhythm ground her. Each bowl she scrubbed clean felt like a small part of a huge accomplishment. She lined everything neatly along the drying rack.

After the dishes were done, she moved to her prep station. She refilled the clear plastic bins she'd emptied that morning: flour, sugar, brown sugar, and powdered sugar. She scooped each one with care, smoothing the top with the back of her measuring cups.

Tomorrow would be another early morning, but knowing her ingredients were prepped made her to-do list a little shorter.

Her delivery order would arrive before dawn. Landon always came early, which she appreciated. After the first week of her scrambling half-dressed out of bed to meet him, she'd given him a spare key so he could let himself in, drop the goods, and continue his route without interruption.

She moved on to writing her to-do list for tomorrow, Rachel's cake at the top. She tapped her pen against the paper, double- and triple-checking the rest.

When the last counter was wiped down, and the display case clean, she swept the entire kitchen and then the front room. She mopped, humming under her breath, letting the motion unwind the last of her nerves. She hung her apron on its hook, grabbed her coat, and turned toward the side exit off the kitchen, ready to faceplant into her waiting bed.

Bang!

A sharp, hollow clatter echoed from the alley behind the bakery. Ginger froze, her pulse spiking so hard that she felt it in her fingertips. The alley would be dark at this hour; just a narrow stretch between her building and the next, cluttered with recycling bins, cardboard boxes, crates, and whatever deliveries had been broken down during the day. Was someone back there? Had Harrison found her? She waited, holding perfectly still, her breath coming in shallow gasps.

Maybe it was the wind, she tried to convince herself.

BANG!

Another one, louder than before. Her chest tightened, but she took a tentative step toward the door straining her ears. Nothing.

'Get it together, girl,' she said to herself. She didn't

survive the Caldwells, flee an engagement, and rebuild her entire life to get jumped behind her bakery in a small, country town in Georgia.

Not tonight, not ever.

Ginger shuffled back through the kitchen toward the register and pulled out her secret weapon: her father's old baseball bat. She'd snagged it from the garage the day she packed her bags and left for Atlanta after college. He didn't know she had it, but she'd figured he would have approved of the intention.

Her tennis muscles hummed with familiar readiness as she crept back toward the alley. *If someone is out there, they're about to regret picking my bakery.*

She pushed the door open with a fury, bat lifted, her heart pounding. A cold gust of wind slapped her in the face. Leaves skittered across the pavement. The alley was dim, lit only by the weak light of a single buzzing streetlamp overhead.

For a second, she saw nothing.

Then, a tiny rustle. Ginger tightened her grip, steadying herself. Something was moving in the pile of cardboard near the recycling bins. One was upturned, its contents spilling out over the alley. She stepped closer, raising the bat higher, expecting a bunch of raccoons to be having a feast judging by the half-eaten sleeves of butter scattered around.

A tiny, spotted shape scrambled out from the butter box.

A kitten.

A small, very dirty kitten who looked up at her and let out a wobbling, pitiful cry, showing her its tiny teeth. Ginger examined it closely; its white fur had a dull patchy mix of black and golden spots. It had no collar, no tags, nothing to signal that it had once been cared for.

Ginger blinked, half relieved, half annoyed. '*You're* the one making all this noise?' she asked.

It toddled forward on unsteady legs, circled through her boots and rubbed its face against her ankle like they'd been lifelong friends and Ginger had simply gotten lost along the way.

'No,' she repeated, backing away, but the kitten followed. Her shoulders softened, loosening her grip on the bat. Something traitorous inside her chest melted.

'What are you even doing out here? Where is your mama?'

It mewed again, a soft, desperate sound. Ginger leaned the bat against the wall and braced her hands on her hips as the kitten glanced up at her with eyes as big as the moon.

'Ridiculous,' she relented, leaning down to scoop it up. The little kitten trembled against her body, small enough to fit in one hand. 'Alright, fine. Just for tonight, until we find your neglectful mama. I got a few words for her, letting her baby make all this noise outside of my bakery,' Ginger fussed, kicking the butter box aside. She did a double take, looking between the box and the cat. It was obvious what to do next.

'Let's go, Butter.'

She tucked Butter inside her coat, where it curled up against her chest and let out a tired sigh. Still armed with adrenaline and a ridiculous amount of responsibility she didn't ask for, Ginger tossed her bat inside and locked up the bakery.

She made the walk down the street to Cinnamon Grove in search of some cat food before heading home for the night. The automatic doors whooshed open at her arrival, releasing a cool rush of citrus-scented air. The interior gleamed under soft white lighting: sleek shelving, minimalist signage, and polished floors. It felt more like a boutique market than a small-town grocery.

Butter's tiny head poked out curiously from under her jacket as Ginger stepped inside. Yellow eyes darted left to right, absorbing the fluorescent brightness and the hiss of the produce misters.

Against the far wall, emerald kale leaves and plump tomatoes sat in wooden crates stamped with the store's logo. Everything looked staged, but not artificial, like someone had taken great pride in their merchandising. Aisles stretched ahead of her, symmetrical and clean. Ginger scanned each one carefully, noting that pet supplies were in the far back corner.

She started in that direction when she spotted a

familiar face in a passing aisle. Heather Hughes stood midway down the tea aisle, long fingers lightly touching the edges of neatly stacked boxes. She was tall and willowy in a way that mirrored Ginger's own height. Her hair was cut into a sleek bob that skimmed her jawline, parted down the middle, the ends tucked neatly behind her ears. There was nothing flashy about her; she was a plain kind of pretty that announced she was a settled and well-kept woman.

A knowing smile overtook Heather's dark, glossy lips. 'Well, look at you!' Her eyes landed on the mound fidgeting in Ginger's motorcycle jacket. 'Is that . . . a kitten?'

Ginger stepped forward, giving Heather a good look at the antsy kitten. 'Found it behind the bakery. I've been chosen.'

Heather leaned closer carefully. 'Look at that face,' she cooed. 'It looks like a baby, can't be older than a few weeks.' She placed a box of raspberry tea on the shelf absentmindedly and leaned one arm against the shelf. 'Your first Fall Festival and you're already adopting animals.'

'Or being bullied by them,' Ginger muttered.

Butter meowed loudly. At that moment, a tall man rounded the corner with an easy stride, glasses resting low on his nose as he skimmed something on his phone. He looked up and his expression softened as he saw Heather.

'Found you,' he said warmly. His smile was immediate and open, the kind that easily reached his eyes. Heather extended one arm toward him, and he stepped into her space naturally, pressing a quick kiss to her cheek before slipping an arm around her waist.

'Ginger,' Heather said, shifting slightly so they stood side by side. 'I don't think you've met my husband, Dr. Preston Hughes.'

Preston Hughes was a middle-aged man built on contradictions. He was slim through the shoulders and chest, yet softened at the middle by a slight pouch that hinted at a fondness for comfort over sweaty discipline. His hair was close cropped and mostly black, though streaks of silver threaded through at the temples and along the sides.

If Ginger squinted one eye, he was handsome enough, but not in a way that demanded a second look. His face was anchored by deep-set eyes that bordered on serious, like a man who listened more than he spoke. A neatly groomed mustache and goatee stretched around his mouth. It hinted at playfulness like he could be lighthearted, but only sparingly. He released his wife and extended his hand. His grip was firm but not overpowering.

'Preston is just fine,' he said in an easy tone. 'Pleasure to finally meet the infamous Ginger Mills. I've been hearing about your bakery project for months.'

'Infamous?' Ginger raised a brow.

'Oh, absolutely,' he replied with a grin. 'Heather has been anticipating your opening day for weeks. Congratulations, by the way. I didn't get a chance to stop by before you closed. We were swamped today at the office.'

'Selling out on your first day, that's amazing, Ginger, really! Cinnamon Falls is lucky to have you,' Heather added in.

Ginger smiled. 'I have you to thank for that. If you hadn't given me Landon's information, I'd still be buying flour one bag at a time.'

Heather waved a dismissive hand, though the compliment clearly pleased her, her cheeks reddening. 'Don't mention it.' She tossed her hair over her shoulder. 'Landon's been delivering this way for years. It was only fair to help you get started. Oh!' Heather clapped her hands joyfully. 'Speaking of getting started.' She straightened, smoothing a lock of hair behind her ear and turning to her husband. 'Ginger here has made a new friend.'

Ginger leaned down, opening her jacket just enough to reveal the small, trembling bundle inside.

'Well, who do we have here?' Dr. Hughes asked, stepping closer. His voice softened as he crouched to get a better look.

'Found it in a butter box behind my bakery,' Ginger explained.

'Preston's a veterinarian,' Heather said proudly.

Dr. Hughes extended his hand slowly, giving Butter

a moment to sniff his fingers before gently brushing them along the cat's head. Butter let out a faint mew but didn't pull away. He carefully lifted Butter just enough to examine the cat, checking its eyes, its gums, and its little ribs. His expression shifted slightly, still calm, but more focused.

'Underweight,' he assessed. 'And probably dehydrated, a little malnourished. I'd want to check it properly, make sure there's no infection, parasites or anything more serious going on. I can take a look tonight if you're free.' He stood to his full height. 'Clinic's just across the way. It won't take long.'

Ginger nodded quickly and he glanced over at Heather. 'That alright with you?' he asked. 'I know you've had a long day with the Fall Festival. I can get the receptionist to drop me home if you don't want to wait—'

Heather waved him off with an easy smile, though there was a hint of fatigue behind it.

'I'll survive,' she replied. 'You go ahead. I'll lock up here and head over once I'm done.'

'Alright then.' Dr. Hughes turned back to Ginger. 'Give me a few minutes to get set up and meet me at my office in the back of Paws and Whiskers Pet Supply.'

Ginger and Heather exchanged a few more pleasantries; lunch plans tossed around with the promise of getting together during the week, before she headed back outside.

She felt Butter snuggle deeper into the crook of her arm, purring softly against her sweater. In the span of a few hours she'd gone from lonely, anonymous baker to a cat lady.

Her life was a walking cliché.

Chapter 4

Austin

'One more, I promise,' Austin lied, raising his phone again as Lillian posed for what had to be the thousandth time in her Cinnamon Queen regalia. She sighed dramatically, her lips pinching together revealing her dimples. She flashed him a dull smile.

'Happy now?' she deadpanned, rolling her eyes. 'Can I please go?'

Austin pretended to consider it. 'One more in front of the car?'

Before Lillian could unleash her wrath, their mother, Katherine, swatted Austin's shoulder with the quick precision of someone who'd raised three rambunctious children and suffered no foolishness from any of them.

'Let your sister go.' Katherine stepped around Austin, her heart-shaped face glowing with pride, and gently lifted Lillian's crown from her head. She smoothed down her daughter's curls, removed the satin sash, and folded both items into a garment bag resting across Matthew's lap. He held the bag tenderly as though it were the day his youngest was born.

It'd only been a year, but it felt like Austin's baby sister had sprouted overnight. He couldn't believe the baby who used to crawl into his bed during thunderstorms was graduating high school, going to dances, wearing lipstick . . . dating. Growing up.

Lillian's ceremony was the first time that the whole family had gathered in the same place for an extended period of time. Austin hadn't meant to, but ever since his father's accident, he'd started keeping his distance. He still showed up when he was needed – repairs on the property, hauling supplies, running errands his father could no longer handle – but he rarely stayed long. Sunday dinners that used to stretch into the night with laughter and old stories had slowly morphed into shouting matches and silent treatments. It was easier on everybody when he stayed away.

'I want you to have fun tonight,' Katherine said, pulling Lillian's coat around her shoulders and buttoning it up to her chin. 'But use your head, young lady.'

Lillian rolled her eyes again, but she didn't pull away. Her date and this year's Cinnamon King, Carl Weathers, Jr., waited politely by the gymnasium doors, hands tucked into his suit pockets, projecting the calm confidence of a boy who hadn't yet realized Austin was watching him like a hawk.

Austin glanced over at his father, who was red-faced and misty-eyed, fighting back tears of his own. Austin felt the familiar pinch in his chest; a mix of pride and fear that struck him every time his sisters did anything major. He'd hardly gotten over his middle sister, Madelyn, being away in college. He wasn't sure if he was ready to let Lillian go just yet.

'It gets dark around those Falls at night,' Matthew choked out, voice thick. 'You tell that boy to make sure he uses his bright lights once you get around to Old Man Milton's.'

Lillian groaned. 'You've been telling me this all week.' She stomped her foot defiantly like she used to when she didn't want to go to church. Austin grinned. At least some things hadn't changed.

He reached out, tempted to squeeze her face or drag her into a headlock, but before he could, Lillian launched herself into his arms, locking her hands behind his back.

'Thanks for coming tonight, Auzzie.' Her voice softened. 'I'm glad I got to see you, I miss you comin' by the house. I wish Maddie could've made it.'

'I've just been workin', that's all, Lils. With Dad out I got to—'

'I know, I know,' she lamented, her brown eyes meeting the floor. Lillian knew first-hand what it was like when Austin and his father were in the same room longer than fifteen minutes. They butted heads, constantly. Matthew was too stubborn to realize there were things he could no longer handle and Austin was too determined to prove that the business was his responsibility now.

'The second Maddie gets out of her midterm she'll be on the first thing smoking back into town.'

Lillian squeezed him tighter and Austin closed his eyes, returning the embrace. He pinched the bridge of his nose, trying not to embarrass the both of them by crying.

'You text me if you need me, alright? I don't care what time it is, I'll be there.' He pressed a kiss to her forehead.

Lillian smiled, pulling back. 'I already have a dad, thank you very much. CJ's a sweetheart.' Austin cut his eyes at Carl, who found an interesting spot on the floor. 'If anything, he needs to watch out for *me*.'

'That's my girl,' Matthew said proudly. Lillian gave her parents one more round of hugs before heading out of the gym and into the cool October night.

The Jacobs family stood together, watching, until Carl's headlights disappeared down Cinnamon Way, taking their last baby with them. The silence that followed felt bigger than the gym.

Austin's parents' attention turned to him. 'Headed to Rosie's?' Matthew asked, voice clipped.

'Yeah, just for a little.'

'I can't believe it's been two years since she passed,' Katherine sighed as they journeyed toward their truck.

'Doesn't feel like it.' Austin waited until his father

maneuvered himself into the driver's seat. Matthew gripped the frame of the truck and hauled himself up with slow, practiced determination, refusing help even though the effort clearly winded him.

Austin didn't offer. He'd learned that lesson the hard way. Matthew Jacobs had always been a proud man. The accident had paralyzed his legs, but it hadn't taken the rest of him, and he made sure everyone knew it.

Austin removed the seat and wheels from the chair, folding the metal frame, then lifted it into the truck bed. The motions came automatically now, muscle memory after a long year. But there had been a time when the process wasn't as smooth, every movement stiff with grief and frustration. Austin tried to fix everything – installing ramps, rearranging the house, reorganizing the business – as if his efforts could erase the accident entirely. His father had made one thing very clear: the business might run through Austin now, but the house – the family – was still his responsibility.

Austin and Katherine had long since learned to keep their opinions to themselves when it came to Matthew's independence, especially if they didn't want their evening to end up with the family at odds. So, he'd learned to keep his distance, and his mouth shut.

Austin closed the tailgate and pulled his mother in for a quick hug, her vanilla perfume comforting.

'Pay our respects to the Roses. We're going to head home. It's been a long day.'

Austin escorted his mother to the passenger side, offering his hand while she maneuvered into the cab.

'Need a ride?' Matthew asked once he settled in the driver's seat, adjusting the modified hand controls.

'It's just down the block. I could use the exercise.'

Truthfully, Austin would have loved a ride, but he needed the walk more. It would give him time to breathe; time to quiet the familiar voice in the back of his mind that kept insisting that if he worked harder, did more, kept everyone safe, things would finally feel normal again.

Katherine reached out the window, collecting his hand in hers. 'Come by for dinner next week. With Maddie comin' into town, it would be nice to have all my babies together. How about tacos on Tuesday? Whaddya say?'

Austin knew it was his mother's way of saying she missed him without actually saying it. It'd been a while since they'd been together as a family, and he wanted to believe that today's peaceful interaction could be a positive indication of the future. Or maybe his father was simply playing nice. He'd have to wait and see.

'Yeah,' Austin replied. 'I'll call you next week.'

His mother nodded, satisfied, and he leaned in to receive another watery peck to his temple. He waved them off and turned down Cinnamon Way, the cool fall air brushing against his face as the truck's headlights disappeared.

The sky had deepened to indigo, stars peeking between the clouds, but Harvest Square was still alive with activity. Rodney McIntire's saxophone crooned over the speakers while families in lawn chairs snapped their fingers, sipped spiked cider, nibbled sweet potato pie and kettle corn. Austin smiled, soaking in the familiar sounds of home.

He was nearing Ginger's bakery when he spotted Sylvester James fiddling with the General Store's front entrance, pushing and pulling the large doors with growing frustration.

Sly stood tall despite his age, denim suspenders stretched tight over his usual uniform of a checkered button-down with brown scuffed boots. Square-framed glasses hung on his nose as he squinted up, lips pursed in irritation. A half-moon of hair ringed his head, the top long surrendered to time. He looked exactly as Austin had seen him a hundred times before, right down to the faint scent of peppermint that clung to him year-round from the red and white striped candies he kept tucked behind his teeth.

'Off the track I think,' Sly huffed, as Austin got near. He planted his hands on his hips, craning his neck upward as if the doors would fix themselves from his intense scrutiny.

Austin stepped in, flipping a small, flat flashlight out of his pocket. It'd been a Christmas gift from Maddie several years back and it'd come in handy more times than he could count. He shone the beam upward and examined the door's mechanism. The problem revealed itself immediately. The rollers had slipped from the internal track, causing the door to drag stubbornly along the floor.

'You're right. Looks like the roller's come off the track. Should be an easy fix. Can you lock it up for the night? I can come back tomorrow.'

'Yeah, but it's hunting season, son.' Sly clucked his tongue, rolling the candy around in his mouth. 'They expectin' these doors to be open at five in the morning.'

Austin shrugged. 'Then I can be here before that. It shouldn't take too long to pop out a few screws and replace the rollers.'

Sly's stern expression melted into a grin. 'That'll save me a call to the company and that pricey service fee.'

'Then I'll see you first thing tomorrow morning, Mr. James.'

Sly adjusted his suspenders with satisfaction. Austin bet that he was already imagining the money he'd save. They shook hands fervently and Austin knew then that he'd secured a coveted spot on the list of people to receive a handwritten Christmas card.

It always featured Sly in matching outfits with his two cross-eyed pugs, Biscuit and Gravy, posed proudly on his front porch. The Jacobs family hadn't received one in three years and the last one had been the source of their laughter for forty days and forty nights. They still had it framed in their living room because it was too good not to preserve. Austin would be crowned Katherine's favorite child if they received another.

Austin continued down the sidewalk toward Rosie's, passing The Maple Bakery. He forced himself not to glance into the windows. Besides, he was sure Ginger must have gone home for the day by now. He imagined her curled up somewhere warm, probably tired, elated to be off her feet.

Up ahead, Rosie's Diner glowed like a beacon in the middle of the block, laughter and music spilling onto the sidewalk. He pushed inside, and was greeted by familiar faces and warm embraces. He spotted Jesse and Will in a corner booth near the back. They waved him over.

Will was polishing off a cinnamon bun when he arrived. They bumped forearms as a greeting and Austin did the same with Jesse across the table.

'The girls are ordering drinks. Do you want a spiked cider?' Jesse offered as Austin found an empty chair and pulled it up to the edge of the booth's table.

Austin nodded. 'Sure, I won't be long, though; just stopping by to pay my respects.'

He nodded toward the Rose family; Rosie's brother Rupert, and her twin sisters, Rebecca and Rubina, were singing a terrible rendition of an oldies rock classic by the jukebox. They traveled to Cinnamon Falls from Atlanta every year during the Fall Festival to have a memorial service for their sister. This one, just like the one before, was filled wall to wall with residents conversing, laughing, and reminiscing over the one and only Rosslyn Rose.

Nia and Morgan arrived, ciders in hand, just as Morgan declared, 'Another Fall Festival in the books.' She turned, taking in all the people. 'Doesn't feel the same without her.'

'I keep thinking she's going to appear from the kitchen any minute now,' Jesse sighed, watching the workers behind the counter wistfully.

'Right? With a fresh platter of cinnamon buns and cider, forcing us to eat more.' Nia wiped a tear escaping her eye. Jesse's hand landed on top of hers reassuringly, and Austin willed his thoughts of Samantha away.

'To Rosie.' Will lifted his mug in the air.

They toasted, cider spilling over the sides, splashing on the table.

'She'd kill us for making a mess,' Morgan laughed, wiping the excess cider away with a napkin.

Conversation drifted, warm and easy, until Nia's eyes brightened. 'Austin, you didn't tell us little Lillian was Cinnamon Queen this year! She looked gorgeous.'

The group gushed over Lils' big moment appreciatively.

'She's not so little anymore,' Austin chuckled, shaking his head. He couldn't believe how quickly she'd grown up. How could it have been seventeen years already?

'And wasn't that little Carl from the Grow Squad as Cinnamon King?' Nia directed her question to Will. Every other Saturday, Will and his father hosted a group of young men who gardened at Reed & Roots, his father's landscaping business.

He nodded, washing down his cinnamon bun with a swig of cider. 'Yeah, they've been dating for a while now. I think since the Daffodil Jubilee.'

'Don't remind me,' Austin grumbled.

'He's a good kid,' Will laughed. 'You got nothing to worry about outta that one.'

'It's not him I'm worried about,' Austin responded, shaking his head. Out of all three Jacobs siblings, Lillian was the one his parents had to keep a closer eye on. 'Especially tonight.'

Austin caught Nia's eyes across the table. The Fall Festival, although special, held lots of bad memories for Cinnamon Falls residents. Sienna Rose had died this night almost a decade ago, and no one, especially Austin, ever forgot it. He'd been Sienna's classmate and could pick her handwriting out of the pile; she'd always leave hearts over her I's. But she was gone, just like her mother, Rosie. He didn't know if his family could survive a devastating loss like the Roses had. He tried to put the thought out of his mind.

Lils will be fine, he told himself.

Morgan rolled her eyes. 'The girl isn't going to do anything crazy, Austin. You were young and in love once, too. Let the girl live a little.'

And you see how that ended, he wanted to say. Instead, he kept quiet, the words lodging a stone in his throat.

Before he could recover, Will poked the wound harder. 'What's up with you and Samantha, man? I haven't seen her around lately.'

Something thumped under the table and cider jumped out of their glasses again. 'Ow! What'd you kick me for—' Across the table, Nia glared at Will, her eyes flitting to Austin. Will looked sheepish as he said, 'Oh, my bad, man. I didn't know.'

Austin sighed. He thought he'd managed to keep their split quiet. He and Samantha had gone their separate ways without melee or fuss. He hadn't thought anyone would notice, but it was clear that he'd been wrong.

'We, uh, broke up a few months back,' he said finally now that all eyes were on him. 'Sometime in April, I think,' he pretended like he didn't know the exact date and time Samantha had shattered his heart. April 19th at 8:59 a.m.

'Sorry to hear that,' Jesse mumbled.

'I'm not,' Morgan said flatly.

Nia's eyes bulged and Austin almost spat out his cider.

'She was too stuck up for you.' Morgan shrugged. 'I never liked her.'

Austin chuckled; it was easier than hurting. It wasn't the first time he'd heard that. He leaned in. 'My mother wasn't that fond of her either.'

'See?' Morgan gestured to the table as if she'd been proven right. 'Mrs. Jacobs and I have always seen eye-to-eye.'

'How're you holding up?' Jesse asked, sincerity lining his voice. 'It's just . . . I been there. I know what it feels like.' Nia snuggled closer to him.

Austin averted his gaze. 'It's all good, just trying to adjust my life back to being a single man again.'

Nia surveyed the crowd over Austin's shoulder. 'I know a few women who would be happy to hear that Austin Jacobs is back on the market. You got your eye on anybody?'

Austin surprised himself with how quickly his thoughts jumped to Ginger; the way she looked today at the parade; her eyes sparkling in the fall sunlight, her smile of genuine joy; the way the skin crinkled around her nose when she laughed.

He took another long sip of cider, the whiskey warming him all the way through, and lied when he said, 'Nah.'

The little yellow house off Cinnamon Way still looked the same. Austin could have taken the short cut, bypassing the street entirely, but after two ciders, he couldn't stop himself from driving past it. His hands steered the truck almost on their own, dragging him toward a place his heart hadn't fully let go of.

The porch light cast a soft gold over the white railing that ran around the perimeter of the house that he'd installed himself. The shutters were still the same deep navy he'd painted one humid July afternoon, sweat dripping into his eyes while Samanatha brought him lemonade in a chilled mason jar.

He remembered thinking: *This is what it feels like, living inside a dream.* Now, another couple lived there, the Johnsons, according to their mailbox. Someone else sat at his dinner table; reclaimed wood from Old Man Milton's barn; someone else laughed in the kitchen where he'd once slow-danced barefoot with Samantha, heart to heart; planting kisses on her exposed shoulders, planning futures he thought were certain.

Through a front window he caught a flicker of movement; silhouettes crossing the living room, settling in for the night. A man's laugh, warm and low, drifted into the evening air from the cracked window. Austin's fingers tightened around the steering wheel.

He tried to tell himself it was fine. He was fine. That the ache in his chest was nothing more than the sting of old dreams dissolving. But the truth sat heavy beside him, unwelcome and unrelenting. He wasn't grieving Samantha, not entirely. He was grieving the version of himself he'd been with her – happier, hopeful, certain, believing in a future he could hold with both hands.

A soft thud of the porch door closing snapped him from the memory. Austin turned his gaze forward, shifted the truck into gear, and pushed his foot on the gas; forcing himself away from the life he nearly had.

The road stretched out ahead, quiet and empty, lined with trees glowing orange under the streetlamps. Cinnamon Falls always looked so peaceful at night. As the house disappeared in Austin's rearview, the familiar grief rose and settled again; not gone, but gentler this time, more manageable.

As Austin turned onto his own street, he was grateful to see his modest, two-story house waiting at the end of the block. It was a work in progress with fresh paint on the siding that didn't quite match the older trim yet. It wasn't the house he shared with Samantha; that one had been planned and constructed with his own two hands. This one he'd bought on his own, a small starter home he was slowly bringing back to life, one room, one repair at a time. It'd been his obsession in the last several months. Every loose hinge, every unfinished wall gave him something to focus on, something he could fix. And in a way, the house filled the empty space Samantha left behind, giving him somewhere to put all that restless energy, the compulsive need to make things right, even when the rest of his life refused to cooperate.

His headlights caught a little silver car parked crooked in his driveway. Madelyn. He huffed a quiet laugh. She'd never gotten the parking thing down.

Inside, his house was dark except for the soft light spilling from the spare bedroom. He peeked in to find his sister curled up in blankets, her dyed auburn hair fanned out behind her head; her mouth hanging open, a trail of slob leading from her mouth to the pillow. She must have sped home from college, but still missed Lillian's big moment.

Austin closed the door gently and padded down the hall to his own room. He stripped down, peeling off his clothes and tossing them into the hamper. He lay in bed, staring at the ceiling, listening to the quiet of the house: the hiss of the heat in the vents, the faint echo of Fall Festival still ringing in the night air.

But, for once, his mind didn't drift back to Samantha or their yellow house.

It drifted to Ginger. He wondered how her first day had ended, and if she'd had fun at the festival today. Even as his eyes began to close, her face lingered in his thoughts.

Chapter 5

Sunday

Ginger

Three-thirty a.m. came too quickly for both Ginger and her newfound feline friend. She pushed herself upright, groaning softly at the hour. Her body protested, stiff from too few hours of sleep, and too many hours of stress. She rubbed the heel of her hand over her eyes, sleep still clinging to her. She reached for Butter, who blinked up at her with offended slowness.

'I know,' she whispered. 'I don't want to be awake either.'

After spending two hours at Dr. Hughes' office the night before, and several hundred dollars later, she had found out that Butter, a Caliby cat, was actually a boy – a very rare boy for his breed.

Dr. Hughes had delivered the news with a broad smile, as if Butter's genetic lottery somehow justified the dent in Ginger's bank account. He'd been given a clean bill of health; Dr. Hughes had gone down the list of treatments like a grocery receipt: bathed, flea-treated, dewormed, vaccinated, and microchipped. He handed Butter back to her, wearing the world's tiniest blue collar. When Ginger's eyes balked at the bill, the technician offered to 'rehome him', but Butter had chosen that moment to burrow into Ginger's sweater and let out a soft mew; a sound that cracked her heart in half.

Ginger's willpower, usually steadfast, and unyielding, didn't stand a chance. She scheduled a follow-up appointment in a few days, scooped him up with one hand, and swiped her credit card with the other, her eyes squeezed shut. She'd worry about the bill in thirty days. Or never. Never sounded better.

She was now sleep-deprived, financially wounded, and irrationally attached to a warm ball of fur snoring on her only sweater, which had been folded into a pillow. Ginger rolled her eyes. Perfect.

Ginger moved quietly around Alexis' guest room – hers until she saved enough money to get her own place. She snapped on the lamp, washing the room with a warm glow against the soft buttercream walls. The space was small, but comforting, filled with the kind of details that made a house feel lived in: the quilt Alexis' mother had sewn, folded at the edge of the bed, hand-stitched with squares of plum, navy, and burnt orange, and the lofty fern drooping from a ceramic pot in the corner.

Butter followed her like a tiny shadow, tail flicking

with curiosity as he explored the floorboards, weaving between the boxes she still hadn't unpacked.

Ginger showered and dressed quickly, pulling on a pair of black leggings and a wrinkled T-shirt printed with cherries. She'd kept her movements light; Alexis and Terrance slept just steps away down the hall, and the last thing Ginger needed was her cousin waking up and asking a million questions about the kitten she'd smuggled home.

She'd have to have that conversation soon, preferably after her coffee and more sleep. She tiptoed into the kitchen, Butter close on her heels, his tiny paws tapping against tile. Ginger flicked on the lights, revealing Alexis' Pinterest-worthy modern kitchen with bright white cabinets with brass pulls, a farmhouse sink big enough to bathe a litter of dogs, and open shelving lined with color-coded drinking mugs. She matched them to her outfits, which Terrance teased her about relentlessly, but she considered it her 'personal expression'.

Ginger doled out a serving of kitten formula the vet had given her into a saucer for Butter. He lapped at it noisily, his tiny pink tongue flicking with wild enthusiasm.

'You have to stay quiet,' she warned in a whisper. 'If Alexis hears you, I'm doomed.'

Butter sneezed. Loudly.

She glared at him. 'Wonderful.'

Butter continued eating, unfazed.

Ginger gathered her things, placing Butter in the

vet-approved carrier; his meows getting louder, threatening. She dashed upstairs to retrieve the sweater she was wearing yesterday. It was a gift from Harrison; organic cashmere reduced to a pet's pillow. She stuffed it into the carrier. Butter quietened immediately.

Carrying her bag and Butter out of the back door with exaggerated stealth, Ginger held her breath as it clicked shut behind her. She watched for a few seconds but no interior lights turned on. She slid inside her sedan, placing Butter's carrier in the seat beside her, and fastened the seat belt into place, exhaling triumphantly.

Today, she thought, *is going to be a good day.*

The sky was still a bruised blue-black when Ginger pulled onto Cinnamon Way, lamps glowing like fireflies along the sidewalk. The air was cool, fog curling low to the ground in thin ribbons. When she turned on Main Street, she spotted a familiar vehicle: Landon's delivery truck, engine running, exhaust fumes curling into the cold air in white puffs, his headlights aimed directly at her bakery.

She perked up, glancing at the clock on her dashboard. It was just after four. She hadn't been expecting him for at least another hour.

'Guess I'm not the only one who doesn't sleep,' she muttered.

Landon was always early and cheerful; chatty to the point of nosy, but harmless. She could count on him to make the long days more enjoyable with hours of stories and unsolicited advice.

Ginger parked along the curb and left Butter sleeping in his carrier when she stepped out.

She pulled her motorcycle jacket tighter around herself and made another mental note to purchase a real coat. The cold air sliced straight through the faux leather. She'd been meaning to buy one for weeks, but between the bakery's inspection, supply coordination, creating menus, and preparing for the Fall Festival, it'd escaped to the back of her memory. It'd warm up by midday, but not by much. The mornings were getting brisker as the sun was setting earlier.

She headed toward the narrow alley between her building and the General Store, the funneled air between the buildings making it feel even colder. She walked briskly, her supportive sneakers cradling her still sore arches while they crunched on a trail of brittle leaves leading to her back door. She passed Landon's truck, not able to see into the cab from the street. She expected to hear his cheerful whistle any second now while he worked, stacking the delivered items in the alley.

The engine hummed steadily, but there was no whistle. No clatter of crates. No movement. No greeting. Just eerie silence.

She entered the black mouth of the alley, pulling out her cell phone and switching on the flashlight. The beam cut through the fog and landed on the back door of her bakery. Then she saw something sticking out of the bakery's open back door.

A pair of legs.

Boots she recognized immediately.

Her steps faltered. 'Landon?' Ginger whispered, her breath fogging the cold.

The legs didn't move.

A piercing spike of dread slid down Ginger's spine. She approached slowly, her heart hammering against her ribs so hard she could hear it in her ears.

'Landon,' she tried again, louder this time. He still didn't stir. She channeled some courage into her voice. 'If you're trying to scare me, it's too early, and I'm not in the laughing mood.'

Her feet felt like cement as she crept closer, until she reached the threshold and froze. Her flour bin lay tipped on its side, white powder spilling across the tiles like fresh snow. Footprints tracked through it in smudged, wide arcs.

Landon lay face down, one arm bent awkwardly beneath him, his head tilted at an unnatural angle. Beneath it, where his temple met the tile, a small pool of blood glistened. Ginger's breath caught in her throat. Landon wasn't joking.

He wasn't even breathing.

He was dead.

'Landon!' She rushed forward, dropping to her knees. The fine powder puffed around her jeans. She grabbed his shoulder and turned him over, his head lolling loosely. His eyes were open but unfocused, staring at something she couldn't see. There was swelling along his cheekbone, an angry bruise already forming near his eye. Fresh crimson coated Ginger's fingers as she cradled the back of his head.

Her stomach lurched and something wooden knocked against her knee. She glanced down at her rolling pin. It lay half-buried in flour near his hip, a faint smear of red along its smooth surface. Her mind couldn't make sense of what she was seeing. She reached for it instinctively, fingers wrapping around the handle. It felt sticky.

Blood.

Her breath hitched violently. The rolling pin slipped from her hands and clattered back onto the tile. The room felt smaller somehow, the air thinner. She looked down at herself: flour coating her knees, blood on her hands, Landon's head in her palms.

Time halted and her whole world narrowed into a pinpoint behind her eyes. She pushed herself up but her legs weren't strong enough to stand. She stumbled backward, out of the bakery until she slammed into the brick wall behind her, crates and empty boxes collapsing under her weight.

'No,' she gasped. 'No, no, no—'

The scream tore out of her before she could stop it. It echoed down the alleyway, slicing through the quiet dawn.

Chapter 6

Austin

Austin pulled alongside the General Store and yawned so hard his jaw cracked. He shifted his truck into park and leaned backward against the headrest, shuttering his eyes closed. He had no idea why he'd agreed to help Sly James before the sun rose, hunting season and a Christmas card be damned. What kind of person agreed to fix a door while the moon was still out? What had he been thinking?

The sky was still a deep navy; the only light came from streetlamps reflecting hauntingly in the low fog curling in the streets. He scrubbed a hand over his face, his eyes sandpaper dry.

'Let's get this over with,' he huffed while reaching over to grab his tool bag. He hefted it over his shoulder when something outside caught his eye, Landon Lawson's delivery truck, parked unusually in the middle of the street, engine idling, his headlights shining into Ginger's bakery.

Austin shouldered his truck door open, stepping out into the cool air. He was just about to walk over when a scream split the air.

Austin froze; ears perked, his breath halting.

As the big brother to two very curious, very oblivious sisters, he knew a scream of danger when he heard one. And he was certain it came from the alley behind Ginger's bakery.

'Ginger.' He dropped his bag; assorted tools clattered along the street, forgotten, and sprinted in that direction. Boots pounding; his heart hammering, fog swirling around him in ghostly curls, he rounded the corner into the alley and found her.

Ginger was pressed against the brick wall, body trembling, eyes wide and wild. She was pale under the alley lights, her breath coming in ragged gulps.

He approached her slowly. 'What happened, Ginger? Talk to me. Are you hurt?'

Her eyes swung over to meet him, fear and recognition colliding on her face. She shook her head but couldn't seem to form words. Instead, she lifted a trembling hand and pointed toward the open back door of the bakery. He followed where her bloody finger stilled and his stomach dropped.

There were legs . . . human legs sticking out of the bakery's back door.

Austin moved toward the body on instinct, years of stepping between his sisters and whatever threatened them kicking in before logic had the chance to stop him. He swallowed hard, creeping closer, taming the galloping horses in his heart.

As he pushed open the door, the dim light slanted into the bakery's kitchen, catching in the suspended dust and revealing Landon's body. He was sprawled on his back, arms jutting out from his sides like a broken doll, resting at unusual angles; his eyes open but unseeing. Beneath his head, a pool of blood had seeped into the flour, turning it into a thick, crimson paste. At first glance, it looked like he'd slipped and lost his balance under the weight of something heavy and knocked over the flour bin. Then Austin noticed the bruise blooming along Landon's cheekbone. His eyes landed on the rolling pin next, lying just inches from Landon's hip, streaked with red.

Austin's pulse roared in his ears.

'Landon . . .' Austin knew he wouldn't answer. He crouched down beside Landon's body, pressing two fingers to the pulse point in his neck. His body was icy, his pulse nonexistent.

Landon was dead.

Austin swallowed again, forcing down the sick twisting in his gut, threatening to march up and out. Outside, he could still hear Ginger whimpering, terrified.

'Is he okay?' she called desperately. 'Please tell me he's not . . .'

Austin pushed himself upward, the room tilting. He braced himself against the doorframe, forcing air into his lungs. He was terrified in a way he'd never been before. His brain was a hive of bees, his thoughts moving at breakneck pace. Closing his eyes, Austin thought about his father, the strongest man he knew. *What would Dad do?* he asked himself.

Open your eyes, a voice inside his head rang out.

Austin obeyed. When he did, Ginger was standing next to him, horror carved into her face. Flour coated her knees. Her hands . . . stained red.

'Oh my God,' Ginger said behind cupped, trembling hands.

Austin scanned the floor again. Flour was smeared in wide arcs. There were faint impressions too, like . . . footprints overlapping each other, indistinct. A bloody rolling pin. It was then that Austin realized that something had gone very, very wrong. This was no accident.

No.

'We need to get out of here,' Austin mumbled, guiding Ginger out of the door and into the alley.

Landon's headlights revealed the shining whites of Ginger's eyes as she exploded, 'Wha— We need to help him! We can't just leave him here like that!'

Austin braced his hands on her shoulders. 'Call an ambulance,' he instructed Ginger. 'Now.'

While she fumbled for her phone, Austin's gaze shifted over to Landon's truck still idling, then back to his body. What had happened between the truck and the bakery? He jogged toward the vehicle and climbed up on the passenger side running board, flipping the flashlight out of his pocket and peering inside the cab.

At first glance, it looked normal: crumpled fast food bags littered the floor, a clipboard rested on the dashboard, pages stuffed into the clip's mouth: some yellow, some pink, signatures scrawled across the bottom, receipts for completed deliveries. He swept the light lower. There was a coffee cup in the holder, red roses printed on the side. He'd know that cup from anywhere, it was a to-go coffee cup from Rosie's. Then the beam landed on the driver's side window. A spiderweb-shaped crack radiated outward from a central point in the glass. And in the center – blood.

Austin discovered the passenger door was ajar. He had enough sense not to touch the handle but noticed a clump of bright red fabric caught in the metal latch, like it'd been ripped from some kind of clothing, but Landon's Valley View uniform wasn't red.

Austin jumped down, his pulse roaring in his ears, and braced his back against the truck. He dragged a hand over his face. What had he gotten himself into? Ginger's shaky voice brought him back to the moment. She was seated on the curb, her elbows resting on her knees.

'This is G-Ginger Mills. I'm at The Maple Bakery on Main Street, and Landon . . . he's – he's not breathing . . . Yes, I checked! He's dead! Send someone out here right now!' She ended the call and buried her face in her hands. Sobs shook through her, though she tried fiercely to quiet them.

It was cutting Austin's heart in two watching her cry. He lowered himself beside her. 'Hey, look at me.'

She didn't, so he gently touched her shoulder. She flinched, but lifted her head, eyes wet and terrified.

'Austin, I . . . He was just lying there,' she whispered, her voice broken. 'Dead.'

Red and blue lights flashed at the end of the block. Tires roared on the open road, heading quickly in their direction.

'My bakery,' Ginger eked out, tears sliding down her face. 'It's ruined.'

'I bet that's Chief Raines,' Austin responded. 'Cinnamon Falls Police will figure it out, they're the best. Then, The Maple Bakery will be back to being the talk of the town.'

He didn't include what he'd been thinking: *It'll be the talk of the town, alright. In more ways than one.*

Chapter 7

Ginger

Police Chief Noelle Raines was a certified bitch. Ginger could tell from the moment she saw her. Ginger thought *she* was rough around the edges, but Raines was a pitbull in blues, barking orders from the moment her truck screeched to a halt outside the bakery. She'd hopped out with the swagger of someone twice her size. Her eyes were sharp as knives, without a hint of sleepiness, as if it wasn't five in the morning.

Her skin was a deep chestnut, smooth, wrinkle-free, enough to guess that she moisturized religiously, or the woman had never smiled a day in her life. Her hair was pulled into a no-nonsense bun at the back of her neck, her uniform tucked with precision. Her boots added zero inches to her height but somehow a terrifying amount of presence.

Raines marched toward them with quick, decisive steps that sounded like a countdown against the pavement. She scanned the street, the alley, the truck, then zeroed in on Ginger with a stare so direct Ginger fought the urge to hide behind Austin seated next to her on the curb.

'Wade, I want a roadblock from Nutmeg Avenue to Cinnamon Way. No one in or out, you got that?' she announced to a pudgy, round-faced officer who scurried out of the passenger seat and appeared next to her.

'Wake the mayor up,' she continued. 'I'll need him here. Oh, and make sure Miss Whitfield from the mortuary is on her way. I want this scene processed ASAP. We need to notify the next of kin before the rumor mill wakes up and beats us to the punch.'

'You got it, boss.' The officer spoke into the radio on his shoulder then pulled on a pair of latex gloves with a smack. Jesse Shaw rounded the truck and Ginger breathed a sigh of relief. Finally, someone she knew.

'Wade, Shaw, I want you to check out the bakery. I'll deal with these two.'

Jesse made eye contact with Ginger, gave a small, sympathetic nod, and continued past. Wade traveled behind him like a shadow.

So much for help.

'I'm Chief Raines. Your names?' Raines snapped, crossing her arms over her chest.

'Austin Jacobs,' Austin said, straightening his spine. His voice was steady, but Ginger could tell that he was rattled. 'I was about to fix the automatic door for Sly James before he opened this morning, when I heard a scream from the bakery. I saw Ginger in the alley and we found Landon . . .' he gestured over his shoulder, 'like that, and then we called emergency services.'

Raines flipped a notepad out of her shirt pocket and scribbled something down. 'Do you know the victim's last name?'

'Lawson,' Austin supplied. 'Landon Lawson.'

Raines scribbled again. 'And you?' she frowned, turning to Ginger, zeroing in on the dried blood on her hands.

'Ginger Mills,' she replied. Her pulse hammered in her throat. She wished she'd had the forethought to wash her hands before the police arrived. She was so distraught, her mind moving in all directions, she hadn't thought about how this looked, how *she* might look.

Landon was dead in her bakery, of all places, and law enforcement knowing her name was not a good thing. If this got out, it would only take a few loose lips for the news to travel to Atlanta, right back to the Caldwells. And if Harrison, or worse, his father, ever found out where she'd gone . . . Ginger didn't want to think of the consequences of her actions.

'I came in to prep for the day's bake and I found him . . . like that.'

'Like what?' Raines asked, her beady eyes roaming

Ginger like she had a flashing sign over her head that read: GUILTY.

'Dead,' Ginger said, marrying her hands together. 'I . . . I tried to see if he was still breathing.'

'You *touched* the body?'

'Yes,' Ginger admitted. 'I thought he might still be alive. I thought I could help.'

Raines nodded to Ginger's hands. 'Blood tells the story. The lab will tell me if this transfer is from touching him or . . . something else.'

Ginger's throat tightened. 'I didn't hurt him. I walked in and found him.'

Raines leaned forward, her voice quieter, sharper. 'Ms. Mills, help me understand what Mr. Lawson was doing at your bakery so early in the morning?'

'He's my delivery driver.' She gestured to the truck parked in the middle of the street. Ginger continued, 'Well, not just for me, he delivers to a bunch of businesses around here. He works for Valley View and Heather Hughes referred me to them because I was buying flour and sweet potatoes by the bag which isn't really feasible for a business and—'

'It's pretty convenient that the victim is your delivery driver, wouldn't you say?' Raines quipped.

Ginger flinched like she'd been slapped. Anger flared in her chest, red hot and fiery. She squared her shoulders to the woman. 'I wouldn't call it *convenient*,' she said. *It's horrifying*, she thought.

Raines hummed, unconvinced. She positioned her

hands behind her back and paced in the street. A power move, Ginger was sure. She was letting them both know they weren't getting out of this any time soon.

Austin and Ginger waited with bated breath for her next question. They met eyes and Austin nodded imperceptibly.

Everything is going to be okay, he was probably thinking.

Ginger shook her head. *No, it isn't.* How could he be Mr. Positivity and Rainbows right now? Ginger sighed audibly. His good guy act was nauseating.

Wade made his way toward Landon's truck. He opened the driver's side door and leaned inside the cab.

'Chief,' he called as his flashlight landed on the window. 'Blood,' he reported. 'A bunch of trash from what I can see. Fast food wrappers and such.' He held up the coffee cup from Rosie's Diner with two fingers. 'Lipstick.'

Raines' gaze cut back to her. 'You wear lipstick, Ms. Mills?'

Ginger's stomach dropped.

'Not at five in the morning,' she snapped, crossing her arms so she wouldn't strangle somebody.

Raines' eyebrow twitched in either amusement or annoyance, Ginger couldn't tell. 'We'll see.'

Jesse reappeared at Raines' side, his voice low. Ginger angled her seated body toward them, listening intently. 'Footprints everywhere inside. Hard to tell the size, looks like a scuffle occurred or . . .' his eyes flicked to Ginger, 'it's been staged to look that way.'

Ginger couldn't stop herself. 'Staged?' she asked, incredulous.

'Means someone wanted this to look like something it's not,' Jesse explained.

'I know what it means,' she grumbled.

Raines turned toward Ginger again. 'How *well* did you know Mr. Lawson?'

'I – barely. I just told you, he delivered ingredients to me a couple of times before. We talked a bit, but nothing serious.'

'Talked a bit, huh?' Raines scribbled again on her notepad. Ginger wanted to snatch it from her hands and rip the papers to shreds. 'Did you two ever meet . . . outside of deliveries? Any romantic involvement?'

Austin sighed. 'Come on, Chief.'

Ginger held her hand up, catching a smear of Landon's blood in the moonlight. She was capable of defending herself. She hadn't gone up against the most powerful family in Atlanta to be pushed around by a two-bit cop in a too-small town, Chief or not.

'Never,' Ginger replied, pushing her hair out of her face so Chief Raines could get a good look at her steely expression. 'And I would appreciate it if you didn't imply otherwise.'

If Raines was offended, she didn't show it. Her arrogant disposition was undeterred.

Austin cut in. 'She didn't do anything wrong. We found him like that. I swear to it.'

Raines turned her irritation on him like a laser beam. 'Mr. Jacobs, unless you're about to tell me you were with Ms. Mills all night, I suggest you let me conduct my interview.' Austin's cheeks flamed and his mouth snapped shut. Raines paused, considering; her eyes roamed Austin with intense scrutiny. 'You're Matthew Jacobs' son?'

'Yes, ma'am,' Austin nodded. 'Like I said, I was fixing the door for Sly James when I heard Ginger—'

'Your father put a new roof on the house next door to mine a few years back. Did some good work. I heard about the accident. How's he gettin' on, alright?'

'Yes, ma'am,' Austin choked out. 'Better than ever.'

'You tell him I asked about him.'

Austin gave her a tight nod. Back to business, she turned to Ginger again, pointing her pen in her direction. 'You need to come down to the station to make a statement.'

'What? Why?' Ginger reeled, panic flooding her veins. She couldn't go to a police station, not now, not ever.

Raines listed on her fingers. 'Because you discovered the body. Because your prints will be everywhere in that building. Because you've got blood on your hands, flour all over your clothes. Because you have no alibi. And because, until I determine otherwise, you are a person of interest.'

Ginger's breath caught. A person of *interest*? The

phrase echoed like a bullet ricocheting in her skull. She was done for. She needed a quick out of this situation pronto.

'Hey, Chief! Chief!' Terrance sprinted down the sidewalk, still in his pajamas. Alexis' printed face smiled at Ginger as Terrance approached, tugging on his pants, badge swinging from his neck. When he reached them, he doubled over, bracing his hands on his knees, his chest heaving.

'Wait a second, Chief . . .' he explained, 'this is Ginger Mills, my wife's cousin.'

Terrance pulled Ginger to her feet and enveloped her into a hug, before pulling back to search her face. 'I got here as soon as I could. You okay? What's going on?' He spun around to his boss. 'I know her, okay? She wouldn't hurt anyone.'

Raines didn't flinch. 'Then she should have nothing to hide.'

On the contrary, Ginger thought. She had everything to hide. The trembles started again, this time in her knees. Ginger could feel her whole life – her fresh start, her dream, her bakery – slipping through her fingers; her world tilting off balance.

Terrance pulled her closer. 'Ging, it's going to be okay, alright? Just answer their questions. I'll be right behind you.'

'I'll go,' Austin offered, his voice firm. 'You stay here, find out what happened to Landon. I'll go with Ginger to the station.'

Ginger looked over at Austin, his eyes – usually warm, infuriatingly bright like nothing bad ever happened in his world – were dark with something else. Determination, maybe, Ginger wasn't sure, and she didn't have time to try to figure it out. Her life was at stake.

Raines snapped her fingers and two no-named officers moved toward Ginger.

Ginger backed away. 'Wait – Butter! I can't go anywhere without Butter.'

'Don't make us have to cuff you, Ms. Mills,' Raines threatened.

Ginger explained, 'He's my cat.'

'Chambers, do something with the cat,' Raines ordered.

'What cat?' Terrance looked at Ginger.

Ginger nodded toward her sedan. 'In the passenger seat. I found him in the alleyway last night. I was going to tell you but—'

Terrance threw his hands up. 'I'm allergic! I can't touch that thing!'

Raines snickered and Ginger wanted to punch herself in the face.

Austin stepped in. 'Me and Butter will be right behind you, okay?'

Raines sighed, bored with the whole ordeal. 'Let's clear it all up at the station, shall we?'

Ginger swallowed, her throat tight. The officers guided her toward the cruiser. At the last second, she turned, looking at her bakery. Her future. Her hard work. Her everything. All of it suddenly felt so far away.

When the door closed behind her, the last thing she saw was Austin, standing tall, jaw set, eyes locked on hers, with Butter's carrier clutched to his chest.

Chapter 8

Austin

Austin paced the length of the grungy lobby of the Cinnamon Falls Police Department for what felt like the hundredth time, one protective hand bracing Ginger's very curious kitten, sitting on his shoulder.

For a cat, Butter was kind of cool. Incredibly tiny, but cool, nonetheless. Austin was more of a dog person; floppy ears, wagging tail, constantly happy to see you. All Butter seemed to want to do was sleep. And when he didn't sleep, he whined for Ginger, or food. The only thing that calmed him down was the opportunity to be nosy. He watched intensely, in silent judgment of every person who came and went.

Austin flipped his cell phone out of his pocket and checked the time. It'd been almost two hours since he'd last seen Ginger get taken away in a police cruiser. He couldn't take the waiting, minutes dragging past with no update. What were they saying to her? Was she okay? Crying? Hurt? He hated that he couldn't storm in there and fix everything, but he knew she wouldn't let him even if he tried.

Ginger wasn't a damsel by a long shot. If she were a storybook princess trapped in a castle, she'd fashion a sword and slit the dragon's throat, relegating Prince Charming to be her butler or something humiliating. Austin found her tough exterior intriguing or else he wouldn't be cradling a finicky cat with an attitude problem at the crack of dawn.

Had Chief Raines found a link between Ginger and Landon? Ginger had seemed genuinely terrified to find Landon dead; he had been too. That sort of horror, no one can fake. Besides, she hadn't been in town long enough to get connected to someone slippery like loverboy Landon Lawson.

Despite Landon being a church-going, inconveniently married man, everyone within the Cinnamon Falls limits knew he was no saint. He kept a revolving door of girlfriends and his wife, Ethel Lawson, on the side. There'd been plenty of women who'd wanted to take Ethel Lawson's place, but year after year, Landon stood in front of the congregation at All Saints Tabernacle, lying to the Lord by pledging his unyielding love to his wife whom he 'didn't deserve'. At church, Austin made sure never to sit by Landon just in case a lightning bolt shot from the heavens. He could not get caught in an adulterous crossfire. His mother would dig him up and kill him again for dying.

Angela Robinson, Angie for short, the station's

receptionist, closed her thick novel with a thunk and leaned over the counter.

'Austin, you're startin' to wear a hole in my floor.'

'My fault, Angie, I'm just worried—'

'About that pretty baker back there?' Angie probed, her eyes widening. Austin knew that look. He would not feed into gossip if he could help it.

'I'm cat-sitting. He's worried,' Austin clarified, gesturing to Butter, who'd finally succumbed to his yawns and fallen asleep. Or he was pretending to be asleep. Austin would bet a hefty amount that it was the latter.

He peeled the kitten off his shirt and cocooned him in Ginger's soft sweater on the chair, placing him back inside the carrier.

'Mm-hmm,' Angie responded with pursed lips. She didn't believe him. Hell, *he* didn't even believe the lie himself. It was more than cat-sitting. He had an insatiable curiosity about Ginger. He wanted to get to know her, for real, not the tough exterior she showed everyone, but the smart, sensitive woman he knew had to exist deep down. He'd seen it in glimpses; a flash of her elusive smile or the few times he'd actually gotten her to laugh.

More than anything, he didn't want Ginger to feel alone in an unfamiliar place. Cinnamon Falls could not compare to Atlanta by a long shot, but he wanted her to see what he saw, the magic, the community, the love. But it would be a hard sell after this morning's fiasco.

'How's your daddy doing?' Angie's question pulled him out of his thoughts. The inevitable topic returned. His father's accident had been a year ago and he was still constantly asked for updates. He knew most people were merely concerned, but for Austin it felt like reliving the trauma again and again.

He gave his customary answer. 'Good, real good.' Angie nodded enthusiastically. 'Complaining more than usual so he ain't lost feeling in his tongue yet.'

Angie sputtered out a laugh. 'Thank God he's alive, though, right?'

'Yeah, thank God,' Austin repeated. It was one of those mollifying statements that people say when tragedy strikes someone else. He'd grown used to it by now. His father was lucky, yes. That much was true. But Austin was still reliving versions of the day that had changed their lives forever in his nightmares.

Angie added, 'That man refuses to let a wheelchair slow him down.'

'He refuses to acknowledge the chair,' Austin corrected fondly. 'As soon as we had those handbrakes installed on the truck, he was gone. I had to add a GPS just to keep up with him.'

Angie leaned closer, laughing. 'Just last week I had to talk one of the rookies out of giving him a speeding ticket.'

'See, that's what I'm talkin' about,' Austin chuckled, shaking his head. 'But, honestly, it's got me thinking about ramps, about sidewalks, and parking spaces.

Half of this town isn't designed for people who move differently. But it shouldn't have taken my dad's accident for me to start noticing, or caring, about that.'

Angie's eyes softened. 'I'm sure your daddy is proud to have a son as thoughtful as you.' Last year, he would have agreed. Now, he wasn't so sure about that.

Within the station, Austin heard a door slam, hard enough to rattle the photo frames along the wall. The thud of boots along the tile floor made his heart drum with anticipation. He saw Terrance first, his lined face still furrowed like he'd aged ten years in two hours. Jesse Shaw trailed behind him, and sandwiched between the two men was Ginger, with an expression that could have sliced steel.

Her posture was straight, rigid, almost military, and her eyes, simmering with frustration, told Austin exactly how their talk had gone. There was a storm brewing. The clothes she'd been wearing were gone, replaced with a Cinnamon Falls Police Department sweatshirt and standard issue sweatpants with a pair of cloth, slip-on shoes.

'Hey,' he said, reaching for her. 'You okay? Where's your clothes?'

'They took them. Evidence, apparently. Where's my cat?' Ginger moved strategically to avoid his outstretched arm. She rushed to Butter's carrier on the chair and dropped into a squat. Butter blinked sleepily up at her from inside, still wrapped in her sweater. 'You fed him?'

'Yeah, we found the formula. Angie gave me a paper cup for him to drink out of.'

'It really was the cutest thing,' Angie added from behind the desk. 'Got a video of it.' She turned her cell phone around, showing Butter lapping formula from a cup that was bigger than his body.

Ginger fingered the bars of the carrier, watching Butter for a long second. She didn't look up when she said, 'They shut down the bakery.' Her jaw clenched. 'Until further notice.'

Angie shooed the detectives out of the lobby and deeper into the station.

Austin tried comfort first. 'It's temporary, I'm sure. They just have to—'

Ginger raised her hand, cutting him off. He noticed the blood was gone.

'Do not,' she snapped, looking up at him with hard eyes, 'start with the silver lining sermon. I swear, if you say one more positive thing before eight a.m. I will run outside and fling myself into traffic.'

Austin blinked. 'I . . . I can be negative. I'm great at negativity.' To prove it, he kicked the plastic chair next to him for good measure. The bolted furniture didn't move, and Austin winced at the pain shooting through his foot. 'I'm a negative expert.'

Ginger huffed, raking a hand through her curls. Waves fell around her shoulders, an ocean of hair shielding her face from him. He wished she didn't look so defeated. In fact he wished, more than anything, that he could say the exact thing – do the exact thing – that she needed in this moment.

Instead, Butter meowed again. Ginger's intense concentration shifted back to her kitten.

'Thank you,' she muttered, 'for watching him. I appreciate it.'

'No problem,' Austin said. He lifted the carrier and Butter was perched at the edge. 'He's a good listener. Better than most people I know.'

Butter showed him his tiny teeth.

Ginger pushed past him with the carrier under her arm. 'I need to talk to Rowan Bell.'

'The wanna-be fortune teller?'

'Yes,' Ginger replied as she stormed toward the exit. 'I'm not letting Raines shut down my bakery and imply that I killed a man.'

Austin stopped in his tracks. 'What?' He pivoted, anger blooming in his chest. *Murder?* That's why they'd kept Ginger so long – they'd been accusing her of murder? Raines had gone too far this time. Had Terrance stood there in silence and watched his wife's cousin get interrogated without defending her?

Austin rapped his knuckles on the counter, his pulse hammering. 'Angie, call one of the detectives back out here for me.'

Angie lifted the receiver to her ear but Ginger tugged at his arm.

'Austin, don't. I just want to get out of here.'

Despite his anger and his instinct to barrel past

the desk and demand answers, he let Ginger pull him out of the station.

Outside, Ginger paced in a tight circle on the sidewalk. 'Raines thinks that I was somehow involved in this, which is ridiculous. But I played it cool in there, got them to tell me some of what they know.' Her eyes flashed in a way that he'd never seen before. 'They kept asking me if I owned any red clothing. They showed me a photo of some kind of red fibers they found in his truck.'

Austin frowned. 'Do you want me to be negative or positive here? I can't tell. And what's this gotta do with Rowan Bell?'

'I saw her yesterday. She was wearing a red scarf.'

'Whoa. Wait, Ginger, maybe you need a minute—'

She spun on him, stabbing the air with her finger. 'I was trapped in a little room with a woman half my size and her two pitbulls for hours. No more minutes. No optimism. No pep talks, Austin. I'm doing this.'

She charged down the sidewalk toward his truck and tapped her foot impatiently when she reached the passenger door. 'Well?' she asked, gesturing toward his locked door.

'Well, what?' Austin crossed his arms over his chest, leaning back with a smirk.

She glared in return. 'My car's been sequestered, are you really going to make me ask?'

Austin planted his feet, hands in his pockets, enjoying this more than he cared to admit. Unstoppable Ginger Mills actually needed his help.

She blew out a frustrated breath. 'Are you going to be my backup or what?'

Chapter 9

Ginger

Ginger didn't want to get in Austin's truck. She also didn't want to admit how rattled she was after spending the last few hours of her morning defending her innocence. But when she had stepped out of the station and realized her hands were trembling so violently that she could barely hold Butter's carrier upright, she had to admit that she was in no shape to drive. And she still didn't know her way around yet; she'd get lost as soon as she left Cinnamon Falls town limits.

Austin, however, could navigate this place with his eyes closed. So she swallowed her pride, each inch of it scraping down her throat like broken glass, and slid into his passenger seat.

Accepting help felt too much like weakness, and Ginger hated feeling weak. Almost as much as she hated feeling scared. And she had to admit, she was terrified. She wished Camille was here, or Alexis, or anybody she had known for more than a few weeks in passing. She had always thought she was tough enough to handle anyone or anything on her own. She wished for her mother's reassuring Detroit drawl, or her father's encompassing hugs. She wished that someone she loved would hold her hand and tell her that everything was going to be okay.

She'd underestimated this place, and Chief Raines especially. Raines was something else; relentless, and unbothered by Ginger's attitude. She tried to dissect Ginger bit by bit, cutting away at her exterior like she was flaying a fish – pelting her with questions about her background, her love life, her business. And for the first time since leaving Atlanta, Ginger seriously wondered if she was truly safe here after all.

But what was her alternative? Tucking tail and heading back to Harrison? Never. She couldn't escape one hell for another, and she couldn't keep running. She had to protect her investment and put an end to this now, and that started with finding out what had really happened to Landon Lawson.

They pulled away from the police station in silence. For once, Austin didn't crack a corny joke to try to fill the quiet with chatter. Their tension pulled taut; Ginger could feel him waiting, patient, steady, understanding, as always.

Austin's truck was undeniably comfortable. The inside held a scent of cedar, sawdust, and faint traces of cinnamon, comforting in a maddening way. It reminded her of her father's garage; summer after summer of watching him tinker on an old Cadillac from his high-school days that he never seemed to get up and running. She melted into the plush leather seat and when Austin turned on the heat, she fought to keep her eyes open, the long morning catching up to her.

Butter meowed from the carrier at her feet. She reached down and pulled him out, fingers stroking his tiny head.

'I know, buddy,' she said. 'It's been a rough morning for the both of us.'

Austin cleared his throat softly. 'Do you want to talk about what happened back there?'

She didn't, not really. But the words crashed out anyway. 'Raines thinks I killed Landon,' Ginger replied, digging her fingers into Butter's soft fur. He snuggled deeper into her lap. She focused on the steady rise and fall of his breathing – anything to keep from seeing Landon in her mind's eye again, the way his body crumpled against the floor, the strange angle of his arms, the blood spreading beneath his head. His blood on her hands. The sticky, coppery substance that dried, flaking beneath her fingernails.

'She asked me flat out like she was repeating her breakfast order.' Austin's fingers tightened around the steering wheel while she continued. 'They saw my hands, the flour, the lipstick and immediately jumped to *me* like I'm some murdering temptress.' She rubbed her palms together unconsciously. The blood was gone now. They were clean. She'd scrubbed them in the station's sink until her hands felt raw. But she could still feel the phantom of it, sticky and warm, on her hands.

'Well, when you put it like that . . .' Austin started, and Ginger cut her eyes at him. 'It's just, I can understand why Raines jumped to that conclusion. It does look suspicious.'

Ginger groaned. 'I know I shouldn't have touched him, alright? I was trying to check if he was breathing. I – I didn't even think about it, I just acted.'

Austin tried to lighten the mood. 'You're not the temptress type, anyway.' Ginger kissed her teeth and he sobered instantly. 'I just mean you're more . . .' He scratched the back of his neck, keeping his eyes concentrated on the road ahead. 'Real . . . not like, flashy or seductive. You don't need all the extras to be noticed, is what I mean.'

'Are you calling me plain?'

'Plain?' he scoffed. 'You? Never. Have you seen your bakery? I'd never call that plain.'

Ginger turned, staring out of the window, cheeks warming. She exhaled, pushing out the knot of emotion churning in her chest. But the image came back anyway: Landon on the floor. The pooling blood. And the awful, sinking feeling that things would never be the same again.

'What happens when word gets out? Everyone is

going to think that I actually killed him, and what am I supposed to do? Who's going to believe me?'

Austin slowed at a stop sign and glanced her way; the early sunlight highlighted the edges of his jaw, the slope of his nose, and the concern etched between his eyebrows. '*I* do. I believe you and I'm going to help you,' he offered. 'You're not doing this alone.'

Something in her chest twisted. 'You really don't have to do that. You don't even know me.'

'I know enough,' he responded. 'I know you didn't kill Landon. I know you worked your ass off to get that bakery open. I know you don't have much family in town, that you're going to need someone in your corner. Plus, I helped build the place, so I have some personal stake in this.'

Reluctantly, she laughed; the sound surprised her at a moment like this. 'Thank you.'

He nodded, his eyes were the color of double chocolate brownies fresh from the oven. 'Anytime.'

The moment was fragile; tiny fissures in a glass wall. Ginger couldn't let it linger. Intimacy was dangerous. It cracked open doors she'd worked hard to keep bolted shut.

Behind them, a tiny car beeped its horn.

Austin tore his eyes away from hers, and turned onto a narrow street toward Juniper Heights. Finally, Ginger felt like she could breathe.

In Juniper Heights, Moonlight's Howl Apothecary was sandwiched between The Velvet Fox, a custom clothing boutique with a flirty fox mascot in a top hat and monocle, and Black Thorn Studio, a tattoo parlor with blacked-out windows and hand-painted ivy that ran along the exterior, roses peppering the vine.

Ginger wasn't sure what she expected to find, but it wasn't a handwritten sign taped crookedly to Rowan's door:

CLOSED FOR A FAMILY EMERGENCY.
Will reopen soon. Or not.
– Rowan.

Ginger stared at the sign in disbelief, her stomach dropping.

'No,' she whispered. 'No, no, no! I just saw her yesterday!'

Austin fell in beside her. 'It could be anything. Maybe her sister needed her, or her cat got stuck in a vent—'

'I know you like to be "Mr. Everything's Going To Be Alright", but everything isn't always a happy co-incidence, Austin.' Ginger stepped up to the door, cupping her hands to see inside. 'Rowan was wearing a red scarf yesterday. I saw it with my own two eyes.' She whirled around to face him. 'Raines showed me the photos of red fibers in Landon's truck, and now she's suddenly gone after Landon dies? Tell me that doesn't seem suspicious to you.'

Austin shrugged. 'It's . . . kind of a reach.'

Ginger shot him a glare and wished her eyes were knives. She folded her arms. 'I bet you she knew Landon. And now we can't ask her a single question because . . .' she gestured in frustration toward the sign, 'she's gone!'

Through the open passenger seat window, Ginger heard Butter meow at her heightened voice. Austin sighed, and gently guided Ginger away from the door.

'Look, I get it, really. But we can't prove you're innocent if we're banging on a locked door all morning.'

'She's involved, I know it,' Ginger said through gritted teeth, her hands curling into fists.

'Well, we can't know that for sure because she isn't here, so . . .' Austin pointed his thumb over his shoulder toward his truck, 'you're coming with me.'

'The hell I am,' Ginger retorted. 'I have a business to save, a reputation to protect—'

'And nowhere you can *legally* go,' Austin reminded her. 'Your bakery is off-limits. Raines made that very clear, and unless you want to get hit with obstruction or trespassing, you're stuck with me.'

Ginger bristled. 'I'm not *stuck* with anyone.'

'Semantics,' he replied breezily. Ginger resisted the urge to slap him with her purse.

Austin kept going, unfazed by her murderous gaze.

'I've got some errands to run. I still have to fix Sly James' front door like I promised. Mrs. Guy needs some shelving rearranged and Calvin Reed requested an estimate for some roof work before winter gets here. We can swing back by here tomorrow.'

'No,' Ginger replied immediately. 'Today. We're coming back later today.'

'What if she's still gone?' Austin countered. 'We can't sit out here all night hoping she materializes.'

He had a point. She hated when he had a point.

'And,' Austin added, softening his voice, 'I'll take you to Rosie's for lunch. My treat. You've got to be starving.'

'Fine,' she replied, tension needling out of her like a deflating balloon at the mention of food. Austin circled around to the driver's side and slid inside the cab, shifting his truck into drive. Ginger took one last look at Moonlight's Howl Apothecary before he drove away, vividly recalling Rowan in her long red scarf yesterday.

Was it truly a coincidence that she had an emergency the day Landon was found dead? Ginger shook her head. She didn't believe in coincidences. Not anymore.

Chapter 10

Austin

They were back to a suffocated silence. Austin was running on a few hours of sleep, four, maybe five, if he counted the twenty minutes where he'd caught some shut-eye in the truck outside of the police station. It was just after nine a.m., and the exhaustion wasn't what made his chest tight with nerves, it was Ginger.

He liked to pretend he was immune to nerves. He built houses for a living, after all. But sitting next to Ginger without talking was enough to reconsider his career path. Lion training, maybe? Something less dangerous than making conversation with a woman who didn't want to be bothered. She sat ramrod straight in the passenger seat, arms crossed. She didn't look at him, out the window, or at anything, really. She just stared straight ahead, her jaw ticking as he got closer to the Cinnamon Falls limits.

'You don't have to babysit me,' Ginger muttered

suddenly, arms tightening across her chest. 'I know you have work to do.'

'Yeah,' Austin said, slowing to turn onto Cinnamon Way. 'And you're part of it today.'

Her eyes finally flicked over to his. 'I am not a job.'

'No,' he agreed, keeping his tone soft. 'But you and I both know you shouldn't be alone.'

She looked away again; her throat bobbed, and that tiny betraying movement let him know that he was right. For a few seconds, neither of them said anything. The hum of the engine filled the cab. Butter, who had no regard for human crisis, let out a groggy meow from the carrier near Ginger's feet.

Austin cracked a smile. 'See? Even Butter thinks I'm right.'

Ginger didn't laugh. 'Let's just get it over with.'

'First stop is Sly James' place,' Austin said. 'It's a quick fix, shouldn't take more than twenty minutes or so.' Ginger didn't answer. 'Then Guy's Grocery. Mrs. Guy said it's a shelf issue. I'm thinking it'll be about the same time frame.'

Still nothing.

He exhaled, shifting his hands on the wheel. 'Look, Ginger. I know you're going through a lot right now, and you don't have to talk about it, but I want you to know I'm on your side. I'm right here with you.'

That earned him a sharp glance. She still didn't reply, but her shoulders dropped a fraction, just enough for him to hope that he was breaking through the glacier that surrounded her. That was victory enough for him.

He pulled onto Main Street, and negotiated bypassing the police barricade with an overzealous officer that'd been set up in the time they'd been gone. It was normally quiet at this hour, yesterday's festival chaos swallowed by an early morning calm. But this year the decorations were still holding on. If Maggie had been alive, there'd be hell to pay. Austin had to remind himself that everything was different now.

Austin parked in front of the General Store and slid out of the truck, stretching the stiffness from his shoulders. It'd been days since he'd had a proper workout. He had to get back to his routine.

Ginger met him on the sidewalk, arms still crossed, examining every movement happening at her bakery with a watchful eye as white-gloved officers rushed in and out.

'It looks so different from here,' she said in a low voice, longing in her sad eyes. 'And I didn't get a chance to bake Rachel's cake! She's going to hate me now that I ruined her son's birthday.'

'I'm sure she'll understand,' Austin offered. He practically had to push her away from the bakery and in the direction of the General Store.

Sly James beckoned him over, keys jingling as he removed the chains from the crooked front doors.

'Mornin', Mr. James,' Austin started brightly with

apologies. 'We had a bit of a run-in this morning.' He nodded toward the hub of police activity next door while Sly looked Ginger up and down like an extraterrestrial.

'I heard,' he said, finally turning his attention to Austin. 'That rookie, Nash, questioned me to high heaven about getting to my own store! Wouldn't tell me a durn thing but wanted to know what business I had on Main Street.'

Mr. James waved Ginger over. 'Come on in.'

Austin stepped inside the vestibule. Ginger passed them, with a nod of thanks, traveling further inside the store. Mr. James warmed his hands against his overalls. When Ginger was out of earshot, he tsked and said, 'Another murder on Main Street, this ain't gon' be good for business.'

'Murder?' Austin feigned ignorance, retrieving his tools from the bag. 'Is that what they're saying?'

Sly twisted his lips, resting his hands on his waist. 'That's what ol' Bones told me, and I heard your bakery chick is tied up in it.' He jerked his chin toward Ginger.

Austin looked past Mr. James' inquiring eyes and found Ginger hovering by the register, her fingers drifting over the shelves, the antique scales, the postcard spinner, and random dog treats. He could still see the tension radiating off her. Unfortunately, she'd been right to worry. Austin hadn't wanted to believe that the town would treat her like a suspect, but if

Harold Bones had managed to tell Sly James about Landon's death and it hadn't even hit noon, there was no telling how much further the rumors had traveled already. He was convinced that Ginger had nothing to do with Landon's death, but for some folks, dying in the new girl's bakery seemed to be the only thing that mattered, as if somehow, Landon had become a faithful saint overnight. As sad as it was, Austin wasn't surprised that a two-timing liar's past had finally caught up to him. He bristled at the thought of Ginger getting mixed up in Landon's mess.

'You think she did it?' Austin asked plainly, his eyes steely, his jaw tight. He was going to put a stop to it all right here and now even if he had to set the whole town straight.

Mr. James rocked back on his heels and stammered, 'I – well, I don't . . . no, I don't . . . well, you know, it's not up to me to determine. The law says everyone's innocent until proven guilty so, you know, who am I to judge?'

'Exactly,' Austin replied, shutting down any further conversation about Landon. 'Give me twenty minutes and I'll have this squared away for you.'

Sly must have gotten the hint. 'I already shut the power off and left the ladder for you so you can get started.' He faltered on his feet. 'I'll just, uh, run on down to Rosie's and grab you some coffee, then.'

'None for me, thanks,' Austin responded without looking up. 'Ginger will take a latte with vanilla foam and a cinnamon bun, though. She's gotta be hungry by now.'

'Vanilla foam and a cinnamon bun, got it.' Sly James slinked away just as Ginger appeared.

'Chilly in there,' she mumbled, watching Mr. James hightail it out of his store and down the sidewalk.

'Just a few more minutes,' Austin assured her. 'You want to sit in the truck?'

'No, I can't stand doing nothing while they trample in and out of my bakery. I need to be productive, do something with my hands to take my mind off it.'

'Good,' Austin replied. 'Hold this.' He handed her his flashlight and shouldered the doors until they were fully open. He grabbed the ladder and took a deep breath. He hadn't realized his eyes were closed until he heard Ginger's voice.

'You alright?' she asked jokingly. 'It won't eat you.'

His eyes popped open. She tilted her head, studying him. 'You look like you're about to wrestle a bear. What's the problem? Chop, chop!' She clapped her hands twice.

'I . . . haven't been on a ladder in a while.'

Ginger scoffed. 'Seriously? You're a contractor who's afraid of heights?'

'I'm not afraid of heights,' Austin retorted.

She arched a brow in disbelief, then she chewed her bottom lip. 'Wait, you *did* have someone come in and replace the ceiling tiles that one time . . .'

Austin nodded. 'I don't really . . . do . . . ladders.'

He could barely get the words out; the memory of his father's broken body flashed through his mind. Time still hadn't healed that wound. He'd stayed far away from ladders ever since.

To his surprise, Ginger didn't use that moment to crack a joke at his expense. Instead, she said plainly, 'Come on, show me.' She braced her body against the ladder. 'I won't let you fall.'

He didn't want to talk about their weight difference; his mother had taught him better than that. He sighed, 'Here we go.'

Austin planted one boot on the first rung, testing his weight. Moisture sprang to his palms. He adjusted his grip and climbed another, and another, until he was facing the top of the door.

He couldn't stop it – the memory flashed through his mind, sharp and unwanted. One bad step. The sickening drop. The crack. His father's defeated groan.

He swallowed and forced the image away.

'I'm right here,' Ginger said, less teasing now, bringing him back to the moment. He scooched to one side of the rung and beckoned Ginger up the ladder.

She hesitated. 'You sure this thing can hold both of us?'

'Get up here before I change my mind.'

Reluctantly, she climbed up to meet him and Austin angled his body so that she could see.

'There,' he said, pointing to the offending roller in

question. Ginger shone the flashlight into the small crack between the door and the glass. 'See how this has been worn down? It needs to be replaced.'

He realized too late that he was just inches from her face. He could make out the raised moles near her ear in the shape of a constellation he was sure he'd seen before in the night sky. Her lips pursed in concentration, pulling her bottom lip into her mouth. Austin tried not to stare.

Her question broke the silence. 'So, you got another one of those circle thingies, or what?'

Austin stifled a laugh. 'Yeah, in the bag.' Ginger made her way down the ladder and he wished for her warmth again. 'I'll need a flat wrench about an inch and a quarter, and an Allen wrench, too.'

'A what?'

Austin shook his head, putting on his big brother hat. 'Uh, long silver thing with matching ends that look like claws and the silver curved rod.'

'Got it.' Ginger handed him both wrenches and she turned on the flashlight again, the beam just under where he needed it.

Austin instructed, 'Up a little more.' The light shifted, barely. 'It's a flashlight, not a rocket launcher, woman.'

Ginger shot him a daggered look. 'Do you want help or not?'

He turned, grinning at the door. 'I always want your help.' The beam steadied, right where he needed it, and he worked quickly. She'd gone still beside him, focusing harder than necessary. He didn't dare say a word to ruin the moment.

First, Austin examined the anti-risers, making sure those were intact. He removed the nut from the roller, noting which way it was inserted, and slid it out of the back of the carriage.

He reached down. 'Circle thingy,' he requested. Ginger handed him a new roller and he installed it with care, making sure everything was aligned. He repeated the action with the other rollers, replacing each one for good measure. He double-checked the door leans and that the locks were properly positioned. He descended from the ladder and jogged to the back of the store to turn the power on again.

'Hit the switch,' Austin instructed Ginger once he was back in the lobby, and she pressed the button against the wall. The doors slid open smoothly, then closed without a hitch.

Sly arrived just in time to see it. He whistled with satisfaction. 'You're a magician, boy! How'd you do it?'

'With the help of my assistant here.' Austin gestured to Ginger and tucked his tools back into their compartments.

Sly laughed and slapped him on the shoulder good-naturedly. 'You two make a good team.'

He tucked a roll of bills into Austin's hand. From what Austin could see, it was more than what this job was worth, but he wasn't going to complain.

Sly turned to Ginger, handing her breakfast. 'Good to see you holdin' strong, dear. As they say, truth will out . . .'

He examined her from top to bottom then said, 'Go on and run back there and find you somethin' to wear.' Sly pointed his chin toward the women's clothing section in the back of the store. 'My treat.' Ginger took the food with a weak smile and a nod of thanks.

The sagging shelves in Guy's Grocery were fixed so quickly that by the time Ginger found the gumption to get out of the car, Austin was already done. He snacked on a protein bar he'd stashed in his center console as they hit the highway toward Reed & Roots Landscaping Company, just outside of Cinnamon Falls main town.

He turned into the expansive yard, angling his truck in the circle driveway. His father had already arrived, his truck parked just ahead of his own, waiting in the yard with Mr. Reed.

Reed & Roots always smelled like freshly cut grass and mulch, even in the throes of fall. The yard was dotted with pavers and half-finished projects, while the greenhouse stood tall in the back of the yard. Austin left Butter sleeping on the dashboard while Ginger had barely stepped out of the truck before a tiny squeal belted across the yard.

'Miss Gingcr!' Angel Reed came barreling across

the yellowed lawn like a heat-seeking missile, curly ponytails bouncing wildly behind her. Austin watched as Ginger's eyes lit up, bracing herself for a crash landing. But Angel skidded to a stop just in front of her, breathless and grinning, clutching a glittery purple composition notebook to her chest like classified material. Austin leaned over to get a peek, only just making out a few of the stickers on the front; one was a skull and crossbones.

'I made you a murder notebook,' Angel announced proudly. 'Because I heard there was a murder in your bakery, and every detective needs a notebook.' She shoved it into Ginger's arms as purple glitter exploded all over Ginger's new flannel shirt.

Austin sucked in a breath, fighting a laugh.

Angel flipped open the notebook, pointing to the first lined page with authority. Austin angled his head to make out the backwards, misshapen letters.

'Rule number one: always retrace footsteps.' Angel turned the page. 'Rule number two: don't forget family and friends.' She flipped the page again. 'Rule number three: suspects lie.'

Angel paused, growing stoic. 'The next page,' she declared, 'is the most important. Are you still listening, Miss Ginger? You can't miss this.'

Dumbfounded, Ginger nodded.

'Rule number four: don't get murdered.'

Ginger stared down at the notebook, then back at Angel, then at everyone standing around, watching.

With reddened cheeks Mr. Reed mouthed, 'I'm so sorry.'

Austin shrugged. He had nothing to offer. It was the same situation if a child offered you a toy phone – you had to play along and answer. Ginger was on her own.

'. . . Solid advice,' Ginger finally said. 'Thank you, Angel, for your expertise.'

Angel beamed, pleased with herself, and Austin couldn't take it anymore. He finally lost the battle, letting out a laugh that should have been a cough. Ginger shot him a look that didn't quite land because the corners of her mouth were turned up, losing her hard-fought battle, too.

Angel continued, unbothered. 'Andrew Guy says the last place someone was before they died is very important.'

Ginger sobered. 'Thank you, Detective Reed.' She attempted to return the notebook. Angel took a step back, keeping Ginger at an arm's distance.

'That's for you,' she said. Angel saluted. 'Call me if you need backup. My whereabouts are here.' Angel took the book and flipped to the last page that read: Property of Morningstar Elementary.

Ginger returned the salute clumsily. 'Ay-ay, captain. I'll take all the help I can get.'

As Angel sprinted off, Ginger tucked her murder book under her arm. Calvin Reed offered his apologies around a hearty laugh.

'I'm so sorry, Miss Mills. That girl's been obsessed with solving murders ever since Ms. Langford passed a few months back over at the Daffodil Inn. She thinks she's Andrew Guy.'

Ginger snorted. 'From the private detective show?'

'That's the one,' he confirmed. 'Damage is this way.' Calvin gestured over his shoulder toward the back of the house.

'Sorry 'bout the bakery, Ginger. I sure do hope they find out what happened to Landon,' Matthew said, offering her a hug, their affection seemingly easy; meanwhile all Austin could get were snarky responses.

'How was yesterday? Heard you sold out,' Matthew continued, maneuvering his chair to keep the pace alongside the group as they ventured around the back of the expansive property.

'Sold out of everything,' Ginger beamed. 'It was really nice until . . .' Her smile dimmed as she trailed off.

'Everything'll work out, kiddo. Don't you worry,' Matthew offered; his hand covered hers reassuringly.

Austin broke away from his father and Ginger, joining Mr. Reed at the back of the house where a tall ladder rested against a gutter.

'The last rainstorm came through here and pulled a bunch of shingles off,' Mr. Reed said, rubbing the back of his neck. 'Found them scattered all over the yard. I knew from the way it sounded that the damage had to have been more severe than I anticipated, but . . .' His voice faded, eyes flicking toward the ladder. 'I haven't had the courage to go up and look.'

Austin already knew where this was headed. Hefting his body on a ladder a few feet off the ground in Mr. James' store was one thing. An unreliable roof was another.

'Like I said on the phone,' Mr. Reed continued carefully, 'I don't know how comfortable you are with goin' up there after everything that happened with Matthew, but—'

Austin cut in quicker than intended. 'It was an accident, Mr. Reed. We're still holding strong.'

Mr. Reed studied him for a moment, then nodded. 'I know, son. Matt's a good man.' He clapped a solid hand on Austin's shoulder, the familiar weight grounding and heavy all at once. 'And you're a good son to keep the ball rolling. I know he's proud of ya.'

Austin swallowed, looking upward skeptically. If it hadn't been for the longstanding friendship between Mr. Reed and his father, he would have turned this job down. But he'd already faced his fears once today. What was another?

Easy money, Austin told himself as he set the ladder into place. He tested that it was sturdy by shaking it once, then twice, for good measure. He knew his father was somewhere watching, eyes trained on him. Before his brain could catch up with his body, and fear hooked itself into his bones, he started climbing.

Each rung felt further than the last. His hands tightened around the metal, knuckles whitening as memories crowded in uninvited: his father's yelp drifting down from the roofline, the scream that followed, then the deafening silence.

Austin paused halfway up. *Breathe*, he reminded himself. *You've done this a million times. It's nothing.*

The roof came into view, sun-warmed and deceptively calm. He climbed the rest of the way, pulling himself onto the shingles. His mind focused as he examined the scene, blocking out the thundering in his heart.

The damage was worse than it looked from the ground. Several shingles had been torn away, nails exposed, edges curling where the wind had shaken them loose. He crouched, inspecting the underlayment and testing the integrity of the surrounding shingles. Everything was still sound beneath the surface, which meant it was fixable. He steadied himself and fished his phone out of his pocket, snapping a few pictures. Then, he climbed back down to where Ginger, his father and Mr. Reed were waiting. He was more than thankful when his feet hit the ground.

'Nothing structural,' he reported, trying his best to keep it together. The rubber band that was squeezing his heart loosened, only slightly. 'Looks like we just need to replace a small section. I'll write up an estimate.'

Mr. Reed nodded, relieved. Austin calculated a

reasonable number for parts and labor and passed the clipboard to his father, who assessed his estimate. He didn't say a word, he didn't need to, just nodded his approval. While he and Mr. Reed ran through the numbers, Austin felt gravity bear down on his shoulders. He had to get out of there.

At that moment, Ginger appeared beside him, her eyes gentle, her touch soft.

'I'm starving,' she said decisively, taking hold of his wrist. The weight of her touch grounded him in the moment. 'And I can use a break from . . .' she gestured around herself, 'all this.'

Austin exhaled, thankful for the excuse to exit. 'Rosie's?' he suggested.

Ginger's lips folded into an easy smile. 'Rosie's.'

Austin said his goodbyes and headed toward his truck; the tension in his chest eased when he climbed behind the wheel. Ginger didn't say a word as she clipped on her seat belt after pulling Butter into her lap. He took her silence as an offering. Ginger hadn't asked him to explain, and that'd meant everything to him.

Chapter 11

Ginger

Ginger noticed the shift in Austin's body language immediately, but he was too nice of a guy to mention to his father, or Mr. Reed, that he was more than ready to get out of there. Watching Austin practically tremble in fear as he ascended the ladder had made her think back to the months when he'd renovated The Maple Bakery, never scaling a ladder himself. He'd hired people for that. The recessed lighting, the high shelves all had been installed by a contractor. But today, he'd conquered not one, but two ladders.

The man who usually filled any second of silence with a joke or casual conversation suddenly had nothing to say, like he'd folded inward, retreating behind something heavier than just the fatigue of an extremely long morning.

She'd learned a long time ago that people talked when they were ready, herself included. But the realization hit her with quiet clarity. For the first time since she'd met Austin Jacobs, she understood that his relentless optimism that sometimes bordered on toxic positivity wasn't a performance, it was armor; and today he'd taken off his breastplate, leaving it in Mr. Reed's backyard.

The drive into town was quick but unhurried. When they entered Rosie's Diner, Ginger felt a wave of unexpected relief. The fifties-style restaurant didn't feel old-fashioned, but vintage. Timeless. The comforting smell of cooked food and the clink of glasses over conversation was like a pocket of normalcy after her otherwise abnormal day.

Ginger had just settled into her seat at the table, joining Austin in watching Butter lap his formula from a saucer with a quiet fascination, when their peace was shattered.

'That is the cutest kitten I've ever seen!' The voice sliced through the diner like a siren, and Ginger's head spun toward a girl rushing over, all smiles and unfiltered enthusiasm, questions firing a mile a minute. Ginger immediately recognized Austin's little sister, Lillian.

She had warm brown skin that glowed with youth. Her hair was pulled into a high ponytail secured with a ribbon tied neatly into a bow that bounced with every movement she made. She wore a cozy striped sweaterdress and a pair of brown cowboy boots. She leaned into Butter without hesitation as if he was the most important thing in the room.

'Auzzie!' she squealed. 'When did you get a cat? No fair, I want one! Wait – is it mine? My birthday's not 'til June!' She lifted Butter out of Austin's grasp, twirling him above her head, enamored.

Butter locked eyes with Ginger, wide and pleading.

'Lils, wait—' Austin said, lunging for Butter, but the girl pulled him away just out of Austin's reach.

'You've had him all day, at least let me—' She stopped short, her eyes flicking to Ginger like she'd realized another human being was beside her.

'Oh,' she said slowly, her eyes trailing Ginger, their empty table save for two perspiring glasses of water, and finally landing back on her brother. 'Ohhhhh,' she said again, brighter this time.

She brought Butter to her chest, cradling him just above her heart. He looked thankful to be stationary. 'This is . . . you're on . . . O-M-G, Auzzie, is this a date? Are we, like, interrupting?'

Ginger felt her face ignite.

'We?' Austin repeated flatly, crossing his arms over his broad chest.

'I mean, it *is* a cute cat.'

Behind her, another young woman approached, just a hair taller with their shared warm brown eyes and her auburn hair tucked into a Cinnamon Falls branded hat. Her calm and an easy smile mirrored Austin's. She had a sporty look about her – an oversized sweatshirt and loose fitting jeans – like she'd played years of softball and made it her personality.

Ginger didn't need introductions. These were Austin's sisters, Madelyn, the oldest of the two, and the youngest, Lillian, Cinnamon Queen.

Madelyn stepped around her sister, revealing herself fully. 'We came to pick up lunch and spotted your truck in the lot. Sorry if we're interrupting—'

Lillian cut in, undeterred by her sister's apology. Her firetruck-red fingernails pointed accusingly. 'Wait, aren't you like, wanted by the cops or something?'

Ginger's mouth dropped open, but nothing came out. 'I—'

'This is Ginger Mills,' Austin said firmly, stepping in without hesitation to save her from further embarrassment. 'And her kitten, Butter—'

'Butter?' Madelyn echoed. She looked down at the tiny cat. 'That's certainly . . . a choice.'

Lillian brought Butter's nose to hers. His tiny tongue jetted out, smearing across the end of her nose. She burst into a fit of giggles. 'I kinda like it. It suits him.'

'I found him in a butter box behind my bakery—' Ginger explained.

Lillian kept going. 'So you *are* the one wanted by the cops—'

Madelyn elbowed her, whispering a warning. 'Don't be rude, Lils.'

Austin cleared his throat loudly. 'Ginger talked to the police this morning, but she's not a suspect—'

'So, like, did you kill Landon, or what? Because Niles Bennett has been online telling everybody about this pull-apart bread . . .' she lowered her voice conspiratorially and covered Butter's ears with her hand, 'that's better than Rosie's cinnamon buns, and I can't lie, I want to try one, but I can't justify buying baked goods from a murderer, know what I'm saying?'

Ginger couldn't possibly become any hotter inside than she already was. It was like someone had turned her internal furnace on full blast, and the flannel shirt she grabbed out of the General Store wasn't helping. Sweat trickled down the small of her back.

She tried to laugh it off; after all, these were Austin's sisters and she didn't want to be rude. If it had been anyone else, she wouldn't have been so nice. 'I wouldn't go that far—'

On the table, her phone buzzed, Alexis' name showing on the screen. She clamored for the device, welcoming the distraction from the awkward conversation.

The young women pulled up chairs, turning their third degree on their big brother as Ginger stepped away from the table, phone in hand.

'Hey cuz, what's up?'

Ginger knew from Alexis' labored breath on the line that it wasn't going to be a good conversation. 'Listen, Ging, I don't know how to say this—'

'Wait, Lex, before you start.' Ginger ventured deeper to a quieter part of the diner. 'I had nothing to do with Landon's death, okay? You know me, I would never do anything—'

Through the phone, Alexis kissed her teeth and stated firmly, 'I'm not worried about that. Terrance told me what went down this morning. I'm sorry about your bakery, but once they clear the scene, you'll be able to get back in there in no time.'

'Okay,' Ginger replied, still not convinced. 'Then what's the deal?'

Alexis sighed. 'Terrance told me you adopted a cat or something?'

'I found a cat,' Ginger clarified. 'Late last night in the alley behind—'

'So, you brought a literal alley cat into my house?'

'Well, I went to Dr. Hughes first. Butter's got all the things to be safe: shots and chips and all that jazz. He's got a clean bill of health—'

'Ging, Terrance is super allergic. He's been sneezing and hacking all day.' Ginger's stomach dropped and suddenly she knew where the conversation was headed. She had never been the type to beat around the bush. She'd rather rip the Band-Aid off and get it over with.

'Are you saying I can't stay at your house with Butter?'

Alexis went silent on the other end. 'The timing is shitty but it's just that Terrance . . .' She sighed. 'We love having you here, cuz, but I can't risk my husband's health or my sanity. This man is acting like he's going to die any second.' In the background she heard Terrance whining about his itchy throat.

'Are you really kicking me out? Tell him to take an antihistamine and grow up!'

Alexis stammered. 'We talked to Morgan, alright? She's all ready for you over at the Daffodil Inn. You can stay as long as you want, no charge. It's absolutely gorgeous, Ging. It's acres and acres of land, imagine waking up to that every day. Little Olive Oil would love it.'

'Butter,' Ginger grumbled.

'I'm really sorry, Ging. It's just temporary, until we can figure something else out, okay?'

Ginger didn't believe that, not for a second. Besides, she'd decided last night that Butter wasn't temporary either. She had no choice but to relent.

Returning to the table, Ginger saw that Lillian and Madelyn were still peppering Austin with questions about Landon Lawson, hanging on every word while they stole fries from his plate.

Madelyn popped one in her mouth while Lillian asked, 'So, like, you saw his legs sticking out of the door, and then what?'

Ginger slumped into her seat.

'Bad news?' Austin asked, directing his attention to her.

Ginger shrugged bitterly. 'I can't take Butter back to Alexis' place. Apparently, Terrance is deathly allergic to a cat smaller than a sheet of paper.'

Austin turned, all serious, his eyes bearing down on her. 'So, what's that mean for you?'

'It means,' Ginger sighed, 'I'm officially homeless.'

The sisters gasped; Lillian clutched Butter to her chest. He mewed helplessly.

'No!' Lillian exclaimed.

'Alexis said Morgan offered me a room at the Daffodil Inn—'

'Absolutely not!' Madelyn shot forward, eyes wide. 'Someone just got murdered there a few months back. Didn't you hear about it on the *Untold* podcast?'

Ginger threw her hands up, frustrated. 'Does anybody in this town die from plain old age?'

'Stay with Auzzie,' Lillian volunteered brightly, letting Butter gnaw gently on her pointer finger.

'Excuse me?' Austin blanched, choking on the water he'd just swallowed.

'What?' Lillian shrugged matter-of-factly. 'You've got the space. She can stay in your guest bedroom, right?'

Madelyn elbowed her sister hard in the ribs. '*I'm* currently occupying that room!'

Lillian rolled her eyes. 'You can sleep at Mom and Dad's. Can't you see the woman is in crisis? Who's the one being rude now?' she sneered.

Austin met Ginger's eyes across the table; a maddening slow smile crept across his lips. 'The guest bedroom is yours, if you'd like. No murderers, I guarantee it.'

Chapter 12

Monday

Austin

Morning couldn't come soon enough. Austin hadn't planned on waking before sunrise, but he couldn't sleep a wink knowing that for the first time since Samantha had left, there was another woman in his home, and not just any woman – Ginger Mills.

In the dawn haze, he lay on the floor, his sweaty back sticking to his workout mat, spent from the weight session he'd just endured. He lay there for a moment, allowing his heart rate to decrease, and listened to the quiet hum of his house. Most of all, he listened for her. The silence felt different; fuller somehow . . . occupied, like the walls were holding their breath. Ginger was just down the hall, in his spare bedroom with the kitten she couldn't part ways with.

After taking a long, hot shower and dressing, Austin crept toward the kitchen and shifted the dial on the wall upward. Golden light rained down from the recessed bulbs above, radiating a faint glow. He loved this room the most; it was the first one he'd renovated once he'd moved in. Sturdy oak cabinets lined the wall, painted a cool sage green. He remembered the weight of the electric sander between his palms as he worked the machine over them until the wood grain shone through.

He started breakfast quickly, turning on the coffee pot first. Ginger's occupation kept her on an early schedule and any minute now he imagined she'd be awake craving caffeine and nourishment. He wanted to be prepared to satisfy all her cravings, and he knew the perfect breakfast to do the trick.

He made sure to preheat the oven and prepared the bacon and sausage on the stove. He sifted pancake mix into a bowl and folded the proteins inside. Tossing in a generous handful of cheese, he combined the mixture together with milk and a hefty serving of maple syrup. Then, he spooned the mixture into a muffin pan and placed it in the oven. It was his go-to recipe when he needed a quick, high protein breakfast while on the go. Plus, it stopped him from slamming back two cinnamon buns at Rosie's every morning.

As he waited for the timer, Austin's eyes drifted toward his living room where Ginger's boxes were stacked neatly on top of one another. He counted only three, one stuffed suitcase, and the cat carrier. The sight hit him harder than he expected in the new light of the morning. Last night there had been the urgency of making sure she had a place to sleep. Now, the reality of it had settled in.

That was all that existed of Ginger Mills; her life reduced to a few boxes in the corner of his living room. She didn't come with any furniture that carried happy memories, no framed photographs or books; nothing that suggested a life lived somewhere long enough to leave roots, just the bare minimum. He didn't want to pry, but it did make something ache in his chest, low and uncomfortable. It made him wonder, who was Ginger, really? Before he could think too hard about it, the faint jingle of Butter's bell chimed from the staircase.

Austin glanced up as the kitten came trotting into the kitchen first, tail high, and Ginger wasn't far behind. He pulled down a mug from the cabinet just as she appeared at the bottom of the steps.

Her hair fell around her shoulders, face bare, wearing one of his old T-shirts he hadn't seen in decades. It hung loosely on her frame, the hem brushing the tops of her knees.

The sight stopped him cold and for a second he forgot what he'd been doing. He forgot about the coffee and the timer ticking behind him. He even forgot how to breathe.

God, she was beautiful, he thought. And her standing in his kitchen, wearing his clothes, it did something strange to his chest. Austin could smell

Ginger across the kitchen; shea butter and something warm, soft and familiar. Something that made the space feel less like the quiet house he'd lived in alone for years and more like . . . a home. The realization settled over him slowly. He liked having her here, more than he probably should.

'Morning,' he said, busying his hands so he didn't look too awkward. He quickly silenced the timer and pulled on a pair of oven mitts, grabbing the muffins and setting them on the counter. Then, he pulled down a shallow bowl for Butter and poured the formula into it, setting it on the floor. The tiny cat ventured over and started happily lapping.

Austin tried very hard not to look at Ginger again. 'How'd you sleep?'

'Great,' Ginger replied. 'Thank you, again, by the way, for letting me and Butter stay here. I – we . . . really appreciate it. You made muffins?' Ginger's eyes flicked to the muffin tin cooling on the island.

He shrugged. 'My dad used to make them for us on busy mornings. He calls it breakfast in a bite: bacon, sausage, cheese and pancakes. I figured we'd need some fuel for the day ahead.'

'Sounds delicious,' she said with a tight smile. 'But I can smell your artificial maple from here.'

Austin rolled his eyes. 'You haven't even tasted it.'

She smirked. 'Don't need to, but I am starving.'

Ginger fingered a muffin and split it down the middle with a fork. Steam curled around the metal, slow and inviting. She took a bite, her eyes shutting. 'I can't believe I'm saying this . . . but it's actually good.'

'Don't sound too surprised,' Austin scoffed.

'No,' Ginger backtracked, an apologetic laugh escaping. 'It's just I can tell the maple's fake. I bet it's pancake syrup.' Ginger searched for the bottle on his counter and her eyes scanned the label. 'Ah-ha!' She held it up to him like a hidden clue. 'Maple flavoring,' she said, pointing to the thin font printed on the very bottom of the label.

Austin chuckled. 'Please accept my sincerest apologies, Maple Queen.'

Ginger tossed the bottle in the trash. 'Apology accepted. I'll stop by my bakery and introduce you to some authentic maple syr—' The thought curled in on itself, halting in Ginger's mouth. He could tell what she'd been thinking: her bakery wasn't accessible right now, and who knows when she'd be able to go back inside?

Austin course-corrected quickly. 'What's up with the maple thing, anyway?'

It was her turn to chuckle as she tucked another forkful of muffin into her mouth. 'My Uncle Maple, Alexis' dad, was originally from Michigan. I'm not sure if you've ever been before but Canada is just across the river. Every Christmas he'd bring us authentic Canadian maple syrup. Sounds kinda stupid but it wasn't Christmas until I saw Uncle Maple.'

'It doesn't sound stupid at all.' Austin pretended not to notice the tears shining in her eyes. Not wanting the moment to end, he implored, 'Tell me more about him.'

'He was my father's older brother, Maurice, but I started calling him Uncle Maple as a kid, and it stuck. We were all much closer when Alexis and I were girls but . . . time, you know.' Ginger shrugged, her eyes downcast. 'He was killed in a car accident when we were teenagers. Alexis took it hard, naturally, but strangely, Terrance reminds me of Uncle Maple in a lot of ways.' Austin waited and a nostalgic smile returned to Ginger's lips.

'Anyway, my mother would whip up all these maple desserts and force me and Alexis to try them. It was like we were little judges on our own personal baking show. I went to culinary school right after high school and did a stint in a few bakeries, but in the past few years . . . I lost the passion for it. When I moved to Cinnamon Falls, I promised myself that I'd bake from my heart again, and my most cherished memories are those Christmases when my mother made her maple pull-apart bread or her no-bake cheesecake bars specially for me and Lex.'

'Paying homage,' Austin commented.

She slapped away the tears that threatened to spill over. 'Yeah. I guess so. Cheaper than therapy.'

The moment had shriveled between them until silence crusted over.

'You don't have to keep upending your days for me,' Ginger said eventually. 'I know you've got a business to run.'

'It'll survive without me for twenty-four hours.'

That wasn't the whole truth. He had a full schedule today, a paint job on Nutmeg Avenue that would take several hours, and an estimate for a full demo at a clothing store in Asheville. The truth was that he wanted this moment more; any excuse to get to know her better, deeper; to understand her without pushing too hard; to share more moments with her like the one that'd just passed. He wanted to figure out why the woman with stories of a loving childhood, parents, and friends only had three boxes to her name.

She studied him then, her eyes narrowing. 'Why are you helping me?'

There it was, that wall again, slamming down around her like a fortress. He leaned back, choosing his words carefully. He had hundreds of them floating around in his head, but he wanted to pick the safest ones.

'Because I don't like seeing good people with their backs against the wall.'

He felt her gaze soften, just a fraction, like a shift in the weather.

'Your muffins are good,' she said flippantly. She forked another out of the pan and shoved the top of it in her mouth. 'Thanks for breakfast.'

'Anytime,' he replied.

'First stop to see Rowan Bell?'

He shook his head. 'Second.' He pointed his coffee mug at her chest. 'First you're going to take off my shirt and put it back where you found it.' Ginger choked on her muffin. 'And *then* we check out Moonlight's Howl. We'll grab your car on the way back. I'm hoping we can sort this mess out today.'

Ginger fisted her hips, swallowing down her last bite. 'It's going to take much longer than that. This is not some sixty-minute scripted show with a satisfying, happy ending. This is my real life, Austin.'

Austin rolled his eyes. 'So, are you taking your murder book, or what, Detective?'

Chapter 13

Ginger

Austin held the truck door open as she and Butter, already napping in his carrier after breakfast, folded into his passenger seat. Ginger flipped on the seat heater, settling in for the ride toward Juniper Heights. Austin's truck was more comfortable than her decades-old sedan – supple leather seats, smooth suspension, and enough buttons and gadgets on the dash to launch a small spacecraft. Austin eased them out of his driveway, and they settled into a quiet rhythm as the neighborhood slipped past the windows.

The night before had been unexpectedly peaceful. She hadn't thought she'd sleep at all in a strange house, especially after such a long, stressful morning. But the spare room Austin gave her was warm, the bed soft enough that she'd sunk into it the moment her head hit the pillow. Butter curled himself into a ball on top of her head, and Ginger surprisingly slept straight through the night. No nightmares. No flashing images of blood on her hands. Just silence. She hadn't realized how exhausted she'd been until morning sunlight spilled through the lacy curtains.

And then there was breakfast.

Austin had been standing at the stove in a thin white undershirt that clung to his stocky frame, the cotton stretched just enough to hint at the solid muscle underneath. The recessed lighting caught his shoulders and traced the strong lines of his arms as he moved, his corded forearms and sculpted biceps flexing easily while he worked the muffin tin. A faint dusting of dark hair shadowed the groove between his pecs.

Ginger hadn't expected that. Or the way he'd looked up at her as she descended the stairs and simply . . . started. Not rudely, or in a way that made her feel uncomfortable. But, long enough for her to notice. Long enough for a slow warmth to creep up her neck as she realized something she'd never let herself consider before: Austin Jacobs was . . . kind of fine. And as she'd been standing there in his kitchen, Ginger suddenly had the strange feeling she'd just stumbled into a moment neither of them had been prepared for.

Now, as the truck rolled through the quiet streets of Cinnamon Falls, she could still feel that look, that strange electric feeling, lingering between them.

As grateful as she was for Austin's willingness to save her from the brink of homelessness, Ginger couldn't help the small knot of caution tightening in her chest. Was Austin's generosity simply traditional Southern hospitality, or was it more? And if it was more, what did he want?

All men wanted something eventually, even the nice ones. She wondered what Austin would request when he cashed in on his quid pro quo. She glanced at him from the corner of her eye as he drove, one hand resting loosely on the steering wheel. He was attracted to her, that much she suspected, it wasn't like the man was blind. But there was something deeper, too. Something she couldn't quite name yet. Austin Jacobs was turning out to be far more complicated than she'd first assumed. And judging by the stretch of road ahead of them, she had plenty of time to figure him out.

With Harrison, she never had to wonder. His want was clear. His courtship, loud: name-brand handbags she couldn't pronounce, hand-picked exotic bouquets, and tropical vacations. Austin, on the other hand, had quietly stretched out his hand when she was drowning, never demanding reciprocation. She'd never forget that.

Austin pointed his chin to the sparkly purple notebook Ginger balanced in her lap, breaking the silence between them. 'So what's the plan?'

'We find out what Rowan's been up to,' she stated matter-of-factly. 'I've been thinking about it all night and I still can't wrap my head around her going missing the same day Landon dies. I mean, you're from here. Does Rowan have any connection to Landon?'

Austin scrubbed his hand over his face and answered, 'Not that I know of. He got around, if you know what I mean, so it's possible he and Rowan could have . . .'

Ginger shook her head. 'Landon told me he was married.'

He maneuvered his truck onto the highway, the engine accelerating as he merged into early morning traffic. 'He is,' Austin said finally, settling into a moderate speed.

'Then, what?' Ginger turned to face him in her seat. 'He just parades around town with floosies and everyone knows?'

Austin shrugged nonchalantly. 'Yeah. It sounds crazy but, wait – did you just say floozy? I haven't heard that word since I was in diapers.'

Ginger chuckled, embarrassed. 'Something my mother would say.'

'So you've got your mind set on Rowan, then?' Austin asked, taking the exit toward Juniper Heights.

Ginger nodded curtly, directing her gaze ahead. 'Yeah, I think so. It makes the most sense.'

He slowed next to Moonlight's Howl Apothecary and nodded toward glass double doors that were still shut tight, along with the same closed sign. 'Let's find out then.'

They crossed the street together in quick strides.

Austin rapped his knuckles against the door, once then twice, before cupping his hands to the glass to peer inside.

A shadowed Rowan made an appearance, her hair wilder than the last time Ginger had seen her. She poked her head out of the door, just barely, angling her body inside the dark store. When Rowan noticed Ginger, her lips twisted.

'You,' she said flatly. 'I should've known.'

Ginger folded her arms. 'Rowan, we need to talk.'

Rowan's eyes flicked to Austin, assessing. Almost imperceptibly he nodded, and her eyes swung back over to Ginger. 'About what? Because I don't have time for—'

'Your alibi,' Ginger cut in, all business. The subterfuge was growing old, and Ginger's livelihood was on the line.

Rowan's eyebrows shot to the sky. 'Excuse me?' she shrilled.

'The night Landon died,' Ginger pressed, unaffected. 'Where were you?'

Rowan threw her head back and laughed once, humorless. 'Is this a joke?'

'No,' Ginger said plainly. 'It's a question.'

Rowan exhaled slowly through her nose, then stepped aside allowing them to enter. 'Five minutes, that's all you get.'

The shop was exactly how Ginger had imagined: a dark, crowded room, with a strong medicinal smell.

Rowan moved restlessly, stuffing items in a canvas tote bag laced across her slim midsection: bundles of dried herbs, a pack of cards with gold trim, a small jar of oil, and a cotton cloth. Ginger's eyes roamed the store but she couldn't see what she was looking for . . .. yet. Where had Rowan tucked that red scarf?

Dark circles hung under Rowan's eyes, and she had a tension about her shoulders that Ginger hadn't noticed before. Her usual flowing layers were replaced with a simple pair of black leggings and an oversized Cinnamon Falls High hoodie like she'd dressed in a hurry, or hadn't slept at all.

'If you must know, I was at the hospital.' Rowan pushed her hair out of her face. 'All night.'

Austin's brow creased, all concern and less accusation. 'Is everything alright, Rowan?'

Ginger rolled her eyes.

'It's my aunt,' Rowan replied weakly. 'She's been sick for a while and took a turn late Saturday night.' Ginger watched her hands. They trembled while she shoved clothes in her bag.

Convenient, Ginger thought. 'And we just so happened to catch you at your shop this morning?'

Rowan's head snapped up, fire in her eyes. 'It is my store, Ginger.'

Ginger didn't blink. 'The police found red fibers in Landon's truck.'

That did it. Rowan went still, freezing mid-motion.

'The last person who was wearing a red scarf outside of my bakery was you,' Ginger finished, waiting on her reaction.

A candle slipped out of Rowan's grasp and clattered to the floor. It rolled away under a mahogany dresser steps away.

Rowan's face flushed, anger blazing hot and fast. 'You think *I* had something to do with this?'

Ginger shrugged. 'I think it's awfully coincidental.'

Rowan let out a bitter laugh. 'You're basing your assumption on my clothes? That was a Natasha Montgomery exclusive,' she snapped.

Ginger frowned, the air slowly seeping out of her sails. 'A what?'

Austin cut in. 'Natasha Montgomery . . . she knits, right? She crocheted my mother a hat one year at the Fall Festival.'

Rowan nodded. 'The scarf was a custom piece. She made it for me as a favor. It adds to my whimsy.' She shrugged.

Ginger crossed her arms. 'What's this got to do with your Saturday night whereabouts?'

'Are you incapable of listening?' Rowan threw her hands up. 'My aunt is dying! I'm on my way back to the hospital right now. Why don't you go question Landon's latest flavor-of-the-week and get out of my damn store—'

'Wait,' Austin interrupted. 'Are you saying Natasha and Landon—'

'I'm saying, if you want to know who killed him, start with the woman who wouldn't quit him, even after Ethel threatened to knock her head off.'

'Natasha and Ethel had a fight?' Ginger breathed. 'Do you know where we can find her now?'

'Last I heard the clothing business wasn't hittin'. Now she's waiting tables over at Prime Society.' Rowan adjusted the bag on her shoulder, giving the two of them an impatient once-over. 'Now, if you'll excuse me.' She shoved past them and held the door open for the pair of them to exit. Ginger and Austin took their cue, and Rowan followed after, locking the door behind them all with a firm twist of the key.

'And for the record, I don't take kindly to being accused of murder.' She spun on her heel and started down the sidewalk, her wild hair flowing after her.

'That went well,' Austin stated, watching Rowan stomp away.

Twenty minutes later they were still outside Moonlight's Howl Apothecary in Austin's truck, iced coffees sweating in their respective cup holders from the nearby gas station. It was just after nine in the morning, and Austin pointed out that Prime Society, an upscale restaurant and lounge, wouldn't open for several more hours.

Ginger sighed, drumming her fingers along the dashboard. Butter playfully nipped at her fingertips while she ruminated.

'Tell me again why we can't just call up Natasha and ask her about Landon?'

Austin laughed listlessly, his head balancing on the headrest. 'You really think you're CFPD, don't you? You can't just go around questioning people thinking they're going to tell you what you want to hear. You're an outsider, Ginger, and I'm not sure if you remember, but everyone thinks you're a murderer.'

'Thanks a lot,' Ginger deadpanned. 'It was almost like I'd forgotten all about it.' She threw her head back against the headrest too, crossing her arms, her mind whirring.

Austin continued. 'You're thinking about who killed him, but I'm thinking about *why* someone would get up at four in the morning and take Landon's life. And why inside of your bakery of all places?'

The thought struck her like lightning. She scrambled for Angel's notebook in the backseat. She flipped through the pages' drawings, arrows, and settled on rule number one: always retrace footsteps.

'What if he wasn't killed at four in the morning? We need to figure out where Landon was *before* he got to my bakery.'

Austin took a long sip of his coffee. 'Then we'll need to split up.'

'Split up?' Ginger echoed incredulously. Butter mewed with disappointment.

'Yes,' Austin said. 'No one is going to talk to you about Landon, not without someone they trust, someone they know. Plus you're a little . . .'

Ginger cut her eyes at him. 'A little what?' she snapped.

'Rough,' Austin finished. He gestured toward Rowan's store. 'People don't like being questioned. But they'll talk your head off if you disguise it as gossip about someone else.'

Ginger huffed. 'I don't have time for petty rumors.'

'The answers are *in* the rumors. Listen, I'll track Landon's last movements. I'll find out where he went before he got to your bakery.'

Ginger nodded, thinking. 'Then I'll talk to Natasha this afternoon once Prime Society opens.'

Austin started to object, but Ginger continued. 'I'll bring Alexis with me. It'll be less . . . intimidating. Besides, Alexis thinks I'm mad at her anyway, so it will give us a chance to bury the hatchet.'

Austin hesitated, then tapped the pages of the notebook resting in Ginger's lap. 'We meet back at the house tonight to compare notes?'

Ginger met his eyes. There was something steady there, unyielding; something that made this feel possible.

'Tonight,' she agreed.

Austin's truck roared to life as he headed back

toward Cinnamon Falls. Ginger placed Butter back in his carrier and rested her head against the window, her thoughts moving as quickly as the passing wild cinnamon trees. Someone had killed Landon Lawson and she was going to figure out who.

And then, she was going to get her bakery back.

Chapter 14

Ginger

Austin's truck disappeared down the street, the low rumble of the engine fading until the neighborhood settled back into its usual quiet. Ginger stood in the doorway a beat longer than necessary, arms folded tight across her chest, watching the empty space where his truck had just been. The moment the sound of the engine vanished, the silence rushed in, sudden like a slamming door. The quiet wrapped around the house, pressing in from every corner.

What surprised her most was how quickly the feeling came. Yesterday, she'd been desperate to be alone, wanting to crawl inside and shut the world out. Now, the stillness felt different. Too big. Too empty. She realized, with an uncomfortable jolt, she'd been counting on Austin's presence more than she cared to admit.

Back inside his house, the air smelled faintly of the breakfast he'd cooked them earlier that morning. Butter padded across the hardwood floors, utterly unconcerned with the weight pressing on Ginger's chest. She kicked off her shoes and dropped her purse on the end of the couch, sinking down on the comfortable, tufted sofa.

Butter leapt beside her, his foot brushing the remote. The television flickered on. A morning talk show swam into view; two anchors detailed the weather, traffic, and introduced a cooking segment that she refused to focus on.

She shot off a text to her cousin: **Drinks tonight? Prime Society?**

The response came quickly: ***I'm down. But you should turn on the TV, channel 6. Now.***

Ginger searched frantically for the remote. She found it wedged perfectly under Butter's behind, who made no effort to move. She shifted him over with her elbow and flipped channels until she reached the right station.

The scene sharpened into focus: a podium, microphones, and flashing cameras. The Cinnamon Falls Police Department seal loomed large behind Chief Noelle Raines as she stepped forward toward the press pit.

Ginger sat up straighter. Annoyed with her change in position, Butter scooted to the other end of the couch. He kneaded the throw pillow there until he found it comfy enough to lie down, curling his tail around himself, shooting daggers toward her with his eyes.

Ginger didn't have time to worry about her cat's temper tantrum. She turned up the volume once a banner scrolled across the bottom of the screen: DELIVERY DRIVER FOUND DEAD.

She sucked in a breath when his picture was superimposed on the screen. Landon Lawson stared back at her – all head and shoulders in his gray work uniform, frozen in a moment that felt far too alive for a man who was gone. His chestnut skin was unblemished. A neatly kept salt-and-pepper beard framed a slim face that was still undeniably handsome, youthful in a way that almost felt unfair, like time had decided to skip past him instead of settling in. His smile was warm and practiced, shoulders relaxed, posture easy, as if he had all the time in the world ahead of him. This was the face Ginger wanted to remember, not the one she'd seen bruised and bloody on her bakery floor.

'I'm so sorry, Landon,' Ginger whispered, wishing she had more than statements of sorrow.

Chief Noelle Raines stood rigid in her uniform, shoulders squared, expression carved from stone. No wasted movement. No warmth. The same woman who looked at Ginger like she'd already decided she was guilty. Behind her stood both Terrance and Jesse, stoic and unmoving. Ginger braced herself for the worst, hoping neither she nor her bakery would be mentioned.

Raines cleared her throat and leaned into the microphone. The soft feedback echoed through Austin's living room. Butter buried his face beneath his paws.

'Early Sunday morning,' Raines began, her voice clipped and professional, 'Cinnamon Falls Police Department responded to a call reporting an unresponsive individual at The Maple Bakery on Main Street.' Ginger groaned. 'Upon arrival, officers discovered the body of Landon Lawson, an employee of Valley View Wholesale Foods.' Her pulse ticked faster with every syllable.

'Preliminary findings indicate that Mr. Lawson suffered a significant head injury and was discovered shortly before four-thirty a.m. by an individual entering the bakery,' Raines continued. 'My investigators observed evidence at the scene consistent with Mr. Lawson's injury, and it has been secured for forensic examination.'

The camera zoomed in slightly, catching the faint tightening around Raines' mouth. 'Based on the condition of the body and the injuries observed at the scene, we currently believe Mr. Lawson's death resulted from blunt force trauma. However, the medical examiner will conduct a full autopsy to confirm in the coming days.' Ginger's stomach sank. 'Detectives are working to establish a full timeline of Mr. Lawson's movements in the hours leading up to the incident, and we are actively investigating Mr. Lawson's background, including his known associates and recent activities. This remains an ongoing investigation, and we are pursuing all viable leads.'

All viable leads. Ginger's jaw clenched. She was one of those leads.

A sharp voice cut through the clamoring reporters vying for Raines' attention.

'Elaine Matthias, *The Cinnamon Chronicle*.' An older woman got to her feet, adjusting the houndstooth blazer around her. She held an old-fashioned recorder as big as her hand, pushing it in the air to get the advantage over the other reporters. Her gray hair was pinned into a French roll at the back of her head. A pair of cat-eyed glasses rested on top.

Raines nodded in her direction. Elaine proceeded. 'Chief Raines, are investigators treating Mr. Lawson's death as a homicide?'

The question landed like a stone in still water. The crowd buzzed with anticipation.

Raines didn't hesitate. 'Given the nature of the injuries observed at the scene, this is being investigated as a homicide,' she said. 'At this time, we are not releasing additional details regarding the evidence while the investigation remains ongoing.'

Ginger's fingers dug into the couch cushion. Elaine nodded once, then pressed again.

'Chief, I want to be frank. It seems we are having déjà vu, don't you agree?' Raines made no movement to acknowledge the statement, only blinked. Elaine continued. 'This is the fourth violent death in Cinnamon Falls—'

'I can count, Elaine,' Raines interjected.

Elaine smirked. 'Then what assurances can you give residents who are concerned about their safety? You have to admit, these brazen attacks are terrifying.'

Raines drew herself up even straighter, pushing her shoulders back. 'We understand the community's concerns. At this time, we are asking residents to remain vigilant, particularly during overnight hours. If anyone observes suspicious activity, we urge them to contact law enforcement immediately.' Elaine and others attempted to interrupt, but Raines waved away their comments. 'Our department is committed to seeking justice for Mr. Lawson,' Raines concluded. 'We ask for patience as we continue our work. You will receive updates as we have them.'

A crescendo of voices rang out but the screen cut to the station logo, the sound dropping abruptly as the broadcast shifted to a news report that was already in progress, a segment about the importance of fiber that promoted a hearty seven bean soup.

Ginger snapped off the TV and stared at the darkened screen, her reflection faint and warped against the glass. Her chest felt tight, like the room had lost all oxygen. Butter lifted his head and crossed the couch toward her. He pressed his warm little body against her thigh, purring softly.

Her phone buzzed. ***Still wanna go out tn? You're a wanted woman.*** Alexis added an emoji with the tongue out. Ginger was not in the mood for jokes.

Her cursor blinked, waiting for her reply.

Raines' words 'remain vigilant' bounced around in her head.

If the town was going to watch her anyway, she wasn't going to sit still and let them decide who she was or what she'd done. She was not a killer and visiting Prime Society was one step closer to proving that.

Ginger replied: **Pick me up at 4.**

Chapter 15

Austin

Valley View Wholesale Foods sat on the outskirts of Asheville, more than an hour outside of Cinnamon Falls. The giant warehouse stretched across acres of land; a hulking sprawl of concrete and steel. Dozens of identical white box trucks stamped with the Valley View logo – a golden sun peeking over green, rolling hills – were parked in tight, uniformed rows toward the back of the property. At the front, an assortment of cars peppered the parking lot of a three-story office building. That was where Austin was headed.

He cut his engine, resting his forehead on the steering wheel, his heart thudding harder than he liked as he listened to the CFPD's press conference. He snapped off the radio broadcast in disbelief. Raines hadn't said Ginger's name, but she hadn't had to; mentioning the bakery was enough. Raines' careful phrasing, the subtle implication that the bakery wasn't just a crime scene, but a question mark. He knew how quickly people in this town filled in the blanks when they were scared; how fast suspicion became truth once it was whispered enough. By tomorrow, folks would be crossing the street when they saw Ginger coming. By the end of the week, someone would swear they'd *always* had a bad feeling about her.

Austin gripped the wheel harder. He wasn't supposed to be here, doing this. This wasn't his lane. He wasn't law enforcement. He wasn't trained for investigations or interrogations. He built things, he fixed what was broken. Most of all, he stayed firmly in his own damn business.

Ginger's face flashed through his mind; those furious eyes, and his doubt burned off like fog in sunlight. If clearing Ginger's name meant stepping outside of his comfort zone, so be it. She needed answers, and he wasn't going to let her down. She needed an ally, especially after Raines had put a target on her back.

Austin flipped down his overhead mirror, checking his reflection. His eyes were tired but determined, and his close-cropped beard was growing grays quicker than he liked. He hoped he looked the same as he had the last time he saw his ex's little sister.

Celine Delaney was the meticulous office manager of Valley View Wholesale Foods and if anyone had a record of where Landon had been, it was going to be her. It'd been a while since he'd seen her. She'd always been respectful, a neutral party even after he and her sister split, and if he was going to make this surprise appearance believable, it had to be coincidence, and not a fishing expedition.

He journeyed across the parking lot, scanning for a police vehicle. Austin hoped he'd beaten CFPD to the punch. He entered the front door, fluorescent lights humming overhead, too bright for a Monday morning. Austin winced, pushing through the tiled lobby toward the carpeted office area, when a guard seated behind a tall oak desk flagged him over. The standard buttoned white shirt stretched across his midsection; the top button undone revealed a black T-shirt underneath that did little to hide a graphic of a cartoon Austin hadn't watched since Lillian was small. His name tag read: Phillip.

'What can I do for you, sir?' he asked, pausing the movie playing on his phone.

'I'm here to see Celine Delaney,' Austin responded, pointing over his shoulder. 'I'm a family friend, just in the area and wanted to surprise her.'

Phillip waved him through without a second thought and resumed his movie. So much for security.

Austin pushed through a set of wooden doors that shielded a hushed carpeted space filled with cubicles. He spotted the receptionist behind a wide desk; a phone hooked between her neck and ear as she flipped through paperwork. She looked up as Austin approached, her eyes sparkling with a practiced warmth, then her smile deepened into familiarity.

Austin was transported almost instantly to a time where they were still on good terms, and would bond over poking fun at Samantha. Her honey complexion radiated against a lilac blouse and her short, voluminous black hair was tucked behind her ears, showing off the matching diamond studs. She pushed her square black glasses up on her slim nose with manicured fingers, revealing a sizable diamond on her ring finger.

'Austin Jacobs,' she said, in a knowing voice. She stood, walking around the desk to meet him. He noticed her protruding belly first, and the reality of how much time had passed slammed into him.

'Long time no see!' she exclaimed, delighted, throwing her arms open for an embrace.

She offered Austin a friendly side hug, bracing her back with the other hand. Austin took a step back, getting a good look at her. 'First of all, congratulations! It has been a minute. How far along are you?'

She rested her hands absentmindedly on her belly. 'She's comin' out of here in just a few weeks.' She held her hand up. 'And don't you start. I want to keep my independence, and my paid time off for as long as I can.'

Austin ran a finger over his lips. He figured he'd get the hardest question out of the way first. 'How's Sam?'

Celine took a labored breath. 'She's good. Busy,' she added at the last second.

'Still in real estate?' Austin asked, annoyed with himself that he wanted more information about the woman who'd twisted his heart out of his chest.

She nodded. 'Yeah, doing really well. Atlanta was the right place for her. She's really making moves in the city.'

Austin wasn't surprised. Samantha had always been ambitious; it was one of the qualities he admired the most about her. It was also the reason they broke up. He swallowed down his feelings, reminding himself he had a job to do. He wasn't here to take a walk down memory lane. Samantha was the past. He had to focus on the present, and that meant finding Landon Lawson's manifest from Saturday night.

'So, what can I do for you?' Celine settled back into her office chair with a huff, resting her hands on her belly.

'I actually have a question about a driver,' Austin said carefully, not elaborating on purpose. 'He missed a couple of deliveries and my new client is getting a little concerned.'

Her expression shifted, not alarmed but cautious. 'Missed? Impossible. Tell me the name.'

Before Austin could respond, her desk phone rang. She frowned, glancing at the display, then pressed the phone to her ear. 'Valley View Wholesale Foods, this is Celine. How can I—' She paused. 'What is it, Phil? I'm with a customer.'

Austin's pulse spiked when he heard the word

'police' drift through the receiver. Celine stilled, her eyes flicking toward the double doors behind Austin, then back down at the desk.

'I've got it pulled up right now . . . Not without a warrant . . . Fine,' she relented. 'I'll be out in a second . . . Tell him I'm pregnant and he'll have to wait until I get there. Who does he think he is, rushing me?' She looked up at Austin apologetically. 'I'm sorry, I have to handle this.'

'Take your time,' he advised, pushing away from her desk, settling into one of the cushioned chairs that lined the far wall.

Celine waddled into a side office and closed the door behind her.

Austin didn't think. He moved. The computer monitor behind Celine's desk was still unlocked; an open logistics screen showed pale blue rows of data: time stamps and destinations, codes and symbols he didn't know. His eyes scanned fast – too fast to comprehend anything – but he knew what he was looking for.

He found a search bar near the bottom of the screen and typed 'Lawson, Landon'. To his surprise, a window was already open with the very information he'd been looking for: Saturday's route manifest. Austin figured the higher-ups at Valley View had seen the press conference by now. A pop-up window showed that a recent print job had been completed. It prompted a question: close or print again.

Austin chose the latter. The noisy printer spat out a duplicate document next to him. He glanced to his left, keeping his eyes trained on the closed door where Celine was just steps away. He heard heightened voices, hoping whatever disagreement she was having continued for a few more seconds while the printer worked. When it finished, Austin snatched his printout from the tray, folded it hastily, and stuffed it under his vest. He jetted from behind Celine's desk just as she opened the adjacent office door. He leaned against the wood coolly, posture casual, hands empty, his heartbeat pounding in his ears.

'Everything okay?' he asked. 'Sounded serious.'

Celine rolled her eyes. 'Nothing I can't handle.'

Austin took that as a cue to get out of there. 'Listen, I can see you're busy. We can talk about the deliveries another time,' he assured her, backing toward the double doors.

'Give me a call later, I can pull up the manifest of your missed deliveries and figure out what's going on.'

'Thanks, Celine. I'd really appreciate that.'

He escorted her to the lobby where he found two uniformed officers he didn't recognize, thank goodness. Austin kept his head low. If it'd been Jesse or Terrance, he would have been screwed.

Only when he reached his truck – doors locked and engine idling – did he allow himself to breathe. He pulled the papers from his jacket, smoothing them across his thigh with hands that wouldn't stop shaking. He stared at the lines of data, adrenaline coursing through his veins.

Times, dates, stops, GPS locations, all were listed in neat rows. He forced his mind to slow down. He analyzed the lines of time stamps, his finger trailing down the column searching for the one he needed.

Lawson, Landon ID# VV-3378. His clock-in time was confirmed at 9:00 p.m. Saturday night. The truck left the Valley View loading dock approximately an hour later, after all items had been scanned, stacked, and logged. His first destination, a convenience store in Asheville.

His delivered items were scanned and signed for, each with its own barcode that included a digital signature crowding the small line. Austin skipped the rows of Landon's Asheville deliveries, more curious to know when he'd arrived in Cinnamon Falls. If he could pinpoint when Landon had arrived at Ginger's bakery, he could prove that Ginger hadn't been there before he arrived.

His finger stilled at a blank stretch of white that sat between two lines of blue. Just before midnight, there had been no GPS pings, just an error message: *Signal interruption, manual override.* The rest of Saturday's manifest had been blank.

Austin frowned and flipped the page. Sunday's manifest was also empty. He expected that, since it was the morning Landon had been found dead. He'd completed no deliveries and the truck hadn't been returned since he left the lot on Saturday night. That tracked with what he'd witnessed outside of Ginger's bakery early Sunday morning. But the gap in time and peculiar phrasing gnawed at him: *manual override*. Had someone turned off Landon's location tracking? Or had Landon turned it off himself?

He flipped backward through more pages to find the Saturday before, and there it was again. A different date, but the same time window where Landon's GPS signal was suddenly overridden at 11:48 p.m.

Celine had only printed two weeks' worth of manifests, but he would bet that the previous Saturday would show the same: a window of time where Landon and his truck were unaccounted for. It was long enough to detour. Long enough to meet someone. Long enough for things to go horribly wrong.

Austin leaned back in his seat, swallowing down the lump in his throat. What if Landon hadn't been killed at four o'clock on Sunday morning like Raines said? He was holding proof of a possibility that it could have happened hours before, late and quiet, after the Fall Festival had died down and Main Street had been deserted; long before Ginger even made it to her bakery early Sunday morning.

Landon could have spent hours lying in the cold, dank alley, alone.

Dead.

But that didn't solve their problem, not entirely.

The question had been staring him in the face since Sunday morning: *If it wasn't Ginger, then who?*

There was only one person who would know more about Landon's whereabouts than GPS tracking: his wife, Ethel Lawson.

Chapter 16

Ginger

Between Alexis' nonstop housewife complaints and petty gossip about celebrities she'd never meet, Ginger finally had a chance to glance down at her phone to see she'd received a text message. She hoped that it was Austin letting her know that he'd figured out Landon's last whereabouts. Next to her, Alexis leaned over, craning her neck to get a glance at her screen.

'Is that Captain Save-A-Ho?' she joked, fingering the pink straw in her colorful cocktail.

Ginger smacked her arm playfully, shielding the phone from her cousin.

Big news, Austin had texted a few hours ago.

Ginger gave the message a thumbs up, too cautious to text him back around Alexis' prying eyes. It seemed as though Austin had held up his end of the bargain. It was her turn now.

'You're the one who left me for dead,' Ginger shot back. 'He's a nice guy.' Ginger couldn't believe she was saying that, but after experiencing Austin's last-minute, no-questions-asked generosity, she had to admit that it was true. He'd surprised her.

If Alexis had asked her just two days ago how she felt about Annoying Austin, Ginger could have written a list as long as her legs. And now, well, things started to change. Ginger didn't really know what that meant, but she did know one thing: 'He didn't leave me stranded, unlike my own flesh and blood.'

Alexis sighed dramatically. 'Are you seriously going to make me apologize again? I already feel like shit about it, Ging. I can't help that my husband is allergic to your cat.'

'It's whatever, Lex. Water under the bridge.' Ginger knew she'd never win a fight with Alexis when it concerned Terrance. Instead, she lifted her cocktail, clinking glasses with her cousin, and returned to the text on her phone.

'Hold up, are you blushing right now?' Alexis shrilled jovially. 'You *like* Austin?'

Ginger's face flamed and she quickly changed the subject. 'I like having a place to stay, thank you very much.'

'Blah-blah,' Alexis responded, gesturing to Ginger's phone. 'It clearly worked out for the best.'

'Whatever, let's get back to you.' Ginger spun in her seat to face her cousin. 'What is your man saying about my bakery? When can I go back in?'

Alexis' smile faltered a notch. 'Real soon. Maybe

tomorrow or the next day. But Terrance says it's still considered an active crime scene. Raines wants to be thorough.'

'Of course she does,' Ginger muttered, scanning the room for Natasha. Ginger had no idea what she looked like, but figured the mistress would reveal herself eventually.

Prime Society was low-lit and romantic; air thick with bourbon and something sweet caramelizing in the kitchen. They were seated at the bar on black plush velvet barstools lined with brass trim. Polished concrete and black walnut accents gave the place a modern feel. At the tables, candlelight flickered golden against the skin of the dinner guests while live jazz hummed softly in the background. Across the restaurant stood a wall of windows that offered a panoramic view of downtown Asheville. Harrison would never have spent more than two minutes in a place like this. But to the people of Cinnamon Falls, Ginger was sure this was as fancy as it got.

'That's her,' Alexis mumbled around her straw, nodding to the waitress who'd just arrived toward the end of the bar. 'Natasha.'

Natasha Montgomery didn't look like a home-wrecking ho. Ginger didn't know what she'd been expecting, but it wasn't a stunning, full-figured woman with soft curves and medium-brown skin glowing under the pendant lights hanging from the ceiling. Her hair was pulled back into a ponytail, the curls flipped upward at the end like a nineties Barbie doll. She folded and stashed her jacket in a cupboard under the bar and swiped a card hanging at her waist on the nearest machine. When she smiled, her glossy lips pulled back to reveal deep dimples carved into her cheeks, giving her a warmth that felt disarming. She looked young and heartbreakingly open.

'Want me to join you?' Alexis asked, nodding toward Ginger's unsuspecting victim, her eyes laser-focused.

'I think I can handle it,' Ginger replied. 'But watch my back.'

Alexis nodded. 'Got you.'

Ginger slid off her stool while Natasha tapped a few buttons on the point of sale system's touchscreen. She approached, waiting for Natasha to make eye contact.

'Hi, Natasha?' Ginger asked, softening her tone when she remembered Austin's advice. As much as this was about her bakery, it was about Landon, and Natasha, too. Despite the whole mistress thing, Natasha had just lost someone she cared for. She would have to navigate this conversation with a finesse and softness she preserved for loved ones, not strangers.

Natasha studied Ginger, placing one hand on her hip. 'Who wants to know?'

'I'm Ginger Mills. I own The Maple Bakery . . .' Something flickered in Natasha's eyes. 'Do you mind if I ask you a few questions about . . . Landon?'

Natasha hesitated, glancing over her shoulder at her coworker who was busy taking orders at the other end of the bar, then nodded.

'I figured this might happen,' she said as she traveled around the bar and gestured toward a pair of empty seats tucked in a quiet corner. She toyed with the multiple gold rings on her fingers. 'What do you want to know? Were you seeing him too or something?' She looked up at Ginger sheepishly like it wasn't the first time she'd had to have this conversation with another woman.

'No,' Ginger assured her. 'Landon was a friend of mine. Well, he delivered to my bakery. We'd talk from time to time. Weather, sports, climate change, you know, the usual, and I was devastated when I heard the news. Were you two . . . together?'

'Landon and I, well, yes, we were a couple.' Natasha paused. 'At least, I thought we were,' she continued after a moment, her voice steady but careful, like she was holding back.

'How did you two meet?' Ginger probed.

'Sometimes he'd stop by here on his route and grab a late dinner. He'd sit at the bar and always ordered the lamb chops with a baked potato and we just started . . . talking. About anything, really. He was like that, worldly. We'd go from ancient Egypt to pop culture, to space exploration. We did that dance for a couple of months and then he asked to take me home one night while I was waiting for my ride out front. I get off at midnight most nights and it's dark in the staff parking lot so he didn't want me to wait alone. That night we talked and laughed and . . . well, we fell in love.'

Ginger felt a presence over her shoulder. She looked up to find Alexis hovering nearby, her arms crossed, eyes narrowed in Natasha's direction.

'You had to know he was married, though,' Alexis barked.

Ginger spun around, wide-eyed, giving her cousin a warning look that said: *Do. Not. Blow. This.*

'I did not,' Natasha shot back. 'Not at first. I'm not from The Falls. I had no idea the kind of reputation he had. I knew he was older, but he was always sweet to me; he listened. He cared. I'd never met a man like that.' She swallowed, fighting back tears. 'I only found out he was married Friday night and we had it out. I couldn't believe *I* was the other woman after *he* courted *me*!'

'How'd you find out?' Ginger asked gently.

'He picked me up late after my shift and there was lipstick on his shirt.' Ginger sucked in a breath. Natasha continued. 'It was dark red, like what old ladies wear. Some shit I'd never be caught dead in. He claimed he had an explanation but I told him to fuck off. I told him I was done. I didn't see him again . . . until I saw the news.'

Silence settled between the three of them. 'I'm so sorry,' Ginger offered.

'Me too,' Natasha replied, knocking away a tear that spilled over.

'One last question, were you wearing anything red Friday night, like a scarf?'

Natasha stilled. 'Nah, I just told you it's not my color. The last time I've seen a red scarf was the one I made for Rowan Bell a couple of years back. I have a clothing business, Knot Your Average Threads, and I make custom pieces for—'

A headless voice shouted, 'Ay, Tash! Need your help back here!'

'I gotta head back.' She stood abruptly, smoothing down the front of her uniform. 'It was nice meeting you, Ginger.' She cut her eyes at Alexis, giving her a brusque once-over that she'd rightfully earned, and left without saying goodbye.

Ginger's thoughts churned as she and Alexis returned to their seats at the bar, not with anger, but with something heavier, the weight of the truth.

Natasha hadn't been lying, Ginger could tell in her eyes. She'd been used and hurt. If Landon had been lying to Natasha, then there was someone else who'd been living with his betrayals every day, too. His wife.

Different from all the other times, Ginger felt no thrill at this revelation; no righteous spark or sudden burst of anxious jitters, just a sober understanding of what it felt like to have your life rearranged because of someone else's selfishness. She knew that ache intimately.

If Ethel Lawson had found out – really found out – about Landon's indiscretions then the motive was clear. Landon hadn't been murdered in a rage killing, but a slow burn of grief, humiliation, and, worst of all, betrayal.

'What're you thinking?' Alexis prodded, signing their dinner receipt with a flourish.

Ginger exhaled slowly, her thoughts folding on each other. She was thinking that the next conversation she had would be harder than this one. But it was unavoidable. She had to talk to Ethel Lawson.

Alexis pulled up in front of Austin's house just after ten. The street was quiet, washed in porch lights and the song of cicadas winding down. Ginger gathered her bag, pausing before she opened the door.

'You sure you're okay?' Alexis asked, one hand still on the wheel. Her voice had softened, the earlier edge replaced with worry. 'That Natasha girl threw me all the way off. Everyone knew Landon was married. And you know how I feel about *my* man. That's why I make sure he's got my face on every piece of clothing he owns. I—'

Ginger stopped her cousin's rant with a raise of her hand. 'I'm okay, really. Thank you for having my back earlier.'

Alexis snorted. 'For being rude and right?'

'Judgmental and dramatic,' Ginger corrected, smiling faintly. 'But thank you for dinner.'

Alexis reached across the console and squeezed her hand. 'Be careful, Ging. And call me if you need anything, anything at all.'

'I will.' Ginger stepped out of the car and shut the door quietly, watching as Alexis backed out of the driveway and pulled away, shaking her head at her cousin's new vanity license plates – MZCHMBRS – before turning toward Austin's house.

She let herself in with the key he'd left for her under the mat. Inside, the living room glowed an electric blue from the television mounted to the wall. Austin was stretched out on the tufted couch, one arm thrown over his head, the other curved protectively around a warm bundle of fur.

Butter.

Ginger moved slowly, toeing off her shoes and crossing the room without turning on a light. Austin's breathing was deep and even, his mouth slightly open, exhaustion etched into the lines of his face. For someone who spent his days holding everything together, he looked startlingly vulnerable like this; a mere mortal after all.

She crouched beside the couch and gently lifted Butter from his chest. The kitten stirred, gave a tiny protesting chirp, then settled once he was in Ginger's arms, purring immediately. His tongue swiped sleepily at her exposed forearms before settling in the crook of her elbow.

'I've got you,' Ginger whispered, stroking one finger down his soft body.

Austin shifted but didn't wake.

Ginger lingered for a moment, studying him. The quiet house, the steady rhythm of his breathing, the absurd normalcy of it all pressed in around her. It felt dangerous and familiar all at the same time – how easy it would be to stay right here and pretend everything was fine, forget all about her bakery, Landon, and Harrison, in exchange for a simple life that ended in hearty dinners and runaway television programs.

She turned away just in time before the thought could root. She didn't have the emotional capacity for that. Austin's place was temporary and she needed to treat it as such.

Upstairs, the guest room was dim and welcoming, everything exactly how she'd left it that morning. Ginger set Butter down on the bed then headed to the bathroom. She washed her face, brushed her teeth, and stared at her reflection, her eyes clearer than they had been that morning.

Her phone buzzed on the counter.

It was a text from Heather Hughes: ***Hey, Ging. I just passed the bakery on the way home and thought about you.***

She typed back quickly: **How's it looking? Are the police still there?**

No. It looked cleared out. Has anyone from CFPD contacted you?

Not yet. Alexis is thinking I can go back either today or tomorrow.

I'll stop by tomorrow then.

Ginger was both surprised and relieved. The day had been heavy, full of questions and half-answers, and the idea of sitting across from someone familiar, someone who wasn't going to ask her to explain herself or defend her innocence, felt like oxygen.

She set the phone down, exhaling slowly. She crawled into bed beside Butter, the kitten curling instantly against her side. Downstairs, the television murmured on. Ginger closed her eyes, holding onto the small comfort of the present, thankful she'd been given a soft place to land.

Chapter 17

Tuesday

Austin

Austin jerked awake. He sat upright with a grunt, stretching out his cramped back.

'Butter?' His voice was rough with sleep. The kitten must've gotten tired of Austin's snoring and found somewhere quieter to sleep. Smart.

He snapped off the TV, bracing for darkness, convinced he'd only been out a couple of hours. Pale morning light seeped through the front windows, soft and blue-gray, stretching across his living room floor.

He blinked. Morning? How long had he slept? Unease stirred in his belly. Butter was gone. And where was Ginger?

Austin was on his feet in an instant. He crossed the living room in two quick strides and yanked the front door open. Cool morning air rushed in. He found Ginger's car exactly where they'd left it the afternoon before, parked beside his truck, dew clinging to the windshield, proof she hadn't gone anywhere. He turned back inside and took the stairs two by two until he reached the top landing. He nudged the guest bedroom door open with his socked foot and let out a breath.

Ginger lay sprawled diagonally across the bed, one toned leg tangled in the comforter like she'd fought it in her sleep and lost. Butter was curled in a tight ball directly on top of her head, their deep breathing in perfect sync.

For a long moment, he stood in the doorway, watching her; the rise and fall of her chest, the way she frowned as Butter's tail tickled her nose. The room smelled faintly of her already, shea butter and something else warm and sweet.

The thought landed fully formed before he could stop it: he wanted more. More chances, more conversations, more time . . . more Ginger.

He told himself that their partnership was temporary; that she was passing through, regrouping until she got back on her feet; and when this was over, she'd move on, and he'd go back to empty rooms and late nights on the couch, alone.

But as he watched her stir, watched Butter grow stronger every day, the idea felt hollow. He had to admit, he liked this. He liked *her*. He liked waking up knowing she was there. Liked that his guest room – usually untouched unless Maddie drove over – had been claimed as her refuge. He tried to keep himself in check, reminding himself that this was a short-term solution; a pause, not a destination. Soon, she'd get her bakery back, her reputation back, and then she'd move on.

It didn't sit right with him. When all of this was over, Austin didn't want to go back to before. He didn't want to just be the place she stopped along the way. He wanted to be her landing place, or at least, he wanted to try; not with pressure or grand gestures, but with effort and consistency.

With startling clarity, Austin realized that whatever this was, mattered. And when the dust settled, he was done pretending to think otherwise.

His phone rang while he poured his second cup of coffee. Above, his houseguests still slept like rocks. It was nearing eight a.m. and he hadn't heard a peep. He was sure Butter would have made his way downstairs by now, demanding sustenance.

Austin took his time answering, watching the phone dance along the countertop while it vibrated. It was his father and he already knew what he wanted without having to answer the phone. Austin gritted his teeth and got it over with.

His father started without preamble. 'Where were you yesterday? You missed the paint job on Nutmeg.'

Austin leaned against the counter, watching birds chase each other outside his kitchen window. 'Mornin' to you too,' he grumbled.

'Austin,' his father warned.

'I'll get to it today,' he said. 'I just had something to do yesterday.'

There was a pause on the other end, his father's version of a disappointed sigh. 'They're expecting you before noon. Don't get caught up in someone else's mess and ruin my good reputation—'

Austin cut him off. 'I gotta run, Dad.'

'Wait, are you still stopping by tonight?' His father's voice dropped lower. 'Your mother's been talking about it for days.'

Tonight? Austin searched his memory, the promise surfacing slowly. He'd agreed to go to dinner at his parents' after Lillian's ceremony. His heart squeezed in his chest.

He was supposed to recap with Ginger tonight. They were going to talk through everything he'd learned about Landon. That conversation felt more important – urgent, even – but it would have to wait.

It'd been months since he'd stepped through the front door of that house, longer since they'd sat down as a family together over a meal. The thought of facing his father, his mother, and his sisters all at once sent a familiar knot of nerves twisting in his stomach. There would be questions; about him, about Samantha, about everything he'd been avoiding.

And then there was Ginger. *I could bring her*, he considered. Would that be too much too soon? He hadn't figured things out with her yet, and now he was considering walking her straight into the most complicated part of his life. His family would descend on her, curious and relentless. They'd grill Ginger like a hot dog on Independence Day.

Was he ready for that? Was *she* ready for that? He didn't think he had a choice.

Austin exhaled slowly, running a hand along the back of his neck.

'Yeah,' he said finally. 'I'll see you tonight.'

His mother whooped in the background: 'Tacooooo Tuesdayyyyy!'

His father gruffed, 'Bring some sour cream, and don't be late.' Then he hung up the phone.

Ginger still hadn't woken up by the time he was ready to leave. He figured it was the weekend's events catching up to her. He scribbled a note on the back of an old envelope he found on the counter:

Running a few errands. Back before dinner.
Taco Tuesday at my parents' if you and
Butter are up for it. No pressure.

He hesitated, then added a smiley face at the end, immediately hating himself for it. He folded the note and left it where she'd see it, next to the coffee maker, and slipped out into the cool morning.

Austin cruised toward Cinnamon Falls with the

windows cracked, letting the damp autumn air roll through the cab. Low clouds clung to the sky, the sun struggling to break through the pale streaks of silver. The ground was still wet with mist, leaves plastered to the asphalt like confetti.

His father had given him a direct order to tend to the Nutmeg Avenue job, but his first stop was CinnaCutz Hair Studio. The shop sat dark and silent, blinds drawn tight, the OPEN sign flipped over to CLOSED. A handwritten note was taped to the door, edges curling from the humidity. Austin leaned closer, frowning as he read 'until further notice' under the closed sign.

He'd never seen Ethel shut the place down before; not for sickness, storms, or even Rosie's death. The unease that had been simmering in his gut sharpened.

He checked his watch – he had over an hour until noon. On instinct more than logic, he headed toward Ethel Lawson's house. He hoped the detour wouldn't take long. He and his father had cleaned her property's gutters a few years back and he remembered the way.

When he arrived, two police cruisers were pulling away from the curb. Austin slowed, keeping his head low as Chambers and Shaw disappeared down the street. His brow furrowed with worry. That wasn't good.

He parked and climbed out, the air thick and cool against his skin. The Lawsons' house looked smaller than he remembered; the paint peeling over the door, porch sagging against the frame, and a gutter dangling uselessly along the roofline.

Inside, Austin fumed; he had yet another reason to resent a dead man. Instead of focusing on his husbandly duties, it seemed as though Landon had let his personal life take a front seat.

As he ventured toward the front door, it opened to reveal Ethel Lawson, wrapped in a cardigan that swallowed her small frame, her shoulders hunched as if she were bracing against more than the weather. Her eyes were red-rimmed, and her expression set in a way that made Austin's chest ache. It was the same way she looked at church when Landon recommitted himself time and time again.

'Austin Jacobs,' she started, voice gravelly, remnants of a smile pushing through her pained expression. 'Tell me you're here to fix somethin' and not share your condolences like everybody else. I've had enough people snottin' and cryin' all over me.'

'Saw the gutter hangin' off when I drove past. Mind if I fix it?'

She studied him for a long moment, then pointed over her shoulder. 'Ladder's 'round the side of the house. Do what you want.' She hobbled over to the rocking chair on her porch and slumped into it, wrapping the cardigan around herself tighter.

Austin worked quickly, grabbing some supplies from his truck. He set the ladder against the house and took a deep breath. This was the third time in a week he was on a ladder after not climbing one for a year. The only thing that had changed in his life between then and now was Ginger.

'You got it,' he said to himself out loud. 'Quick and easy.'

Austin ascended until he reached the offending roofline, steadying himself.

The spike and ferrule gutter system was ancient, and he remembered his father begging Ethel to let him update it years ago. Austin retrieved a hidden hanger and placed it in the lip of the gutter. With a zip screw he drilled the gutter into place, making sure it was secure with a tug before moving over and doing the same to a few more spots.

Satisfied, he descended the ladder and heard Ethel release a deep, rattling cough that didn't sound good at all. When he reached the ground, and walked to the front of the house, he found Ethel still on the porch, one hand pressed to her chest, breathing shallow.

Austin folded himself into the rocking chair next to her. 'You okay?' he asked gently.

She waved him off. 'Bronchitis been gettin' worse.' A phlegmy cough escaped that sounded like it hurt. 'Doc called it COPD or something. Forty years of smokin' finally catchin' up to me. I can't lie, I wish I had one now, though.' She brought two wrinkled brown fingers to her lips and pretended to puff a cigarette.

They sat in silence for a moment. Finally, Austin said, 'I'm sorry about Landon.'

Ethel didn't flinch, just shrugged. 'The detective that just left said the same. Said his name was Chambers. You know him?'

'No,' Austin lied, shaking his head.

She continued. 'He yapped on and on about how devastated he'd be if it'd been his wife who died. To be honest, we were only married on paper at this point. We haven't been a proper married couple in years. Landon didn't even live here.'

Austin's mouth dropped open. Ethel and Landon weren't together? *Why all the theatrics in church, then?* he wondered. *What was he trying to prove?*

He hesitated to broach the subject but asked, 'So you knew about the other women, then?'

Her mouth twisted. 'Of course I did. This town talks.' She stared out into the street. 'And I ain't blind. I saw how those women flirted with Landon when they thought I wasn't lookin'. As long as it didn't come to my front door, I convinced myself that I didn't care what he did in his free time.'

Austin couldn't imagine the helplessness she had to feel to stay in a loveless marriage. 'There was a time, though . . .' she grinned with a far-off smile, trapped in a memory, 'when we were in love. We were together for sixteen years until . . .' Tears misted her eyes. 'Landon was electric; funny, vibrant, and such a good listener. I always felt like . . . he got me.

I didn't have to explain myself all the time. He accepted me for who I was. I'm fifteen years his senior, you know. I'd forgotten about love until I met him. I was forty-nine and free when we got married. What do they call that? A tiger?'

'A cougar,' Austin supplied.

'Right,' Ethel continued. 'Everybody warned me I was makin' a mistake. But I ain't never been stupid. I knew a time would come when he'd find someone younger, someone more his speed. Someone who wasn't so sick and weak all the damn time.' Ethel shook her head. 'Soon as I turned sixty, everything changed.'

'Is that why the shop is closed down?'

She nodded, another cough racking through her frail body. She closed her eyes briefly, her breathing returning to normal. 'If I don't find someone to help, I'll have to shut it down for good. I can't stand all day like I used to . . . can hardly breathe as it is. But that's the least of my worries. I've got insurance paperwork and funeral planning to get straight. Gage is on his way to meet me.'

'Gage Whitfield from the mortuary?' Austin clarified.

'Yeah, he's helpin' me set everything up for the funeral on Friday.'

'Already?' Austin asked. 'I just saw the press conference . . . have they released his body?'

'That's what they were just here tellin' me. Gage

called right after. That reminds me, I need one more pallbearer. And I would've asked your dad but . . .'

Austin nodded, agreeing almost instantly. He had been no fan of Landon, but he couldn't say no to Ms. Ethel, especially at a time like this. 'Sure, Ms. Ethel. Anything you need.'

They were quiet for a long moment.

'It shoulda been me. It was supposed to be me.' Ethel shook her head and tried to stand on trembling legs. Austin jumped up to help, but she swatted him away. She leaned heavily on the chair's arm and pushed herself to her feet.

'Thank you, Austin.' Her rheumy brown eyes latched onto his. 'You're a good boy. Tell your father I said that.'

'Yes, ma'am,' Austin replied. 'I will.' He watched as Ethel turned slowly and shuffled into her house.

After a moment, he backed off her porch and settled back into his truck. As he drove away, the last of his doubt dissolved.

Ethel Lawson couldn't have killed her husband. She could barely stand on her own without assistance. Whatever secrets Landon kept, whatever mess he'd made of his life, his wife hadn't ended it.

Still, the question remained: *Who killed Landon Lawson?*

Chapter 18

Ginger

Ginger woke to Butter's puny paws pressed deep into her forehead, his adorable spotted face scrunched into a menacing look, meowing nonstop.

'Alright, alright already!' Groggy with sleep, Ginger struggled to sit up, her legs tangled in the sheets and comforter. Butter paced in a tight circle next to her, unleashing another set of cries that let Ginger know that he was starving and she was moving way too slow for his liking.

'Five minutes,' she requested, to which Butter only cried louder.

'Fine!' Ginger relented, pushing the covers off and crossing the room, rubbing the sleep from her eyes. She fumbled through the drawers and threw on Austin's old high-school wrestling T-shirt that fell around her knees, soft from a thousand spin cycles, and smelled like fresh cedar and soap.

She grabbed her cell phone and descended the stairs,

Butter trailing her every move like an impatient shadow. She checked the time, nearing ten a.m.

'Austin?' she called, but no one answered her back.

The house felt oddly quiet; empty in a way that made her notice every creak. Her feet were cool against the tiled kitchen floor as she retrieved Butter's bowl and formula. He paced hungrily, eyes locked on hers as if sheer willpower would make her move faster.

After her demanding kitten was fed, she moved on to caffeine. An envelope stuck out on top of the coffee pot. She recognized Austin's handwriting.

'A note?' Ginger asked aloud. 'Is he ninety-five years old? He could have just texted me.' Ginger scanned the note; her finger trailed over the smiley face he'd drawn, the corner of her mouth lifting.

'Feel like tacos tonight?' Ginger asked Butter, who was too busy eating to answer. 'Tacos it is,' she confirmed, while he continued to ignore her. Butter flicked his tail in her direction, never looking up from his bowl.

Her cell phone clattered against the countertop. It was Terrance; she hoped for good news.

'Hey, Ging,' he said. Wind whistled in the background like he was currently driving. 'Was callin' to give you an update. Raines gave the all-clear for you to resume business as usual. Fair warning, it is a bit of a mess.'

'I expected that,' Ginger responded, preparing

herself mentally for all the cleaning she'd have to do today. Moreover, she had to prepare herself for seeing the place where Landon died. As badly as she wanted to reclaim her bakery as her sanctuary, she wondered if things would ever be the same. If every time she entered her back door, would she think of Landon? Would she only be able to remember Sunday morning? Could she bake in that kitchen again? Could she bake again at all?

'You there?' Terrance asked, when she'd gone quiet too long, lost in her thoughts.

'Yeah,' Ginger said. 'Thanks for the heads-up.'

'And Ginger? Sorry 'bout the whole cat thing.'

'Don't mention it.'

Ginger white-knuckled the drive to Main Street, anxious for what she might find. Her mind insisted on drumming up the worst possibilities: another body, more blood, flour drifting through the air like snow, or worse, Chief Raines waiting inside ready to slap handcuffs on her wrists.

When she finally turned onto Main Street, the familiar storefronts came into view, dressed in the easy charm of autumn. Wreaths of rust-colored leaves hung on the doors, pumpkins of all sizes clustered along the doorsteps. Halfway down the block sat The Maple Bakery, its cheerful pink and white awning looking painfully normal beneath the mid-morning sun.

She was surprised to find a parking space free, and pulled into it easily. All the other spots were taken, meters glowing red signaling they were in use. All except for one, directly in front of her bakery like it was the origin of the plague.

She grabbed Butter's carrier and stepped out of the car. The bakery's windows reflected her uneasy expression back to her. For a moment, she stood there staring at the door, remembering the way she'd burst through it on Saturday morning expecting nothing more dramatic than prepping dough. She'd had a good day that day. She had been happy.

And in just a few hours everything had changed. Her fingers curled instinctively against her palm and for a second she could swear she still felt Landon's blood there, sticky and warm. She forced the thought away and walked around the side of the building, through the alley and toward the back door.

Yellow caution tape was arranged in an X, stretched over the back entrance. The sight was like a knife twisting in her chest. This wasn't a crime scene. It was her bakery, her livelihood. Ginger grabbed the tape and swiped it down in one swift motion, rolling it tightly around her fist until it crinkled into a bright yellow ball. Shoving her key into the lock, she paused for a long breath before turning it. The door creaked open and the smell hit her; the familiar scents of her bakery were still there: flour, sugar, vanilla, but something underneath it all felt disturbed. Her heart sank as she stepped inside the doorway.

Ginger was thankful the blood had been cleared and there was no longer a dead body waiting to be discovered. She pushed past the memory of Landon lying in the same place, his body twisted against the floor, the dark pool spreading beneath his head. For a moment the phantom image lingered anyway. Ginger set Butter's carrier down on the counter, forcing herself to breathe and move further inside.

Flour still coated the kitchen floor, churned and trampled in the melee since she'd been away. Footprints crisscrossed in every direction – heavy boot prints, narrower shoe prints, some overlapping and smeared. They snaked from the back door all the way through the kitchen and Ginger followed them slowly onto the service floor, which looked even worse.

Her small cafe tables had been shoved aside, chairs overturned as if someone had searched beneath them. Cabinet doors hung open along the wall where she kept supplies; the neat rows of baking tools were disturbed, out of place. The police had gone through everything: drawers were half open, boxes shifted, flour dusted across surfaces that once gleamed. Her bakery, her carefully tended, lovingly built bakery, looked like a storm had torn through it.

For a moment Ginger just stood there in the middle

of the destruction. She pressed her lips together, blinking hard as the sting of tears reached her nose before they sprang to her eyes.

How had everything gone so wrong?

Before this, every time she had entered through the bakery door, she'd felt a spark of pride in her heart that she'd manage to slip from under Harrison's proverbial thumb, escaping a life she hadn't realized was suffocating her until it was almost too late. Seeing her business destroyed brought back all the memories she'd been blocking out.

Five years with Harrison had looked perfect from the outside: money, stability, the kind of security Ginger never knew growing up. Bills were paid early, no wondering if her card would be declined at the register. But the Caldwell world had rules. Expectations. Invisible lines that tightened the longer she stayed. She'd learned a little too late that love was a cruel kind of magic; an illusion so convincing you didn't feel the trap close until you were already inside of it. She'd watched it happen to Camille first.

Her fierce, powerful, sharp-tongued best friend had softened into someone quieter, careful, tamed. She'd changed almost overnight. She had scheduled her life around Theodore's calendar, jumping up from their coffee dates the second it reached the top of the hour. Watching her had felt like seeing a candle's flame extinguished.

Before the Caldwell brothers came into their lives,

Ginger and Camille had laughed at women who lost themselves in the pursuit of marriage and motherhood; whose conversation always circled back to their husbands or children, with hardly a mention about their own goals or ambitions. They had sworn to each other that they'd never shrink. But the closer Ginger grew to Harrison, and away from Camille, the clearer it became: she was going to be next.

Ginger refused to follow in Camille's footsteps, hiding her imminent betrayal deep in her heart from her best friend. It was the biggest secret she'd ever kept from anyone, including her parents, who'd grown to love the settled version of her, connected to old money and prestige.

One chilly February night, Ginger walked away with three months' worth of her allowance, a burner phone, and Harrison's engagement ring. Now, her finger brushed the faint line circling her finger, the ghost of what once held a treasured family heirloom: his mother's emerald.

What once felt like an anchor had become her ticket to freedom. The moment she stepped foot in Cinnamon Falls, she'd sold it without hesitation, using the money to fund her dreams: The Maple Bakery; an idea Harrison would have most certainly sneered at if she had ever dared speak it out loud.

She could imagine him now: 'A bakery?' He would've guffawed around a mouthful of dinner wine. 'What do *you* need to bake for?' It was almost like he thought she'd endured culinary school for shits and giggles. The idea of Harrison Caldwell's fiancée being anything other than a perfect trophy was absurd. She'd never needed a lot anyway, and being with Harrison, she'd lost sight of that; of what *really* mattered most: her happiness, and, most of all, her freedom.

Ginger took another long look around the wrecked shop. Flour everywhere. Chairs overturned. Cabinets rifled through. The Maple Bakery wasn't some pipe dream, not anymore. It was a real place and she refused to let her dream die.

Ginger trekked through the kitchen and grabbed the broom from the small storage closet up front.

'No one,' she muttered, starting to sweep, 'is going to take my happy ending from me.'

In his carrier, Butter meowed impatiently. Ginger knew if she let him out now, he'd be more of a nuisance than a help, so she kept him there until she was finished with the floors at least.

The steady scrape of the broom filled the silence as she began sweeping the flour into careful piles. Each stroke pushed pale clouds into the air, the fine powder settling over the counters and the toes of her shoes. She followed the trail of footprints toward the back door, sweeping it into larger, uneven piles.

The steady rhythm helped. Push. Gather. Push. It felt like she was gaining a bit of control back once she could see her pink tile shining through.

Then, her broom caught something, trapped between the bristles snagging the floor with a dull scrape. Ginger paused mid-sweep and frowned, nudging the excess aside with the broom's edge. Beneath the powder, a small flash of bright orange plastic peeked through the mountain of white. She crouched, brushing the flour away with her fingers. Ginger picked up the orange thing. It was light, no heavier than a bottle cap, with ridged edges, a little bigger than a fingertip, with flour packed inside the hollow center; a cap of some sort.

She turned it over slowly in her fingers, lifting it toward the kitchen light. At first she wondered if it was a piping tip, the kind she used for rosettes or delicate borders, which would normally have a raised manufacturer's logo on the side and a small hole at the bottom for buttercream to flow through. This one had neither.

Why would something like this be in her bakery? Maybe it'd been tracked in by one of the officers, or dropped by the paramedics when they came for Landon. That made the most sense. Still, the bright orange cap looked oddly out of place.

She leaned down, bringing the cap to Butter's carrier. 'What do you think?' she asked, letting the curious kitten sniff it. Butter leaned forward, nose twitching. Then he sneezed before retreating to the back of his carrier.

Ginger laughed softly. 'Alright, you're over it. Message received.'

She set the tiny cap on the counter next to the mixing bowl, then returned to sweeping.

A knock sounded at her back door. Ginger straightened, her heart skipping at the sudden noise.

Whoever it was didn't wait for a response. The door pulled backward and Heather stepped inside a moment later, taking in the chaos of the bakery with wide eyes. Heather wore a soft knit cardigan over a cream-colored blouse, sleeves pushed to her forearms like she was perpetually ready to help.

She cupped a hand over her mouth. 'Oh my God,' she breathed. 'Ginger . . .'

Her gaze swept across the kitchen. The piles of flour at Ginger's feet. She craned her neck to see the main floor past the kitchen.

'They really tore through the place,' Heather said, her eyes roaming over the chaos.

Ginger let out a tired breath, leaning against the broom. 'Didn't leave one drawer unopened.'

'How're you holdin' up?'

Ginger shrugged, though the motion felt heavier than she intended. 'I've had better mornings, that's for sure.'

For a moment, neither of them spoke. Then Heather stepped further into the kitchen, carefully setting her purse on one of the cleared countertops.

'Well,' she started, rolling up the sleeves of her cardigan another inch. 'You can't open with the place looking like a tornado passed through,' she said. 'Where do you keep the mop?'

Ginger stared at her for a second before a grateful smile tugged at the corner of her mouth.

'You don't have to help. This is . . . a lot and you've already done enough, Heather.'

Heather waved the comment away like it was nonsense. 'Ginger Mills,' she said firmly, grabbing a soiled rag from the counter, 'I watched you build this business from nothing but one mixer and a whole lot of stubbornness. The least I can do is help you sweep the place up.' She glanced down at the floor that still had streaks of white left over. 'Besides,' she added, wringing out the rag, 'if we work together, we can have this place looking halfway respectable before lunch. What do you say?'

Ginger looked around at the bakery again, and for the first time since she'd walked through the door, it didn't feel quite so overwhelming.

Chapter 19

Ginger

'So, what's happening with you and Mr. Fix It?' Heather asked, slicing into a piece of grilled chicken. They were seated at the small eat-in table, Ginger's bakery sparkling like it was opening day again. She'd managed to sweep and mop the floors; getting up all the flour was the worst part, her knees would be screaming at her for the next few days. While Ginger concentrated on her floors, Heather straightened all the drawers, cleaned the counters, dishes, and cabinets.

Famished from all the hard work, Heather ordered lunch from the Golden Grille. Meanwhile, Butter balanced along the window ledge beside her, eyeing a pair of playful squirrels running back and forth on the sidewalk.

Ginger balked. 'Excuse me?'

'A little birdie told me you two have been spending quite a bit of time together. You didn't tell me you two were . . .' She smiled suggestively.

'Were what?' Ginger was not going to do the heavy lifting for her.

'You know . . . together . . .'

'We're not. Austin is helping me out, that's all. He's letting me stay at his place until—'

'Is that what the young people are calling it these days? "Helping you out"?' Heather air-quoted.

Ginger fought her smile. 'It's nothing serious. Austin and I are friends.'

Just a few days ago Ginger would not have considered Mr. Toxic Positivity a friend by any stretch of the imagination. But now she didn't know what to do about the butterflies in her stomach when she thought about him. So, she put them out of her head for now.

'Friends,' Heather repeated, sounding skeptical, a playful lilt to her voice. 'Well, maybe you and this *friend* of yours can join Preston and me for dinner one night.' Ginger started to protest, but Heather continued. 'Austin's mother and I used to go to school together, but we haven't talked in ages. It would be nice to know how the Jacobs family is doing, especially after Matthew's injury. That family is solid.' She blew out a breath. 'I'd be lost if something like that happened to Preston. I can't imagine.'

There was a subtle shift in conversation. The laughter from earlier thinned out, replaced by something heavier, more reflective. 'Tragedy changes people,' Ginger offered carefully.

Heather nodded; her gaze drifted toward the window, unfocused. 'It does, sometimes for the worst, especially in a small town like this. People are saying all kinds of awful things about Landon.' Heather picked at her salad, stabbing a runaway cherry tomato with her fork. 'Like that he was careless and selfish.'

Ginger added in, 'From what I've learned these past few days, Landon had quite a reputation for a supposed married man.' She recalled Natasha's forlorn expression last night. Landon's death had hit her hard, especially since the last words they shared were during a heated argument.

'Learned from who? He loved Ethel,' Heather responded.

'He had a funny way of showing it,' Ginger replied. 'I talked to Natasha Montgomery last night and she said she had no idea Landon was even married.'

'Natasha,' Heather harrumphed. 'Bullshit. All those girls knew. They might have laid down with him once or twice, but in the end, Landon was loyal to Ethel. They had an understanding.'

Ginger snorted before stuffing part of a volcano roll into her mouth. She knew at least one woman who would disagree; two if Ethel Lawson knew what her husband had been up to before he died. 'If loyalty means screwing anything with legs, then sure.' Ginger shrugged.

Heather bristled. 'Loyalty doesn't always look romantic. Sometimes, it's simply showing up when they need you. He took Ethel to all her appointments, waited with her for hours, paid for her medications out-of-pocket when insurance dragged its feet. He even worked double shifts when she cut her shop's hours a couple of months back.'

'Is Ethel sick?' Ginger inquired, recalling the brief moment she'd encountered Ethel on Saturday.

'Extremely,' Heather replied. 'Can barely walk without getting winded, all that damn smoking in her younger years. Landon waited on her hand and foot. He did—'

'What he was supposed to do,' Ginger finished. 'He was her *husband*, Heather. He stood before God and his family and made lifelong vows to her. Chauffeuring her to appointments and paying for her meds was the least he could do.'

Heather quipped, 'Well, you're not married so I don't expect you to understand.'

Ginger recoiled. That felt like five fingers to the face. 'I've been engaged before. I know what it's like to commit to someone.'

Heather quickly regrouped. 'You're right. I'm sorry, I know it doesn't excuse things, and it sure doesn't erase the hurt he caused along the way, but Landon was a good man. He didn't deserve to be killed.' Tears sprang into her eyes.

Ginger reached across the table, placing a reassuring hand over Heather's. She hated when people cried. It almost always made her want to as well. 'I didn't realize you and Landon were close. I apologize for speaking out of turn about your friend.'

Heather swallowed. 'We'd been friends practically all our lives, since our teenage years when I transferred to Asheville Prep, but we lost contact after high school. Decades later, I opened Cinnamon Grove and my store was assigned to his delivery route. I looked forward to seeing him every week. Everything's going to be so different now.'

Ginger stared down at her plate, appetite waning. She knew what it was like to long for normalcy, to go back to a time that was simpler. And now that her bakery didn't look like a tornado, she was more than ready to get back to her routine.

'I'm not going to let this stop me,' Ginger assured her. 'One way or another, I'm going to find out who killed Landon and restore my bakery's good name.'

Heather looked nauseated. 'You're a grown woman and I know I can't convince you to stop your witch hunt, but you should stay out of it, Ging.'

'I'll be careful, you've got my word.'

Heather nodded, satisfied. 'I should get going. Preston should be finished at the office by now.' She reached across the table and enveloped Ginger in a tight hug that stole her breath.

Ginger thanked her again for all her help and walked her through the kitchen and toward the back door where she noticed Heather's handbag sitting on the counter.

'I meant to tell you earlier, that bag is gorgeous!' Ginger said, nodding toward the maple brown leather structured shoulder bag with gold-toned hardware she was slipping on her arm.

Heather held it out for Ginger to admire. She smiled, clearly pleased. 'Don't you just *love* it? Vintage! And I got it for a steal!'

A bag like that was never on sale. Ginger had the same one in a different shade still in a box back in Atlanta. She was sure Harrison had tossed all her belongings by now or sold them. The latter, she was sure.

Ginger questioned, 'A steal? From where?'

Heather leaned in. 'The second-hand shop over on Pine Street, A Penny For Your Thoughts. Milo Penn owns it. You ever been?'

Ginger's stomach squeezed, but she kept her expression neutral.

'Never heard of it,' she lied, her palms dampening by the second. She vividly recalled the day Milo Penn bared his yellow teeth, nearly snatching the emerald off her ring finger after they haggled on a price that was way under what it was worth. She was desperate and he could read it all over her face. She remembered signing her real name on the receipt. A rookie's mistake. Did Milo let it slip to Heather that Ginger had been to his shop just a few months before? She wouldn't know but that didn't stop her from wondering. Ginger had told herself that everything would be okay and that Penn would more than likely keep her identity a secret. Besides, Cinnamon Falls wasn't that big. Of course people shopped at the same places. Heather's purchase was simply a coincidence.

'You should check it out sometime. You'd be surprised what people give away,' Heather said airily.

Ginger nodded, changing the subject. 'Thanks for lunch, Heather. I really appreciate everything. My mind was spinning in circles these last few days, so this was a good distraction.'

'I'm glad. Call me later,' she said over her shoulder before jetting down the alley toward Main Street.

Ginger grabbed her purse from the counter and paused. The small orange cap she'd set there earlier was gone. She scanned the pristine countertop before glancing toward the hefty trash bags they'd filled during their cleaning frenzy. Somewhere between sweeping, mopping, and sanitizing, it must have been tossed out with the rest of the debris. Shrugging it off, she reached for her keys as Butter trailed dutifully behind her.

The sun felt brighter as Ginger drove back to Austin's place, her earlier unease fading. As she pulled into the driveway, she noticed his truck was still gone. She let herself into the quiet house and released Butter from the carrier. He crisscrossed through her legs affectionately.

Dinner was a couple of hours away, which gave her the perfect task to fill the time. Her hands were growing restless from her lack of baking. She fetched items from Austin's pantry, and to her surprise, he had everything she needed: real butter, good vanilla, brown sugar that hadn't fossilized in the back of a cabinet. She preheated the oven, thinking about Mr. and Mrs. Jacobs; about first impressions and gratitude. She knew the exact recipe she'd make, one that Uncle Maple would approve of.

Butter supervised from his place on the carpet, watching as Ginger moved around the kitchen: measuring, whisking, folding batter. The rhythm steadied her breathing, grounding her in something she understood completely.

The front door opened just as she'd removed the pan from the oven, setting it on the countertop to cool: a vanilla poundcake topped with pecan streusel.

'Ginger?' he called. 'I'm h—' Austin stopped short in the doorway, gym bag slung over one shoulder, eyes flicking from Ginger, to the mixing bowls, to the cake.

'You didn't have to do all that,' he said after a moment, crossing the kitchen and resting his hip against the counter. Up close, she could see the faint scrape on his knuckle, a splash of paint on his forearm, the tiredness he tried to mask with a half-smile. His voice was gentle, almost cautious, like he didn't want to scare the moment away. 'My mom would have been thrilled with something store-bought.'

Ginger shrugged, hyper aware of the flour dusting her clothes, and the loose curl that had escaped her bun. She wiped her hands on a towel.

'It's the least I could do,' she offered.

'You don't owe us anything,' he said gently. 'It's just dinner.'

'I know.' She met his eyes. 'That's why I made it. You gave me a place to stay. You've been good to me and to Butter.' Butter chose that moment to meow loudly as if summoned.

Austin huffed a laugh. 'He's an angel.'

'He's a menace,' Ginger countered with a mock frown.

The moment quieted and they shared a look – soft and unguarded. Something unspoken passed between them; warm, tentative, and charged. Austin stepped back, giving her space again like a man very aware of how close he'd drifted. He pointed over his shoulder, breaking eye contact.

'I'm just going to grab a shower and I'll be ready in twenty minutes?'

Ginger spun and tended to the cake. 'Sure. I'll be ready.'

When he bounded up the steps, Ginger released the breath she'd been holding.

The drive to his parents' house was wrapped in golden evening light. The neighborhood shifted as they turned off the main road; trees taller, lawns wider, houses set back from the street. His parents' home sat proudly at the end of a curved drive; a brick facade, white columns framing a wide porch that ran around the exterior of the home, warm lights glowing behind tall windows. A ramp was bolted to the siding, ascending from the driveway toward the house. The yard stretched wide and manicured, the kind of place that hosted large family gatherings filled with laughs in the summer.

'This is beautiful,' Ginger said as Austin parked.

Austin shrugged, but the pride shone behind his eyes. 'Dad planted that tree himself.' He pointed to the large oak in the front yard, its tangled branches stretching toward the sky.

She lifted the cake carefully from the backseat, the scent of toasted pecans clinging to her clothes. They climbed the steps together, and Austin set down Butter's carrier before he knocked on the door.

Ginger felt her phone buzz in her pocket. She shifted, holding the cake out for Austin to hold while she fished it out. He took it from her instinctively, his fingers brushing hers for just a second too long. She opened the message and the number was unfamiliar, no contact name or photo attached.

It read: ***Hello, Virginia.***

Ginger's world tilted off its axis. Her fingernails dug into her palm, and her pulse rang loudly in her ears, drowning out the distant traffic on Austin's parents' street, the evening chorus of Cinnamon Falls going about its business.

A rock settled in her gut. She'd been found.

The front door swung open and Austin's mother appeared in the doorway, her silky black hair billowing in the evening breeze. She smiled wide, eyes bright with welcome as the warm scent of cilantro and spice met her and Austin on the porch.

'Ginger! Welcome to our home!'

Chapter 20

Austin

Seated next to him at the farmhouse-style table, Ginger looked like she'd seen a ghost. Austin stole a furtive glance around the table to see if anyone else had noticed. The Jacobs household carried on as normal, loud and chaotic. Lilian and his dad were belly laughing over last year's unfortunate Thanksgiving incident featuring a scorched turkey and a visit to the emergency room, while Maddie and his mother looked on, shaking their heads, failing to hide their smiles. In the corner, Butter lapped at his formula, flicking his tail defensively at Rocky, the Jacobs' elderly golden retriever, who sniffed curiously around the tiny cat.

The room itself felt like home in a way Austin rarely thought about until someone new was inside of it. Wide-planked hardwood floors worn smooth over time. Framed photos lined the walls: his parents on their wedding day, the girls at various awkward stages of childhood, Austin holding a catfish far too big for his hands while his father looked on proudly. The dining room smelled of cumin, lime, and roasted corn, comfort layered over the memories.

Austin stuffed the last corner of his taco in his mouth, his gaze landing on Ginger again; the stricken expression hadn't left. If anything, it'd deepened.

What happened between the moment she climbed out of the truck and now? Austin watched as she glanced down at her phone, then up at the ceiling, blowing out a careful, controlled breath. She reached for a sip of water and laughed at the right places, a soft polite sound that didn't reach her eyes, giving the impression that she'd been following the conversation. A performance.

Austin knew that look. She was worried. Distracted. Dare he say . . . scared?

Had someone threatened her? Austin wouldn't be surprised. Ever since Raines mentioned The Maple Bakery during the press conference, he'd known the backlash would be swift. Cinnamon Falls operated on assumptions; whispers passed over coffee cups and checkout counters.

But the woman he'd known for the last six months wasn't scared of anyone. She'd already been questioned by detectives. That, he assumed, would be the hardest part, and she'd faced Chief Raines with grace. What could have rattled her this badly?

It dawned on Austin that he wasn't privy to every

facet of Ginger's life. Even if she was living under his roof, there were many aspects of her life that he didn't know about.

Would I ever? he wondered. *Would she ever trust me enough to let me in?*

Just as he was about to reach out to her, Ginger shifted, pushing her chair back slightly.

'Excuse me,' she murmured. 'I need the restroom.'

She didn't wait for a response or directions. Austin tracked her as she crossed the dining room and disappeared down the hall. The bathroom door clicked softly behind her. The moment it did, the energy at the table changed, filling the room with an uncomfortable silence.

'So,' Lillian said brightly, leaning forward with her elbows on the table. 'She's kinda intense.'

'Lillian,' his mother warned, though there was curiosity in her voice, too.

Madelyn tilted her head, probing, 'Is she always this quiet?'

Austin swallowed down his taco with a swig of beer. 'She's had a rough few days.'

Matthew scoffed. 'That's an understatement. Raines practically put a bullseye on the girl's back after that press conference.'

Austin's thumb rubbed the edge of his beer bottle. He didn't like this: dissecting Ginger when she wasn't there to speak for herself. But he also understood the concern. This was his family, their home, and he'd brought a stranger into it. A stranger who had the suspicion of murder hanging over her.

'She's staying with you,' Matthew added, pointing his fork at Austin. 'Is that why you missed the job on Nutmeg?'

Austin groaned. 'She is not the reason.'

'Why didn't you tell us?' his mother probed.

He leaned back in his chair, crossing his arms, his eyes trained on the restroom door. He wondered how much of this conversation she could hear, or if she was slumped on the floor in a pool of her own tears. Maybe dinner with his family was too soon, too overwhelming.

'Because I'm grown. And because Ginger needed help and I—'

Madelyn cut in. 'You sound defensive.'

'You're interrogating me!' Austin shot back.

His father studied him quietly for a moment then said, 'We're asking because it's obvious you care for her.'

The words landed heavier than Austin expected. Was he *that* obvious? He did care; more than he meant to, more than he understood, and that terrified him because he couldn't answer the questions stacking up in his own head – the same ones, he was sure, his parents had.

Why did Ginger leave Atlanta? Why had she flinched at her phone like it might bite? Worst of all, what was she running from?

'Son, what do you *actually* know about her?' his mother asked, reaching across the table to take his hand.

Austin opened his mouth, then closed it, realizing he knew nothing about Ginger Mills. He knew her name and that she had some semblance of a family, Alexis and an Uncle Maple. He knew that she had an adorable cat and that she could bake her ass off. But that was nothing. Any stranger who had two eyes and a mouth could deduce that from a five-minute conversation with her.

Frustration burned behind his eyes. He hated that they were right; hated that Ginger hadn't trusted him with more. Most of all, he hated that he couldn't defend her the way he wanted to without knowing the full truth for himself.

'I know she didn't kill anyone,' he said firmly. 'And right now, she deserves some grace.'

Silence settled in again. Katherine squeezed his hand.

Finally, his father nodded. 'Then that's what we'll give her.'

Austin exhaled, tension draining just a notch.

Matthew changed the subject, pushing roasted corn around on his plate. 'Don't forget Thursday morning you're meetin' me at Old Man Milton's . . .'

Austin was half-listening now. His thoughts were on a spin cycle about Ginger. For the first time since she'd walked into his life, Austin wondered if whatever she was hiding might be bigger than either of them was ready for. He glanced down the hallway toward the bathroom, unease creeping in.

What could be bigger than murder?

Chapter 21

Ginger

Ginger leaned back against the bathroom door, wishing she was anywhere but here. The space was tight and immaculate, all crisp white baseboards and pale blue walls, with a pedestal sink pressed close to her hip and above it a round mirror with a scalloped edge.

A framed watercolor painting of wildflowers hung slightly crooked above the toilet, and a faint scent of lemon cleaner and vanilla lingered in the air. She clutched her phone like it might leap from her hands and expose her all on its own.

Hello, Virginia.

The words glowed on the screen, devastating in meaning. Her heart hammered so loudly she was sure someone on the other side of the door could hear it. Austin's perfect mother. His sisters. His father. Austin. Through the wall she could hear all of them laughing at the table, unaware that Ginger's past had just reached through time and wrapped its cold, dead fingers around her throat.

She sucked in a breath and turned on the faucet, splashing cool water against her face. Once. Twice. Three times. She stared at her reflection in the mirror: her skin was flushed, her mouth trembling, despite her best effort to steady it.

Was that what she'd looked like at the dinner table? No wonder Lillian was giving her the stink eye. She looked like she'd just escaped from a mental hospital.

Get it together, she told herself, smoothing down the edges of her damp hair. *You're embarrassing yourself.*

She dabbed at her cheeks with a paper towel, pressing until the sting of it grounded her. She needed to walk back out there, sit down, smile, and be normal. She needed to make a good impression on Austin's parents.

Why does that even matter right now?

She huffed out a humorless laugh. Austin annoyed her, constantly. His relentless optimism, the way he acted as if the world could be fixed if you just showed up with the right attitude and a smile.

And yet he'd opened his home to her without hesitation. He'd carried her boxes, her life, up his stairs and hadn't demanded any answers. He fed her kitten. He'd given her space without pushing, support without any strings. He hadn't left her alone on Sunday when everything collapsed around her. He'd stayed. Over and over again, he'd stayed.

The last man who did that was Harrison, she reminded herself.

Harrison, who started as charm, steadiness, and safety, too. Harrison who'd paid the bills and kissed her forehead and promised a future so clean and polished that it looked perfect from the outside. Harrison, who'd slowly replaced her independence with comfort, her opinions with convenience, her voice with silence. She'd mistaken control for care. And now here she was again, standing in someone else's bathroom, eating another family dinner, wondering if she was about to repeat history.

A muffled burst of laughter drifted through the walls. Her absence had to be noticeable by now. They had to be asking questions. She could feel it. She imagined Austin fielding them, defending her with half-answers.

Guilt burned behind her eyes. She needed to get back out there, but she couldn't. Because if Harrison had found her, if he was close, then none of this was safe. Not Austin. Not the bakery, and definitely not Cinnamon Falls. Had Milo Penn ratted her out? He was her only connection to the outside world. How had Harrison found her?

I could run, she thought. How would she get past Austin? And where would she go? She couldn't go back to Alexis' place, not with Butter, and she wasn't leaving her kitten behind. She was out of options.

Her hands shook as she scrolled through her contacts. There was only one other number saved besides her family. Camille. She hesitated only a second before pressing the button, lifting the phone to her ear just as her friend answered.

'Hello?' Camille asked.

'Cam, it's me,' she breathed, her voice barely above a whisper.

Silence stretched on the line, long enough for Ginger to hear her own heartbeat thudding in her ears, long enough for her to think that she'd made a terrible mistake.

'You've got a lot of nerve calling me.' Camille's voice was piercing and brittle, hurt wrapped tight around every word. In the background, she heard Camille's son, Julian, giggling as a cartoon blared through the television. Ginger's chest cracked open; she was missing everything. She wondered how big he'd gotten or if he'd learned any new words in the months she'd been gone.

'I know. I'm sorry. I just got a message and someone used my real name and I thought—' Her voice wavered. 'I thought it had to be you.'

'You thought that *I'd* contact you?' Camille snapped. 'After what you did?'

Her words stung the most because they were true. Ginger swallowed hard, her throat burning. 'I didn't mean to hurt anyone,' she said, the confession worn thin from repetition. 'I was drowning, Cam. I couldn't stay a minute longer.'

'You humiliated me,' Camille shot back, her anger

flaring. 'You humiliated all of us! Do you have any idea what it's been like here? They think you're *dead* in a ditch somewhere!'

'I'm sorry,' Ginger whispered again, uselessly. 'I never wanted to hurt you. We're . . . family.'

Camille's laugh cut through the line right into Ginger's heart. 'Save it. You made your choice. And if you know what's good for you, you'll stay gone.'

Ginger's stomach dropped, dread bloomed cold and heavy. 'What do you mean?'

'Harrison's losing it,' Camille said flatly, no anger in her tone, only certainty. 'He's on a rampage. He wants answers. He wants you. And he's determined to find you.'

The bathroom felt too small, the air too thin, the walls too close. Ginger's hand slid along the cool porcelain of the sink as her knees weakened.

'Please, Cam,' she begged. 'You can't tell him where I am—'

'Stay gone,' Camille interrupted. 'If you have any sense at all, you'll disappear. For good this time.'

The line went dead. Ginger stared at her phone as the screen faded to black. Spots dotted behind her eyes and her knees finally gave out, buckling underneath her. She tried to hold onto the sink, fingers slipping, but she slid down to the cool tile floor. She pressed her fist to her mouth as a sob tore free. Tears spilled hot and fast, blurring everything: the life she'd left behind, the friendship she'd shattered, Austin's quiet kindness, the warmth of his family, the safety of his home, the comfort of his soft bed, the fragile life she'd stitched together in Cinnamon Falls.

She cried for the woman she used to be.

For the friend she'd lost.

For the choices she couldn't undo.

Most of all, she cried because she knew, deep down, that no matter how safe Austin felt, no matter how badly she wanted to stay, Harrison's shadow was already reaching for her.

And sooner or later, he would catch up.

Ginger finally peeled herself off the floor when she heard scratches at the bathroom door. Butter's tiny meows grew louder with every passing second, and somehow his cries – not her panic or fear – were what pulled her together. She could not embarrass her kitten under any circumstances. She took one last look at her reflection and unlocked the door.

Butter was waiting. He looked up at her expectantly from the hallway, tilting his head, studying her with solemn judgment, before issuing a demanding meow. She reached down, pulling him into her chest, and he rewarded her with a lick to her chin.

'I'm alright,' she reassured him with a soft caress down his back. 'Everything's okay,' she said again, more for herself than him.

The house was quiet. She turned the corner, surprised to find that dinner had been cleared away. The room that had been alive with laughter and filled with food was empty. All their plates, silverware, and drinks had been removed and replaced with an untouched set of china stacked neatly at each place setting.

Rocky padded over and nudged Ginger's knee with his wet nose, herding her toward the back of the house, and she followed him through the dining room toward the deck.

Beyond the glass doors, the Jacobs' backyard was wide and welcoming. A generous stretch of manicured grass rolled out from the deck like a soft, green carpet, well cared for in a way that boasted regular Saturday morning trims. The paved deck itself felt like an extension of the house, anchored by a stone fire pit and a built-in outdoor kitchen with a stainless steel grill and wide counters. Ginger could imagine the summer cookouts that happened here.

Further out, a set of cushioned reclining chairs sat positioned toward the tree line that pressed close around the property. The sun hovered low, dipping behind the burgundy and tangerine trees, painting the yard a honeyed gold. Fireflies blinked to life, one by one, tiny sparks drifting through the dusk air; warm enough to stay a while.

The Jacobs family had migrated outside, settling around the fire pit that crackled and popped in the center of the paved deck. Oversized red Adirondack chairs circled the flame. One empty chair sat conspicuously open between Austin and his father.

Lillian and Madelyn stood around, roasting marshmallows on long wooden sticks, their faces glowing in the firelight. Once they were satisfied, they smashed the marshmallow between two graham crackers and scurried away into the yard. Rocky burst through his dog door and waited for Ginger on the other side, tail wagging expectantly. She found the latch for the sliding door, took a deep breath, and joined them.

Austin turned immediately. His gaze swept over her, quick and searching, and when they met eyes he mouthed, 'You alright?'

She nodded slightly, not wanting to make more of a scene than she already had. Mr. Jacobs beckoned her over, patting the empty seat next to him. Up close, Matthew Jacobs was an imposing figure. She could tell he was bigger than Austin, broader through the shoulders, with the kind of stocky build that suggested a lifetime of physical labor rather than a love for the gym. His flannel jacket hung open over a faded Jacobs & Sons T-shirt. His wheelchair was positioned close to the fire pit, the toes of his boots meeting the exposed brick. They were scuffed at the toe and laced snug, like he might stand at any moment given half a chance. It struck her that he wore them out of habit, not hope or defiance.

'We had to send ol' Rocky in for you, girl,' Mr. Jacobs said, concentrating on his marshmallow that was becoming more charred by the second. 'Thought you got lost.' Rocky settled in on the other side of Mr. Jacobs' chair as he finally pulled the marshmallow from the flame and inspected it with a satisfied nod.

'Just had a family matter to tend to,' Ginger said, the lie slipping out too easily.

She wondered how Harrison would react if she had the guts to just pick up the phone and tell him that she was done. Camille had tried that once, and Theodore had only thrown more money at her, sucking her in deeper.

She settled into the chair, Butter tucked against her thighs, the fire warming her knees. The flames danced, sparks lifting into the night like tiny prayers.

'Auzzie, set the movie screen up!' Madelyn yelled, sinking into one of the reclining chairs in the middle of the yard.

'Be right back.' Austin squeezed Ginger's knee before walking away.

Ginger stilled, his innocent display of affection warming her all over. His touch had been brief, barely there, just a quiet press of reassurance. Her breath caught anyway. It reminded her of her father, years ago, when they were in crowded places or unfamiliar rooms. It was a grounding thing. A promise that he wouldn't go far, and if he did, he'd return.

She watched Austin cross the yard, laughing as his sisters heckled him, and felt the weight of the gesture settle in. It hadn't been accidental or meaningless. The small squeeze told her everything he hadn't said out loud yet: his feelings were growing.

And the realization scared her far more than she wanted to admit, because some part of her knew that her feelings were, too.

'Family's a bitch,' Mr. Jacobs quipped, bringing her back to the present. His gaze drifted into the yard. Lillian shrieked with laughter as Austin untangled himself from a long extension cord, the sound echoing over the acres of woodland. 'Luckily, I've got a good one. I can truly say I'm blessed in that department.'

'You have a beautiful home, Mr. Jacobs. Thank you for inviting me to dinner.'

He waved her compliment away like it was a pesky mosquito. 'That's Katherine's doing. She's the magic behind all this.' He gestured around himself, his marshmallow cooling on the stick. 'I just foot the bill,' he chuckled.

A comfortable silence drifted between them, punctuated by the snap of the fire and distant laughter.

'You and I talked briefly while Austin was renovating the bakery, but not a lot,' Mr. Jacobs said, and Ginger steeled herself. 'Tell me, where you from, Ginger?'

'Atlanta,' she said. The word felt heavy. 'By way of Michigan.' That felt better.

'Mm,' he nodded. 'You're a city girl.'

'I was,' she responded. 'I guess in a way I still am.'

He studied her then, in a way that felt careful and

kind. 'Cinnamon Falls must have been a culture shock for you, then.'

'A little bit,' Ginger replied, a laugh filtering through her words. 'But I'm kind of liking it here.'

He smiled. 'Austin kind of likes you, too. For all his strength, my boy's sensitive. Wears his heart on his sleeve, even if he pretends otherwise. Ever since he was young I could read what he was thinking all over his face.' He chuckled softly, then sobered. 'Samantha leaving knocked the wind outta him. Took him a while to come 'round. I'm glad to have him back.'

Austin had never told her about anyone named Samantha. An ex? Ginger's curiosity piqued. 'I didn't know,' she admitted.

'He didn't tell many people.' He poked at the fire with his stick. 'Truth is, I've been hoping someone would come along and make his life feel settled, like Katherine did for me.'

She nodded, unsure of what to say. Mr. Jacobs poked at the fire again, embers snapping and curling upward into the setting sky. A blanket of indigo was stretching closer and closer.

'Austin's got a lot on his shoulders right now.' His voice was casual, but the weight between them felt like it was something he was worried about every day. 'Jacobs & Sons has grown faster than either of us expected. Jobs keep comin'. Bigger ones, more responsibility.'

'Is that why it's Jacobs & *Sons*?' Ginger asked, more of an observation than a question.

He smiled at her then, warm and wistful. 'I was positive we'd have more kids. A coupla boys to fill out the crew. But, uh, life had other plans.'

Ginger glanced across the yard where Austin and Madelyn were wrestling opposite sides of an inflatable movie screen, while Lillian offered zero assistance and plenty of commentary.

'It used to be just the two of us,' he continued. 'That was enough back then.' He paused, his lips downturned like he'd tasted something sour. 'Before I got hurt.'

She turned toward him. She'd heard from Heather, but she wanted to hear it from him. 'If you don't mind me asking, what happened?'

Before he could respond, Mrs. Jacobs stepped out on the patio, a cold beer clutched under her arm and a glass of wine in her hand. She pressed a kiss to her husband's temple before extending him the beer, and settling into the chair next to him. Mr. Jacobs immediately softened, his posture relaxed.

He leaned back in his chair, gaze drifting toward the fire as if it held a memory. 'I fell off the roof last year. One bad step changed everything.' His voice was layered, steady on top, but there was something raw underneath. 'Hardest part wasn't the pain, it was the acceptance. I had to learn how to let people help me . . . to let someone else take the lead.'

'I think Auzzie took it harder than all of us,' Mrs.

Jacobs chimed in. She leaned over, patting her husband's leg. 'We were all so tight and then he and Samantha called it quits, it seemed like one blow after the other. He could have broken my heart in two when he stopped comin' around. Tonight feels like old times.' She nodded toward her children, tears misting her eyes.

Ginger was shocked. The Jacobs family seemed so close-knit. Ginger couldn't imagine Austin staying away from his mother or his sisters for months at a time. She'd built a fantasy in her head of perfect Austin spending long, golden summers with his flawless family filled with large weekly dinners and belly laughs floating late into the night.

Together, the three of them watched as Austin succeeded in setting up the inflatable screen, throwing his arms up in triumph while his sisters applauded sarcastically. The opening credits of a nineties action comedy flickered to life across the lawn.

After a moment, Mr. Jacobs spoke again. 'Can I ask you something?'

Ginger's shoulders stiffened.

'And you can tell me to fuck off if you want,' he continued. 'I'd get it.'

'Matty,' Katherine warned over the lip of her wine glass.

'What? I thought we were sharing,' Mr. Jacobs joked.

'It's okay, go ahead,' Ginger replied, clutching Butter a little tighter.

'Did you kill Landon?' he asked plainly, his eyes locking onto hers.

'Matthew Austin Jacobs!' Mrs. Jacobs squealed. She swatted at her husband's arm, but he didn't react. Mr. Jacobs held Ginger's gaze like he could see through her.

Ginger made sure not to break eye contact when she answered. 'No,' she said, just as plainly with no hesitation, no qualifiers, or fillers. 'I didn't.'

Finally, after what seemed like minutes, he nodded. 'That's all I needed to hear.'

Ginger pushed air through her teeth, releasing the breath she'd been holding. In the nick of time, Austin jogged back toward them.

'What'd I miss?' he asked, dropping into his seat. He reached for Butter, who hissed at being removed from Ginger's lap.

Mr. Jacobs took a sip of his beer, a smile playing at his lips. 'That's our business.'

Austin shook his head. 'Figures.'

Later, as Austin and Ginger walked to the truck weighed down with leftovers and Butter's carrier, she replayed Mr. Jacobs' words: *Austin kinda likes you, too.* Then her thoughts trailed to Samantha. What made her leave a guy as nice as Austin, and where was she now?

Chapter 22

Wednesday

Austin

Wednesday morning came too soon. Austin frowned, rubbing the sleep from his eyes and stretching out the muscles in his back and legs that had gone stiff. He was lying on his back, one leg hanging over the edge of his bed.

What happened last night?

He remembered stepping out of the shower and agreeing to meet Ginger downstairs for a nightcap. It'd been too long since it was just the two of them without interruption, and he was anxious to share what he'd learned about Landon. He wanted to know what she'd found out about Natasha, but he must have fallen asleep somewhere between the shower and changing into his pajamas. He glanced down at himself. He'd slept only in a T-shirt and briefs, one foot tangled in the leg of a pair of striped pajama pants.

Austin knew he'd felt tired after dinner, but not

pass-out-as-soon-as-his-head-hit-the-pillow kind of tired. Despite his awkward position during the night, he felt refreshed, and judging from the aroma of brewing coffee wafting upstairs from his kitchen, Ginger had slept well, too.

He was growing used to having her around, his family's opinions be damned.

He fumbled for his phone on the nightstand, but the screen was black. Dead. He plugged it in using the charging cord hanging next to his bed and the screen brightened, revealing that it was just past nine a.m. A text chimed from his father, asking him to check out a sink at Bones' Barbershop around noon. It was a good thing he didn't have any morning jobs or else he'd be giving his father something else to fuss about.

Austin readied himself in his ensuite bathroom before heading downstairs to join Ginger. She was seated on one of the barstools, leaning over at the kitchen island, coffee mug cradled in both hands. Her hair was twisted into a bun at the top of her head. She was barefoot in a pair of navy blue sweatpants that looked too big for her because they were his. The elastic was rolled at her hips, revealing the fleece lining inside. He instantly recognized his high-school wrestling T-shirt that was knotted in a tight ball at her waist, revealing the soft slope of her back. Austin bit down hard on his lip to stop the blood from flowing elsewhere.

'Good morning, sleepy head,' Ginger said, turning toward him. Her long, dark lashes fanned against her cheeks while her eyes roamed him, down then up.

She was unfairly gorgeous. Her toffee brown skin all but glimmered in the sunlight filtering in from the kitchen window over his stove where he noticed something had been prepared in a covered pan.

'Good morning,' Austin choked out. 'How'd you sleep?'

He ventured toward the coffee pot, stepping over Butter who was sprawled in a sun spot, refusing to move. Austin crouched down and rubbed his belly and Butter stretched, rotating until Austin scratched him all the way around.

'So spoiled already,' Ginger grumbled, shaking her head.

'You made him this way,' Austin countered.

'Says the man on his hands and knees giving him morning scratches.'

'It's more like a squatting motion,' Austin clarified.

She pointed her chin toward the stove. 'Made you some breakfast since we both KO'd after dinner last night.'

'I didn't realize I was so tired.'

'Me neither. Not getting up to go to the bakery has thrown my sleeping pattern all the way off.'

Austin lifted the top off the pan, revealing fried eggs and bacon. Nearby on a plate was a large stack of pancakes.

'You ate already?' There was no way all that food could be for just him.

She lifted the mug to her mouth again. 'Was waiting for you,' she said nonchalantly, like she hadn't spent her morning cooking when she could have been sleeping. Austin decided not to go there. He realized that Ginger was not a woman of many words, but everything she felt came out in her actions. Cooking him breakfast, baking a cake for a no-pressure family dinner were all small acts of consideration. She didn't have to say it, Austin knew that he was getting closer to defrosting her heart.

'Thank you,' Austin said, busying himself with plates and silverware, stopping himself from reaching over the island and kissing her. It'd been months since a woman had cooked for him, even longer since he had someone to share a meal with that wasn't his family. He could get used to this.

Austin doled out breakfast and they ate in a comfortable silence, mostly because he didn't know what else to say. And that was a first for him.

'We were supposed to exchange notes last night, remember?' Ginger reminded him. 'You texted me "Big news" on Monday and I can't wait a second longer.'

'Right,' Austin said, shoveling the last of his pancakes into his mouth. 'For starters, I stopped by Ethel Lawson's place.'

'And?' Ginger asked, her eyes widening.

'She didn't kill her husband.'

Ginger deflated, her shoulders slumping.

'She could barely stand long enough to talk to me. She's got COPD and there's no way—'

'She could have killed him physically,' Ginger finished, shaking her head, reminding herself of the conversation she'd had with Heather just yesterday. Suddenly she straightened as if she'd been hit by a burst of inspiration. 'But she could have arranged it.'

Austin shook his head. 'Ms. Ethel didn't sound angry about Landon's indiscretions at all. She was very cavalier about it all.'

'You *asked*?' Ginger said, her mouth falling open in shock.

''Course I did. This is an investigation, right?' Austin joked. 'She said they had an understanding. Ms. Ethel's fifteen years older than Landon and she knew he'd want someone younger as she grew older.'

'That doesn't give him the right to cheat on her so publicly—'

Austin held up a finger, stopping her. 'We talked about that, too. She said as long as it didn't come back to her front door then she was fine with Landon having a little fun on the side. She also said they hadn't lived together in a long while.'

Ginger shook her head. 'Understandings are fragile. It wasn't like he was just having a little bit of fun here and there. According to Natasha, she was under the impression that Landon was her *man*, and I don't think she was lying about that.'

'You sure?' Austin asked.

Ginger nodded emphatically. 'Yes. Why would she? She was devastated that *she* turned out to be the other woman. She said they had it out Friday night and that was the last time she'd seen him before he . . .'

Austin frowned. 'Seems pretty convenient.'

'You weren't there,' Ginger replied. 'I saw the pain in that girl's face. She loved Landon.'

'Ethel loved him, too.'

Ginger sighed. 'Then somebody's lying.'

'Or it could be someone else entirely.'

Ginger shook her head. 'Who would care that much about a cheating delivery driver to kill him? It had to be someone close to him.'

'Rowan mentioned that Ethel and Natasha had words, remember? She said something like Ethel almost knocked her head off. If they knew about each other . . .'

Ginger's eyes lit up. 'What if they conspired together . . .'

'No way,' Austin responded. 'Ethel is practically an old lady!'

'We're missing something. None of this is adding up.'

'Shall we consult the murder notebook?'

Ginger carefully lifted the glitter-covered pad and opened it to the first page. 'We've retraced his foot-steps and talked to his family and friends.'

Austin reached over, flipping to the next page,

showering Ginger in a wave of glitter. 'Suspects lie,' he said, tapping the page.

Ginger twisted her lips, brushing glitter off her T-shirt.

Austin stifled a laugh. 'I'm telling you, Natasha has the motive and, according to Landon's manifest, she had the opportunity, too.'

'Then you talk to her,' Ginger advised. 'Maybe she was telling me what I wanted to hear.'

'Fine, I'll go today,' he said.

Ginger spun in her seat, grabbing both their plates and depositing them in the sink. She turned toward him, her waist on display again. A diamond-studded crescent moon hung from her navel.

'Thank you for inviting me to dinner last night. Your family . . .' she gestured around herself, 'your home, is beautiful.'

'Thank you for joining me,' Austin replied. 'I was hoping you didn't hate it, especially after the way my dad interrogated you.'

Ginger chuckled. 'I wouldn't say it was an interrogation necessarily. But he doesn't play about you, that's for sure.'

'I hope he didn't make you uncomfortable. My dad can be a little blunt at times.'

'No, nothing like that.' Ginger leaned against the sink, crossing her arms over her chest. 'He was kind and honest. I could appreciate that.' She hesitated before saying, 'He told me about Samantha.'

Austin froze mid-motion while bringing his glass of orange juice to his mouth. 'What?'

'Samantha,' Ginger repeated. She looked up at him sheepishly through her dark lashes. 'I figured she was an ex.'

Austin blew out a breath. This was *not* how he thought he was going to start his morning. But he might as well get the hard conversation out of the way. He had nothing to hide. It was over between him and Samantha and he wanted Ginger to know that . . . just in case she was wondering.

'Yeah, she is,' he admitted, knocking back a swig of juice to coat his mouth, which had gone dry. He decided on the abbreviated version. 'We were together for a few years. I wanted to get married, she didn't.'

'He didn't tell me any details, just that you stopped coming around after the accident and then you two broke up.'

Austin sighed, the tingle in his chest hurting a little less the more he explained. 'It was hard being in all the places we used to frequent without her. It felt like a piece of me was missing.'

Ginger nodded. 'I know exactly what you mean.'

'That reminds me.' Austin walked through the kitchen toward the front door where his coat was hanging in the closet. He pulled out the crumpled papers he'd hidden in the pocket on Monday, Landon's manifest.

'Samantha's little sister works for Valley View. I

managed to get my hands on Landon's manifest from Saturday night. It goes back two weeks.'

Ginger's eyes widened as she joined him on his side of the island. Austin spread the papers out on the counter, leaning close, their shoulders almost touching.

'Your ex's sister?' She scanned the papers hungrily, her eyes zooming line by line. 'She just gave you this information? No questions asked?'

'Not exactly,' Austin replied, a mischievous smile spreading across his face.

Ginger held her hand up. 'I don't even wanna know.' She turned her attention to the pages again. 'Tell me what this means. What are these numbers and symbols?'

'Here.' Austin tapped the page. 'This is the time stamp where Landon's GPS signal was lost on Saturday night, 11:48 p.m. His next check in wasn't until he reached Cinnamon Falls, then his GPS turned back on around one a.m. His truck mysteriously loses the location tracking every weekend at the same time.' Austin flipped the pages to the week before Landon was killed. 'See? Same pattern.'

Ginger looked up at him. 'That gives us a huge window of time. Landon could have already been dead for hours by the time I made it to Main Street on Sunday. Austin, you just made my morning!'

Ginger scooted closer, her eyes trained on the pages. Austin pivoted, allowing her to close the gap between them. He could smell her body wash, floral and enticing, drawing him in. He didn't care about Landon or the manifest anymore. She was in his personal space, again. With just one small reach he could bring her face to his. He watched as she trailed her finger down the page, studying each line like she was memorizing facts for an exam. She pulled her bottom lip into her mouth, concentrating, and Austin braced himself, gripping the edge of the island for balance.

In his mind, he'd knock all the papers to the floor. Ginger would grab him by his shirt and smash her face into his. They'd make love, right there on the kitchen island.

Instead, Ginger turned; her face was mere inches from his. To his surprise, she didn't look away and instead returned his gaze, her eyes playfully narrowing. He didn't know how long they stayed like that, surveying. It could have been six or sixty seconds, Austin couldn't tell. A smile tried at the corners of her lips and everything dropped out of Austin's mind. Everything except for one thing: the fear in those same beautiful brown eyes at dinner just the night before.

Austin hadn't forgotten about last night. There was something Ginger wasn't telling him, something she'd been afraid of, and before he could go any further, he had to know. His timing wasn't the best, all things considered, but there was no way he could continue whatever this was without knowing.

'Ginger,' he whispered, raking her with his eyes,

wishing he was the kind of man who could throw caution to the wind. He prided himself on always thinking with the right head, his brain, no matter what the other one was screaming at him. And it damn sure was screaming.

Her pouty pink lips were a breath away from his. The moment he'd been fantasizing about was primed and ready, in the palm of his hand.

And he had no choice but to watch it flutter away.

Without hesitancy he asked, 'Who texted you last night?'

Chapter 23

Ginger

Ginger realized a little too late that she hadn't been this close to Austin before, shoulder to shoulder, their bare arms touching just so.

She was close enough to detect a faint scar that ran along his jawline, beneath his neatly trimmed beard, close enough to spot the brown in his eyes, morsels of caramel floating in pools of dark chocolate; close enough to hear the quiet steadiness of his breath, the want radiating from him, drawing her in like a moth to a flame. Her body had succumbed way before her mind could catch up, and before she could stop herself, she was nearly underneath him.

She'd been denying it; pretending he was just conveniently kind. But standing there – barely a whisper between them, her pulse resounding in her ears – she felt the truth of it settle in her belly, low and undeniable.

She *liked* Austin. Hell, she wanted him. Right here.

Suddenly, it all rushed back to her. She missed being held; she missed the safety of a man, someone who wanted her without conditions. Her body had remembered what love was supposed to feel like, even if her heart had learned to be cautious.

His hands hovered near her waist, not touching, but waiting. Always waiting. That undid her more than anything. She wished he would grab her, pull her body to his, and kiss her. But Austin would never do that. He was too much of a gentleman.

All she had to do was move a fraction of an inch and her mouth would be on his; their quiet morning cascading into something deeper, something meaningful.

And then he said her name, smooth as spun sugar on his tongue. His eyes studied her face like he could see the thoughts in her mind: them, horizontal on the kitchen island, lost in a passionate kiss.

All of a sudden, he asked, 'Who texted you last night?'

When Ginger was seven years old, she watched her mother's antique gold mirror shatter to pieces during their move from Michigan to Atlanta. She hadn't wanted to move. She'd made it clear from the beginning, when her mother pulled her out of school to have an 'important conversation' with her. She cried. She stomped. She screamed. But nothing she did stopped her parents from packing her room up bit by bit until it was just four bare walls.

She remembered standing on the staggered concrete steps that led to her home, what used to be her home. Her father lost his footing on the final step and the mirror slipped out of his hands. It exploded once it hit the sidewalk, shards of glass skittering across the concrete and into the street; tiny fragments of memories lost, never to be found again.

In her mind, Ginger watched her daydream repeat the same pattern, shattering to pieces before her eyes.

She placed two palms to Austin's solid chest and pushed backward, just enough to breathe, just enough to snap out of passion's glittery realm and back into reality.

His heartbeat was steady beneath her palms, his body warm enough to sink into. But she pulled away anyway, lacing her hands behind her back where they belonged.

'It was Camille,' she said quickly. Too quickly. 'She's my best friend back in Atlanta.'

Austin's expression softened immediately, concern replacing rampant want like a switch inside of him flipped. 'Was everything okay?'

Ginger nodded, suddenly thirsty and lightheaded. She dropped onto one of the nearby barstools.

'Yes. We don't talk much anymore. Her situation isn't . . . safe. Her husband monitors her phone calls, her texts, everything. Getting a message from her out of the blue, it spooked me. And I needed to talk to her. I couldn't do that at the table in front of everyone.'

'Understandable,' Austin replied. No suspicion. No second-guessing. Harrison, on the other hand, would have questioned her from sun up to sun down.

Relief washed over her but the lie was bitter on her tongue. 'When we talked it was more of the same. She doesn't want to leave. She has a son so I get that she can't just pick up and disappear when there's a kid involved.'

Austin studied her for a beat. She had no idea what he was thinking. 'Did she need help? You were in there for a long time.'

Her stomach tightened. 'Just moral support. There were lots of emotions. It wasn't a short call.'

Austin watched her like he was weighing something. He looked over his shoulder at Butter, who'd found another sun spot under the living room window, then back over at Ginger. 'I just need to know one thing.'

Ginger couldn't stop herself from biting her lip.

'Okay,' she said gently, wishing she knew where this was leading if it wasn't upstairs to his bedroom.

'Is somebody going to show up at my house thinking I stole a future that belonged to him?'

Austin's tone was jovial, but his eyes were stone. He wasn't playing around.

Ginger swallowed. 'No, it's nothing like that. I promise.'

She couldn't tell him about the weird text, or about Harrison. Not yet.

He seemed to accept her answer, his shoulders loosening a fraction. He stepped back, giving her space, and the distance between them somehow felt colder than before. He turned to head up the stairs, but stopped on the first landing. She watched the muscles in his back as he turned toward her.

'I've got some work to do at Bones' over on Main Street today. When I'm done I'll swing past Prime Society and see what I can find out.'

They were back to business. Ginger cleared her throat, wiping her damp palms on her – Austin's – sweatpants. 'I have Butter's follow-up appointment with Dr. Hughes this afternoon. I'll see you tonight?' She hated how desperate she sounded.

He nodded. 'We'll have dinner.'

Once she heard Austin's footsteps above her head, Ginger slumped onto the barstool, cradling her head in her hands. That was *too* close. She had to be more careful.

Chapter 24

Austin

Bones' Barbershop sat about halfway down Main Street. The red, white and blue pole sporting spiraling stripes spun slowly, signaling it was open for business. Austin snagged a coveted spot behind a black coupe he knew belonged to Will Reed. A Cinnamon Falls patrol vehicle drove past and maneuvered in front of Will's. Austin watched as Reggie Nash hopped out and headed into the barbershop. Austin did the same with one person on his mind: Ginger. Her words from breakfast were still bouncing around in his head.

I get that she can't just pick up and disappear . . . Austin couldn't help but wonder if that's what Ginger had done. Disappear. As much as he hated to admit, his family had planted a bug in his ear about her. Was everyone around him seeing something he wasn't? And was he an idiot for giving her the benefit of the doubt?

The bell above the door jingled when Austin pushed

inside. It was a place he'd known his whole life; Saturday mornings spent with his father, waiting his turn in the cracked vinyl chairs, listening to the older men talk about football, weather, women, and everyone else's business.

Austin spotted Will Reed behind the counter, sleeves rolled up, a wrench in hand. He looked relieved when he saw Austin.

'Thank God,' Will muttered. He reached over to give Austin a dap. 'Pipe under the bowl's been leaking again.' Will jerked his chin toward the back and made his way over to Reggie Nash who was draped in his chair.

'I got you,' Austin said, nodding to Reggie across the room. He returned with a nod of his own, a silent but friendly greeting.

He grabbed his toolbag and ducked into the narrow hallway that led toward the wash station. The barbershop continued to stir as usual, clippers humming and the low murmur of conversation buzzing through the wall.

Crouching beneath the sink, Austin rolled up the sleeves of his flannel shirt. He carefully pushed the bucket that had been catching the water out of the way and flipped out his flashlight. The leak was immediate, splashing him between his eyes. It was clear the vacuum breaker was as old as the sink itself, rusted to the exterior, a constant leak dripping from the pipe. Austin affixed his wrench to the rusted bolt when he heard the bell chime above the door, Bones' distinct voice carrying easily down the hallway.

'I'm tellin' you,' Bones said, his voice disjointed like he was in the middle of eating something. 'My money's . . . on the bakery girl.'

'Ginger or something, right?' a new voice inquired. 'I heard her cinnamon buns are better than Rosie's.'

Austin froze. He turned slightly to get a view of the door and spotted Alvin Grady, the retired postmaster, following behind Bones toward the service area.

'Shut yo' mouth!' Bones bit back. 'Just because she's new in town, everyone is fallin' over themselves to get to her bakery. I don't trust it. Landon's been deliverin' to Main Street for years. This girl shows up, pushes Marsha Pickens outta her prime spot, sets up shop, and then boom. Landon's dead. Don't sit right wit' me.'

'Don't look at me.' Austin heard Reggie Nash next. 'I'm just here to get my hair cut.'

'Mm-hmm,' Bones grunted.

Will interjected. 'Come on now, that's one hell of a leap. Even for you, Bones. Plus I heard Marsha's got a bigger place over in Asheville.'

'Thank goodness for that,' Bones responded. 'Heard that girl was hellbent on opening that bakery before Fall Festival. Then Landon falls dead the next morning? You don't gotta be Sherlock Holmes to connect the dots.' Austin's hand gripped his wrench harder. 'She coulda been one of Landon's side pieces. He liked 'em young and pretty. And she's got that look to her, like she's hidin' something.'

'I'm sure she was questioned already,' Will offered. 'And the police didn't arrest her.'

'Yet,' Bones scoffed. The words landed like a slap to Austin's face. 'The town's gone too soft. Everybody wants to play nice, but I been 'round long enough to know outsiders bring baggage. You don't just pawn a ring and reinvent yourself in a place like Cinnamon Falls unless you're runnin' from somethin'. You remember that Cameron guy from a couple months ago?'

'He pretended to be Eleanor Langford's nephew or somethin'?' Alvin asked.

'Mm-hmm,' Bones said. 'And look what happened to Eleanor. Dead as a doornail.'

Austin stood. He placed his wrench back in his bag and slung it over his shoulder, fists curling at his sides. He made sure to stomp up the hallway so that Bones and his audience could hear him coming.

Their conversation died as he reached the doorway. Bones looked up from his seat mid-sentence, surprise flickering across his face. He flipped his wrist around to look at his watch.

'Oh, Austin,' he said brightly. 'I didn't know you'd come in.'

'Just back there fixing your vacuum breaker. You'll need a new one.'

Bones nodded. 'I'll call the manufacturer today and have them send one out to me.' He extended his hand for Austin to shake. 'Thank you, young man. I'll let you know when it comes in.'

Austin avoided his hand and Bones tucked it around the newspaper open across his lap. An article about Landon's death was on top.

'I couldn't help but overhear what you said about Ginger.'

A beat passed and no one moved. Clippers paused. The shop went quiet.

Bones adjusted in his seat on the couch. 'I – I'm just saying what folks are thinkin'. Whole town's talkin' about it.'

'That so?' Austin asked. His voice was even-tempered, and that was what made it worse. Beads of sweat sprang to Bones' forehead.

'The whole town's accusing Ginger of murder? That's news to me.' Austin looked over to Reggie Nash to confirm, but the officer had gone silent, squinting at a distant spot on the wall where a slim crack ran into the ceiling.

'I think Bones is just saying what he's been hearing—' Will explained.

Austin cut him off. 'Oh, I heard him. I heard him accuse a woman of murder with no proof, based on gossip, and the fact that she's new.'

'Look, Austin, I didn't know you had feelings for the girl. I'm just sayin'—'

Austin edged out his words through gritted teeth. 'She lost her business overnight. She was interrogated for hours and has been cooperative every step of the way. She hasn't done a damn thing to deserve her reputation being dragged through the mud by a room of grown men speculating for entertainment.'

Mr. Grady coughed awkwardly.

Bones opened his mouth and shut it. 'I ain't mean no harm, son.'

Austin shouldered his tool bag once more. 'Intent doesn't really matter once the words are out there.' Bones tried to respond but Austin kept talking, shutting him up. 'Call my father when the new vacuum breaker comes in. You gentlemen have a nice day.'

The bell jingled as Austin pushed open the door to leave. Outside, the air felt sharper. Austin stood on the sidewalk for longer than necessary, jaw tight, heart pounding, debating whether to finish his errands for the day or grab Bones around his collar.

After a while, his anger bled into something else. Disappointment. According to Bones, Cinnamon Falls had already written Ginger off, and he'd been defending her blindly.

He climbed into his truck, gripping the wheel. Prime Society was a car ride away and he needed answers before this town decided Ginger's guilt for her.

Chapter 25

Ginger

Dr. Hughes' office was cramped, smelling of disinfectant that worked triple time to cover the ever-present pet odor. Alexis squirmed in the plastic seat next to Ginger as a husky and its equally plump owner passed, while Butter stared daggers at her from his position perched on Ginger's shoulder.

'Be nice to Aunt Lexy,' Ginger whispered, trying not to laugh.

'You're enjoying this,' Alexis responded, narrowing her eyes at Ginger, looking over her magazine. 'Your cat is imagining skinning me alive and you're laughing.'

'You did put us out on the street.'

'The two of you were *rehomed*,' Alexis clarified. Ginger swatted her shoulder playfully. She replaced the magazine in the waiting-room rack and pulled out her phone, beginning to scroll on a social media app.

'So,' she started casually, never looking up. 'Are you going to tell me why you invited me to your cat's appointment knowing my man is allergic, and also, why you look like you've just survived a hostage situation?'

'First of all, your man needs to grow up. Second of all, I needed my cousin today.' Ginger raked a hand through her hair and Alexis pulled her sunglasses down her nose, giving her cousin her full attention. 'Austin and I almost kissed this morning,' she confessed.

'Almost?' Alexis shrieked.

'Yes, almost,' Ginger said, lowering her voice as the vet tech called another pet's name. The dozing Shih Tzu puppy across the lobby perked up, his tail wagging furiously. Ginger waited until they were gone to continue. 'And then right before we were going to kiss, he asked me who texted me during dinner last night.'

Alexis grimaced, pushing her sunglasses over her eyes again and slouched back in the chair. 'Of course he did.'

'I panicked,' Ginger admitted. 'I told him it was Camille.'

'Well,' Alexis said slowly, her thumb pausing on her phone screen mid-scroll, 'was it Camille?'

Ginger started, 'Well, it wasn't technically a lie—'

'And what would you call it?'

'A half-truth.'

'Which is worse!' Alexis cried. 'Way worse!'

Ginger shifted Butter from her shoulder to her lap and turned toward her cousin. 'We went to dinner with his family last night. I got a text and I had to excuse myself from the table. He notices *everything*! He's not stupid, he knows something is off.'

Alexis pulled her sunglasses off and studied Ginger carefully, her eyes sweeping over Ginger's face. 'What did the text say?'

Ginger hesitated and unlocked her phone. She opened the text thread and turned the screen toward her cousin. A new message popped up, more threatening than the last.

Hello, Virginia.

You can't disappear forever.

Alexis' face drained of color. 'What in the hell is this, Ging?'

'I don't know who it is,' Ginger whispered. 'No one here knows my real name. No one.'

Alexis was sitting up now, alert. She reached over and grabbed Ginger's free hand. 'I'm letting you know right now, I'm telling Terrance.'

'No,' Ginger said quickly.

'Ginger—'

'I really do think it's Camille . . . or someone connected to Camille. I just need to give her time to cool off. If Terrance gets involved now, it will just blow everything out of proportion. I don't want any of this to come back on Camille, or worse, Julian. The Caldwell brothers are not forgiving men.'

Alexis pressed her lips together, clearly unhappy. 'Raines has got the whole force working overtime for info and Terrance talks like she's ready to nail your ass to the wall. What if this has something to do with Landon's murder? If someone is threatening you, that's motive, Ging. That could clear you.'

Ginger pulled her lip into her mouth, considering. Finally, she held her phone out. 'Just take a picture of the number.'

Alexis snapped a picture of the contact details.

'Butter Mills!' the vet tech called from behind the desk across the room.

Ginger lifted her hand, signaling that she and Butter were ready. She pulled her kitten closer to her, giving him a kiss on the top of his head, grateful for the grounding weight of him.

The vet visit went smoothly; almost too smoothly considering how chaotic Ginger's life had been in the last few days. Butter passed every test with flying colors, earning a clean bill of health and a clearance for solid food. She was grateful that at least one thing in her life wasn't on the brink of unraveling.

Afterward, Alexis suggested stopping at Guy's Grocery and, for once, Ginger didn't argue. She and Butter had been eating Austin out of house and home the last few days and the thought needled her, even though he hadn't complained one bit. He'd given his space, safety, sweatpants, and kindness so freely, all without asking for anything in return.

She had to bake for him again to show her gratitude.

As they shopped, her mind kept circling back to that morning – the way his hand hovered at her waist, the way his breath was steady and even. Their almost-kiss replayed in her mind constantly, warming places inside her that had gone cold months ago.

And the most unsettling part of it all? She wasn't angry about it. If anything, it scared her how much she wanted to stay in Cinnamon Falls. Which was why she'd decided that she couldn't keep hiding. Austin deserved more than half-truths and carefully edited versions of her past. He deserved honesty, even if it cost her the fragile safety she'd found in his home.

She had to be honest with him. Tonight.

Ginger didn't know how he'd take the news. She didn't know if he'd listen the way she hoped, or if her truth would finally push him away. If it did, she'd swallow her disappointment, and hope that Morgan would honor her offer of a room at the Daffodil Inn. She told herself that she was prepared for the outcome, but she wasn't sure if she believed it.

Austin had mentioned offhandedly that he liked chocolate. Ginger smiled as she reached for cocoa powder, sugar, and espresso powder, already forming the plan in her head. She'd bake a three-layer dark chocolate fudge cake, each sponge separated by rich chocolate frosting, with a glossy ganache poured thick over the top. Decadent. Comforting. A peace offering and a way to soften the truth she was finally ready to tell. Whatever happened tonight, she wanted him to know one thing for certain: her feelings were just as real as his. She *liked* Annoying Austin.

Ginger reached for a bag of semisweet chocolate chips when she heard it: whispers. She spun on her heel, half expecting someone to be standing right behind her. The aisle was empty. Then she heard it again, just ahead of her, low and urgent.

There was someone close, conversing. She pushed her cart further down the aisle, moving slowly, then crouched near the endcap of frosting cans. On the next aisle over, two older women were huddled together.

Mrs. Guy wore the signature green Guy's Grocery apron stretched over her ample breasts. Her gray hair was pulled back into a sensible bun; her arms looked strong and capable crossed tightly over her chest as she leaned in to listen. The woman beside her was considerably thinner, almost fragile. Her coat hung off her frame like it belonged to someone else. Her posture curved inward, shoulders rounded as if the weight of the world had physically bent her. One hand trembled faintly as she rested it on the handle of her cart. Ethel Lawson.

Ginger held her breath. Whatever they were saying wasn't meant for public consumption.

'I just don't know how I'm going to keep everything running,' Ethel said, wiping her eyes with the back of her hand. She inhaled deeply, a wheezy cough rattling in her chest. 'Landon handled all the heavy lifting.'

Mrs. Guy murmured sympathetically. 'You're doing the best you can, Ethel.' Seeing her again, Ginger knew now that Austin had been right. There was no way Ethel could have killed her husband. She hardly had the stamina to stand let alone plan a grisly murder.

'It's going to be hard for a while,' Mrs. Guy continued. 'When I lost Gilbert I didn't know how I'd keep this place afloat. You take it one day at a time. It'll get better.'

'Doesn't feel like it. Especially after that girl showed up at my house.' Ethel shot Mrs. Guy a knowing look.

Ginger stilled, straining to hear more.

'That waitress?' Mrs. Guy asked. 'What was her name? Natasha?'

Ethel nodded with pursed lips. 'Banged on my door Friday night like she was entitled to answers. She demanded that I prove I was his wife. She was convinced I was his momma covering for his ass.'

Mrs. Guy jumped back. 'The nerve of her!'

'I told her to her teeth,' Ethel said, 'that he was almost fifty years old and *married* to me. I told her if she had a problem, she needed to take it up with him.'

Ginger gripped the bag of chocolate chips so hard it threatened to pop.

Mrs. Guy crossed her arms over her chest. 'Y'know, Ethel, I told you about him a while ago. I don't know how you've put up with him for so long. What did Landon's no-good ass say?'

Ethel shook her head. 'You know I called him up right after I dismissed her off my damn porch. He apologized profusely and said he'd take care of it.' Mrs. Guy rolled her eyes. 'He told me that he'd pick me up for church on Sunday morning like always.' Ethel's voice wavered. 'He never showed, and when the police came later that day . . . I knew something was wrong.'

Mrs. Guy drew closer to her friend. She glanced around then asked, 'You think she had something to do with it?'

'I know she did,' Ethel said flatly before releasing a cough that shook her entire body. 'That girl killed my husband.'

Ginger backed away slowly, her heart pounding so hard it hurt. She barely registered Alexis calling her name at the end of the aisle.

Inside her bag, her phone buzzed:

You ruined our lives. Now we'll ruin yours.

Ginger's breath came fast and shallow. Her hands shook as she held her phone, dread curling low and heavy in her stomach.

We? The cold boot of reality slammed into her. The Caldwells had found her.

She flipped the phone around, showing her cousin.

'That's it. I'm callin' Terrance,' Alexis said, bringing her cell phone to her ear.

Ginger realized that her priorities had to change from now on. It wasn't about finding Landon's killer anymore. She couldn't outrun her truth forever.

Chapter 26

Austin

By the time Austin made it to Prime Society he was already too late. The newest spot in town should have been alive, music spilling out of the front door with laughter curling off the rooftop patio. Instead, red and blue lights pulsed against the tree-lined street like a warning flare. Two Cinnamon Falls Police Department patrol cruisers sat nose-in, parked horizontally across the road like barricades. Yellow police tape fluttered from a street sign, snapping in the evening breeze.

Austin slowed in his truck just as he reached the turn near Diamond Jack's Casino, making a quick left into the connecting parking lot.

This was not good. He hurried into the casino, showing his I.D. at the door and pushing through the entrance. Inside, Diamond Jack's was buzzing, alive in an atmosphere all its own.

The air hit him first, perfumed with citrus layered

over the earthy undertone of cigar smoke and expensive cologne. The plush wine-colored carpet was springy beneath his boots, the casino thrumming with controlled chaos. Slot machines chimed and chimed again, coins clattering like applause. Laughter burst from a blackjack table. Somewhere nearby, a woman squealed in victory.

For a half second the urge hit him to feed a few spare dollars into the nearest machine to try his luck, but he had to find Natasha. Something was happening next door at Prime Society and he had to find a way to get around the police barricade. The restaurant and casino had to have been connected by a breezeway somewhere in the building, and he hoped that there was still a way through that hadn't been blocked off by police.

Austin weaved through the crowd. He played a game of 'Excuse me' and a few bonus rounds of 'Sorry 'bout that' until he reached the elevator. He rode it up with a couple who were too lovesick to notice someone else was in the elevator with them. When the doors slid open, he made a right, confident he'd found the corridor toward Prime Society, but he walked straight into a uniformed officer with a mean scowl and too little patience. The officer planted herself squarely in his path, arms crossed, expression carved from pure irritation. Her gel-slicked hair gleamed under the fluorescent lights, shellacked beneath her CFDP hat.

'Can I help you?' she asked flatly, hooking her thumbs in her belt loops.

Austin lifted his hands and added a slur to his words for dramatic effect. 'Ssssorry, I thought thisss was the way to the bathroom.'

She didn't blink, just pointed one finger with an extra sharp red nail over his shoulder, her glossy lips pursed. 'You passed it.'

Austin didn't need to turn around to know that the restroom sign was directly behind him. 'Wrong turn,' he joked, shrugging his shoulders.

Her returned smile was thin, the kind that warned he was already on borrowed time. Austin ducked into the empty bathroom and stood by the sink, gripping the porcelain edge, counting his breaths for a total of three minutes, long enough not to look so suspicious. Once he slid out of the bathroom, the officer was further down the hall, her back turned as she conferred with someone unseen.

Austin doubled back toward the elevator and punched the button for the roof. When the doors opened at the top floor, he was welcomed by the cool evening air and silence. He was surprised to find it empty, save for a lone bartender, leaning against the railing, a limp joint resting between his fingers. Austin would have missed him entirely if it weren't for the pungent smell and the smoke curling around his hiding place.

'Bar's closed,' he called to Austin without turning around. 'We open at six. You've got about fifteen more minutes,' he said, flipping his wrist around to read his watch.

'I'm with the police department,' Austin said smoothly, the lie sliding off his tongue easier than it should have. 'Does that stairwell take me back down to Prime Society?'

The bartender startled, straightening immediately. 'Oh, my bad.' He crushed the joint beneath his shoe, giving Austin a sheepish look, his cheeks flushing. 'Yeah, just down here. Second floor.' He stepped aside quickly so that Austin could pass, giving him a toothy grin.

Austin smirked as he dipped inside the stairwell and took the steps two at a time. He paused at the second-floor landing, peering through the narrow rectangular window at the door.

Prime Society was swarming with uniformed officers. Some snapped pictures, others dusted and conferred in clusters. The bar looked gutted, chairs overturned; little yellow tents marked spots along the bar top.

No one looked up as Austin spun the doorknob and eased inside the door. He stayed close to the wall, shoulders hunched despite his height, hoping that his black fleece jacket and dark wash denim would help him to blend in. Given his stature he could have passed for a plain clothes officer if anyone bothered to look twice, which thankfully, no one did. His eyes swept the building for Natasha, but could not find her in the crowd.

He heard Terrance Chambers' voice first, carrying over the low murmur of the scene. He was close, just a few feet away. Austin mustered up the courage to peek around the corner and found Terrance questioning a young, visibly nervous bartender. He twisted a rag in his hands, shifting his weight from one foot to the other.

'Walk me through her routine again,' Terrance asked, calm but relentless.

The young bartender swallowed, his Adam's apple bobbing in his throat. 'Natasha clocks out around eleven. Sometimes earlier if it's slow, or later if we're busy. Her boyfriend usually picks her up.' He gestured vaguely.

Terrance whipped out a piece of paper, holding it up to the bartender's face.

'Is this the boyfriend?'

The bartender twisted the rag tighter, his hand growing white around the edges. 'Yeah, that's him.'

'What's he pick her up in?'

'A big white delivery truck, it's hard to miss. He drives for Valley View.'

'He picked her up every night?' Terrance pressed.

'Most nights,' the bartender said with a shrug. 'They'd leave together, that's all I know.'

Someone else said, 'That lines up with what we pieced together in Landon's manifest.'

Austin turned, keeping his head down, his heart pounding. He and Ginger had figured that much out together. They weren't too far behind the police. He whipped his phone out of his pocket to text Ginger when a sudden grip clamped down on his shoulder.

Austin spun around to face the person, ready to spit out another lie about the elusive restroom when he came face to face with Jesse Shaw. His stomach dropped.

'Well,' Jesse said, snapping off a pair of latex gloves, eyes sharp. 'Looks like someone's lost.'

Austin exhaled slowly.

Jesse asked, 'Wanna tell me what you're doing here?'

'Same as you,' Austin replied. 'Getting to the bottom of Landon Lawson's murder.'

Jesse shuttered his eyes closed and clamped his thumb and pointer finger over his nose. He whispered to himself, 'Does a police investigation mean anything anymore?'

'I'll leave,' Austin started. 'I just wanted—'

'To help Ginger, I know, I get it. But you need to get out of here before someone sees you.'

'Me?' Austin scoffed. 'I'm a patron of this establishment who got a little too tipsy and turned around. My good friend here, top cop Jesse Shaw, is walking me back to the casino.'

Jesse rolled his eyes and grabbed Austin under his arms like he was an unruly guest, dragging him toward the exit, which was no easy feat. The men were similar in build, but since Jesse hadn't grunted or broken a sweat yet, Austin realized he wasn't doing enough during his workouts. He needed to get on the Jesse Shaw workout routine stat. They passed groups of policemen all of whom gave Austin the briefest of glances, shaking their heads, before returning to their conversations.

Jesse planted Austin at the exit.

'What are you all doing here?' Austin mumbled.

Jesse's expression didn't soften. He grunted, voice low, 'We're canvassing.' He sighed, rubbing a hand over his jaw. 'Raines thinks the murder weapon might've been ditched here.'

'Did you find anything?'

'We're still looking. Natasha was the last confirmed person to see Landon alive,' Jesse replied. 'We'd be idiots not to turn over every stone.'

'What about Ginger? Is she cleared then? You must have Natasha in custody if you're doing all of this—'

'She's next to be questioned.'

The words landed like a punch.

'Come on, man. This has got to be like, harassment or something,' Austin snapped. 'You just said you've got a suspect, but you're still circling Ginger. Why?'

Jesse's eyes flicked toward the crowd of officers who were still busy canvassing. No one was looking their way. 'Raines doesn't do tunnel vision when it comes to murder. She's thorough. She looks at everything, everyone, all at the same time. And she doesn't like being lied to.'

'Ginger didn't lie,' Austin said instantly.

Jesse studied him for a long beat. 'You sure about that?'

Austin bristled. 'Of course I'm sure. I asked—'

Jesse's eyes searched the floor. He huffed out a deep breath. 'Did she tell you . . . everything?'

Austin clamped his mouth shut, his jaw tightening. The noise of the bar seemed to drop away, leaving only the low buzz of the lights overhead and Austin's heart beating in surround sound in his chest.

Jesse looked at him sympathetically. 'Talk to your girl, man. I don't want to be the one to—'

Austin shook his head defiantly. 'She's got nothing to lie about.'

Jesse sighed. 'You want the truth? Or you wanna stick with whatever version she told you?'

Austin hesitated, just for a second, toying with the idea of either pulling out his cell phone and calling Ginger right then, or punching Jesse Shaw in the face. He couldn't decide.

'Yes,' Austin growled, his curiosity getting the best of him.

Jesse leaned in, lowering his voice. 'Her name isn't Ginger Mills.'

The floor tilted underneath Austin's feet.

'It's Virginia Millford,' Jesse continued. 'Reported missing out of Fulton County since March of this year. She was engaged to Harrison Caldwell, son of Elias Caldwell.'

Austin blanched. 'The jeweler Elias Caldwell?'

Jesse nodded and added, 'The family is offering a hefty reward for her return, or their family heirloom they're positive she's stolen. Atlanta PD is gearing up to make their way to Cinnamon Falls as we speak.'

Breath left Austin's lungs in a rush of air, leaving him heaving.

Jesse glanced over his shoulder then back at Austin, his voice lowering. 'If they find her, you could be charged with harboring. You need to go before Raines sees you.'

Austin didn't argue. He didn't ask questions or defend Ginger. He turned and walked out, his thoughts splintering.

Virginia.

Missing.

Reward.

Stolen.

Harboring.

Go.

All the moments replayed in cruel clarity: the texts she flinched at, the palpable fear in her eyes. The way she looked at him like she couldn't decide whether she wanted to stay or run at the same time.

Austin trudged through the building toward his truck. The commotion from the casino didn't affect him anymore, all of it background noise to the thoughts that collided in his mind.

Ginger had lied to him. Not only that, she'd put his safety at risk.

With a lead foot, Austin floored it back to Cinnamon Falls. Normally, he would have taken the scenic route, rolled the windows down, and let the scent of the wild cinnamon trees seep into the cab, something that brought him comfort, grounding him. But he barely registered as they whipped past his speeding truck in dark streaks.

Austin didn't slow for the curves. He didn't notice the evening's waning sunlight, stretching shadows long and thin across the road. All he could see was her, standing in his kitchen wrapped in his sweatpants that hung low on her toffee brown hips. He had desperately wanted to kiss her this morning. And that was the problem because beneath that rampant want had been a splinter of doubt; that voice in the back of his mind, nagging at him – the question he couldn't answer: *Who was Ginger Mills?*

A part of him wished he was the kind of man who acted on impulse instead of caution. Recklessness had its perks. It would have been easier. But reason had saved him before. It'd kept him upright when Samantha left. It'd kept him from falling off the edge when his father's accident turned his world inside out. It just wasn't doing him any favors tonight.

The house lights were on when he pulled into the driveway. It was a sight that he'd grown fond of the past few days. It meant Ginger was home. It meant laughter, warmth, someone waiting. Tonight, it twisted the knife deeper.

He threw his truck into park, his stomach in knots, hands gripping the steering wheel. He thought he would have cooled down by now, he hadn't. The anger was sharper, cut with disappointment so deep it made his chest ache.

Give her a chance to explain, a small voice urged.

But how many chances had he already given her?

They'd spent days together. Shared meals. Shared space. She'd sat at his family's table. She'd laughed with his sisters. She'd listened to his father's stories. And not once – not once – had she mentioned that Ginger Mills wasn't even her real name.

Virginia. It didn't even fit her personality. Or maybe it fit her too well, Austin didn't know.

Inside, the house smelled distinctly of chocolate. Butter was resting on the living room sofa, his sleepy yellow eyes blinking up at Austin when he walked through the front door. Austin scratched at his head absently as he passed, barely registering the cat's low purr. As he rounded the couch, he could hear Ginger humming in the kitchen while she worked. He leaned against the doorway, taking her in before she noticed he'd arrived.

She had jeans on today, Austin observered. Not his high-school sweatpants. Her hair was down, effortlessly glossy curls cascading over her shoulders. Her lips were painted with a soft pink lipstick that made her complexion glow. Mascara darkened her lashes. Austin's eyes slid over to the island where a dinner setup was waiting: two plates, two wine glasses. What was the occasion? A conversation? A confession? Another performance? A chance to lull him closer with more lies?

With oven mitts too big for her hands, Ginger pulled a large chocolate cake free from the oven. She turned and bumped the oven door closed with her hip. That was when she noticed him. She looked up and froze, her smile flickering before settling back into place.

She looked hopeful, a little nervous, like she'd been waiting for him.

'Austin, hey.' She gestured to her cake. 'I remember you said you liked chocolate so I—' She stopped short, eyes narrowing. 'Are you okay?'

No, not even close.

'No, Virginia. I'm not.' He watched as color drained from her face. 'You lied to me,' he continued, the words tasting bitter as they left his mouth. 'You lied about everything, who you are, what you're doing here in Cinnamon Falls. You dragged me – dragged my family – into something dangerous.'

Anger and hurt tangled in his chest until he couldn't tell one from the other. The image of police lights outside of Prime Society flashed through his mind; Jesse's voice, his disagreement with Bones just a few hours ago, the weight of the truth crashing down on him all at once, his heart crumbling in his chest. She'd lied to him. She'd embarrassed him.

Hurriedly, she placed the cake down on the island, stripping the mitts from her hands. 'I was going to tell you,' she said, panic edging her voice. 'Today. I set everything up so we could talk—'

'You should've told me sooner,' he said, shaking his head. 'From the start. Or when I asked you just this morning if someone was going to show up to my house.'

'I didn't know how,' Ginger pleaded. 'I didn't want to lose—'

'Don't,' Austin cut in. 'Just don't.'

He couldn't hear another almost-explanation, couldn't stomach another half-truth dressed up as fear. Silence stretched between them, thick and suffocating, while he toyed with the idea of telling her everything he'd learned from Jesse.

Butter wandered into the kitchen, meowing loudly, hungry and oblivious. Austin watched him for a second, grateful for the distraction. Truthfully, he was starving too, just not for food. He'd give anything to go back to an hour ago when he was standing in Prime Society. He should've minded his business; gotten in his car and returned home, ignorant and happy.

'I think you should leave,' Austin said finally, his heart aching. He funneled some strength into his voice. 'I called Morgan. The room is still available for you at the Daffodil Inn.'

Ginger fisted her hips. 'You're kicking me out?'

'Atlanta police are looking for you, Ging . . . I mean, Virginia. The first place they'll check is here.'

'Who would connect me to you?' Ginger had gone white as a sheet. Her eyes filled but didn't shed.

'We've been gallivanting all around town, looking for answers about Landon. Everyone's seen us together. It's only a matter of time before someone opens their mouth and they end up on my front porch.'

'Alright,' she conceded. 'If that's what you want.'

'I do,' Austin lied.

She nodded, swallowing hard, then headed toward the stairs.

Austin scooped Butter up and held him close. Butter licked Austin's chin while he scratched between the kitten's ears.

'Gonna miss you,' he whispered. Butter let out a soft mew and buried his face in Austin's neck.

Footsteps thundered down the stairs and Ginger appeared in the kitchen again. A suitcase, Butter's carrier, her purse crammed in her arms. She reached for Butter and placed him gently inside his carrier, her hands shaking. She'd packed too quickly, like she'd practiced this kind of goodbye before.

'I can come back for the rest?' she asked. The tears had disappeared. Her armor was back on.

'I'll drop it off in the morning,' Austin replied.

She steeled her chin and nodded, passing Austin without looking back. At the door, she paused. 'I hope you know I never meant to hurt you, Austin.'

He couldn't look at her. If he did, he might break.

The door closed behind her with a final, echoing click. The sound ricocheted through the house. Silence rushed in to fill the space she'd occupied just moments before; it felt cavernous without her.

Austin's gaze drifted over to the island, the untouched plates, the waiting, unfilled wine glasses. The cake she'd baked, still warm and perfect. Beside it sat a glossy chocolate topping ready to be poured over the top. A beautiful future that had been one honest, maybe uncomfortable conversation away.

It hit him all at once; the restraint, the hurt, the exhaustion of choosing logic over his feelings. He told himself that he was doing the right thing by protecting himself and his family. But the truth of it was, he hadn't pushed her out because she'd lied. He'd pushed her out because letting her stay meant risking everything; his safety.

The pressure built behind his eyes. Sorrow twisted into something jagged: anger. At her. At himself. At the fact that he couldn't fix this with a couple of screws and a steady set of hands. He hated to admit to himself that there was nothing he could do. This was unfixable.

Austin grabbed the nearest glass and hurled it against the wall. It shattered on impact, exploding across the kitchen floor, the sound cracking through the quiet like a gunshot.

All he wanted to do was protect her, and instead,

just that fast, he'd lost her, standing alone in the wreckage of a choice he wasn't sure he'd ever forgive himself for.

Chapter 27

Thursday

Austin

Austin took the long way out to Old Man Milton's farm, the back roads still slick with morning dew, fog hanging low over the fields. The sky was barely awake, soft gray bleeding into a pale gold. The quiet pressed in around him hard enough that he couldn't outrun his thoughts. He didn't reach for the radio, and the engine of his truck wasn't loud enough to drown them out. It was just him and the steady hum of tires on asphalt and the ever-present ache deep in his chest.

He fisted a yawn. He had tossed and turned all night, sleeping only in snatches. Every mile he traveled carried him further from the kitchen where Ginger stood with that damn cake in her hands; those too-big oven mitts, hope settling over her face, right before he'd snuffed it out. The image of her looped in his mind against his will: the way she'd looked at him, the hurt in her eyes. He'd done that.

He clenched the steering wheel, jaw tight.

He'd told himself last night that he'd done the right thing. There were lines you didn't cross, no matter how good the person on the other side of it seemed. Protecting his family meant pushing her away before things got worse.

But the words didn't stick. Beneath his anger, there was a sick feeling of regret that sat in his gut, refusing to move. He hadn't given her a chance to explain. He'd reacted the way he always did when something felt out of his control – with a hammer. He shut it down, locked it out, and would deal with the fallout later. It was easier for him to be decisive than to be vulnerable.

Except later was now. Austin swallowed, eyes burning as the fog thinned and the road stretched ahead of him. The quiet morning had a way of bringing hindsight and stripped his excuses bare, and the worst part of it was that he didn't miss the truth. He missed her.

He glanced over at the cake balancing in his passenger seat, along with the rest of Ginger's belongings she hadn't packed last night. He navigated his truck into the gravel driveway of the Daffodil Inn, hoping someone would be awake. It was early, just a bit past seven a.m., but he couldn't stand to look at anything that belonged to Ginger. It hurt too much.

He trudged up the steps, the cake heavy in his hands, and knocked softly. Through the glass-paned door he noticed someone in the hallway. Mr. Taylor, Morgan's father, opened the door quickly and stepped into view.

'Good timing, I was just about to head out. Is this for our new guest?' he asked, eyeing the belongings in Austin's hands.

Austin nodded. 'Yes, sir. I promised to deliver the last of her things.'

'Would you like me to wake her up?' He gestured over his shoulder toward the staircase that led to the second floor.

Austin knew Ginger was up there, just a few feet away. He could feel her. He imagined her sprawled across the bed, her legs tangled in the sheets, Butter sleeping directly on top of her head. His heart ached at the memory.

'No, sir.' Austin managed a smile. 'I just wanted to make sure she got her stuff.'

'Uh huh,' he responded, his doubtful eyes roaming Austin like he could see the pain written all over his face. 'We'll make sure she gets it. I can't guarantee she'll get any of the cake, though.'

Austin knew he should've laughed. It was the polite thing to do, but he could barely muster the smile on his lips.

'Thanks, Mr. Taylor. I appreciate it.' He handed over Ginger's belongings, his hands now just as empty as his heart and his home.

'No problem, son. Give Katherine and the girls my love. Matthew hanging in there?'

'Better than ever,' Austin replied.

'Good to hear it,' Mr. Taylor responded.

'I'll, uh, get out of your hair,' Austin said, turning toward his truck again. 'Gotta meet my dad over at Old Man Milton's.'

'Oh, yeah?'

Austin nodded. 'We're sourcing some wood to make Mayor Tate's new custom desk for his office. Mr. Milton told my dad he had some oak that he was willing to part with.'

'You'd better get a move on then. Old Man Milton and those roosters wake up before Jesus.'

That made Austin chuckle, and he was grateful to feel something other than regret. 'Sure thing. See ya 'round, Mr. Taylor.'

'Oh, will I see you at Landon's funeral tomorrow?'

'Yeah,' Austin replied. 'Ms. Ethel asked me to be a pallbearer.'

Mr. Taylor nodded his head in approval. 'You've turned out to be a good young man. Tell your daddy I said so.'

Austin gave him a tight smile. 'Thanks, Mr. Taylor. I will.'

Old Man Milton's farm sat at the edge of Cinnamon Falls, acres of land rolling outward until the weathered fence line blurred into the horizon. Autumn had settled over the property like a warm quilt. The fields glowed in shades of amber and rust, and a scatter of maple and oak trees had begun shedding crisp leaves that skittered across the grass whenever the wind picked up.

The property felt endless in the quiet light, stitched together by dirt roads worn smooth by decades of truck tires, booted feet, and the steady impact of hooves. The air carried the familiar smells of turned earth, drying hay, and wood smoke drifting from somewhere nearby. Three curious and rambunctious roosters, Shadrach, Meshach and Abednego, roamed the grassy end of the property, Milton's self-appointed overseers. Stacks of rough-cut lumber rested on sawhorses, boards sorted into neat piles, waiting for the right hands – the right project – to bring them to life.

Austin pulled in behind his father's truck. He wasn't surprised that his father had beaten him there. Matthew's chair was positioned beside a long slab of wood laid across sawhorses; he had a travel mug of what had to be coffee in one hand. He looked solid this morning in his standard uniform: jeans, flannel jacket bearing the Jacobs & Sons logo, and heavy boots.

'Morning,' Matthew said, squinting up at Austin against the sun. 'You look like hell.'

Austin grumbled a greeting, grabbing his own thermos filled with coffee out of the truck. 'I feel worse.'

Matthew nodded toward an incoming vehicle. 'We can talk about that later.'

Moments later, a blacked-out SUV arrived. Mayor Sterling Tate stepped out of the backseat, polished as ever in pressed slacks and a sport coat that didn't look like it belonged anywhere near dirt or sawdust. He glided across the field, his Oxfords gleaming, and shook their hands with fervor, flashing a politician's smile.

Sterling Tate was a far cry from former mayor Asad Lyons, a born and bred Cinnamon Falls resident, but Tate's reputation was solidifying among the town. When Maximillian Greaves' scheme to buy the Daffodil Inn unraveled, Tate made sure the town knew exactly on which side of the law he stood on. He publicly urged the District Attorney to pursue the maximum sentence allowed for the murder of Eleanor Langford, determined to send a clear warning to any crooked developer with plans to encroach on Cinnamon Falls: they'd be wise not to get too close.

'Morning, gentlemen,' he boomed, his voice echoing across the property. 'We're missing someone,' he observed.

'Milton's around here somewhere,' Matthew responded. 'Feedin' chickens or whatever farmers do first thing in the morning. He told me we could get started without him.'

'Fair enough,' Tate smiled again. 'Let's proceed, shall we?'

They walked the stacks together, Austin running his hand over grain patterns while his father talked wood like poetry; how walnut's elegant, rich grain would stand the test of time, and how pine would be too soft for a man trying to rebuild the town's trust.

'What about this one?' Austin suggested, stopping at a wide slab of dark walnut.

'Strong. Grounded,' Matthew said, slapping his hand on the grain. 'Won't warp under pressure.'

Sterling nodded, impressed. 'Speaking of staying grounded . . .' He turned to Austin. 'How's Ginger doing? Chief Raines has informed me that she's become a bit of a . . .' He searched the ground for the words. 'Flight risk.'

Hearing her name thrummed the cords in Austin's heart. 'I wouldn't know. I haven't heard from her.'

Matthew took a loud sip of his coffee and Sterling studied him a beat too long. 'Is that so?'

'Yeah,' Austin said evenly.

'Hm.' Sterling clapped his hands together. 'Raines should be reaching out to her soon for some quick follow-up questions so let's hope she gets things sorted.' He turned back to the wood. 'Let Milton know I'll take the walnut. You'll send me the bill?'

Matthew nodded. 'We'll work it out and I'll have it over to you before the weekend.'

'Excellent,' Sterling responded. 'Gentlemen, I have to run. I trust I'll see you tomorrow for Mr. Lawson's homegoing?'

'We'll be there,' Matthew said.

Before long, Sterling Tate was gone. When the dust settled, Matthew let out a low whistle. 'You know it's probably illegal to lie to the mayor, right?'

'It's not like I was under oath.' Austin rolled his eyes. 'Besides, it's the truth. I don't know how she is.'

'What changed? Last time I saw you, you had hearts in your eyes and two new roommates.'

'It's complicated,' Austin said instead, not wanting to relive last night's nightmare. He pushed his father toward the direction of their vehicles.

'Lay it on me,' Matthew responded, his arms spread wide. 'I've got nothing but time.'

'We had an argument,' Austin admitted. 'I asked her to leave.'

His father let out a low whistle. 'That must've been one hell of an argument.'

'Yeah, well, she lied to me, even after I asked her for the truth, flat out.' He paused and watched his father scrub a hand across the back of his neck. 'Don't tell me you agree with her.'

'I'm on your side, always,' Matthew said. 'It's just . . . I looked that young lady in the eyes. I could tell there was something she wasn't telling you, and it must've been something big for my generous son to put her out on her ass.'

'I didn't put her out,' Austin clarified. 'She's safe.'

Matthew chuckled, bringing the mug to his mouth

again. 'You want to know how I know you still love her?'

Austin scoffed. 'Dad, come on—'

'Even after she hurt you, you didn't turn her in.'

'I know what everyone's saying about her, alright. But I know she didn't kill Landon.'

'I'm not here to judge you, son. I told you, I'm on your side.' Matthew rested his hands on the wheels of his chair then asked, 'Why don't you come over for dinner tonight? I don't want you alone.'

'Nah.' Austin shook his head. 'I just need some time to sort everything out.'

'We're your family, Auzzie. Your mother and the girls love it when you come around . . . when we're all together.'

Austin shifted his weight, suddenly uncomfortable beneath his father's gaze. The gravel crunched under his boot as he looked away toward the far fence line. 'I know, it's just . . .'

Matthew sighed softly, the sound carrying more patience than frustration. 'Ever since the accident you've been avoiding me.'

Austin turned back sharply. 'How can you say that? I'm at your beck and call. Anything you need, I get it done.'

'Oh yeah,' Matthew responded. 'I'll give you that. You're busting your ass to keep the business afloat.' He readjusted, sitting up straighter. 'But that's not the same thing as showing up.'

Austin didn't respond and Matthew's voice softened. 'I want my son back.' The words landed like a blow to the chest. He'd never heard his father be this candid about his emotions. 'Me getting stuck in this chair . . . Maddie heading off to college . . . Samantha leaving right after . . .' He shook his head slowly. 'It was like the whole family scattered overnight. And somewhere in all that, you went into hiding.'

Matthew continued gently. 'Lils winning Cinnamon Queen brought us all together again. For the first time in a long time it felt like the house was full.' He paused, watching Austin carefully. 'As much as you don't want to hear it, Ginger brought you back, too. Tell me the other night didn't feel like the old days,' Matthew said tenderly. 'Like we were a real family again.'

His father was right. Tuesday was special. The house had been loud and warm, alive in a way Austin hadn't realized he'd missed until he was standing in the middle of it.

Austin shook his head, trying to brush off the weight of the moment. 'Let me find out this chair is making you soft.'

Matthew barked out a laugh. 'I'm serious. I haven't seen your mother that excited to cook dinner in ages. When's the last time we sat on the deck, huh? Or watched a movie on the big screen?'

Austin didn't answer. He didn't have to. Matthew leaned forward slightly. 'We're stronger together. I know you know that.' He studied his son's face. 'I can see the hurt in your eyes. Let us be there for you for a change.'

Austin swallowed down the emotions rising in his chest. 'I didn't appreciate you talking to Ginger about Sam. That was my business to tell.'

Matthew kissed his teeth, maneuvering his chair around Austin. 'We just had a Hallmark moment right there and *that's* what you want to talk about?'

'Everything isn't a moment. You gotta stop watching all those romance movies with Mom,' Austin laughed. 'And yes, that's what I want to talk about.'

'You're my son, your business *is* my business. And she deserved to know.' He rolled closer. 'You hadn't brought a woman to the house since skinny little Samantha. I needed to feel her out, make sure she understood you came from good stock.' Matthew thumped his fist against his chest with a grin.

'Some good that did,' Austin grumbled.

'So, where is she?' Matthew pushed.

Austin didn't look at him. 'I don't know.'

'Good.' Matthew nodded, satisfied.

'Good?' Austin questioned.

'If you were truly done, you'd tell me where she was hiding out.' Austin opened his mouth to reply but his father beat him to the punch. 'I don't know what happened last night, but I do know this. I know a scared woman when I see one. Scared people don't need judgment, they need protection. I know you'll do the right thing by Ginger.'

'I already did enough damage,' Austin muttered.

Matthew reached out and Austin lowered to meet his gaze. His father clapped a hand on his shoulder, his grip firm. 'Then fix it. I know you know how to do that.'

Chapter 28

Ginger

Ginger woke beneath a canopy of white linens as morning light filtered in through curtains she didn't recognize. The room was washed in blues – the walls, quilt, and even the hand-painted trim, too bright for an early morning. It made her wince and her head throbbed dully, as if her body had already captured everything her mind was trying hard to forget.

For a moment, she lay still. She listened as the Daffodil Inn came to life around her, the unfamiliar creaks of the old cabin stretching awake: the distant rush of running water, the soft thud of footsteps below. Somewhere, a hum of conversation brewed and birds sang, cheerful and unbothered, threading through the cracked window.

Then, memories started rushing in. Austin's voice; hurt, furious, and final. *I think you should leave.*

Ginger's throat tightened as she rolled onto her side.

She pressed the heels of her palms to her eyes, breathing through the sharp ache blooming in her chest.

There was so much she hadn't told him: the conversation she overheard at Guy's Grocery, Natasha showing up at Ethel's door in the middle of the night. She didn't get a chance to tell him about the texts, or about the life that'd she been trying – fumbling – to shape into something safe enough to hand over. The story, her truth, had been ripped from her mouth and twisted before she had the chance to tell it.

And now she'd lost him.

Ginger had never been much of a crier, but this town was making her soft. She felt the urge to bawl in this moment. Back home, crying over a man would have earned her hours of teasing from Camille.

But Austin wasn't any man. He was a good one, a rare one. Someone that she actually liked, not for what he had or could give her, but for who he was when no one was watching.

Austin was steady, kind, and infuriatingly earnest. He showed up without being asked. He looked at her like she was worth protecting. He saw stars in her eyes and not the scars she carried.

She dragged in a shaky breath and pushed herself upright. She thought about calling him, but that meant she'd have to look at her phone, and she hadn't done that since the night before, the threatening texts still there. She'd have to deal with it sooner or later. Later, preferably.

A countdown sounded in the deep recesses of her brain.

Her gaze flicked to the empty pillow beside her, then the foot of the bed. No Butter. He'd probably escaped and wandered off in search of Daphne, Morgan's dog, or breakfast, whichever came first. After a quick shower, Ginger pulled out some clean clothes, settling on the pair of Austin's oversized sweatpants that she had packed in a rush. She pressed the soft fabric to her fingers, the cotton smelling faintly like his soap, before pulling them on and cuffing the waistband at her hips so they didn't drag on the floor. She followed the smell of brewing coffee downstairs, her heart heavy, knowing that with each step forward, she was walking away from a life that no longer included Austin.

The kitchen was already alive by the time Ginger made it down the stairs. Butter skidded across the hardwood floor, batting playfully at Daphne's tail while a black cat lounged regally atop a chair, unimpressed by the chaos unfolding beneath it. Butter tumbled into a potted fern, emerged triumphant, a leaf blocking his eyes, and darted back toward Daphne again.

The chef, Lionel, noticed Ginger first. He had been the first person who greeted her last night when she arrived on the porch of the Daffodil Inn with a tear-streaked face and an unruly kitten. He had taken her things without question and ushered her inside the quiet cabin, noting that her room was ready for her. An excited border collie had barreled down the steps, sniffing her furiously before allowing her to move any further.

'You'll have to excuse the security,' Lionel had grumbled, grabbing the dog under the collar and wrestling her away from Ginger. 'Daphne gets a little excited by new people.'

Now, he stood at the kitchen island, a flour-dusted apron tied tightly around his middle. His goatee was expertly trimmed, his eyebrows creased, an expression that suggested he was perpetually grouchy. He was slicing an enormous and familiar cake, the knife gliding gracefully through the glossy ganache.

'She lives,' he said, not taking his eyes off the chocolate masterpiece.

Both Nia and Morgan looked up from the kitchen table at the same time. Their eyes surveyed Ginger from top to bottom. The pair were buried under wedding chaos: photographs, papers, and jewel-toned fabric swatches spread around, along with what looked to be a seating chart. Nia sat cross-legged in the chair, her hair piled atop her head. Morgan leaned back, sharp-eyed and observant, lips pursed in a way that let Ginger know she had something to say.

'Your cat is crazy,' Morgan announced in a flat tone.

Ginger scooped Butter up before he could make another pass at Daphne, planting soft kisses to the top of his head. He wriggled indignantly in her hands.

'He's a sweetie,' Nia countered, reaching over to scratch Butter between the ears. The black cat seated beside her let out a low, offended groan.

'And who's this?' Ginger asked, gesturing toward the grouch wrapped in black fur beside Nia.

'She's Midnight,' Nia responded brightly.

Ginger dipped Butter toward her. 'I'm Ginger, and this is my cat, Butter.'

Midnight stared through the pair of them, then turned away and began to lick her paws, uninterested.

'She said it's nice to meet you,' Nia supplied.

Ginger squinted. 'Why do I get the feeling that she didn't say that at all?'

Morgan snorted. 'And you would be correct. Midnight hates everyone, don't take it personal.'

As if on cue, Midnight leapt gracefully from the chair and disappeared down the hallway, tail flicking in disdain. Lionel placed two generous slices of decadent chocolate cake in front of Nia and Morgan.

Ginger froze, finally registering what she was seeing. 'Is that . . . ?'

'Yessss,' Morgan said, moaning happily once the cake reached her mouth. 'And it's absolutely sinful. Forget Ben Carson, girl, you're the one with the gifted hands!'

Nia nodded vigorously in agreement once she got a mouthful of her own. She pointed her fork at the cake. 'Honestly? Austin is an idiot for not wanting this. I can eat that whole thing right now. You put your foot in this, girl!'

Ginger's heart twisted a little more. She'd meant to share that with him. It had been her apology, everything she hadn't had the courage to say whipped, baked, and glazed. Austin must have dropped it off early before she'd woken up. She guessed he was really done with her now. There was no going back.

Nia reached across the table and squeezed her hand. 'This cake is the best thing I've tasted in my life. Will you make it for my wedding next weekend?'

Ginger blinked. 'You want me to bake your *wedding* cake?'

'Would you prefer me to get on my knees? I'm literally begging you,' Nia said, her hand squeezing Ginger's tighter.

A small, fragile piece of Ginger unclenched. 'Of course, yeah,' she said, a smile breaking over her face, tight and unfamiliar for all the crying she'd done. 'I'd be honored.'

Morgan grinned, nudging Nia in her side. 'Harboring a fugitive has its perks.'

'I am not a fugitive.'

Nia whistled, pursing her lips in disbelief. 'That's not what *I* heard.'

Ginger frowned. 'And what did you hear?'

'Lots.' Nia looked up at her sheepishly. She flattened her hands to the table, her words coming out all in one breath. 'That you left your man with no explanation, changed your name, and sold your ring to Milo Penn of *all* people, to open that bakery of yours.'

There it was, Ginger's truth laid bare. The truth she'd been hiding from Austin had already spread all around town if Nia, Cinnamon Falls royalty, had heard it. Great.

Ginger bristled, but Nia continued. 'I'm not judging you girl, but your life's a mess. No shade, I've been there.'

Ginger laughed weakly. 'A mess' was putting it lightly. 'And you're not worried about "harboring a fugitive"?' Ginger air-quoted the words, turning her gaze to Morgan.

Morgan waved her off. 'Please.' She jammed her thumb in Nia's direction. 'I've got protection. CFPD wouldn't dare mess with us right before the Queen's wedding.'

Lionel cut in. 'Not like it would be the first time you two been arrested.'

The women both swiveled in their chairs, facing him. 'Excuse me, I'm a changed woman,' Nia clarified, holding her left hand in the air, showing off her engagement ring. Lionel huffed in a way that showed he wasn't convinced.

They spun back around to face Ginger. 'Besides,' Morgan continued, 'my man's brother has a lawyer on speed dial who can get anybody outta jail, fugitive or not.'

Relief fluttered through Ginger. She was sort of protected, but that still didn't change the fact that Austin was gone, her name was still connected to a murder she hadn't committed, and her ex was circling. She joined them at the table. Lionel placed a slice of cake in front of her along with a steaming mug of coffee.

Ginger dug in. The ladies were right, it was a damn good cake if she said so herself. Moist in all the right places, the ganache decadent and silky smooth. It was her best work.

'Give it time,' Morgan said after a little while. 'I know it hurts right now, but just let it settle. You did the hard thing. You started over. Don't dwell on the mistakes.'

'You were in survival mode. You sold that ring to restart your life,' Nia added softly. 'I've done my fair share of running too. You're not alone in that.'

'I just didn't know what else to do,' Ginger mumbled around a forkful of cake.

'But Milo Penn?' Morgan added, grimacing. 'Girl, what were you thinking?'

'I needed the money,' Ginger admitted, her eyes downcast. 'I didn't care how I got it, or what it cost.'

'Getting it back is going to cost you double,' Morgan said flatly. 'The man's a snake.'

Ginger had never thought about getting the ring back. But if she returned the ring then she could make things right with the Caldwells. The texts would stop, they'd call off the manhunt, and Austin might forgive her.

The forgiveness part was a long shot, but she at

least had to tell her side of the story to his face. He deserved that.

Nia flinched as her phone let out a high-pitched ping, signaling that she'd received a notification.

'Jesse,' she said, studying the screen. 'He says turn on the TV.'

All four of them jumped up and jetted toward the living room. There first, Morgan fished for the remote in the couch cushions and punched the power button. The wood-paneled television struggled to life, the picture swimming into view.

'The news,' Nia directed while Morgan flipped between channels frantically.

She landed on the right one and silver-haired Elaine Matthias filled the screen, her expression dubious. The ticker at the bottom read: SUSPECT APPREHENDED.

Elaine's gravelly voice reported, 'I'm here at the Cinnamon Falls Police Department where Natasha Montgomery has been brought in for questioning in connection with the murder of delivery driver Landon Lawson. It is alleged that the two were in a romantic relationship and Ms. Montgomery, a bartender at the new restaurant-lounge Prime Society, was the last person to see the victim alive . . .'

Morgan gasped, clasping her hand over her mouth.

Ginger's heart sank. 'No,' she whispered. 'How?'

'You know her?' Nia questioned.

Ginger shook her head. 'I talked to her just a few days ago. She told me she and Landon were together.

She said the last time she saw him was Friday night. She—'

Nia held her hand up and gawked. 'Wait, you talked to a *murder* suspect? Alone?'

Morgan jumped in. 'No wonder the police lookin' for you! You just making your way around Cinnamon Falls, missing person be damned.'

'I know the Wonder Twins are not talking,' Lionel quipped. 'You two were gallivanting all around The Falls trying to figure out what happened to Rosie. And if I recall correctly, the two of you were also perp-walked into that very station.'

'That was different,' Nia sniffed and Morgan nodded emphatically beside her best friend.

'She seemed like a nice girl. She was so heartbroken about Landon,' Ginger said.

'I'd be heartbroken if my sugar daddy just died too,' Lionel added with a cackle, slapping hands with Morgan on the couch.

'I think their relationship was deeper than that,' Ginger countered. 'She found out he was married Friday night and when I talked to her she looked really hurt. She told me she broke up with him, but that was all.'

'Did you expect her to tell you the truth?' Morgan scoffed.

Ginger explained, 'Landon was killed on *Saturday* night. Why didn't she just kill him right then and there on Friday when she found out?'

'Maybe she needed time to make a plan,' Nia suggested, shrugging her shoulders.

Ginger shook her head, still not convinced.

On the screen, there was a wide shot of Natasha getting walked into the police department. Several officers created a barrier around her, forcing back the reporters who were clamoring to push a microphone into her face.

Nia turned to face Ginger. 'Looks like you're in the clear!' she whooped, then snapped off the TV. 'Jesse said Prime Society will be restored in time for the bachelorette party tonight! Everything is working out just like you said it would!'

Nia and Morgan embraced, their happy squeals piercing Ginger's heart.

But for Ginger this wasn't over. Not by a long shot.

Hours passed slowly. The bright light softened into a pale autumn afternoon, shadows stretching across the living room floor as the sun dipped behind the trees. Outside, a breeze rattled the branches of the tree in the yard, sending the occasional crisp leaf skittering across the porch. The faint scent of chocolate mingled with the steady warmth of the house.

Nia and Morgan had barely moved from the kitchen table, entrenched in their debate about which photos would be chosen for the centerpieces, and which ones belonged in the slideshow. The table had slowly filled with evidence of the day's passing – empty coffee mugs and plates that held crumbs of sandwiches.

Ginger joined them, but she felt slightly removed, like she was experiencing everything from behind a pane of glass. Watching Nia and Jesse's love story unfold through photographs made her heart ache. When had she become this woman?

Ginger fingered a shot of Nia and Jesse, heads thrown back in unguarded laughter. Jesse's arms curled easily around Nia's waist while she playfully swiped ice cream across his nose, her smile easy and wide. There were other people in the background of the photo, blurs of movement and color, but the center of the shot belonged to the pair of them, lost in their own world, unaware of anyone else around them like nothing else mattered.

Morgan glanced over, her face softening at the picture. 'That one has got to be included, don't you think? Just look at them.'

Ginger turned the picture around to Nia and her eyes sparkled in a way that let Ginger know there was a tender memory attached to it. She reached for it and Ginger handed it over.

'I love this picture of us. This was at the Daffodil Jubilee. If Landon wasn't in the background I'd include it.' She hesitated, then tossed it back into the pile of unused photographs.

'You sure? It's such a nice picture,' Ginger said. 'You guys look really happy.'

Morgan agreed. 'We can get Jabari to photoshop Heather and Landon out. I'm sure he wouldn't mind making a few edits.'

Ginger pulled the photo toward her again and concentrated on the background. Morgan was right. Just off Nia and Jesse's shoulder stood Heather Hughes and Landon Lawson. Landon had one hand braced behind Heather's back, and he looked to be whispering in her ear. Whatever he'd been saying made Heather blush, her hand cupped over her mouth delicately. But it was something else that stopped Ginger cold.

Heather was wearing a red striped sweater; not just any red either. It was the same deep, unmistakable shade as the fibers found in Landon's truck.

Ginger's mind spun. There were plenty of women in Cinnamon Falls with red sweaters – the color was everywhere, in scarves, jackets, it painted the whole town during the fall season.

Ginger thought back to her lunch with Heather just a few days ago, recalling how fiercely Heather had defended Landon.

What if . . .

The thought crept in, impossible to ignore. What if Natasha wasn't the only woman seeing Landon? The thought of Natasha sprouted another memory in her mind.

The Saturday after the Fall Festival, when she went to Cinnamon Grove in search of cat food, Heather had stood in the aisle while they conversed, her lips painted a deep, passionate burgundy. The color had stood out then, too.

She recalled Natasha's words about the lipstick mark with startling clarity: *It was dark red, like old ladies wear. Some shit I'd never be caught dead in.*

'When did you say this picture was taken?' Ginger asked, the fine hair along her arms rising as a chill swept through her body. Her pulse thundered in her ears.

Morgan glanced up, puzzled. 'Just a few months ago. Why?'

Ginger knew what she had to do next. She pulled out her cell phone and scheduled a dinner date tomorrow night with the only person who could give her answers: Heather.

Chapter 29

Austin

Fix it, I know you know how to do that.

His father's advice was like a specter following him all the way down Old Man Milton's driveway, onto the two-lane highway, into town, and finally into First Falls Bank.

Mrs. Josephine Simmons had been his family's accountant for as long as he could remember. She'd sat in the last office to the left. Austin followed the cranberry-colored carpet worn thin from footsteps until he reached her door. She sat behind her desk signing a stack of papers with a flourish.

'Jo-Jo!' Austin greeted, not waiting for an invitation to walk inside.

Mrs. Josephine looked up, her expression folding into a warm smile. 'Auzzie! Look what the cat dragged in! Matt didn't tell me you were stopping by today.'

She rounded her desk and enveloped him in a hug that always smelled of fresh linen and peppermint.

'I'm here on a solo mission, Jo-Jo,' Austin explained, settling into the chair across from her. 'Hopin' you can help me out with something.'

She eyed him cautiously, her thick eyebrows scrunched into a frown framing her black and white striped glasses. 'Why don't I like the sound of that?'

'I need to make a withdrawal.'

'Alright,' she replied, an edge of curiosity in her voice. Mrs. Josephine pushed aside a stack of papers and reached for her calculator, fingers hovering over the worn keys. 'How much?'

Austin pulled a folded piece of paper out of his pocket and slid it across the desk. Usually, he didn't handle the finances for Jacobs & Sons, that was his mother's lane. Austin built things, kept them running. So he could only guess how much Ginger's bakery had cost based on the labor he'd performed.

Josephine unfolded the paper and balked. 'Austin, where do you expect to get this kind of cash on short notice?' He didn't answer, thinking the solution was painfully obvious. 'Certainly not here. I'd have to put in a request to Asheville Regional, and even then—'

Austin didn't have time for that. 'How much can I get right now?'

'Twenty grand, max,' Josephine replied, her eyes narrowing.

Austin bit his lip, his mind whirring. That wasn't enough. Not even close.

'Austin Jamal Jacobs, what are you mixed up in?'

He tried to answer, but Mrs. Josephine cut him off, pointing her pen at him. He hesitated, which was the wrong thing to do with Mrs. Josephine.

'And don't you dare tell me it's nothin'. I've known you since you were knee-high to a grasshopper. You've never come in here asking for money like this unless something's wrong. And you smell like trouble.'

'It's for a friend, Jo-Jo,' Austin admitted. 'She's in a tough spot.'

Mrs. Josephine looked down at the amount on the paper, then up at Austin again. 'A friend, huh?' she inquired sarcastically. 'And what does your father have to say about this . . . *friend*?'

'He's the one who gave me the idea.' It wasn't a total lie, but it wasn't the total truth either.

Mrs. Josephine sat back in her chair, crossing her arms over her chest, never taking her eyes off him. 'You were always a terrible liar,' she muttered. Finally, she sighed, giving in.

'You can take the twenty today. I'll give you a form to take to Asheville in the morning. You'll have to sign some papers, lots of them, and they'll have the rest prepared for you.'

'I kind of need it like, now, Jo-Jo.'

'Oh,' she said slowly. She straightened up in her seat, a smile tugging at the corner of her mouth. 'You're serious about this girl.' Austin didn't answer because he didn't have to. She glanced down at the analog clock on the edge of her desk. 'I'll call Franklin

Spears over at Asheville Regional,' she said, already dialing. 'I suggest you get a move on. If you leave now, you might catch him before lunch. And trust me, you do not want to come between that man and a Caesar salad.'

She hooked the phone between her neck and ear and scribbled something on a slip of paper, handing it over. 'Take that to Brandi at the window.'

'Thank you, Jo-Jo. I owe you.'

'Mm-hmm, that's what all you Jacobs men say.' Mrs. Josephine shooed him out of her office. As Austin walked away he heard her say, 'Hey, Frank, it's Josephine Simmons at First Falls . . . I know it's close to your lunch hour but I need a favor . . .'

There was only one place to sell a family heirloom in all of Cinnamon Falls, at Milo Penn's second-hand shop, A Penny For Your Thoughts. If Austin returned the ring, Harrison could call off his dogs in pursuit of Ginger and then there'd be one less person out for her blood. Settling the matter of her guilt or innocence in the eyes of Cinnamon Falls residents was another issue entirely.

That thought prompted another: since when had the police cared enough to cross county lines to locate a piece of missing jewelry? Elias Caldwell could have them in his back pocket, attaching a hefty payday for the return of the ring. Tonight, Austin was hoping to cut off the Atlanta PD before they reached town.

A Penny For Your Thoughts sat at the very end of Pine Street, an older part of Cinnamon Falls that most people didn't frequent, sandwiched between a cash checking office and a video rental store that had closed down decades before, its sun-faded sign still boasting 'New Releases'. The whole place had an unsanitary feel, like something dusty out of yesteryear that could have been swept into a proverbial trash can and set out on the street for pick-up.

Milo Penn was a snaggled-tooth crook notorious for price gouging and Austin knew this conversation wouldn't bode well with the man who'd haggle the white off rice. A renowned vagabond before settling down in Cinnamon Falls, Milo Penn used to be the weird guy who lived in a run-down trailer at the edge of town. He collected all sorts of knickknacks from all his so-called hitchhiking adventures; things he traded for, things he coaxed out of desperate lenders who needed the cash more than their prized possession.

Penn didn't fall for begging or pleading, or even tears. He only spoke in cash. Yesterday, Bones mentioned it was a ring that Ginger had pawned, and if she really was Harrison Caldwell's soon-to-be wife, Austin knew it would be a tough negotiation for its return, but he'd come prepared. He didn't know when he became this person, but there were lots of things that post-Ginger Austin had done these past few days that would've shocked pre-Ginger Austin, including this.

He stepped inside, immediately accosted by the sharp stench of raw onion, and the unmistakable smell of something else. He grinned, his plan falling into place easier than he expected.

He inventoried the place: glass cases lined the walls with clocks that had stopped ticking years ago; chipped, forgotten china; knock-off handbags; and faux designer clothes. There were racks overflowing with jeans, jackets, sweaters, T-shirts, and skirts. A foggy glass counter held gold chains dull with fingerprints, silver and gold rings that had long lost their luster. Austin couldn't imagine that Ginger's was one of those.

Penn was seated behind the counter eating an enormous deli sandwich. Thick white rings of onion spilled out of the sides of soft deli bread, dropping onto the thin paper underneath with a splat. Penn hustled to grab some of the runaway onion, and bright yellow mustard oozed between his pudgy fingers when he grabbed it. His tongue flicked out of his mouth, displaying a mess of mushed food trapped between his lips. He brought his fingers to his mouth and looked up with low, bloodshot eyes just in time to see Austin approaching the counter.

'Well I'll be damned. If it isn't Jacobs and one son slumming it on the old end.' Milo hesitated, thinking better of licking his hands in front of Austin, and found a stack of napkins next to his keyboard. He threaded the napkins through his thick fingers and smiled, revealing a row of black gums gripping a handful of yellowed, brittle teeth.

'What can I do you for?'

'A friend of mine sold a ring to you. I'm here to get it back.'

Milo took the time to wrap up his sandwich, before releasing a belch that should have been categorized as a weapon of mass destruction.

'Let's hope I ain't already sold it. What's it look like?'

'Don't know,' Austin admitted, fanning away the stench, which did no good in the stuffy store. 'Her name's Virginia Mills, some folks call her Ginger.'

Milo coughed out a patronizing laugh. 'Oh, that sounds *real* familiar.'

He ducked behind the counter, pulling out an overflowing three-ring binder. He opened one side, hefting a mountain of carbon copy receipts to the other. He trailed a dirty fingernail down a receipt log and stopped on a line Austin couldn't read upside down.

Milo tapped the page with finality. 'Yeah, she was here a while back.'

'I'd like to purchase whatever she pawned.'

'Purchase? No, no, no. This bad boy's staying right here with me. I'll let ya take a look at it, though.'

Milo licked his lips hungrily. With great effort, he

heaved himself off the chair and reached under the counter. He fiddled with something out of Austin's sight before planting a small velvet box between them.

Austin felt a strange tightening in his chest, not knowing what to expect. This was a Caldwell jewel, not something he could buy from a department store's website on sale. With the cash weighing heavy in his bag, he braced himself for whatever he might find.

Austin flipped the lid open. The light from the grimy overhead bulb caught the stone, betraying its opulence. Inside, perched on a cushion, sat a large, vivid green emerald surrounded on both sides by crescent-shaped diamonds. Its color and clarity made the room feel alive, catching the dull light with quiet intensity. Smaller diamonds ran around the band set in cool platinum, the metal gleaming underneath the proud stone.

'Almost ten carats that is.' Milo nodded to the emerald. 'She said it's been in the Caldwell family for centuries, and that there emerald came from Zambia.' He fumbled over the pronunciation. 'You ever been there?'

Austin shook his head.

'Me neither. Looked it up m'self. A realllll pretty thang.'

'I'll take it for what she sold it for.'

Milo blinked like the thought of a transaction at this moment was foreign.

'Maybe you didn't hear me, Jacobs and one son. The ring's not for sale.' He snatched it from Austin's fingers, shoving it back into the cushioned box. Austin felt his heart go with it. 'You comin' in here thinkin' you can bargain with me on a piece like this? This platinum alone . . .' he jerked his thumb toward the box, 'that emerald is worth more than what you or that cripple's got in the bank.'

And there it was: the version of Milo Penn that Austin knew well. The scum of the earth. 'What I bought it for was chump change. I'd rather sell it to somebody with much deeper pockets.'

Austin leveled Milo with a glare, deciding what to do next. He could reach over the counter, grabbing a fistful of the man's greasy shirt and make him repeat what he said around a knuckle sandwich. But he used his words instead.

Austin squared his shoulders. 'You remember last winter?' he asked, fixing his gaze on the man's triple chin.

Milo frowned, brow tightening. 'Lots happened last winter—'

'You were very grateful to have me fix that busted pipe in your back room.' Austin pointed his chin over Milo's shoulder. 'Funny thing, I remember finding something else in that back room.'

His voice was calm, but there was steel underneath it. Enough to drain the color from Milo's face and make the fine hair on his arms stand up. Austin didn't need to spell it out, but he would, just this once; a warning.

Austin nodded toward a narrow hallway over Penn's shoulder. 'I remember that a certain someone was growing a particular kind of . . . plant.' A curious glow peeked out under the black curtain that doubled as a privacy door, a handwritten sign that read EEMPLOYE'S ONLY taped to the rod. He had smelled the marijuana the second he walked in and Penn's enormous sandwich and bloodshot red eyes only confirmed it. 'The ring is hot.' Austin nodded to the box gripped in his fingers. 'Atlanta PD is on their way right now to snatch up Virginia. It won't take long for them to find you.'

'You wouldn't,' Milo growled, his chins rippling with anger.

'I don't mind snitching, not one bit. So, I would hand the ring over if I were you.'

Milo gulped, eyes flicking to the door as if law enforcement was ready to swarm his establishment any second.

Austin continued. 'Matter of fact, I won't even have to, someone will do it for me. Landon's funeral is tomorrow. The whole town will be there. All I need to do is let it slip to ol' Bones that Milo Penn's got that exotic—'

Milo held his fat fingers up in surrender. 'Fine!' he snapped, flipping out Ginger's signed receipt. Austin grinned.

'I want cash, too. Not a check or some IOU.'

'Milo,' Austin tsked. 'You sadden me.' He pointed to the logo on his chest. 'We built half of Main Street. You know I'm good for it.'

Austin flipped the banded bills out of his bag and slid the correct amount across the counter.

Milo eyed Austin, then the cash, before hungrily seizing it, dragging it behind the counter and away from eyesight.

'Alright,' Milo said, eyes shifting quickly. 'You go on now.' He shoved the velvet box back toward Austin and waved him off like a man trying to act casual after losing a bet.

Austin pushed the box into his pocket and turned away. At the last second, he pivoted, grabbing Milo with a force he didn't know he possessed. He tangled his fist in the collar of Milo's greasy T-shirt, cutting off his airway. One-handed, he pulled the bulbous man over the counter, his belly flattening to the glass.

'Let . . . me . . . go . . .' Penn choked out, but Austin squeezed tighter. Milo's jowls reddened beneath his ashy, cracked skin.

'And the next time you reference my father, you'll sing his praises. Got me?'

Wordlessly, Milo nodded. Austin released him with a heave and Penn scampered behind the counter, staying put.

Austin turned toward the door after saying, 'A pleasure doing business with you.'

He walked out into the chilly night, ring secured, blood pumping with relief. He didn't regret a thing besides the fact that he hadn't punched Milo square between the eyes.

Chapter 30

Austin

All it took was one Google search and Austin had found Harrison Caldwell. An old link led to a social media post from some place called The Gilded Room. Its description read: Where Legacy Meets Luxury.

Austin tapped on the picture to make it bigger. The man's square face filled the screen of Austin's phone, in polished, high-resolution confidence. It showed a man with deep skin, salted temples, a blinding white smile, a tailored suit that probably cost more than Austin's truck, and one arm draped possessively around a woman who'd, without a doubt, slept in Austin's sweatpants just the night before: Ginger.

Only, she didn't look like Ginger here. This woman was Virginia.

She looked immaculate. Curated. Polished. Her hair was blown smooth and glossy, disappearing in long sheets behind her back. Her makeup was flawless, drawing out the intensity in her eyes, her posture angled just so toward the camera. She wore a sleek black dress that silhouetted her slim frame. It screamed money and access. Her tight smile gave Austin the impression that she was there merely for decoration, not romance. She looked like a woman being displayed.

The caption read:

Spotted last night at #TheGildedRoominATL
@ecaldwellthejewel @virginiais4lvrsxo
Thursday nights are for ladies who know their worth.
Private tables. Invite Only.
#AtlantaElite #PowerCouple #ThursdayattheGilded
#OldMoneyEnergy

Austin stared at the screen longer than he intended, his concentration on Ginger. He tried to tap her username but the link was broken, her profile long since deleted. So this was the version of Ginger the world knew. The one Harrison had claimed.

What had he done to her? The Ginger he knew was a world away from this version of her. In the months he'd known her, she'd never worn a dress, only ripped jeans or, lately, his sweatpants. Her hair had never been blown out straight. It was always in bouncy curls pulled up into a bun, or down around her shoulders. Her unblemished skin glowed without the makeup that aged her in the picture. Her lively brown eyes were darker, almost black in the low lighting.

He scrolled to the comments beneath it: fire emojis,

champagne glasses, and admiring remarks from people whose last names sounded like they belonged on skyscrapers or law firms. People who lived a life and spoke a language that was foreign to Austin; one he didn't care to know or learn.

Austin swallowed hard. In his mind, the image of Ginger yesterday morning crashed violently into the version of her on the phone. The woman who was barefoot in his kitchen, wearing his sweatpants, hair trapped in a lopsided bun, laughing softly while Butter weaved between her ankles. She was real. Warm.

The woman on the screen looked like she was trapped in a glass, drowning. His thumb hovered over the photo, grazing the pixels that made up her cheek. Then he locked the phone with a sharp click.

The Gilded Room was nestled inside Magnolia Reserve Country Club. A place that sat behind wrought-iron gates that opened with quiet efficiency, with manicured hedges clipped on either side of the driveway. When he arrived, four hours later, Austin eased his truck close to the bumper of an unsuspecting elderly woman in a slow-moving ruby red Cadillac, painfully aware of how out of place his mud-caked pick-up looked against the sparkling luxury sedans and glossy SUVs idling in the circular drive.

No one stopped or questioned him when he maneuvered around the building, which opened up into a small parking lot. Austin backed into a space that had the best view of the entrance and the shortest distance to the exit, just in case.

The club itself was all white columns and wide verandas, Southern grandeur and tradition on full display. Subtle touches of the season softened the elegance; tailored arrangements of garlands featuring eucalyptus, magnolia leaves, and deep magenta dahlias were interwoven between white pumpkins that lined the entry steps. Glass lanterns flickered at the base of each column. Crystal chandeliers glinted through tall, arched windows. Laughter spilled out into the evening from the attached terrace in soft, curated bursts as couples conversed around the heated lamps; the faint scent of cinnamon and spiced cider perfumed the air. The women wore tasteful backless dresses almost like the incoming chill wouldn't dare penetrate a place as carefully insulated from the outside world as this.

Fix it, his father had said. Austin exhaled through his nose, not knowing how he would approach this situation. He wasn't there to fight. He was there to atone, something Ginger hadn't had the chance to do. He fished the velvet box from his pocket, taking one last look at the stunning emerald, just as a shiny black Rolls-Royce cruised into the parking lot.

He spotted Harrison Caldwell immediately. He emerged from the backseat: tall, lean, and effortlessly elegant in a gray tailored blazer and slacks. He handed his champagne flute to someone inside the car, then held his hand out for a woman.

Austin saw her legs first. Light brown calves supported a pair of thighs that fought the fabric of a deep ruby dress that matched the ring on her finger. Her hair was styled into a sophisticated roll at the back of her head. Though breathtakingly gorgeous, her expression was the same as Ginger's had been in the photo – taut, steely, and unforgiving.

Another man stepped out, taller only by a hair. Theodore Caldwell. The woman must be Camille.

Austin watched their car get valeted as the group made small talk with the black-and-white-suited workers, who waited patiently while they filed inside.

Austin shoved his door open and trekked through the parking lot in quick strides before doubt could catch up to him.

Once inside, a woman offered to take his jacket, white gloves held out, ready to receive his offering.

'I, uh, won't be long,' Austin stammered, pushing his hands into his pockets.

To his left, a concierge tapped on a tablet. Austin realized a little too late that he was being catalogued from the ground up. The man's eyes trailed him slowly, from his work boots, to his faded jeans, to his fleece jacket, then finally face to face.

'Reservation?' he asked, in a clipped tone behind pursed lips.

'No,' Austin admitted. 'I'm here to meet someone.'

The concierge looked like he'd swallowed something sour. 'The Gilded Room is members only—'

'I won't be long,' Austin countered, craning his neck above the crowd. The Caldwells couldn't have gone that far.

'I'm afraid that won't be possible—'

'I just need to have a quick conversation with Harrison Caldwell.'

That did it. The concierge did a motion with his fingers, flourishing his arm in the air with a twist. Two burly men appeared from the shadows, subtle but unmistakably hired as security. One of them stepped forward, his eyes too close together, his thick neck disappearing into a collar buttoned under his massive head.

'Sir, you need to step aside.'

Austin didn't move, only widened his stance.

'I just drove four hours,' he said evenly. 'I'm not leaving without a word with Mr. Caldwell about Ginger Mills.'

The guard's hand closed around his elbow and Austin planted his feet.

That was when he saw her. Samantha stood just a few feet away. She was mid-laugh at the bar next to Harrison, her head tipped back slightly, the sound caught somewhere between carefree and rehearsed. For a split second Austin didn't recognize her. Time had softened the edges of the girl he remembered, replacing them with something sleeker. It was like he was hearing her with different ears.

Her dress shimmered; a cascade of silver beading that clung to her slim, taupe frame. The neckline swept high along her throat, delicate chains layered across her chest like armor, each strand glinting as she shifted. She looked expensive, like she'd always belonged here.

Her arm was threaded loosely through Harrison Caldwell's and the sight hit Austin like a sudden drop in the road. Samantha lifted her glass, but froze halfway to her lips as her eyes landed on Austin. She looked from the security guard beside him, then back to Austin again. He saw her laughter die and something twisted in Austin's chest. Seeing her now should have meant nothing, but it didn't. He told himself the feeling creeping under his ribs wasn't jealousy, it was irritation, or maybe anger, that his long night was about to get even longer.

Samantha held his gaze before she lowered her glass. The noise of the bar seemed to dim around them, and Austin realized he wasn't the only one surprised to see the other still standing.

Austin watched as Samantha untangled herself from Harrison's embrace, heels clicking sharply against the floor as she moved toward the entrance.

'What is going on?' she demanded as she approached.

The concierge looked like he might collapse on the spot. 'Mrs. Caldwell, this gentleman—'

'Mrs. Caldwell,' Austin scoffed, shaking his head slowly.

At the bar, Harrison turned, his expression shifting

as the scene unfolded, from confusion to irritation, then something deeper. Darker. Camille and Theodore turned too, curious to see what had captured Harrison's attention.

Samantha stopped a few feet from Austin, her composure cracking at the edges. 'What are you doing here?' she hissed. 'How did you even find me?'

'Relax, Mrs. Caldwell. I'm not here for you,' Austin spat.

'I'm not . . . we're just dating—'

'You didn't correct the concierge,' he shot back. 'But I can't call you that?'

'You know damn well what I'm trying to say—'

'Excuse me.' Camille stepped forward and pointed directly at Austin. 'You. What are you doing here?'

The security guard still had a hand on Austin's arm. Austin shrugged him off and straightened his clothes where they'd wrinkled under the man's grip. He met her gaze.

'I need to talk to your brother-in-law about Ging—Virginia Millford.'

Camille went pale and Theodore noticed instantly. He moved forward, placing himself slightly in front of Camille, his body angling protectively between her and Austin.

'Camille,' he said, suspicion hardening his tone. 'Do you know this man?'

'No,' she replied quickly. 'But he said he's here about Virginia.'

Theodore studied Austin carefully as if he was trying to place where he'd seen Austin before. 'He's not on the force. At least, I've never seen him before. You with APD?' Theodore asked.

Camille ignored him, stepping closer to Austin, her voice dropping low enough that only he could hear.

'Is she—' The question caught in her throat. 'Is she okay?'

'Yes,' Austin replied. 'She's okay.'

The tension in Camille's shoulders released as she exhaled a shaky breath. Then she turned sharply toward the security guards lingering nearby.

'Move,' she ordered coldly. 'Now.' They disappeared as quickly as they arrived, leaving the four of them standing in the sudden heavy silence of the party, Harrison Caldwell watching from across the room with growing interest.

The other Caldwell brother swaggered over. His attention fully locked on Austin, eyes raking him over.

'S'there a problem here?' Harrison asked, his voice smooth but edged with irritation as he looked between the four others. Samantha brushed her hair out of her face, returning to her beau's side faithfully.

'He says he knows Virginia,' Theodore filled his brother in without taking his eyes off Austin.

Harrison's expression piqued with interest, then he extended his hand. 'Harrison Caldwell,' he said coolly. 'And you are?'

Austin took the offered hand. Harrison's grip was

firm; the kind of handshake meant to establish dominance before a single word was spoken. 'Austin Jacobs.'

Harrison's mouth twitched. 'Never heard of it.' He gave a sideways glance at Theodore, who gave a lazy shrug.

'I've heard plenty about *you*,' Austin replied.

Harrison's brilliant smile thinned enough to reveal the steel beneath it. 'So,' he said slowly, 'where is Virginia?'

'She's safe,' Austin said.

'That wasn't the question,' Harrison countered. He stepped forward, moving around his brother and sister-in-law, closing the gap between them, teetering on the edge of entering Austin's personal space without touching him. A deliberate move, a test. Something dark flashed across his face. Austin saw it happen, the moment understanding dawned behind his eyes. He held his ground, every nerve in his body thrumming with anticipation.

'Let me guess,' Harrison said quietly, his voice dipping low enough that the insult carried weight. 'You're sleeping with her.'

Camille gasped, her delicate fingers flying to her mouth.

Austin didn't flinch, didn't dare look in Samantha's direction. 'I can't imagine why that's your business anymore.'

Camille stepped forward, cutting through the tension before Harrison could respond.

'Then what're you doing here?' she demanded, her voice tight with urgency. She searched Austin's face. 'Where is Virginia?'

Austin reached into his jacket pocket and for a moment no one spoke. He pulled out the small velvet box. Harrison's eyes lit up in recognition, watching as Austin flipped the lid with his thumb to reveal the deep green, emerald ring within.

Harrison's hand moved instantly but Austin was faster, leaving the man grasping at the air. 'Where did you get that from?' he demanded.

Austin shook his head, holding the ring by his waist. 'Call the search off and it's yours,' he said, unblinking.

A current of electricity ran through his body. 'We good?'

The men were silent, standing nearly nose to nose now. Harrison's fury simmered beneath the surface, his shoulders tight, his breathing measured. Austin remained still, composed, unmoving.

'We're good,' Harrison conceded, swallowing down the fire Austin knew was building in his chest. He snatched the box from Austin's fingers, bringing the ring to his face, examining it in close detail.

Austin didn't wait. He turned to leave and could feel their eyes burrowing into his back.

'Yo,' Harrison called out. Austin stopped but didn't turn. He didn't have to, to know the look on the man's face. He followed Austin, his voice quieter now, colder. 'Take care of her.'

Austin kept walking and didn't look back.

Outside, the air hit him, warm and fragrant. For a stolen moment, Austin breathed, letting the noise of the bar fade behind the club's heavy doors. Then he heard a distinct sound: the click-clack of heels on concrete getting closer.

Camille appeared beside him, slightly out of breath, tears shining in her eyes.

'Wait, Mr. Jacobs,' she said. Her fingers grazed the sleeve of his jacket, stopping him. 'Please.'

Austin turned to face her, full on. Up close, she was even more striking, but the polished Caldwell confidence was gone. She had the solemn look of a woman who hid her sadness deep within.

'She called me, y'know. Just a few days ago. Tuesday night?' She turned, looking at the doors behind her before returning to Austin. 'Said that someone had been texting her some crazy shit. She wanted to know if it was me.' Her eyes dropped briefly to his empty hands. 'You show up here with my family's ring in your pocket.' Her voice hardened. 'Where is she? Is she here with you?' Her eyes swept the parking lot, cataloging every car, as if Ginger might appear from behind one of them.

What crazy texts? Austin wondered.

'She's in Cinnamon Falls—' Austin said, almost finishing his sentence with 'with me'. Camille's gaze snapped back to his face. 'She's safe,' he added. 'She talks about you a lot . . . I'm assuming you're Camille Caldwell.'

That earned him half a smile. 'How'd you know?'

'You're cut from the same cloth,' Austin replied.

Camille draped her arms around herself, the chill breaking through the fortress of warm air that surrounded the country club like a bubble. Theodore appeared in the doorway. Even from a distance Austin could feel the tension radiating off him.

'Camille!' he called for her.

Her feet turned to go, but her eyes stayed on Austin's.

Austin remembered everything Ginger had told him about Camille; about the careful life she lived now, the one where every decision had its consequences. He nodded slightly toward Theodore standing in the doorway. Austin could feel the hate coming off him in waves.

'If you ever need some place safe . . .' Austin paused just long enough to make sure she understood and lowered his voice even further. 'We'd love to have you in Cinnamon Falls.'

Camille didn't respond, her steely gaze locked on his. Then, a small tilt of her head let Austin know she was listening; a single, nearly invisible movement, but Austin saw it, and he knew she understood.

'Camille!' Theodore's voice cut through the night again, sharper this time, and she finally turned.

Theodore embraced his wife once she reached the door, pulling her back inside.

Austin drove back to Cinnamon Falls with his

hands gripped tight on the wheel. He thought he'd feel victorious, on top of the world. Instead, it was an aching emptiness that crept back in, agonizingly slow.

He knew he'd done a good thing, settling Ginger's debt with Harrison Caldwell. But that didn't solve the mystery surrounding Ginger Mills. Camille had mentioned that Ginger had been receiving texts. She'd never mentioned them to him, which brought back the question that had sat squarely in his gut the last couple of days: *What else was Ginger hiding from him?*

Chapter 31

Ginger

When Ginger had left Atlanta, she hadn't thought about packing party clothes. She'd stuck everything she thought she would need in her suitcase, packing light, including only the essentials.

But now that Morgan and Nia had invited her to Prime Society for Nia's bachelorette party that evening, she realized she had nothing to wear besides a faded pair of black jeans and Butter's favorite black sweater he'd been using as a pillow since the day she found him.

Which was how she found herself standing in only her undergarments in Morgan's bedroom, while Nia and Morgan decided on an appropriate outfit.

'Absolutely not,' Morgan declared, yanking the black sweater from Ginger's hands and tossing it haphazardly on the floor. Butter pounced on it happily, burying his face into the folds. 'You are not wearing grief chic to a bachelorette party! I won't allow it!'

'It's all I have,' Ginger muttered, feeling more self-conscious by the second.

Nia laughed from the bed, lying sideways, zipped in a stunning sapphire blue satin minidress. The plunging neckline and ruching at the waist gave her an irresistible hourglass shape.

'Ginger, tonight is about celebrating love. Mine, specifically. We can't have you moping around in all black. Save that for Landon's funeral tomorrow.'

Morgan thrust an indigo wrap dress in Ginger's face. 'It's a little big for you, but we'll just wrap it tighter, no one will be able to tell. It sparkles, it's forgiving, and if you cry, it won't show, trust me.'

'That sounds very specific,' Ginger said, stepping into the dress. Morgan walked around her, tying the straps in a tight knot at her side. It had a tasteful slit, displaying a peek of thigh.

Outside, a horn blew, announcing that their ride was waiting.

'That's Will,' Morgan said with a smile. 'Let's go, ladies!'

Nia pushed herself off the bed and smoothed out her dress. Morgan grabbed her handbag and Ginger fastened Morgan's heels around her ankles. Thank goodness they wore the same size. She wobbled a bit before her glide returned, fluid and familiar. It'd been months since she'd had a reason to be in heels. Before she left Atlanta, she'd spent almost every day in them.

In such a short time, Cinnamon Falls had changed her life, and her wardrobe.

Outside, a midnight black car glimmered under the moonlight, idling in the driveway.

'Your chariot awaits,' Will said with a suave air, flourishing his arms over the classic car. His long locs were twisted away from his face, secured at the back of his head by a holder. The slim man was dressed impeccably in an all-black outfit.

Morgan pressed a kiss to his lips while Nia slid into the backseat after greeting Will with a hug.

'Ginger, right?' Will asked brightly. 'It's nice to see you again.'

'Likewise,' Ginger responded. 'Is this a Cadillac?'

Will nodded and puffed out his chest. 'It's a 1959 Cadillac Eldorado Biarritz Convertible. I restored it myself. It's all original parts, but custom paint—'

Morgan pushed Ginger toward the car. 'He could stand here and talk about his damn car all night. We've got places to be.'

On the ride to the party, Nia pestered Will with a litany of questions about Jesse's plans for his bachelor party that same night. But, despite the constant harassment, he kept his lips sealed.

By the time the ladies made it to Prime Society, Ginger was buzzing with anticipation. She hadn't partied since well before she'd left Atlanta, and she was ready to take her mind off everything for just a few hours. She didn't have to check the mirror in the car before getting out, she knew she looked amazing. Morgan had blown out her natural hair into soft curls that kissed her bare shoulders, and Nia had enhanced her features with a smear of shadow across her eyelids, blush over her cheeks, concealer brightening her under-eyes. Ginger swiped on lip gloss just as they approached the front door.

Prime Society glowed against the night. Bass heavy hip-hop music thumped through the walls, the vibration thrumming beneath their heels as they were escorted past the main bar to a private room tucked behind thick, velvet curtains.

A crowd of women Ginger didn't recognize cheered when Nia stepped inside, embracing her with tight hugs and cheers of unbridled joy. The only people she knew were Alexis and Angela, the receptionist from the police station. She looked different outside of her normal, bulky police uniform. Her layered, dark hair spilled over her shoulders in voluminous curls, and long lashes brought out the intensity of her eyes. She sported a teeny-tiny dress that showed off her shape. Ginger was surprised when she greeted her with the familiarity of an old friend.

'Ginger! So good to see you again!' she exclaimed, hugging her tightly.

The private space pulsed with low amber lighting, a curved leather banquette wrapping the room and a mirrored wall reflecting the bottles lined up behind their private bar. Overhead, a neon sign glowed.

Under a pair of pink lips it said: CHEERS TO BAD DECISIONS.

'Your man spared no expense tonight!' Morgan yelled to Nia over the music.

Alexis handed Nia her first shot and she promptly gave it to Ginger, pointing to the sign overhead. Nia's shot was quickly replaced, and Morgan raised her own glass to the crowd of gorgeous women.

Balancing on her toes in a pair of spiky heels atop a velvet chair, Morgan pulled her tight dress down around her ample hips.

'To Nia Bennett-Shaw! Cinnamon Falls royalty and wifey-to-be to an insanely ordinary man.'

Nia swatted at Morgan's legs. 'Morgan!'

Morgan sobered. 'In all seriousness, I am so glad I get to celebrate this moment with you. After everything we've been through together, I feel so blessed to witness your love persevering. Ladies, let's cheers to a lifetime of happiness, laughter, and love!'

Nia clinked glasses with her best friend, eyes shining. The women cheered and Ginger knocked her shot back before she could reconsider. They laughed, loud and free, and for the first time in days Ginger felt the knot loosen in her chest.

Music spilled out of the room as the night wore on. They danced until their feet hurt, laughed until their cheeks burned, and drank until they could no longer feel their hurting feet. Somewhere between her third cocktail and the last round of shots (which Morgan insisted were necessary for spiritual reasons) Ginger found herself slouched into the arm of the soft banquette, nursing a bottle of room-temperature water.

She wondered if the other ladies could feel the room slowly rotating. She wanted to ask but no one was paying attention, too busy egging on a woman who was showing Nia a move that she credited for making her first child.

'You're awfully quiet,' Morgan noted, sliding into the booth beside her, leaning into her side.

Ginger toyed with the bottle in her hand. 'I'm having a good time,' she started. 'Thank you, Morgan, for inviting me out tonight.'

'Better than you sulking in my living room while Lionel fed you endless slices of pity cake.'

Ginger opened her mouth to protest, but that was precisely how she had planned to spend her evening.

'Exactly,' Morgan laughed, knowing she was right.

Alexis slid in on the other side of her, pulling her slinky dress over her hips. 'You've got to stop beating yourself up, and don't tell me you're not thinking about Austin, because it's written all over your face.'

Ginger hated that it was that pathetically obvious. She was at a full-blown bachelorette party: great music, even better food, and an open bar, all the makings for an unforgettable night and still, she was miserable.

'I just . . . can't believe how much I fucked up.'

'Unburden yourself. Right here, right now,' Morgan demanded.

Ginger shook her head – a mistake because that made the room spin faster. 'I didn't leave Atlanta because of some nasty break-up,' Ginger admitted. 'My fiancé, Harrison, was like Prince Charming. He took good care of me, gave me anything I ever asked for.'

Morgan cut in. 'Yeah, I don't see the problem.'

'Exactly,' Ginger responded. 'No one did. But behind closed doors he was controlling . . . I couldn't go anywhere without his approval and, worst of all, I watched my best friend wither away. After she had her son, it got worse and let's just say—'

'You saw the writing on the wall,' Morgan finished.

Ginger nodded, tears springing to her eyes before she could stop them. 'I had to leave, Morg. I . . . I couldn't become that woman.' Morgan clutched her hand as she continued. 'I remembered Alexis telling my mom about Cinnamon Falls, a place so beautiful it looked like it came right out of a storybook. I came here in the middle of the night with only a suitcase, a couple of boxes of books, and my engagement ring. It was mine . . . I earned it. I spent weeks on Alexis' couch, hiding, terrified that he'd find me and drag me back to the estate, so I started going by my childhood nickname, Ginger.'

Alexis chimed in, 'I told her she couldn't spend her

life in fear. She needed a healthy outlet. Before Harrison, she used to love baking, even went to culinary school. So I asked her to bake a cake for Terrance's birthday. It was so good we convinced her to open a bakery that very night.'

'Then you sold your ring?'

'The next day,' Ginger said. 'I just wanted to feel like myself again, not some scared little girl afraid of her own shadow all the damn time. I wanted to be free, and the only thing that had ever made me feel like that was baking. What's the crime in that?'

A sob bubbled up in Ginger's throat. Before she could stop it, it clawed its way out, ripping through her chest, the tears spilling over. She tried taking deep breaths, which only resulted in hiccups between more gut-wrenching sobs; she was thankful the music covered her cries.

Morgan sat quietly, rubbing slow circles on Ginger's back.

When she'd quieted down some, Alexis muttered, 'Way to kill the vibe.'

Ginger punched her shoulder playfully, wiping her tears away with her other hand. 'I'm trying to be honest here.'

'You don't owe us anything. But have you told Austin all of this?'

'I wanted to last night, but I guess someone else beat me to it.'

Ginger watched as Morgan's eyes found Nia, who

was dancing on top of a table, belting out lyrics to a hip-hop song with Angela. Morgan nodded toward her best friend with a wistful expression.

'She was a runner, too, you know. When Sienna died, Nia left for Atlanta. I didn't hear from her for six agonizing years, and then Rosie died. A double fuckin' whammy, but as sick as it sounds, her death brought Nia back to me . . . to us . . . to Cinnamon Falls. If Jesse and Nia can work out their issues, I know you and Austin can too.'

Ginger shook her head. 'You didn't see his face last night. He was so angry with me.'

'Just give him some time,' Alexis assured her. 'If you really care about him, fight for him. Because let me tell you, he won't stay single for long. The women in Cinnamon Falls are like bloodhounds.'

Ginger sat up straight, her head swimming. 'What if he doesn't forgive me?'

Morgan raised the bottle of water to Ginger's mouth, making her take a sip. 'Then at least you'll know you tried.'

Ginger took a reluctant sip, glancing around the room at the love and laughter surrounding her. Something steady anchored her in place.

'Okay,' she said finally. 'I will.'

'Good, because I am way too invested in this love story.' Morgan pulled Ginger into a hug and nodded toward the water bottle. 'Now drink. We can be brave tomorrow. Tonight, we dance!'

Ginger gulped down the rest of the water and rooted herself in the moment. Finally, she held a night in her hands that didn't feel like an ending, but a fresh beginning. And she knew exactly what she had to do.

Chapter 32

Friday

Ginger

Ginger had a headache that spanned the length of her body. She cracked one eye open at a time and winced. Pale blue sunlight slipped through the sheer curtains. Her body felt like it was still slumped on the couch at the bachelorette party. Her tongue was sandpaper, her limbs heavy, and every movement felt delayed.

She groaned, rolling softly onto her back, the room swimming with her. 'I'm never drinking again,' she murmured. Butter tiptoed on the pillows behind her head before settling into a new position. His whiskers tickled her forehead as he released a deep, sleepy purr.

Today was Friday, Landon's homegoing service. Ginger slapped her phone, which was resting on the bedside table, shaking it awake to reveal the time. It was just before seven-thirty. She struggled to sit up, her brain feeling like she was underwater. Everything in her wanted to collapse back into bed, but she couldn't make Nia or Morgan late, especially not for this.

After an icy shower that made her nerve endings stand on edge, she felt marginally more human. Downstairs, Nia sat hunched at the table, sunglasses on despite being inside, nursing a mug of black coffee. Morgan looked equally in disarray as she leaned against the counter, chewing on a slice of burnt toast with the enthusiasm of a sloth.

'I hate everyone,' Morgan muttered.

Nia lifted her mug in solidarity. 'If I ever suggest tequila again, please bind my ankles and throw me into the river behind the house.'

Ginger sank into a chair, accepting her own mug of coffee that Lionel slid over to her. The coffee was strong, thank goodness, and steaming hot. Ginger took a tentative sip, thanking Lionel with a gracious tip of her head.

'Fun night?' Lionel relished, his voice too loud.

Ginger snorted, then winced. 'Define . . . fun.'

Lionel placed a hand on his hip, his lips pursed. 'Y'all are too young to be actin' like a bunch of old women. Who has a bachelorette party on a Thursday night anyway?'

'I didn't want to have one at all,' Nia admitted. 'Jesse and I were supposed to take a staycation instead. Go to Blue Ridge and see the mountains. You know, spend one last weekend together as just . . . Nia and Jesse before we become the Shaw family,' Nia finished with a far-off look.

Morgan rolled her eyes. 'I think I'm going to throw up again.'

Nia threw a napkin at Morgan. It caught the air instead and zigzagged to the floor, landing on top of Butter's head, cloaking his tiny body completely. He released a pitiful meow and Ginger leaned down, uncovering her cat.

'But . . .' Lionel rolled his hands, prompting Nia to continue.

'Well, Landon died. Jesse's been workin' overtime and couldn't get off so he paid for a room at Prime Society for me and the girls. Tonight, he's taking me to dinner. Let's cross our fingers no one else dies in Cinnamon Falls so I can get some quality time with my man.'

Her eyebrows wiggled suggestively and Morgan gagged behind her hand.

Back in her room, Ginger chose to wear one of Morgan's simple black shift dresses; modest and unassuming. She belted the middle, cinching her waist, and pulled her hair back into a low bun. She didn't have the strength to do much makeup beyond concealer and mascara. She hoped she wouldn't be noticed.

But that hope fizzled the moment she stepped inside the church.

All Saints Tabernacle, a small two-story white building, sat along a curved road. Cars of all kinds were parked along the street, some creating their own spaces in the fields of grass next to the church. Nia aligned her car behind another.

'Niles said he saved us some seats, so we'd better hurry,' Nia said, their modest heels clicking along the road as the ladies followed the crowd heading into the church. They ascended a set of concrete stairs that led to a set of arched double doors.

Pews were packed in from wall to wall, every cushioned seat filled. People lined the side aisles and stood along the back crowding the entries and exits. An organ near the pulpit bleated out a sad tune.

As Ginger walked down the center aisle behind Morgan and Nia, conversations stilled mid-sentence. She felt eyes latch onto her, quick glances, then longer looks that didn't bother to hide their scrutiny. Some were curious, others suspicious, others openly hostile, lips pressed tight, eyebrows colliding. The stink eye came from every direction.

Ginger kept her gaze forward, not daring to look a single soul in the face, shoulders squared, spine straight. When she finally slid into the pew next to the Bennett family, she folded her hands tightly in her lap, fingers laced. Her chest felt constricted, the air in the church suddenly heavy, like the walls had crept inward when she wasn't looking.

At the front of the sanctuary, Landon's photo rested on an easel, surrounded by a dazzling wreath of white lilies, their petals pristine. More flanked his white casket, lining the floor in careful symmetry, in stark contrast to the absolute mess he'd left behind.

In the photo, Landon looked younger, happier; eyes bright and full of mischief like he'd just finished cracking a joke before the photographer captured his photo. That was the version of Landon she'd remember; the easygoing, charming man who'd talk her ear off about anything that came to his mind. The man who stood in her bakery long after the supplies had been delivered, offering unsolicited business advice at the crack of dawn. He always volunteered to taste test new recipes for her Fall Festival menu, critiquing her pastries as if he'd studied under a master chef once upon a time. It was hard to believe that the man pictured was the same one whose secrets dragged them all here today.

Ginger swallowed hard, eyes burning as the organist played louder, the low notes swelling in the small space. Murmurs rippled through the congregation as Ethel Lawson appeared at the back of the church. The older woman was cloaked in uninterrupted black; black dress, black gloves, black stockings, and low-cut black heels. A black fascinator sat askew on top of her head, its delicate netted veil covering most of her face. She looked incredibly small beneath the weight of it all. With one trembling hand, she wheeled a portable oxygen tank behind her; with the other she leaned heavily on a wooden cane, each step measured and seemingly painful, as she journeyed up the aisle. Men rose from the pews instinctively, offering their arms, murmuring soft assurances. Ethel waved them off with sharp, stubborn flicks of her wrist, jaw set beneath the veil. She would not be helped. Then, a familiar figure pushed through the crowd, catching up to Ethel.

When Ginger recognized Austin, her stomach sank as if the floor had fallen out beneath her. Nia's hand clamped down on her knee, a silent confirmation that she saw him too.

There he was.

Handsome simply wasn't enough to describe him. Austin was dressed in a slim-cut black suit, defined lines accentuating his broad shoulders and lean frame. The jacket hugged his torso just enough to make the rippling muscle beneath visible. His white shirt was crisp, collar neat, black tie perfectly knotted. He had trimmed and shaped his beard with care, revealing the strong line of his jaw. His hair was neatly sponged, not a coil out of place.

Ginger couldn't tear her eyes away. She wanted to run to him, to touch him, console him. Instead, she stayed planted in her seat. Now was not the time.

Austin reached Ethel and placed a gentle hand on

her shoulder. She turned, prepared to refuse him like she'd done all the others. For a moment, Ginger thought she would fight her way up the aisle toward her husband, alone. But then Ethel stilled, studying Austin through the veil, her posture softening, shoulders leveling with relief. Slowly, she released her grip on the cane. Austin took it without a word, tucking it under one arm. With the other, he extended his elbow. Ethel hesitated only for a second before slipping her arm through his.

They continued up the aisle, slow and steady, the church collectively holding its breath as they passed each pew. When they reached Landon's casket, Austin handed Ethel her cane and took a respectful step backward, giving her space. Austin stood just off her shoulder, his large hands clasped in front of him, head bowed.

Ethel collapsed forward with a quiet, broken sob, one gloved hand pressed to the closed casket. The sound of her grief cut through the room sharper than any eulogy could have. A few sympathetic sniffles echoed in response. Someone blew their nose. The organist softened the music, letting it taper into silence, and the hush that fell over the sanctuary was palpable. Ginger had never borne witness to something so incredibly heartbreaking.

The service passed in a blur. Ginger sang hymns she hadn't sung since her mother dressed her in itchy socks and frilly dresses. She was surprised it all came back to her like muscle memory. Scriptures, the eulogy, and kind words were read that all felt inadequate for the shameful loss of life.

By the time the final prayer ended and the congregation began to stand, Ginger felt wrung out. The quiet murmur of voices filled the sanctuary as people gathered their coats and programs, shuffling toward the exit.

Ginger slipped out with Nia and Morgan, keeping her head down. She wasn't sure she could face the burial. The thought of watching Landon lowered into the ground – the finality of it – made something churn in her stomach. She pushed open the heavy sanctuary doors leading to the vestibule.

'Ginger?'

She turned at the sound of her name. Rachel pushed through throngs of people, clutching her purse at her side. 'Oh my gosh, I've been looking everywhere for you,' Rachel said, slightly breathless. 'I'm so sorry I didn't make it by the bakery last Saturday. I feel terrible.'

Ginger blinked, caught off guard, relieved it'd only been Rachel and not someone ready to give her a piece of their mind for daring to show up at Landon's funeral.

'It's okay, Rachel. With everything that happened—'

'No, it's not,' Rachel insisted, shaking her head. 'I promised my son that cake and I completely disappeared on you. I just feel awful about it all.' She leaned in closer. 'We had to put Princess Pawlina down Saturday night, worst timing ever.' Her face crumpled. 'Can you imagine? The night before your son's tenth birthday.'

Ginger's heart sank. 'I'm so sorry, Rachel.'

Rachel nodded, blinking back tears quickly. 'Preston handled everything so well,' she said softly. 'He sedated her first with lidocaine, just enough to make her feel comfortable, made sure she didn't feel a thing.' She let out a shaky breath. 'I stayed there with her the whole time, I didn't even realize how late it got. I just . . . couldn't leave her. I didn't want her to be alone, y'know.'

Ginger winced sympathetically. 'That sounds awful.'

'It was,' Rachel said. 'I was completely out of it. Pawlina was like part of our family. I could barely drive home. I almost begged Preston to sedate me, too.'

Despite the heaviness of the day, Ginger felt the corner of her mouth lift. Rachel glanced over Ginger's shoulder toward the entrance doors.

'I have to get in the procession,' she said, already backing away. 'We're heading to the cemetery now.' She reached out and squeezed Ginger's arm affectionately. 'Are you going to Rosie's later?'

Ginger nodded. 'I think so.' She looked for Morgan

and Nia but they'd gotten lost in the crowd. She was sure they would attend the repast later on.

'Good,' Rachel said. 'Let's talk then, okay? We'll figure out another time for the cake.'

'Of course,' Ginger said softly.

Rachel gave her one last apologetic smile before hurrying toward the entrance, disappearing into the flow of mourners. Ginger watched as Rachel pushed open the doors, revealing the early afternoon sun and giving a clear view into the parking lot. A slow line of cars had begun forming.

That was when she saw Austin outside, his back turned toward her. He stood behind the hearse parked near the stairs, making small talk with passersby. For a moment, hope flared. Her legs carried her out of the doors and down the stairs, her heart fluttering in her chest.

She stopped on the bottom step and one of the men Austin had been speaking to scurried off, climbing into the driver's seat of the hearse and disappearing inside the vehicle like she was Typhoid Mary.

Austin turned, politeness on full display, but when he noticed Ginger, his expression drooped. Up close, she could see how wrecked he looked. His eyes were red-rimmed, his jaw set tight, exhaustion etched into every line of his face. She didn't have the right to ask where he'd been or why he looked like he hadn't slept; she was sure she looked the same way. He'd probably been out late partying with Will and Jesse.

She didn't know where to begin or what to say, so she figured the best place to start was with an apology.

'Austin, I—'

'Don't,' he warned. 'I can't talk here, not right now.' His voice was controlled, empty, void of emotion.

'I know you're busy,' she responded quickly. 'I just . . .' She struggled to come up with the words. 'I wanted to explain myself. I didn't get a chance to tell you—'

He gestured widely to the hearse. 'I'm kinda in the middle of something right now, Virginia. Can we do this later?'

Ginger bristled, clenching her teeth. 'I'm meeting Heather for dinner tonight. Can we meet up after? At Rosie's or—'

'Yeah, sure. Later, alright?' Austin said with finality. He turned to close the trunk of the hearse, Landon's bright white casket already loaded inside. He trekked up the stairs and back into the church. Just like that, he was gone. It was a good thing she was at a funeral because no one questioned why she was standing on the steps of the church with tears falling down her face.

Chapter 33

Austin

Austin stood next to Gage Whitfield behind the idling hearse, waiting for Reverend Amos to appear before heading to the gravesite. He looked across the adjacent field, squinting his eyes against the late-morning sun that flashed against polished hoods and windshields, scattering light across the packed gravel lot where cars and trucks wedged together wherever space allowed. Looking back at the church, white lilies crowded the steps of All Saints Tabernacle, their sharp, sweet scent clinging to the air until it felt thick enough to taste.

Austin shoved his hands deep into the pockets of his suit pants, shoulders tight from lifting and heaving Landon's casket. The weight of it hadn't just been physical. It settled somewhere deeper; along the back of his neck where the tension refused to lessen, and the hinge of his jaw that was sore from clenching, his chest tight from holding everything in.

Exhaustion was deep set in his bones, a dull, grinding fatigue that sleep couldn't solve, but he still had hours stretching ahead of him. He'd left Atlanta late the night before with only adrenaline, stubborn resolve, and an energy drink the color of alien piss keeping him upright behind the wheel. Once home, he'd caught a couple hours of sleep, which felt like minutes, before he shaved, pulled on a suit, and drove to the church to carry another man's body into the ground. He couldn't tell if the fog in his head came from the lack of rest or from the week's whirlwind of events crashing down on him all at once.

Just five days ago, he'd been someone else. Someone hopeful, someone who could fix any problem thrown his way. A man who prided himself on trusting his instincts, who trusted the people around him. But now, he didn't know what he thought, and he didn't recognize himself. By every measurable standard, he was doing just fine. But his heart? He didn't know how he was going to fix that. He couldn't sand down, reinforce or replace that. It just sat there, a cracked rock in his chest, pulsing hard with something he couldn't quite name. He'd felt a twinge of it before with Samantha, but nothing as encompassing as this. Anger didn't fit, neither did grief. Betrayal came the closest, but even that felt too clean of a word for what twisted through him when he thought about Ginger.

He'd spotted her before the service, flanked on

both sides by Nia and Morgan. The three of them looked exactly how he felt, ragged. And he was sure it wasn't because they'd spent all night with a pedal pressed to the floor on an open highway. He regretfully had to decline Jesse's invitation to his bachelor party, and from the looks of the guys, they'd had just as much fun as the women.

When Ginger found him after the service, he hadn't been able to look her in the eye. He'd felt it then, that pull to go to her, to ask if she was okay, to hear her say his name. But the disappointment rose faster. He scurried inside the church until she walked away, not trusting that he had the strength to tell Ginger how he was feeling.

Beside him, Gage Whitfield, one half of the Whitfield Family Mortuary, shifted his weight, the gravel crunching beneath his shiny black hard-bottomed shoes. His sister, Grace Whitfield, was the town coroner while Gage handled funeral services. Between the two of them, there was never an off day in Cinnamon Falls.

Gage was a big man, dark-skinned and solid. His black suit looked like it'd lived too many services with him, the fabric stretched at the elbows and knees, the jacket pulling tight across his middle while he moved. He flipped a carton of cigarettes out of his jacket pocket and held one out to Austin, who refused with a quick shake of his head. Gage shrugged, unfazed, and tapped the bottom of the carton against his palm before sliding a cigarette free. He tucked it between his lips, then dug around in his pants pocket for a lighter. When the flame finally sparked, he cupped it with one broad hand, shielding it from a breeze that carried the mumbles of voices from the church's open doors.

He inhaled, then exhaled slowly, smoke curling up and dissipating in the sunlight.

'Hell of a send-off,' he said around a plume of smoke. 'I didn't think Landon had this many . . . friends.' Austin took a half step back out of the smoke's path, his eyes drifting to the church doors where people lingered in small knots. Still no Reverend Amos. Austin took a glance at his watch. He was in no rush, but he was still anxious about the possibility of running into Ginger again.

'Death always draws a crowd,' Austin responded.

He watched as Gage's eyes followed a gaggle of tearful women as they streamed out of the church in a blur of black form-fitting dresses and smeared mascara. He wondered how many of them were surprised to find out they weren't Landon's number one. His thoughts slid to Ethel, how she clung to her husband in both life and death. She'd been loyal to the end, even when the truth gave her every excuse not to be. He scanned the thinning crowd for her, half expecting to spot her small, hunched figure again, but didn't see her anywhere. He wouldn't blame her if she'd left before the burial; she'd already been through enough.

Gage let out a quick huff, smoke slipping from the corner of his mouth. 'Ain't that the truth.' He flicked ash toward the gravel and said, 'You did good in there. Pallbearer duty's no joke.'

Austin nodded. 'Just felt like I owed it to Ms. Ethel,' he replied.

Through the hearse's wide back windows, Austin fixed his eyes on the casket. He still couldn't reconcile that the Landon who used to openly weep over his beloved wife's unlimited forgiveness was the same man whose body was sealed inside polished wood, and about to be lowered into the ground.

Gage caught his look, tilted his head, studying Austin out of the corner of his eye. 'He ain't gon' get up if that's what you concerned about.' He chuckled dryly, taking another long pull and blowing the smoke above his head. He scratched at his jaw, his joking tone slipping. 'It's messed up how he died. No matter what people thought of him . . . Nobody deserves to be killed.' Gage shuddered.

'It was a nasty head wound,' Austin said. 'I keep thinkin' it could have been any one of these women who finally caught Landon slipping and had enough of being girlfriend number two.'

Gage shook his head. 'The blunt force wasn't what killed him. Raines was too eager for that press conference, but Grace had noted the cause of death that same day.' Gage pushed one finger in the side of his neck. 'Lidocaine. Injected straight into the bloodstream. It wasn't no accident either. Somebody knew exactly where to stick 'em.' He lowered his voice, shuffling closer to Austin, cigarette smoke cocooning them. 'Personally, I think it was Ethel. I don't believe that old lady shtick for one second.'

Austin turned fully toward him, gesturing to the church. 'Ms. Ethel? You saw her in there, she could barely make it down the aisle without oxygen. How could she pull herself into Landon's truck and stick him with a needle? Where would she even get something like that?'

Unbothered, Gage countered, 'Didn't have to be her, exactly. I saw that young waitress gettin' arrested on the TV. Ethel coulda paid her to do it.' He choked out another plume of smoke. 'And don't underestimate folks just 'cause they're old. I bet she's on a cocktail of meds.'

'You're talkin' like she keeps syringes next to the peppermints in the bottom of her purse,' Austin shot back.

Gage smirked. He took one last drag on the cigarette and ground it into the gravel with the toe of his shoe. 'You'd be surprised what you can get your hands on around here.'

Austin shook his head, more unsettled than amused. 'You're trippin'.'

'No, *you're* trippin'!' Gage tilted his head, studying Austin more carefully. His tone softened. 'I've known you for a long time, man, so I can keep it real with you. What's going on with you and the baker chick? You barely said two words to her a few minutes ago. Bolted inside the church like a bee stung you. I heard you two were . . . you know . . . something changed?'

Austin's shoulders tightened. The words were trapped in his chest, tangled with too many others he couldn't unpack; not here, not behind a hearse with Landon's body crystalizing a few feet away. He kept his eyes on the gravel. 'It's just not the right time.'

Gage's mouth curved into a grin, his eyes nearly disappearing behind his full cheeks.

'So what's the deal?' he pressed. 'Y'all two on the outs, or . . . ?' He waggled his brows. ''Cause if you're not chasing that anymore, I might have to shoot my shot.'

Austin turned slowly toward the man, his expression flat, jaw hardening once again. He liked Gage. He'd grown up with him, known him all his life, but right now, he didn't care about their history or that he was on church grounds. After the night he'd just had, it wouldn't stop him from putting five fingers to his face even with the good Lord watching.

Gage lifted both hands in surrender. 'Calm down, I'm kidding, mostly.' He snorted. 'Besides, I hear she could be a murderer and I know I'm in the business of the dead, but I'm not tryin' to clock in early, you know what I'm sayin'?' He drew a cross over his chest.

'Come on, man. Don't go there,' Austin grumbled. He was so sick of the Ginger-is-a-murderer gossip. When would it end?

'I'm just saying what the people are saying,' Gage replied, shrugging. 'The whole town's buzzin' about her and Natasha.'

'You should know by now. Cinnamon Falls always gets it wrong.'

Finally, Reverend Amos made his way down the steps, his black robe billowing behind him. He walked toward a limousine parked behind the hearse and climbed inside.

'That's our cue,' Gage said, turning and walking toward the driver's seat. Austin slid in beside Gage as they slowly made their way out of the parking lot toward the cemetery, hazard lights flashing, signaling to motorists passing by that he was part of a funeral procession.

At the last second, Austin noticed Ginger, Morgan, and Nia walking along the road, their eyes trained on the hearse as it passed them, continuing on to the gravesite. Austin couldn't help but stare as All Saints Tabernacle, and Ginger, shrunk from view.

Chapter 34

Ginger

After the service, the drive back to the Inn felt endless. Ginger passed the time by torturing herself, replaying the conversation with Austin on a loop in her head, if she could call it that. His cold distance felt worse than anger.

Finally, Lionel pulled into the familiar gravel driveway of the Daffodil Inn. An empty CFPD police cruiser was parked out front and Ginger knew exactly who was waiting inside for her. She'd been expecting Chief Raines since she'd left Austin's place on Wednesday night. She was surprised it'd taken her this long to reach out to her again.

'Need me to wait with you?' Lionel nodded ominously toward Raines' truck.

'I'm okay,' Ginger replied, swallowing down her nerves. She had nothing to hide, not anymore.

'If Raines is going to keep questioning you, you should really look into getting an attorney.'

'I didn't do anything wrong.'

Lionel shook his head disapprovingly. 'Famous last words,' he grumbled. 'It's your life, I guess.'

'I'll be fine, really.'

She muttered a quick thank you and shoved the passenger door open, stepping out. She watched Lionel turn around and head back toward Cinnamon Falls without her.

Inside, the Inn still smelled like fresh coffee. Butter scampered down the hall like he'd been waiting for her to arrive, his little paws skidding across the hardwood. He unleashed a dramatic meow as if he was warning her about her visitor.

Ginger scooped him up and steadied herself before stepping inside the rustic kitchen. She saw Mrs. Taylor first, sitting at the head of the farmhouse-style island, her fingers laced around a mug of tea.

Chief Raines was standing at the opposite end of the room, leaning against the far wall, her thumbs casually hooked in her belt loops, a folder tucked under one arm. Ginger knew this was not a casual visit.

'Ah, here she is now,' Mrs. Taylor said, flourishing her arm in Ginger's direction. 'I wasn't sure if you were going to Rosie's after the service. Chief Raines here had a few questions for you and I wasn't letting her upstairs without a warrant.' She shot Raines a tight smile.

Across the room, Chief Raines huffed a short, annoyed breath.

'Thank you, Mrs. Taylor,' Ginger said as Morgan's mother passed her on the way out of the kitchen, giving her shoulder a slight squeeze.

'I'll just be on the porch if you need me.'

'I won't be long,' Chief Raines assured her.

'I wasn't talking to you,' Mrs. Taylor mumbled loud enough for only Ginger to hear.

Chief Raines watched Mrs. Taylor with narrowed eyes until she was out of the kitchen, then the front door opened and slammed shut.

'Have a seat, Ms. Mills. Let's talk.' Raines gestured for Ginger to take a seat, but didn't move to sit herself. Ginger lowered onto the bench. Raines concentrated on Butter, who turned in a slow circle on the table before curling into a tight ball, his eyes trained on the police chief.

'About?' Ginger inquired. 'I watched the news yesterday, you've already got Natasha in holding, right? What would you need to talk to me about?'

Raines' lips twitched as if she was stopping herself from smiling. 'We've got enough to keep Ms. Montgomery there while we sort a few things out.' She paused. 'But something isn't adding up, and I think you could help me out.'

Raines reached into her folder and slid a photo across the table. It stopped under Butter's paws, who batted it away defensively. It fluttered to the floor but Ginger had seen enough to know it was a crime-scene photo of her bakery, Landon's booted feet sticking out of her back door. Ginger swallowed down the memory of that day, Landon's blood sticky on her fingers, the way his eyes held ghosts.

'Your prints are all over this bakery,' Raines said with an edge to her voice.

'It's *my* business—'

'In your sworn statement, you stated you were alone with the victim before Mr. Jacobs arrived, prompting you to dial emergency services—'

'I told you everything that happened.'

Raines flipped another page out of her folder: a photocopied article from a food magazine that featured a bakery where Ginger used to intern in Atlanta. The black and white paper showed a young Ginger frosting a three-tiered cake, deep in concentration. 'And now I find out that Ginger Mills isn't even your real name.'

Silence dropped between them. Ginger gripped the bench beneath her. Raines watched her carefully, measuring every reaction.

'You want to explain to me why I had to learn about Virginia Millford from someone else?'

Ginger held her gaze. 'I stopped being Virginia Millford months ago. I didn't think it mattered.'

Raines let out a breath that almost sounded like a laugh. 'After a murder in *my* town? Oh, it matters.'

She straightened to her full height, pacing the kitchen. 'You came here with no real history, opened a business in cash, and managed to renovate a property that – what – cost about eighty thousand dollars' worth of work?'

Ginger said nothing, biting down on the inside of her jaw to keep herself from talking.

'We tried to track the source. That kind of money doesn't come from nowhere.' Raines braced her hands on the side of the table. 'It led me to Milo Penn, you know him?'

Ginger's stomach dropped and Raines' eyes steeled. 'You sold him an emerald ring. Do you remember that, Ms. Mills?' She tilted her head. 'A family heirloom apparently, worth a pretty penny. I'd estimate way more than eighty grand. But, why do I get the feeling that none of this surprises you?'

Ginger's heart thudded, but her face remained still.

'I've got the state police on my line claiming one of my people is a missing person suspected of theft. Would you happen to know anything about that?'

'Why are you here, Chief Raines?'

'Because you lied to me. And I'm not sure if you know, but that's sort of like, a crime.'

'I didn't lie—'

'At the very least, you're hiding something, and that makes you a threat to my investigation.' Raines leaned in. Butter hunched low on his front legs, his pointy little teeth threatening to reveal. 'Tell me what you know about Landon Lawson's murder, the real truth this time, and I won't return Chief Kirkland's call. I'm sure he'd be more than happy to send a couple of detectives from APD to recover their missing person.'

'I told you Sunday morning, and I'm telling you now, I don't know anything.'

Raines scoffed and pushed away from the table, studying Ginger wordlessly for a long moment, as if she was deciding whether she believed her. Then, she straightened, gathering her photos and coolly placing them back in the folder.

'We'll see about that.'

Raines kept her eyes on Ginger as she rounded the table toward the exit. 'If you remember anything about that night, I suggest you don't wait until it's too late to tell me. Once Fulton County has you, there's nothing I can do.'

Raines' boots echoed against the tile as she stalked out of the room without looking back. Ginger heard the front door swing open and shut; Mrs. Taylor and Raines exchanging tense goodbyes.

Ginger sat there for a moment, the weight of it all pressing in around her. She wondered whether she should have told Chief Raines everything she knew: about Natasha and Mrs. Ethel, about the strange orange cap she'd swept up just a few days before, or the picture of Heather and Landon she saw that looked as if they were more than friendly.

Would Raines have ratted her out to the APD, anyway? Ginger wouldn't put it past her, but she couldn't sit here and do nothing either. She needed answers, and fast.

After a long, hot shower, Ginger dressed quickly, pulling on a cream blouse and a pair of jeans. She blow-dried her hair, letting it fall loose over her shoulders without a style. She corralled it in a headband, swiped on some lip gloss, and added a touch of mascara.

Her phone buzzed on the dresser. For a split second, a zip of hope flashed through her heart. Austin. Maybe it was him. Maybe later had arrived and he was ready to talk. She needed to talk to someone who could help her make sense of everything floating around in her head.

She lunged for her phone, her heart climbing into her throat as she unlocked the screen. The message wasn't from Austin but from the same unknown number: ***This is your last warning. Get out while you still can.***

Ginger stared at the words, her fingers trembling. Last warning? The phrase crawled across her skin. The others had been unsettling, cryptic and threatening in a vague way, but nothing like this. This one felt final.

She typed back before she could stop herself: **Or what?** Her thumb hovered over the screen as she waited. Maybe they'd slip, reveal themselves, or give her a clue as to who they were. Three dots appeared on the screen. Someone was typing. Her heart hammered in her ears.

The dots disappeared. Ginger watched and waited – one second . . . five . . . ten . . . but there was no response.

Butter suddenly leapt onto the countertop, the soft thud making her jump. She exhaled shakily. 'Okay,' she said to her reflection in the bathroom mirror. 'That's it.'

Her pulse was still racing as she snapped a screenshot of the text thread and sent it to Alexis: **Please tell me your man has an update?**

Alexis responded quickly: ***He said it's a local number. A burner phone most likely.***

Ginger stared at the message. A local. Not Camille. Not Harrison. Not some ghost from her past stretching across miles. It was someone here, in Cinnamon Falls. A chill snaked down her back. It could have been someone who was sitting behind her at the funeral that afternoon; someone who might have walked past her in the parking lot; someone who'd been watching her all along.

Her gaze drifted toward the dark window, the quiet hills outside suddenly feeling less peaceful than they had before.

If there was one thing Ginger knew for certain now, it was that she didn't have much left to lose.

State police were closing in, she'd already lost Austin, and her business was holding on by a thread. All the odds were against her, but she wasn't running, not again.

She squared her shoulders, grabbed her keys, and headed for the door, her stubborn resolve burning hotter than her fear.

Chapter 35

Austin

As Austin expected, it was nearing standing-room-only at Rosie's Diner by the time he arrived. Most of the people who were at the service had gone straight there, skipping the burial completely, less concerned about Landon's last moments above ground, and more concerned about getting a booth with a clear view to observe everyone else's grief.

Death had a strange way of bringing out the worst in people and Austin wasn't sure that he'd realized that until just now.

From outside the diner, he could smell roasting coffee and cinnamon sugar working double time. Once he stepped inside, heads whipped in the direction of the door, the noise level dipped, hushing to a whisper. It came as no surprise that everyone was expecting him to arrive with Ginger.

Gage stepped in behind him, smirking, and raised his hands to the ogling crowd. 'I know, I know. I can't believe it either. Not one, but two handsome men in the same place? Single ladies make some noooooooise!'

The room erupted in a chorus of groans. Plates clattered, silverware scraped, and conversations resumed in low, eager murmurs.

Austin looked over at Gage, extending his hand for a dap. 'Thanks, man. I owe you.'

Gage brought him in for a one-armed hug. 'All good, I like the attention. Gives these vultures something new to look at.' Gage found open seats at the bar next to Harold Bones. Austin would rather eat a denim jacket than sit next to the town gossip.

He scanned the room and caught Jesse's eyes first, who was standing near the counter with Will and Morgan, Nia tucked between them, her arm looped through his. The women glared daggers, their eyebrows pinched together in a fashion that signaled to Austin he was not welcome. He noticed Ginger's absence immediately, his heart untangling with relief. He could breathe. Jesse gave a brief nod and Austin lifted his hand in return, neutral and controlled, acknowledging the line drawn in the sand.

He found his parents and sisters near the back wall, taking the open seat that, a year ago, his father would have filled. Katherine immediately reached for his arm, squeezing it like she needed the reassurance that he was still alive.

'You alright?' his mother asked softly.

'Yeah,' Austin responded, though it came out automatically. He was always okay. He had to be.

He picked up the menu he'd seen hundreds of times before just for something to do with his hands and pretended to scan the options, hoping that it'd signal to his family not to ask about her. He wanted to go back to what his life was like before Ginger Mills stormed into it.

It had been what he'd found attractive about her at first, the storm. While Austin was all sunshine and warm breezes, Ginger was torrential rain and whipping winds. She ripped up the things he'd safely buried – no more ladders, the yellow house, his dad's injury, his break-up with Samantha – exposing them to the elements.

He couldn't hate her, not entirely. Because of her, he'd gotten on a ladder, three times over, since his father's accident. He'd shared dinner with his family without it resulting in a fight. Because of her, he hadn't driven past the little yellow house in days, too consumed in the present to brood over what he used to have. Seeing Samantha the night before hadn't affected him. He was free. The realization gut-punched him. Things around him hadn't changed, he had. And it was all because of Ginger.

His father leaned back in his seat, eyes sharp. 'Didn't see Ginger come in.'

It was what everyone in the room wanted to know: *where was Ginger?* His jaw tightened but he didn't respond, murmuring in a way that acknowledged he'd heard his father, but wouldn't comment on her absence.

Across the table, Lillian tilted her head. 'Is she coming?'

'Don't know,' Austin said evenly.

Maddie opened her mouth anyway, but before she could push, a voice floated overhead.

'Austin!' Rachel Greene appeared beside their table, clutching a plastic bag of to-go food at her side.

Austin forced a polite smile. 'Hey, Rachel.'

She glanced around the table, giving a friendly wave to his family, then leaned in. 'Have you seen Ginger? I was hoping she'd be here.'

'I haven't seen her since the service.'

Rachel nodded solemnly. 'I wanted to talk to her about making little Dougie's cake. We had to put Princess Pawlina down Saturday night and I forgot all about it.'

Katherine placed her hand over her chest. 'Are you doing okay, Rachel? Do you need anything?'

'I'm doing much better now, thank you for asking. But, putting your family dog down the day before your child's birthday was a zero out of ten experience. I do not recommend.'

'What happened to her?' Lillian asked with wide, sympathetic eyes.

'We're still not sure. Preston thinks she must have ingested something bad. Her blood sugar dropped and Pawlina wouldn't eat and that's just not like her at all. She was just layin' there lookin' so pathetic. Doug finally convinced me to call Dr. Hughes and I felt terrible, calling him out of his bed like that. Poor thing looked half asleep when we showed up. I felt even worse because Heather had to come too, and I felt right awful 'bout dragging them both out so late.'

'Rest in peace to the princess,' Madelyn chimed in.

Rachel hung her head in solidarity. 'I've been a wreck all week, missed half of little Dougie's party on Sunday. But I have to say, Preston took real good care of little Miss Pawlina. Since she was so small he sedated her with some lidocaine and she trotted right into those pearly gates. We picked up her ashes today.'

Rachel dropped her bag of food and wasted no time pulling a pink urn out of her purse, admiring it longingly. The Jacobs family reeled backward at the same time. 'I'm just so used to carrying her right here.' She patted her shoulder bag. 'Feels weird without her sittin' there.'

Lillian gagged, cupping a hand over her mouth. 'I'm going to throw up.'

Madelyn kicked her under the table, clipping Austin's calf in the process and sending a jolt of pain up his leg. Katherine shot them all withering glances and Austin stuffed his laugh back down.

Rachel didn't seem to notice. She replaced the urn and adjusted her purse strap on her arm. 'Anyway, you tell Ginger to call me, will you? I really want one of her cakes, my family is still talking about it.'

'I will,' Austin replied, his voice distant.

Rachel moved on, drifting toward the front door. Austin stared after her, his thoughts racing. She'd just made it to the door, sidestepping so another patron could come inside.

Heather Hughes walked in, her husband tight on her heels. Rachel threw her arms around Dr. Hughes' neck while Heather looked on, smiling.

Heather noticed Austin watching across the room. Her smile widened as she approached the family's table. Austin didn't remember seeing Heather at the funeral, but the church was so crowded, she could have been there for all he knew. She was wearing a red sweater, stripes of burgundy travelling across her arms and chest. Where had Austin seen that color before?

'We're popular today,' Madelyn quipped just as Heather approached.

'Kat,' she began, throwing her arms open toward Austin's mother, who stood to offer her a hug. 'It's so nice to see you all, despite the circumstances and all.' She moved on to Austin's father, her eyes stopping short at his chair. 'It's been ages since I've seen the whole Jacobs crew together. Y'all doing alright?'

'Better than ever,' Matthew replied in a customary tone. 'How're you and the doc? We heard all about Princess Pawlina.' He nodded toward Rachel, who still had Heather's husband cornered at the entrance.

'Doing fine,' she said. 'I can't wait until his truck is out of the shop so I don't have to change my plans every time someone's dog accidentally eats something fatal.' She turned her attention to Austin. 'I'm glad I caught you. Ginger is having dinner with Preston and me tonight and I figured it was only right to extend the invite to her beau.'

Austin swallowed, ears flaming. 'Thank you, Mrs. Hughes, but I'll be with my family tonight.'

Lillian didn't glance up from her phone when she kissed her teeth. 'No, you're not—'

Katherine jumped in, saving Austin from another explanation about Ginger's whereabouts. 'Um, Madelyn is heading back to school so we're having dinner as a family tonight. Thanks for the invite, though, Heather.'

'Of course,' Heather replied, her smile not faltering. She waved politely. 'Y'all take care of yourselves. Call me sometime, Kat. I'd love to hear from you.'

Katherine nodded with a look that let Austin know that Heather would absolutely not be hearing from her. Heather's manicured fingers trailed up Matthew's shirt sleeve, before she walked back toward Dr. Hughes, saving him from Rachel's conversation.

Madelyn leaned in once Heather was out of earshot. 'I thought you didn't like Mrs. Hughes?'

Katherine watched the woman with hawk eyes. 'I don't.'

Matthew groaned. 'Not this again. She was just being friendly.'

'What?' Lillian pressed, finally looking up from her phone, suddenly interested in the conversation once gossip had been introduced.

'I keep telling you about being *friendly* with that one, just like I told Ethel, and now look at her.'

Matthew grinned back. 'I only have eyes for you, my dear.'

'Ethel Lawson?' Austin clarified.

'Mm-hmm,' his mother responded, leaning in. 'Landon was a happily married man until he started delivering to Cinnamon Grove. Next thing I know, he and Ethel were livin' apart.'

Matthew replied, 'I hate to speak ill of the dead but Landon was no saint, Kat. He ain't done nothin' he didn't want to do.'

Katherine rolled her eyes and their conversation drifted elsewhere: Landon's funeral, Katherine's dinner plans, and Madelyn's long drive back to Atlanta, but Austin wasn't listening. The chaotic sounds of lunch crashed all around him, but he hardly noticed, lost in his own thoughts.

He sat back slowly, the realization settling over him like a cold sweat. Heather's red sweater was the same shade as the fibers he'd seen in Landon's truck. His mother's comment, *Landon was a happily married man until he started delivering to Cinnamon Grove . . .*

Then Rachel's, *I felt even worse because Heather had to come too . . .*

Gage's voice echoed closely behind: *Lidocaine.*

There were two things Austin knew for certain: Heather and Landon had been together Saturday night. Secondly, if Ginger set foot into Heather's house tonight, she'd be walking into danger. And he was running out of time.

Chapter 36

Ginger

The Hughes residence sat back from the road, lights glowing behind tall windows as dusk fully settled into the night. From the outside, it looked like the kind of place that could be featured in a home magazine: brick siding washed in warm amber light, stately white columns holding up a screened-in porch, swept clean save for a pair of matching rocking chairs that sat on either side of a navy blue painted door, wind chimes whispering in the gentle evening breeze.

Ginger parked her car along the street and made the short walk across the paved driveway, past the two-car garage, and toward the front door. She wiped her palms on her fitted jeans, damp with droplets of condensation from the chilled bottle of white wine she clutched. Her mother had taught her never to show up at someone's house for the first time empty-handed, and Heather seemed like the kind of Southern, traditional woman who would appreciate the gesture.

Ginger had her own motive for the wine outside of tradition. The thirty-dollar investment paled in comparison to what Ginger was going to walk away from this dinner with: the truth. She might have been three sheets to the wind the night before, but she recalled, in startling clarity, the picture of Heather and Landon at the Daffodil Jubilee. And that wasn't all.

The red sweater. The burgundy lipstick. Her comments about Landon.

All of it crashed together in Ginger's mind and she hadn't been able to shake the feeling that there was something her friend, her confidant for the last several months, hadn't been telling her.

Ginger reached for the door knocker, a monstrous H the size of her hand. She lifted the brass knocker and let it fall back against the door, the sound echoing throughout the home.

'Coming!' Heather's disembodied voice floated through the door, cheerful and distant. A moment later, she pulled open the door with a flourish.

A cool gust of wind rushed past Heather's shoulder, ruffling her hair. Ginger fought to keep her mouth from dropping open when she noticed the sweater: a rich red like the inside of a pomegranate with wide, burgundy stripes cut cleanly across a soft fabric. It skimmed Heather's frame and was tucked neatly into a pair of denim jeans that hugged her long legs just right.

Her brown skin looked airbrushed beneath a wash

of foundation and Ginger zeroed in on the burgundy lipstick that ringed her mouth; the shade mirroring the stripes in her sweater. Heather's lips curved, revealing a welcoming smile.

'Ginger, come on in!' She beckoned her inside, sweeping her arm inward.

'Thank you for the invite,' Ginger replied, holding out the bottle of wine. She stepped inside, taking inventory of Heather's spotless home.

'You shouldn't have,' Heather gushed, taking the wine from Ginger's hands. 'We'll have some with dinner.' Ginger closed the door behind her and Heather turned to walk her inside.

Ginger followed, close on her heels. 'I love this sweater on you!' From the door, it had looked velvety soft like cashmere, but Ginger knew fine fabrics.

Harrison had generously replaced her wardrobe when they had begun dating. Out of all the clothing he'd bought, the only thing she still had was her good cashmere sweater. Up close, Heather's sweater had an unnatural sheen with identical fibers. It was not cashmere. Ginger knew because she had the authentic version in black, crafted with Italian organic cashmere yarn, elegant and subtly luxurious. She'd seen that sweater every day for the past six days because it was now Butter's favorite pillow.

'I think I have the same one in black! Is this Luxe Meridian?' Ginger reached for the tag but Heather spun around at the last minute and Ginger's hand caught her hem instead, her fingers brushing against the sweater. It felt rough against her fingers.

'You have a good eye, Ginger!' She plucked at her sweater. 'Got it the same day I found that vintage handbag at Penny For Your Thoughts. I couldn't believe it!'

Heather pranced in a circle showing off her fake sweater and Ginger pretended to be impressed, zeroing in on a place on her back where the stripes met, jagged and uneven like it'd been repaired at some point. 'It looks great on you!'

'Thank you,' Heather beamed. 'Now, let's eat before Preston has a conniption.' She shooed Ginger further inside her home.

Straight ahead, a long hallway extended into the house with black and white family photos lining the wall; professionally shot, coordinated, smiling faces frozen in chosen moments. Off the hallway, Ginger caught a small glimpse of the living room; thick white carpet with fresh vacuum lines held a sectional sofa arranged around a low walnut-colored table. The room looked comfortable in theory, but untouched.

'Your home is beautiful.' Ginger wasn't lying. The Hughes home was immaculate in the way that looked purposeful rather than lived in. Nothing looked out of place or accidental. It reminded her of a luxury hotel: impressive, pristine, and just like Cinnamon Grove.

It was a stark difference from Austin's home. The Jacobs' home felt alive, like good memories lived in the walls. It reminded her of her own childhood: the heat of the oven, maple desserts cooling on counters, and old-school records that played well into the night.

Preston Hughes' voice floated from somewhere upstairs. 'Is that her, love?'

'Yes,' Heather responded. 'Just in time. Dinner's almost ready, dear.'

'Be right down,' Dr. Hughes said.

Ginger took a seat at the rectangular table beneath a modern chandelier. There were four place mats and four sets of silverware. Two brass candleholders rested at either end of the table.

Moments later, Ginger heard footsteps overhead that then descended the staircase. Preston stepped into the dining room, tall and composed in a button-down shirt, sleeves rolled to the elbows.

'Ginger!' He extended his hand. His grip was firm, not aggressive. 'Nice to see you again. I'm glad you could join us.' He looked between his wife and Ginger and the open place setting. 'Waiting on one more?'

Heather rushed around the table to clear it. 'I ran into Austin earlier and invited him to join us tonight. Doesn't look like he's going to make it, though.'

'Oh, at the funeral?' Ginger fished. Austin could barely say two words to her but seemingly could have an entire conversation with Heather.

'Uh, no,' Heather responded, gathering up the extra plates and silverware. She scurried out of the room and into the kitchen.

'We didn't attend the funeral,' Preston took up where Heather left off. He reached for a corner of bread waiting in a basket in the center of the table. 'Decided to hang back and enjoy our weekend. It's not often that I'm off work on a Friday. Heather's been busy roasting that chicken all day. We stopped through Rosie's to pay our respects to Ethel, though.'

Ginger didn't know if she was in any position to ask, but she did anyway. 'Church was too crowded?' she inquired. Just a few days ago Heather had been the president of Landon's fan club. She said that he and Preston were good friends, but they didn't attend his funeral? What type of friends were they?

Preston shook his head in agreement. 'Don't really do the crowds well,' he muttered around a piece of bread. 'And we just couldn't see him like that, y'know. Boxed up, gone. It would've felt too real.'

Heather appeared next to her, doling out a serving of white wine. In the kitchen, a timer beeped.

'Pres, do you mind taking the chicken out of the oven? The mitts are on the island. Don't try to take it out without them,' she warned, shaking her head.

Preston wiped his hands on a napkin and pushed back from the table. 'Sure,' he responded happily.

'That one thinks he's Superman. He's probably burned all his fingertips off by now.'

'I heard that,' Preston joked, walking through the opening toward the kitchen.

They dined on herb-roasted chicken with glazed

carrots and garlic mashed potatoes. The conversation was gentle and ordinary. They talked about the weather, Nia's upcoming wedding, and all sorts of Cinnamon Falls gossip that skimmed the surface between fun and danger without expressly naming it.

'So,' Preston started, pouring himself another serving of wine. 'Tell me, how are you liking Cinnamon Falls so far?'

'The Fall Festival was great,' Ginger responded. 'Lots more fun than I expected. The whole Cinnamon King and Queen thing and meeting everyone . . . we don't have stuff like that where I'm from. Small towns really commit to their traditions.'

Preston chuckled. 'Oh, they love a good crown around here.'

Heather smiled, but it didn't quite reach her eyes. She dabbed at the corner of her mouth, careful not to disturb her lipstick. Ginger watched that lipstick, the peculiar shade of it, the same shade as her sweater, the same shade as the fiber in Landon's truck, and couldn't take the pleasantries anymore. She had to know.

Ginger reached for her water glass and took a sip, buying herself a break in the conversation. 'Speaking of things people talk about,' she said lightly, cutting into a piece of chicken, 'it's been hard to ignore all the rumors about Landon, especially today.'

Heather's fork paused midair briefly, before continuing on to her mouth. Preston leaned back in his chair, and said, 'Hard to miss, I suppose. Half the town thinks they're some kind of amateur detective, most of them pointing the finger at you or that waitress from out of town. It's all a bunch of gossip.'

'Gossip or no, the police have Natasha in custody,' Heather said quickly, her tone tightening. 'It's pretty cut and dry if you ask me. She was having an affair with a married man and she killed him, that's the end of it.'

Ginger tilted her head. 'You know that to be true?'

Heather's jaw flexed. 'Don't tell me you believe her sob story about her not knowing Landon was married?'

'She told me she didn't,' Ginger replied. 'She said she found out on Friday night.'

The soft clink of silverware stopped. Across the table, Heather's gaze sharpened. 'You *do* believe her! Oh, my goodness, I didn't think you were that gullible, Ginger.' She laughed patronizingly. 'I would've thought you of all people would be elated that the CFPD arrested Natasha. Don't you think you've been under enough scrutiny?'

Ginger shrugged. 'I don't like seeing innocent people falsely accused.'

'I heard she's hardly innocent.' Preston gestured for Heather's plate and she handed it over.

'Finished?' Preston asked Ginger, his hand outstretched. She definitely wasn't finished. Not yet. She declined to hand over her plate just yet, waited, and watched Preston walk into the kitchen before she turned to Heather.

'I don't think it was Natasha. There's just . . . too many coincidences.'

'Like?' Heather said, one skeptical eyebrow raised. 'Lay it on me, Andrew Guy, P.I.'

'Like the red fibers the police found in Landon's truck. They kind of looked like the sweater you're wearing now.' Heather's face didn't move, but something flickered behind her eyes that Ginger could only compare to an animal realizing it'd been trapped.

'Red is a popular color,' she responded evenly.

'Burgundy lipstick is too.' Heather's fingers tightened around the stem of her glass. Ginger's gaze dropped deliberately to Heather's mouth.

'Natasha mentioned seeing lipstick on Landon's shirt, dark red. It wasn't her shade, trust me.' Heather tucked her lips out of view. 'Said it was the kind *older* women wear.'

Silence swallowed the room. From the kitchen, Ginger heard the sound of silverware scraping plates, then running water.

Heather's voice came out lower now. Colder. 'You're treading on dangerous ground.'

'Am I?' Ginger asked, feigning ignorance. 'Because from where I'm sitting, it looks like *you* lied to *me*. You've been lying to cover your own ass. Landon wasn't just seeing Natasha, was he? I saw a picture of you two at the Daffodil Jubilee a couple of months ago. You looked like more than friends if you ask me.' Heather stilled, her eyes locked on Ginger's.

Ginger continued. 'Landon was scheduled to deliver to my bakery Sunday morning, which means he had to have been with someone late Saturday night after Fall Festival. Rachel Greene told me your husband euthanized her dog Saturday night. I know where Preston was, but where were you? My gut is telling me you didn't wait in his office like a dutiful wife would.'

Heather stood abruptly, her chair scraping against the hardwood floor.

'You need to leave. Now,' Heather snapped.

Preston entered the dining room, drying his hands on a dish towel. 'Everything alright in here?'

Ginger didn't look at him, keeping her concentration on Heather.

His gaze shifted between them, as he moved to Heather's side of the table. 'What's going on, babe?'

'She's accusing me of murder, that's what's going on!' Heather replied, her tone wounded, her eyes blazing with fury.

Ginger stood slowly to meet Heather's height. 'You killed Landon because he was seeing Natasha. And you couldn't stand playing second fiddle to a girl half your age!'

Preston went still and, for a beat too long, no one moved.

Then he smiled. It wasn't the polite, neighborly

one from earlier. It carried a sinister weight and Ginger's stomach hollowed out.

Why didn't she think about accusing a woman of murder in her own home before she opened her big mouth? She glanced at the distance between the table and the front door. It was too far. She was trapped.

'Heather didn't kill anyone.' Preston took one slow, deliberate step toward Ginger, his grin widening in a chilling way. 'Because I did.'

Chapter 37

Austin

The Cinnamon Falls Police Department looked deceptively calm in the late afternoon light. Austin slid into a parking space and jumped out, not bothering to shut the door behind him. He jogged toward the station and pushed through the glass doors. No one looked his way when he entered, too entrenched in the scene before him.

Natasha Montgomery stood near the front desk, her wrists free, mascara smudged under tired eyes. An impeccably dressed attorney hovered beside her, a leather briefcase tucked beneath one arm.

Chief Raines stood a few feet away, posture rigid, lips pressed into a thin line. Jesse leaned against the counter, arms crossed, jaw tight. Austin slowed to catch the tail end of their conversation.

'. . . lack of sufficient evidence to hold her,' the attorney was saying. 'We expect a formal apology from this department.'

Raines didn't blink. 'You'll get what procedure allows.'

Natasha glanced up; for a brief second her eyes locked with Austin's. Confusion flickered there. Maybe fear, or vindication. Then, she was ushered out of the door.

'Well, that's great.' Jesse exhaled hard through his nose.

Raines adjusted the folder in her hand. 'We'll pivot. Re-examine timelines. I want to speak with Ginger Mills again.'

Austin stepped forward. 'No.' It jumped out of his mouth before he could stop it. It hung in the air between them. Both officers turned toward him as if they had just noticed he was in the room.

Raines' eyes cooled instantly. 'Excuse me?'

'You don't need to talk to Ginger,' Austin said, evening out his tone. 'You need to find her.'

Jesse straightened. 'What are you talking about?'

'She told me she was going to Preston and Heather Hughes' house for dinner tonight.'

Raines' stoic expression didn't change. 'And why would that concern us?'

Austin forced himself to slow down, to make the pieces tumbling around in his head sound less like a conspiracy theory, and more like the cold, hard truth. 'Because Landon was killed with lidocaine.'

Silence. Neither Jesse nor Chief Raines acknowledged his statement. They simply stared at him. Raines was the first to break the silence, stepping closer toward him. 'How in the *hell* do you know that?'

Austin hesitated. He couldn't throw Gage or Grace under the bus.

'Doesn't matter how,' he improvised poorly. 'What matters is, Heather's husband is a vet and he put Princess Pawlina down that night. Rachel Greene told me she called Preston out of bed but Heather had to come too since they are sharing her truck right now.'

'Slow down,' Raines said, her stare hardening. 'Heather has no known connection to the victim beyond being members of the community.'

'What if Heather was seeing Landon, too? Those red fibers found in his truck? I saw Heather wearing a sweater today in that exact shade. Her burgundy lipstick—'

Jesse sucked his teeth. 'That's weak. Circumstantial, and speculation.'

'You expect us to act on gossip and a couple of coincidences?' Raines asked.

'Isn't that how you usually come to your conclusions?' Austin listed on his fingers. 'First it was Harvey Briggs, then that Brewster kid, Natasha Montgomery, and now you're back onto Ginger. No disrespect, but you're chasing your tail here, Chief. This is a real lead.'

Jesse squared his shoulders and Austin knew he was approaching the glaring line between walking out of the station on his own or ending up in a holding cell.

'Can you just ride by and make sure she's okay?' Austin said, voice breaking slightly at the edges. 'If I'm wrong, I'll take the heat. But if I'm right . . .' Raines didn't move. 'I don't want to tell you how to do your job, but you can't afford an unsolved murder right now.'

Chambers stepped out from the shadows, clearly having heard enough of the conversation. 'What's going on?'

Jesse filled him in quickly. Chambers looked at Austin. 'You sure about this?'

'No,' Austin admitted. 'But I don't want to wake up tomorrow morning and see my girl's face on the news and realize that I was right and didn't do a damn thing about it.'

Raines crossed her arms. 'I knew it! It *was* you that made APD call off their arraignment, wasn't it? You returned the emerald she stole to the Caldwells.'

Austin clamped his mouth shut. Raines' eyes flashed with anger and Jesse glanced at Chambers. They stood in a square, chests out, egos prominent; no one was backing down.

Chambers took a look at his watch and said, 'We're technically off the clock, boss.'

'And I'm not going anywhere without my partner,' Jesse responded.

A long beat passed as Raines studied Austin, calculating.

'If it turns out to be nothing,' she said slowly, 'you

will not step foot in this building without being charged with obstruction. Do you understand me?'

Austin nodded immediately. 'Yes, ma'am.'

Chambers pushed Jesse ahead of him and toward the door. 'Let's ride,' he said.

Austin exhaled for what felt like the first time in hours.

Chapter 38

Ginger

Ginger's pulse roared in her ears. '*You* killed Landon?'

Preston sighed as he slumped into a chair, like a man exhausted by the inconvenience. 'I had no choice.' He casually rested his elbows on the table. 'My wife isn't subtle when she's unhappy. I've known about her and Landon for months and was waiting for the right time to . . . intervene.'

Heather looked stricken, like she'd throw up any minute. Her back was pressed against the wall, one hand clutching her abdomen. 'Preston, I—'

He ignored his wife, keeping his steely concentration on Ginger, his expression almost sympathetic. 'Landon thought he was clever, but men like that never are. Insatiable bottom feeders,' he snarled. 'Couldn't keep his hands to himself.'

Ginger's stomach churned. 'If you knew about the affair, why kill him?'

Preston lifted a pointer finger in the air. 'I stopped

him,' he corrected. 'He wasn't going to ruin my reputation and everything I built if word got out that *my* wife was screwing the town man-whore. Heather made a mistake and I had the opportunity to fix it.' Preston reached out, gesturing for his wife's hand.

Heather audibly swallowed, trepidatiously stepping forward. 'I didn't mean for it to go on for as long as it did, Pres. I was breaking it off with him Saturday night, I swear.' Her hand trembled as she slid it into his. He snapped his fist closed, smashing her fingers together, yanking her forward. Heather squealed in pain.

He brought her terrified face to his, nose to nose. He smiled again, bringing his free hand to her chin, his thumb caressing her cheek slowly. 'I followed you, watched you for weeks. Tracked your location with my phone. Every step you took, I got a notification. All those times you claimed to be working late, doing inventory, stocking shelves, and all the while you were screwing Landon right under my nose. Of all people, the goddamn delivery driver.' He scoffed, haughtily. 'When I've given you all of this.' He gestured widely to the spotless dining room. 'Y'know, the first time I thought it was a mistake. We've been together a long time. I could forgive a mistake, sweetie. But then it kept happening, and you *kept* lying to me.' Preston's fingers tightened around Heather's chin, squeezing; the pads of his fingers whitening. Heather whimpered as tears rolled down her cheeks.

Nothing was stopping her from stepping backward, freeing herself, but she stayed rooted to the spot, petrified of her husband.

'Preston, please . . .' she begged.

'When Rachel called Saturday night it felt like the stars finally aligned in my favor. I knew you wouldn't be able to resist sneaking out to see him. Main Street would be empty that time of the night, I'd be tied up with Rachel.' He chuckled, amused with himself. 'That runt Pawlina went down so quickly that it felt like a sign. I finally had the chance to catch the both of you in action.' His eyes closed like he was revisiting a memory. 'The look on your face when you realized it was me who snatched you out of his truck . . .' Preston grunted; a pompous laugh fell from his mouth. 'The shock in his eyes right before my fist hit his face.' He shivered, enjoying the memory of taking Landon's life. 'Whew, that satisfying wet sound his head made against the glass. I imagined that moment for weeks.'

Heather was shaking now, barely keeping herself upright. 'Pres, please. It'll never happen again.'

'Oh, I know it won't,' he cooed, rubbing his nose gently against hers in a sickeningly affectionate way. 'All it took was a little anesthetic and that lying bastard is six feet deep. I have you to thank for it, baby. You were the one who told me about your young baker friend who was starting over.' His murderous gaze shifted to Ginger. 'You were right. She was the perfect scapegoat and everyone ate it up.'

The quakes that had begun in her knees extended to Ginger's hands. She could barely speak, her teeth were chattering so intensely. 'You . . . framed me?'

'I had no choice!' Heather sobbed. 'I begged you to let it go . . . that day you found that syringe cap at your bakery. I knew it wouldn't take you long to put it together. I tried texting you, threatening you, anything to get you to leave town, but you just wouldn't go!' Heather pleaded, her chin still locked in her husband's hand, wincing.

Ginger's head spun, trying to make sense of the world around her. Her heart ached in her chest, but she didn't have time to feel. She needed to act. There was only one way to get out, the front door. But how was she going to get past two lunatics? She had to distract them somehow, keep them talking. Her next thought she knew was idiotic, but it was the only thing she could come up with: don't back down.

She steeled herself. 'I told you then and I'm telling you now.' Ginger studied the pair of them. 'I'm not going anywhere. This is my home now. Everyone is going to know who really killed Landon, and I'm going to get my reputation back.'

Preston shook his head, that sinister smile returned, chilling Ginger impossibly deeper. His eyes were black, no semblance of a soul behind them. His lips turned down in an exaggerated frown. 'I really wish you hadn't said that.'

No one moved. Then, Preston lunged across the

table, clawing for Ginger's arm. She leapt backwards, her chair toppling to the floor. Preston's nails dug into her arm before she could yank it out of his reach. His nails raked across her forearm, beads of crimson popped on her skin.

'Don't,' Ginger pleaded, looking between Preston and his wife.

Heather moved next, coming at her from the opposite direction. Ginger put her back against the wall, trapped, surrounded on both sides, as Preston raced around the table. She was too late, and he was too fast. The room tilted as he tackled Ginger to the floor. The sudden impact drove the air from her lungs, stars popping behind her eyes when her head collided with the hardwood. She thrashed, kicking, but Preston had her pinned down.

'Hold her,' he growled.

Heather scrambled forward, clutching Ginger's wrists, her face twisted with desperation. 'I'm sorry . . . you shouldn't have come.'

Ginger heard the sound of a package opening, paper ripping free from plastic. Preston pressed his knees on either side of her body, locking her in place.

'It'll be just a little pinch,' Preston whispered.

Ginger watched as the orange cap of a syringe rattled to the floor beside her, just like the one she'd found in her bakery. She thrashed as Heather's nails dug into her wrists. She was trapped.

Her breath came in ragged gasps. 'Austin knows!'

she screamed, her last-ditch effort at saving her life. She didn't know if her statement was true, but shouted it anyway. 'He knows where I am! He'll come looking for me!'

'It'll be too late,' Preston said, his breath hot on her neck.

Ginger cried when she felt the needle prick her skin. Her life: Michigan, her parents, Alexis, Uncle Maple, Camille, Harrison, Butter, Mr. Jacobs, Austin flashed through her mind in quick succession. It was over for her. This was where she would die.

'CFPD!' The front door exploded inward.

Red and blue lights flooded the room. Preston barely had time to stand before the taser hit him. His body locked, convulsing as he shook violently before collapsing beside Ginger. Heather shrieked and suddenly Jesse was there, shoving Preston face down as officers swarmed inside.

Ginger scrambled to the nearest corner, breathless, while Heather was dragged backward out of the dining room with cuffed wrists, sobbing hysterically.

'Don't hurt him!' she howled. 'Please, don't hurt him!'

Everything moved in slow motion. Ginger brought her knees to her chest. She couldn't stop herself from shaking. She was freezing. Why was it so cold?

The next face she saw was Terrance. His voice sounded like he was underwater when he said, 'It's over, Ging. You're safe.'

Another figure stood over Terrance's shoulder. The edges of his silhouette blurred, but Ginger would know him even if her eyes were closed: Austin. He reached for her and Ginger reached back, one trembling hand outstretched.

She was pulled to her feet, the living room whooshing past her in a blur of color. She collided with his strong chest, enveloped in his cologne.

Austin came. She was safe.

She didn't remember anything after that.

Ginger surfaced slowly, like rising from the depths of a deep, dark pool. The first thing she registered was the steady cascade of beeps to her right. The second was the sterile smell: bleach, plastic, and something faintly medicinal that clung to the back of her throat. Her eyelids felt like they were weighted, and when she pried them open, the ceiling above her was a blank, fluorescent white.

For one terrifying second, she didn't know where she was.

Then everything rushed back in flashes: Heather's screams. Preston's confession. The needle sinking into her skin. Jesse bursting through the door. Her chest seized as she jerked upright; a wave of dizziness crashed over her, sending her back down to the bed under her. Hands reached for her immediately.

'Whoa, whoa – easy!' Morgan's voice floated in from her right.

'Ginger.' That was Nia. 'Don't scare us like that.'

Ginger blinked, her eyes adjusting to her surroundings. They were all there: Morgan, in a pair of purple silk pajamas, mascara smudged under her eyes. Nia, still in her funeral dress, her hair falling loose around her shoulders like she hadn't bothered to fix it. Alexis stood near the window, composed, but tight around the edges; arms folded like she was holding herself together by sheer will.

Angel stood at the foot of the bed smiling triumphantly, showcasing a wide gap where her two front teeth should have been. Her coat shifted strangely around the middle. Inside, something moved.

'Is that—'

Before Ginger could finish, Angel dramatically opened her coat. Butter's spotted head popped out of her sleeve and tumbled onto the bed.

'I smuggled him in,' Angel whispered proudly, her missing teeth giving her a spittle-laden lisp. 'He didn't cry once. I think he knew to be quiet. He's very brave.'

Butter sprinted toward Ginger, curling in the space between her shoulder and neck, a steady stream of mews leaving his mouth. She dug her fingers into his warm fur and a watery, pitiful laugh escaped before she could stop it.

'What happened?' Ginger asked, her voice hoarse.

'You fainted,' Nia said gently.

'You're at Cinnamon Falls Medical,' Alexis added. 'They want to monitor you, concussion protocol.'

Angel chimed in, 'And Mrs. Heather and Dr. Hughes are going to jail. Like, real jail with bars and everything.'

'Preston confessed to everything,' Nia added. 'He said he assaulted Landon when he found Heather with him Saturday evening, but the blow to his head didn't kill him. Preston used Landon's key and dragged him into your bakery.' Nia placed one finger to her neck. 'Lidocaine administered intravenously. Landon was dead in minutes. Jesse said he could barely stomach watching him talk so cavalier about killing Landon and framing you.'

Morgan chimed in, 'Wade found a pair of Preston's shoes that matched the flour footprints in your bakery. It's over.'

The words settled in slowly. A shaky breath left Ginger's lungs.

'Heather?' Ginger asked.

Nia shook her head. 'Won't say a word. But they found a burner phone in her purse. Your number was the only contact in it.'

Angel came around to Ginger's side of the bed, stroking Butter. 'Congratulations, you solved the mystery.' Ginger managed a weak smile. 'But,' Angel continued in a stern voice, her hands planted on her hips, 'you did not follow my instructions. Rule number four was the most important one! You almost got murdered!'

Morgan snorted. Ginger reached out and squeezed her small hand. 'You're right. I should have listened.'

Angel beamed at her validation. As the warmth of the room surrounded Ginger, she couldn't help but notice the missing piece of her heart.

Her voice came out smaller, more tender than she wanted. 'Where's Austin?'

The shift was subtle. Morgan and Nia exchanged a look and Alexis' jaw clamped down.

Morgan cleared her throat. 'Angel, baby? Why don't you go find your dad in the waiting room? Me and Auntie Nia will be right out.'

Angel's face fell, poking her bottom lip out. 'But I want to hear the grown-up part.'

'Go, young lady,' Morgan said gently but firm.

With a dramatic sigh, Angel scooped Butter back into her coat. 'Okay, but I'm coming back,' she warned. She slipped out of the room and the silence returned.

Ginger's heart pounded in her ears as her thoughts turned for the worse. Had something happened to him? Was he hurt and in the hospital too?

'Please just tell me. Where is he?'

Alexis stepped closer to the bed. 'He's not here, Ging.'

The words landed like a physical blow.

Nia said, 'After everything, he went to the station to give his statement.'

'And?' Ginger pressed.

Morgan hit her with the finisher: 'We haven't seen him since.'

'He did do one thing right,' Alexis said. 'He returned your ring to Harrison Caldwell. He got APD and Raines off your trail. It's over, Ging. All of it is over.'

Something inside her chest caved inward. Her throat tightened as tears stung her nose. The machines continued their indifferent beeping and she swallowed hard, pushing down everything she was feeling inside. Burying it in a box she vowed never to open again.

'I feel fine,' she said abruptly, pushing the blankets aside. 'I want to leave.'

'Absolutely not,' Alexis declared. 'The doctor needs to clear you first before you go anywhere.'

'I'm not staying here,' Ginger insisted, forcing some authority into her voice. 'I'm going home.'

Alexis opened her mouth to argue, but Morgan shook her head.

'Alright,' Alexis started. 'We'll step out and let you get dressed. But if you pass out again, I don't care if I have to drag you by your follicles back here myself.'

They filed out quickly and Ginger pushed herself up. She swung her legs over the edge of the bed. The tile floor was cool against her bare feet. Her head swam, but she ignored it. Her clothes were folded neatly on the chair beside her and she reached for her jeans first.

As she lifted them, something clattered to the floor. Her phone. She stared at it for a long second before picking it up. Her fingers trembled as she unlocked it and scrolled through her contacts. His name was first.

She pressed 'Call'.

It rang once. Twice.

Voicemail.

Her stomach dropped. She tried again.

Voicemail.

And again.

Voicemail.

The room blurred and she tried to speak, but her words dissolved into a sob. Her shoulders shook as it tore out of her: the relief, the fear, the terror of almost dying, the impossible thought of losing Austin for good.

'I'm sorry,' she choked out. 'I'm so sorry.'

The door opened quietly. In three quick strides Alexis crossed the room and wrapped her cousin in her arms. Ginger collapsed into her shoulder, crying harder.

'We're going home, Ging,' Alexis said softly. 'You don't have to be strong anymore. Just let me get you home.'

And for the first time in her life, Ginger let someone else carry the weight.

Chapter 39

Eight Days Later

Saturday

Austin

Margaret 'Maggie' Shilling and Rosslyn 'Rosie' Rose would have been standing up in their graves if they had the opportunity to see how picturesque Harvest Square looked for the Shaw wedding.

Autumn had saved its best weather for the occasion; that rare October balance that was cool enough for the air to feel crisp against the skin, but warm enough that no one needed a coat. It was the kind of evening where breath just barely ghosted in front of your lips and the scent of fallen leaves and cinnamon drifted through the air.

String lights crisscrossed in the tangled branches of the old maple trees overhead, glowing a soft honey gold as dusk melted into a lavender sky. Mason jars filled with baby's breath and eucalyptus hung from shepherd's hooks, their glass catching the light and scattering tiny reflections across the brick walkway.

White folded chairs lined the aisle in neat rows, each dusted in pale yellow rose petals. At the end of the path stood a wooden arch wrapped in trailing ivy and blush roses, the greenery swaying faintly in the evening air. Behind it, the familiar storefronts of Main Street glowed. In the distance, Town Hall's clock tower chimed, the sound carrying across the square.

This was Cinnamon Falls at its finest.

Austin adjusted his tie, the charcoal suit hugging his shoulders just right. He'd trimmed his beard again this morning, clean lines and sharp edges; taking extra time to make sure his coils were moisturized. He wasn't sure who he was trying to impress, maybe himself.

He desperately wanted to feel normal again. But nothing in his life had been normal since last Friday.

It'd been eight days since Preston Hughes had been dragged out of his own dining room in handcuffs. Eight days since Austin had seen life leave Ginger's eyes as she collapsed in his arms. Eight days since Austin walked out of that hospital, never looking back.

He told himself it'd been necessary, that he needed time. He'd spent the week hiding in plain sight. He'd taken jobs in Asheville: starting a demolition of a cafe off Biltmore Avenue, fixing a split beam in a bungalow, installing custom shelving in a boutique that charged way too much for bootcut jeans. He left before sunrise and came home after dark, boots caked in dust, too tired to think. Too tired to feel.

Except, he always thought. He always felt. Every nail he drove, every board he installed, every problem he fixed felt like a reminder.

Fix it, I know you know how to do that. His father's words echoed louder and louder each night he spent without her.

He checked in with Jesse once. 'She's home,' he'd said.

The second time: 'She's asking about you.'

Austin avoided Main Street. He avoided his family. Bones' Barbershop, Rosie's, the Daffodil Inn. Because if he saw her he didn't know if he'd fold or walk away again. And he wasn't sure which would hurt more.

Angel had on a periwinkle dress; baby's breath had been twisted into her hair. She skipped down the brick aisle, curls bouncing, cheeks rosy, tossing petals with an exaggerated seriousness, pausing mid-aisle to make sure they landed correctly.

The crowd released a soft laugh that resounded over the street. It felt like the entire town was here, witnessing pure love in the eyes of their own. Will stood behind Jesse, who was rigid as a board in a deep navy suit. His eyes never left the end of the aisle.

The music swelled, and Nia appeared. For a brief moment in time, Austin forgot his own mess.

Nia was stunning in a flared lace dress; her long veil twinkled in the light like winter's first frost, drifting behind her. Jesse's face broke open when he saw her, his fist flying to his mouth, tears spilling over as his bride approached in slow, deliberate steps.

They shared vows about devotion, the power of friendship and forgiveness. Nia choked back tears through hers while Jesse's voice cracked only once. When they kissed after being pronounced husband and wife, Harvest Square erupted; a symphony of rejoicing that Austin relished in.

It felt new and shiny like hope had finally been restored to Cinnamon Falls, and Austin's heart straddled that weird space between happiness and longing.

The reception spread across the square. Long farmhouse tables were cloaked in white linens while Rodney McIntire played soft acoustic tones as Angie's dreamy voice floated over the music and laughter rolled through the air.

Austin busied himself at the customizable ice-cream bar. The Cinnamon Scoop had gone all out: dozens of silver tubs gleamed with options like cinnamon swirl, butter pecan, and honey lavender ice cream to name a few. Toppings and sauces were laid out in crystal bowls. Guests of all ages built their custom creations like budding architects, stacking their scoops higher and higher.

Austin was deciding between caramel swirl or chocolate drizzle when he felt her. He'd seen her earlier, just before the start of the wedding, guarding the six-tiered chocolate cake like a sentry. Now, he allowed himself to look, eyes scanning the crowd.

He turned just slightly and saw Ginger standing a few feet away, nursing a small cup of ice cream. They hadn't spoken in days, only seeing her in his memories. And they did no justice to how she looked right now.

Her shoulders and collarbone were exposed in a soft purple dress. Her hair was up in a mess of curls, wisps of hair falling out of the bun. Her lips were stained pink from the strawberry ice cream melting slowly in the cup she held, the small spoon resting between her delicate fingers.

There were things he wanted to say, things he should have said, should have done. He had the chance right now, but did she hate him? Was it too late? Austin couldn't tell.

Just then, she turned in his direction. When her eyes connected with his, an electric jolt shot through his body like there was an invisible string between them, tugging them closer and closer.

The truth slammed into him. He loved her. He knew that, as sure as the morning sun would rise over Barkwood Bridge.

She moved first, taking a hesitant step forward. Austin did the same, one step at a time until they met in the middle.

'Hi,' she said softly.

'Hey,' he replied. 'You look . . .' he started, then

stopped, unsure if he should begin with a compliment or an apology. 'Beautiful.'

The corner of her mouth twitched. 'You look nice, too.'

Silence stretched between them, wide and awkward.

'I called you,' Ginger said hesitantly, fiddling with the spoon, then sitting her cup down on a nearby table.

'I know.'

'You didn't answer.' Her brows pinched together.

'I know,' Austin repeated.

Her shoulders dipped slightly. 'Why didn't you stay?'

'Why did you lie?'

The question hung heavy – the crux of their relationship laid bare.

Ginger took in a ragged breath and shrugged. 'I was scared. You're a good guy, Austin—'

'Don't give me that.'

She held her hand up. 'Please, let me finish.'

Austin planted his feet and listened.

She gestured around herself. 'You've been raised your whole life in this small town where everybody knows you, respects you, depends on you. You're the guy people call when something breaks or goes wrong. The fixer.' She met his eyes again. 'You're always smiling, always calm, always so damn positive, like nothing ever bothers you.' Her voice softened. 'And it terrified me.'

Austin frowned, but made sure not to interrupt. 'A

lot of things have gone wrong in my life, Austin. A lot.' She swallowed. 'And every time someone said they were going to take care of things for me, it turned out what they really meant was that they were going to control me.' She wrapped her arms around herself. 'So when you kept offering to help . . . to fix things . . . I started to see it as the same thing: another man deciding what was best for me.' Austin opened his mouth but she shook her head. 'And I was wrong. I hurt you.' She glanced down, then back up at him. 'And I'm sorry for that.'

Austin toed loose gravel with his shoe. 'Lots of shit has gone wrong in my life too, Ginger.' He rubbed the back of his neck searching for the words. 'After my dad's accident, everything changed overnight. The business, the house, my sisters, my ex – suddenly everyone was looking at me like I had all the answers.' He exhaled slowly. 'The truth is I was pissed. Scared. Angry at the whole damn world.' He met her eyes again. 'But the business couldn't stop. My family couldn't stop. I didn't get the luxury of falling apart, of starting over in a new place. I had to get up, face each day, and be the man my father . . . my family needed me to be.' A quiet beat passed. 'I guess I got used to being needed. It felt like proof I was doing something right.' He gave a small laugh. 'And then you showed up and you didn't need me for a damn thing.'

Ginger sputtered out a laugh, knocking away the

tears that were falling. 'I needed a place to stay,' she joked. Hearing her laugh made his heart soar.

'You're different from any woman I've ever met. I wanted to protect you, keep you close. When you lied to me about your past . . . it gutted me.' The words hung there. 'It sent me right back to that place I'd been trying to outrun for years. That feeling that no matter how much you prepare, everything can fall apart without warning. I don't know if I can survive being blindsided again.'

Ginger took another tentative step forward. 'I wasn't trying to blindside you. I was trying to protect myself.'

'I know that now.' He took a step too, closing the distance between them. He could see her clearly now, more than he ever could before.

'Can we try again?'

Austin nodded and Ginger stuck her hand out. 'I'm Virginia Patrice Millford, most people call me Ginger. My past is messy and I've made a lot of mistakes, but the only thing I've done right in my whole life is move to Cinnamon Falls and meet you, Austin Jacobs. I've spent a long time fighting just to survive, and this place, this little country town, makes me want to live.'

Austin pressed the back of her hand to his mouth. 'Nice to meet you,' he replied. 'I'm Austin Jamal Jacobs. I fix things for a living. For a while there I had the silly notion that I could fix people, too. I discovered I don't forgive so easily . . .'

Ginger looked up.

'And I don't love so easily either.' Her breath hitched in her throat. He took her face in the palm of his hand. 'But I love you, Ginger.'

The words felt terrifying and inevitable all at once.

'You do?'

'I tried not to,' he joked.

'Didn't work?'

'Nah, and there's nothing I can do to fix it.'

The music around them shifted to something slower, softer. He brushed his thumb along her cheek. He leaned in slowly, giving her time to pull away, but she didn't. Their lips met gently at first, tentative, testing. Then deeper. It was the kind of kiss that felt promising, like second chances and retribution, and everything they'd ever lost coming back to them all at once.

Ginger pulled back when she heard Alexis shouting from across the grounds, 'I told you so!' She tipped her head back, laughing, and Austin couldn't remember a time when he'd been happier than this moment.

As Harvest Square glowed all around them, Austin wrapped his hands around her waist and pulled her close.

This time, he wasn't letting go.

I Loaf You A Lot

Ginger's maple pecan pull-apart bread
(NOT to be confused with Rosie's cinnamon buns)

Buttery soft layers of homemade dough covered in cinnamon sugar and pecans finished with a sinful drizzle of maple glaze.

Servings: 8
Prep time: 20 mins | **Bake time:** 40 mins
Rise time: 1hr 30mins | **Total time:** 2hrs 30 mins

Equipment needed: stand mixer, 9x5 inch loaf pan, pastry brush, sharp knife

INGREDIENTS

Dough:

- 3 ¼ cups all-purpose flour
- ¼ cup granulated sugar
- 1 packet of instant yeast
- 1 tsp salt
- ¾ cup whole milk, warmed
- ¼ cup unsalted butter
- 2 large eggs
- 1 tsp vanilla extract

Filling:

- ½ cup dark brown sugar packed
- 1 tbsp ground cinnamon
- ¼ cup unsalted butter, softened
- ½ cup toasted pecans, finely chopped
- 1 pinch of salt

Maple glaze:

- 1 cup powdered sugar
- 3 tbsp authentic maple syrup (Ginger's note: not pancake syrup with maple flavoring!)
- ½ tsp vanilla extract
- 1 pinch of salt
- 1-2 tbsp of milk or cream

INSTRUCTIONS

1. **Make the dough:** In the bowl of a stand mixer, combine flour, sugar, yeast and salt. Add warm milk, melted butter, eggs and vanilla. Mix on a low speed until the ingredients combine. The dough should be soft and slightly tacky.

   Transfer to a greased bowl, cover and let rise in a warm place for 1 – 1hr 30mins or until the dough has doubled in size.

2. **Prepare the filling:** In a bowl, combine brown sugar, cinnamon, pecans and salt. Set aside softened butter.

3. **Shape the loaf:** Grease a 9x5 inch loaf pan. Lightly flour a clean work surface, punch down the dough and roll the dough out. Pat it into a large rectangle, then use a floured rolling pin to roll it into a sharper rectangle around 12x18 inches. (The rectangle does not have to be perfect.)

   Spread the softened butter evenly over the dough, then sprinkle the brown sugar mixture evenly over the surface. Use a sharp knife or pizza cutter to cut the dough into 12 even squares. Stack the squares loosely on top of one another, then cut the stacked dough into 3 or 4 sections.

   Arrange the stacks upright inside the loaf pan. Don't worry if it looks messy, it creates the gooey pull-apart texture.

   Cover loosely and let rise for another 30-45 minutes until puffy.

4. **Bake:** Preheat the oven to 350°F (approx. 180°C) and bake for 35-40 minutes until the top is golden brown and the center is cooked through. Let cool in the pan for 10-15 minutes before removal.

5. **Glaze & serve:** Whisk together powdered sugar, maple syrup, vanilla, salt and enough milk to make a smooth glaze. Drizzle over the warm loaf and add another helping of toasted pecans (if you'd like). Serve warm & enjoy!

Ginger's note: Store the bread covered at room temperature for up to 5 days. Reheat gently in the oven, or single servings in the microwave.

Acknowledgements

Dear Reader,

Come on in and sit down! It's time for another episode of 'Why Writing Acknowledgments Feels Like a Humiliation Ritual'. No, but seriously, why does thanking people feel like writing an acceptance speech for an award I haven't won? The second-hand embarrassment needs to be studied.

Truthfully, I have one person to thank, Shannon, baking extraordinaire. Thank you for all your help with Ginger's recipes and making sure I used all the correct words and processes. Watching baking competition shows paid off a little, but your expertise really saved Ginger (and me). (I still want your recipe for cinnamon buns! *threatening*)

To Charlotte, Kate, Tamsin, Gabby and all the

people at Simon & Schuster UK who worked tirelessly to make this book great, I appreciate you dearly. Thank you for taking a chance on this little world, and what a place it has become!

I must also thank my brain for still functioning after writing three books back to back. If you've read the same sentence fifteen times in this book, no you didn't. And I don't want to hear about it.

To my family and friends, thank you for bearing with me after I ignored your calls and buried myself under my laptop. Your patience and support means more than you'll ever know.

Now, onto the real person to thank: you. If you've been with me since book one, I am so grateful you've decided to stick around in Cinnamon Falls. I'm also very happy to know you haven't gotten murdered. (Spoiler: we've still got a few more books to go so you might be next.) As the hip-hop pioneers, Wu-Tang Clan say, "protect ya neck".

See you in book four!

Bringing a book from manuscript to what you are reading is a team effort, and Simon & Schuster UK would like to thank everyone who helped to publish *The Maple Bakery Murder.*

Editorial
Charlotte Osment
Gabriella Nemeth
Gail Hallett

Copyeditor
Tamsin Shelton

Proofreader
Ollie Cotton

Marketing & Publicity
Kate Kaur
Sabah Khan

Sales
Olivia Allen
Jade Unwin
Sorcha Mulligan
Katie Sormaz
Heather Hogan
Madeline Allan
Jonny Kennedy
Richard Hawton & the rep team

Audio
Alice Twomey
Sarah Allen-Sutter

Design
Pip Watkins
Jill Tytherleigh (map)

Production and Operations
Karin Seifried
Mike Messam

Rights
Amy Fletcher
Ben Phillips
Ruby Love

Finance and Contracts
Luke Shaller
Isabel Ireland
Keely Day
Meshach Yeboah